# WOL OF THE IRISH SEA

*Conchofer Ó Briacon*

*24/12/22.*

# WOLVES OF THE IRISH SEA

### VOL. I

## ASCENT TO POWER

CONOR BRENNAN

This novel is a work of historical fiction.
Although most of the characters, places and incidents portrayed in it are factually correct,
much of the work is of the author's imagination.
The reference maps are based on the authors interpretation of the places at the time.

Published by Conor Brennan.

ISBN: 978-0-6454716-4-9

Editor: Robin Seavill

Cover design, illustration, maps and interior formatting:
Mark Thomas / Coverness.com

*For Demi*

IRELAND

# Viking Era Britain & Ireland

VIKING
TERRITORY

SCOTLAND

DUNKELD

SEIL

STRATHCLYDE

NORTHUMBRIA

LIEURPOL

JORVIK

DANELAW

THE
WELSH
KINGDOMS

CHESTER

MERCIA

TAMWORTH

LONDON

WESSEX

CORNWALL

BRITAIN

# PROLOGUE:

## THE HUMBLING
## OF THE HIGH KING

*Tara 862 AD*

The biting wind rose around the Hill of Tara and sent a shiver up the spine of the Prince of Meath, Flann Sinna. He faced a great host of men surrounding the palisades of the fort of the High Kings, and both he and this great army were waiting patiently for a resolution to be brought about. Either an accord would be reached between Flann Sinna's father, the mighty Mael Seachnaill mac Mael Ruanaid, and Aed Findliath, the leader of the Northern Ui Neill, or a final battle between their forces would ensue. Flann grimaced to himself. The mighty Ui Neill, descendants of Niall Noigiallach, one of the greatest kings in Irish history, now reduced to infighting and ignominy. It sickened him to see such disharmony.

The host that Aed Findliath had gathered was significant, some five thousand men, and Flann Sinna did not fail to notice the worried look that briefly crossed his father's countenance at the sheer size of the force assembled.

It had also perturbed Flann how Aed Findliath was able to move such an army through territories supposedly loyal to his father – with no advance word – until they were fully camped inside the borders of the Kingdom of Meath. Had his father received early warning he could have called upon his under-kings and demanded reinforcement, and if they had all answered in time, his host would have dwarfed that of the Northerners. In these strange times though, old allegiances were uncertain.

A brief flash of anger crossed Flann Sinna's mind when he thought of his uncle, King Cerbaill mac Dunlainge of Osraige, and his brother-in-law Ivar Ragnarson, also known as 'The Boneless' of Viking Dublin. As the closest allies to his father geographically, both had received word of what was occurring in Tara, but neither had responded. They were his father's sworn men, and both had enriched themselves over the past couple of years at his side, subjugating the Eoghanachta of Munster and plundering the southern kingdoms. Flann had repeatedly raised objections to his father. Instead of allying with such treacherous and ambitious under-kings like Cerbaill – despite being related through marriage – they should have dealt with him and his like once Munster was subdued. Over the years Cerbaill had leveraged power between Tara, Dublin and Munster for his own ends. Flann had suggested they should have marched on Osraige and laid waste to his lands, or at least gathered hostages to ensure his loyalty. Perhaps they should have even replaced him entirely with some of his more amenable kin?

His father had dismissed his concerns and was as effusive in his praise for the fighting skill of the men from Osraige as he was for their assumed loyalty. And as for the Vikings in Dublin, the whole city should have been sacked, in Flann's view, and every Viking – man, woman and child – slaughtered or sold into slavery. He felt that this was what they deserved; they had savaged the entire island of Ireland for several generations and stationed permanent colonies on the Irish coast. Flann could not condone any such alliance, but it was not his choice.

His father had married off Flann's sister Aibreann to Ivar the Boneless in the hope of strengthening alliances with the Vikings. In the short term it had bound them together, but it had also alienated some of his under-kings and driven them into the arms of Aed Findliath, who would have no truck with the foreigners. In private moments Flann admitted to himself that the Northern Ui Neill king may have the right of it. Although he would never counter his father publicly on policy, he agreed with the Northerners on their position on the Vikings, that they were pagan warlords one and all and never ever to be fully trusted.

*

When word of Aed Findliath's host had finally reached him, Mael Seachnaill had hastily dispatched men on horses to Kildare and Dublin to raise hosts – but no men came. Some of his own under-kings of the Southern Ui Neill had not deigned to show either. In the week allowed to him before Aed Findliath's arrival, Flann's father had been able to summon a total of fifteen hundred men to man the palisades of Tara. Flann weighed it up. If it came to battle here today, the Northerners – despite having to fight uphill – would surely take Tara and slaughter the defenders. Alternatively, if the Northerners decided to just sit there, they could potentially starve Mael Seachnaill's forces into submission within a moon's turn.

The arrival of this army had taken the High King completely by surprise, and he had not laid down supplies for a protracted siege. And despite his father's pronouncements of faith in Cerbaill Mac Dunlainge and Ivar the Boneless, Flann Sinna harboured grave doubts of any relief arriving from those quarters. Strangely, if anything, the Vikings were more likely to come to their aid than the men from Osraige, which angered and saddened Flann in equal measure. Why had his father taken the loyalty of Osraige and Dublin for granted? Years ago Mael Seachnaill would have predicted the political and militaristic moves of both his rivals and allies long in advance of any potentially dangerous situation. He would not have stayed High King of Ireland for sixteen years amidst a sea of enemies and rivals if he had not considered all possibilities.

The issue of the marriage of Flann's sister to the heathen savage Ivar had been a bone of contention between Flann and his father for a couple of years now. Aibreann, a beautiful maiden of sixteen years, had been married to Ivar in 858 to secure the loyalty of the Vikings of Dublin in the fight against Munster. Mael Seachnaill had felt that this marriage might also dissuade the Vikings of Limerick, under the old barbarian Ceitl Flatnose, from joining the fray on the side of the Munstermen; the Vikings of Limerick at least nominally owed their allegiance to the Vikings of Dublin after all.

Ivar and his even more barbaric brother Olaf were joint rulers of Dublin. The legend of their father Ragnar Lodbrok awarded them a sort of mystical air amongst the heathen savages of the Irish Sea and simultaneously earned them some degree of loyalty amongst the Danes and Norse across the Viking world. Flann's father was initially going to marry his daughter to Olaf the White but elected to go with the far younger Ivar, as she would then be his first wife as opposed to Olaf's third. Flann had to smile at that. His father in his prime had always considered the future shrewdly, whether it be on the battlefield or the marriage bed. For slavers and pagan savages, Flann admittedly found Ivar to be the more reasonable of the two brothers and if his sister had to be married for affairs of state, Ivar was the lesser of two evils.

Flann's reverie was broken with the emergence of the king of the Northern Ui Neill from the soldiery surrounding Tara Hill. Aed Findliath was a big man and strode forward like one born to kingship. His long brown hair, waving in the breeze, was held in place with a simple golden crown. He did not carry a shield but was armed with two short swords held in scabbards at his hip. He also kept a dagger close to his chest, and rumour had it that he always had another dagger concealed in his sleeve. Usually in the presence of a High King a subject would be expected to leave their weapons to one side, but Flann knew that to ask for Aed Findliath to disarm with that host at his back could potentially be dangerous.

Mael Seachnaill had elected to meet Aed Findliath, with Flann at his side, some hundred yards from the walls of the fort, just outside the barricades. He had discussed this with Flann and had given his reasons for this particular ploy. Although well past his prime, Mael Seachnaill was still a big man, and it was important that the host standing behind Aed Findliath should see him as the more imposing of the two. It was a cheap trick, an illusion of the gradient, but his father deemed it wise none the less. Flann himself was larger than both kings and would serve as bodyguard to his father should Aed prove treacherous. From where Flann and his father chose to wait, they had a clear view to the gates of the fort, and were within the range of the archers on the wall, should negotiations go ill. Aed Findliath halted ten feet from Flann and his father. He waited, staring at Mael Seachnaill. Flann's father had warned him to say nothing, but to wait and see what Aed Findliath had to say. After a casual glance at Flann Sinna, Aed Findliath locked eyes firmly on the High King, his arms folded, an invisible cloak of contempt married with arrogance enshrouding him. Neither king spoke a word for a full minute, then Aed Finnliath smiled and stared into the sky at a murder of crows circling overhead. "A good day for the carrion birds, old king, they must expect a battle today."

Mael Seachnaill shifted his stance and cocked his head but uttered no response. More long, uncomfortable seconds passed while the two kings of the Ui Neill glared at each other, taking each other's measure.

A slow smile broke across Mael Seachnaill's face. "You are always very pleased with yourself, Aed, aren't you, boy?" he goaded.

Flann could see Aed Findliath bristle at being referred to as a boy, when in actuality he was a veteran of dozens of battles. Mael Seachnaill continued. "Your father was a reasonable man, Aed, and it is true that we had our differences, but we always treated each other with respect, and did not turn up with hosts of men in each other's lands unannounced. Why are you here?"

"You became High King of Ireland," Aed Findliath answered in a low voice, "on the death of my own father Niall Caille, as is the tradition of the two greatest tribes of the Ui Neill. I accepted you as High King for a number of years. I admired you when you united all of the tribes of the Southern Ui Neill under your banner. I admired you when you captured that heathen savage Turgesius and sentenced him to die in Lough Owel. But you have lost your way, old king."

He paused. "You ravaged the lands to the north, people that were under my protection. You demanded unfair tribute from my kin. You rallied the entire country behind you, went north and sacked Armagh, the seat of our Christian faith. The worst crime of all, though, is your continued allegiance with the Vikings of Dublin."

*And there it is,* thought Flann Sinna, *the real crux of his argument.*

"Olaf the White and Ivar the Boneless are two demons in human flesh, and to make allegiance with these pirates and marauders is intolerable. Yet you have no reservations about making war on your own people with these heathens at your back." Aed Findliath spat in disgust on the ground and waited for a response.

Flann's father looked pained and uncomfortable. He was an elderly man, past fifty, and years of warfare had taken their toll. At that moment Flann Sinna knew that one way or the other, Aed Findliath would gain concession from this show of force. All he could do as a loyal son was to wait and learn their fate.

"Aed Findliath, your concerns are valid, but the Vikings are here to stay whether you like it or not. They have large towns around the Irish Sea with tens of thousands of people under their control. They possess vast fleets, and their sons and daughters have been marrying our sons and daughters for two generations."

"This was YOUR doing!" Aed Findliath exploded, jabbing a pointed finger at the High King. "You have failed us! You should have marched on every settlement from Limerick to Cork to Linn and Dublin and burned them out. They are never going to be a part of us. They are murderers and slavers and wish nothing but ill upon our people. Every year more and more of their kind come and make their homes on our island. Once I am High King and you are deposed, I will rally a force and we will drive the Norse and Danes into the sea!"

His last words were delivered with such passion and anger that soldiers all around eased their weapons from their scabbards and a murmur of unease ran through the assembled hosts.

Mael Seachnaill stared at the enraged northern king and nodded, his eyes downcast. "We could argue points here all day," he responded, his voice wavering due to tiredness and defeat. "I am sick of war and would have peace. There will be no killing of my people here today. I repeat, Aed son of Niall, – why are you here?"

The list of demands set down by Aed Findliath was astonishing. The old man seemed to shrink before Flann's eyes on each requirement.

Mael Seachnaill was to vacate his kingship this day before the Liath Fail stone, the ancient stone upon which all Irish High Kings were crowned and where Aed Findliath would be sworn in. This was highly unusual; traditionally this would happen at the time of Mael Seachnaill's death. The Ui Neill had always alternated the High Kingship on the death of an incumbent through a conclave of the lesser kings of the tribe. Aed Findliath demanded that this be circumvented, and Mael Seachnaill would retire immediately or his people would be put to the sword and his land would be ravaged. Mael Seachnaill took a moment or two to grasp the enormity of this, before acquiescing with a subdued nod.

His wife Land would become the wife of Aed Findliath, not on the hour of his death, but now. Land – the mother of Flann Sinna and his siblings – would be divorced from Mael Seachnaill and travel north with the Northern Ui Neill and their Breffni, Ulaid and Dal Riadan allies. This concession was also against the ancient traditions of the Ui Neill, and was equally humbling and galling. But again, the old king acquiesced with no protest. The third condition was that from that day forward, no king of the Ui Neill could ally with Vikings in war against other Irish kingdoms. Mael Seachnaill also accepted this with an indifferent shrug. Flann knew that deep down any alliances between the Southern Ui Neill and the Vikings of Dublin were purely political, and so in itself it was not such a difficult one to swallow.

*

It was the final condition, though, that sent his father to his knees with the enormity of it. From that day hence, no member of Clan Colman, the most powerful of the Southern Ui Neill tribes, could ever be High King. Flann should have raged against this but seeing his father on his knees only drew sadness from him. Mael Seachnaill tried to object, stating that the Kings of Meath would surely never rally behind anybody else other than Flann of Clan Colman. It was at this point that Aed Findliath struck his cruellest blow. Donnchadh mac Aedacain stepped forward from the ranks of the Northern Ui Neill army, a satisfied smile twisted like an ugly worm across his broad face. He was an under-king of the Southern Ui Neill in his own right, and the leader of the Caille Follamain tribe. He owed his allegiance to Mael Seachnaill. Aed Findliath proclaimed that it was he, Donnchadh, and his progeny from this day forth who would become the principal line of the Southern Ui Neill and if this command was disobeyed or any treachery took place, Aed Findliath would march south once more and ravage Meath and massacre its people.

At this final blow, all Flann Sinna could do was help his father, the once mighty king, Mael Seachnaill mac Mael Ruanaid, back behind the palisades of Tara and to the warmth of his fire. Mael Seachnaill's people were saved, but his power was now utterly broken.

It was later in the year 862, on the winter solstice, when Mael Seachnaill son of Mael Ruanaid, son of Donnchad, son of Domnall; descendant of Niall of the Nine Hostages, passed away peacefully at the fort of his son Flann Sinna. Feilimidh the druid composed a lament for the great king:

"There is much sorrow everywhere; there is a great misfortune among the Irish. Red wine has been spilled down the valley; the only King of Ireland has been slain."

None of the Kings of Meath attended the funeral, nor did any of the Northern Ui Neill. Even Flann's own mother was denied passage south to see her first husband buried. He was laid to rest at the monastery at Kells. Flann Sinna swore a vow upon his father's grave: he would take back the High Kingship, whatever it took, and bring the Northern Ui Neill to heel. All treachery suffered by his father and Clan Colman would be answered tenfold. He lived only to make it so.

# PART 1

## THE RISE OF
## FLANN SINNA

# DRAMATIS PERSONAE:

**Aed Findliath** (*Aid-fin-lee-at*) – King of the Cenel nEoghain and the Northern Ui Neill. Son of Niall Caille and father of Niall Glundub.

**Aengus mac Donnchadh** (*Ang-gus-mac-dun-ic-ah*) – Son of the King of the Caille Follamain tribe of Meath and hostage and cupbearer to Flann Sinna.

**Aibreann ingen Mael Seachnaill** (*Ab-rawn-ingen-male-shock-nail*) – Sister of Flann Sinna and wife of Ivar the Boneless.

**Aidan mac Fergus** – Head of Flann Sinna's guard and distant cousin from a cadet branch of Clan Colman.

**Ainbith mac Aedo** (*Ann-bith-mac-aid-oh*) – King of the Ulaid and Dal Riadan tribes and under-king of the Northern Ui Neill.

**Alfred** – King of the Saxon Kingdom of Wessex and enemy of all the Viking warlords in Britain. Known as Alfred the Great.

**Ardal** – Young warrior and scout of Clan Colman.

**Bairid Ivarsson** (*Bar-id-ivar-son*) – Eldest son of Ivar the Boneless, first generation of the Ui Imair Norse-Gael clan.

**Bjorn Ragnarsson** (*Byorn-ragnar-son*) – Eldest son of Ragnar Lodbrok also known as Bjorn Ironside, fearsome Viking warlord and explorer.

**Brunbolg Headtaker** (*Brun-bulg-head-taker*) – Physically gigantic Viking warlord, subject to the influence of Ivar the Boneless.

**Cathal mac Conchobar** (*Caw-hal-mac-con-co-bar*) – King of Connaught.

**Ceallach mac Cearnach** (*Kyell-och-mac-kyarn-och*) – King of the Breffni tribe and under-king of the Northern Ui Neill.

**Ceitl Flatnose** (*Ket-tel-flatnose*) – Ancient King of Limerick with alliances in the Hebrides and Scandinavia.

**Cerbaill mac Dunlainge** (*Ker-ball-mac-dun-langa*) – King of the province of Osraige, Uncle to Flann Sinna and powerful political player.

**Cinead mac Alpin** (*Kin-aid-mac-alpin*) – A legendary deceased Scottish king who vied for power amongst other Norse and Scottish chieftains.

**Conchobar mac Murchu** (*Con-co-bar-mac-mur-ku*) – Son of the captain of the contingent of warriors assigned to protect Clonmacnoise monastery from attack.

**Congalach mac Finnachta** (*Con-gal-och-mac-fin-och-ta*) – King of Argialla and under-king of the Northern Ui Neill.

**Constantine mac Aed** – Scottish Prince and nephew of Queen Mael Muire.

**Constantine mac Cinead** – King of Scotland and older brother of Mael Muire, High Queen of Ireland.

**Diarmuid mac Aguire** (*Dear-mid-mac-ag-wear-ah*) – Warrior of Osraige under Cerbaill mac Dunlainge.

**Domnall mac Aed** (*Donal-mac-aid*) – Eldest son of Aed Findliath and Prince of the Cenel nEoghain and the Northern Ui Neill.

**Donnchadh mac Aedacain** (*Dun-na-ka-mac-aid-a-cawn*) – King of the Southern Ui Neill and the Caille Follamain tribe.

**Donnchadh mac Flann** (*Dun-aca-mac-flann*) – Prince of Clan Colman and the Southern Ui Neill, later to become known as Donnchadh Donn, or Donnchadh of the Brown Hair.

**Eithne ingen Aed** (*Eth-knee-ingen-aid*) – Daughter of High King Aed Findliath and princess of the Northern Ui Neill, married to Flann Sinna.

**Flann Sinna** (*Flann-sin-na*) – King of Clan Colman, one of the major Southern Ui Neill tribes.

**Flannacain mac Ceallaig** (*Flan-na-cawn-mac-kyal-ig*) – A Southern Ui Neill under-king and King of North Brega in Meath.

**Fogartach mac Tolarg** (*Fo-gar-toch-mac-tol-arg*) – Prince of South Brega and hostage and cupbearer to Flann Sinna.

**Geroid** (*Ger-oh-id*) – Lord Abbott of Clonmacnoise monastery.

**Giric mac Roth** – Powerful Scottish chieftain and usurper of the power of the line of Cinead.

**Gormlaith ingen Flann** (*Gorm-la-ingen-flan*) – Daughter of Flann Sinna and wife to Niall Glundub.

**Gormlaith Rapach ingen Murchada** (*Gorm-la-rap-och-ingen-mur-kada*) – First wife of Aed Findliath the High King.

**Guthrum** – Viking warlord of immense power, enemy of Alfred the Great of the Saxons.

**Halfdan Ragnarsson** – (*Half-dan-ragnar-son*) – Leader of the Great Heathen Viking army that sacked Britain, son of Ragnar Lodbrok and older half-brother of Ivar of Dublin.

**Harald Fairhair** – King of Norway.

**Hvitserk Ragnarsson** (*Vit-serk-ragnar-son*) – Renowned warlord and brother to Ivar the Boneless.

**Ivar Ivarsson** – Middle son of Ivar the Boneless, first generation of the Ui Imair clan.

**Ivar Ragnarsson** (*Ivar-ragnar-son*) – Known as Ivar the Boneless throughout Europe. Joint King of Dublin with Olaf the White his older half-brother and notorious Viking warlord. Founder of the Ui Imair dynasty.

**Land** – Wife of Mael Seachnaill and mother to Flann Sinna. Queen of the Southern Ui Neill.

**Lugaid** (*Lug-ad*) – Clan Colman warrior in the Clonmacnoise garrison.

**Mael Muire ingen Cinead mac Alpin** (*Male-mwir-a-ingen-kin-aid-mac-alpine*) – Daughter of famous Scottish King Cinead mac Alpin and wife to High King Aed Findliath. Mother to Niall Glundub.

**Mael Padraig mac Mael Curarada** (*Male-paw-rig-mac-male-coo-ra-rada*) – King of Argialla.

**Mael Seachnaill mac Mael Ruanaid** (*Male-shock-nail-mac-male-ruin-ad*) – Father of Flann Sinna, King of Clan Colman and the Southern Ui Neill and High King of Ireland.

**Murchu mac Diarmuid** (*Mur-ku-mac-dear-mid*) – Clan Colman warrior and officer in charge of the defences of Clonmacnoise monastery.

**Niall Caille** (*Niall-kile-ya*) – Deceased King of the Northern Ui Neill and former High King of Ireland. Father of Aed Findliath.

**Niall Noigiallach** (*Niall-noi-gee-allak*) – Also known as Niall of the Nine Hostages. Semi-legendary ancestor of all Ui Neill nobility.

**Oitir Auislesson** (*Ot-teer-ow-shla-son*) – Viking warlord and leader of the Isle of Mann.

**Olaf the White** – Much older half-brother of Ivar the Boneless and Joint King of Dublin.

**Ragnar Lodbrok** – Infamous long-deceased Viking warlord, brother of Turgesius and father of many Viking rulers and chieftains.

**Sean mac Brian** – Warrior of Osraige, serving King Cerbaill mac Dunlainge.

**Sichtfridh** – Youngest son of Ivar the Boneless, first generation of Ui Imair.

**Sigurd Ragnarsson** (*Sig-urd-ragnar-son*) – Notorious Viking warlord of Denmark and Frisia, half-brother to Ivar the Boneless.

**Thorstein Olafsson** (*Tor-stin-olaf-son*) – Surviving son of Olaf, nephew of Ivar the Boneless and cousin to the Ui Imair dynasty. Called Thorstein the Red.

**Tolarg mac Ceallaig** (*Tol-arg-mac-kyell-ig*) – King of South Brega and under-king to the Southern Ui Neill.

**Turgesius** (*Tur-geese-e-us*) – Deceased Viking warlord, brother of Ragnar Lodbrok and founder of the city of Dublin.

**Ubba Ragnarsson** – Leader of the Great Heathen Viking army that sacked Britain, half-brother to Ivar the Boneless.

**Uincent** (*Inch-ent*) – Gnarled chieftain of Clan Cairbre, subject to the King of Clan Colman of the Southern Ui Neill.

# CHAPTER 1

# THE MARRIAGE TO
# EITHNE, DAUGHTER OF AED
# (876 AD)

Flann led from the front of the caravan, the spear tip amongst his warriors and extended family. The captain of his guard, his cousin Aidan, had insisted that he take his leisure in the wagons alongside his son Donnchadh and his daughters Gormlaith and Eithne; but he had declined. It would not do to be seen by the men from the Northern Ui Neill to be weak and pampered, amongst the women and the baggage. It was important that he was perceived as a warrior to be respected and feared. It had taken a week of travel to traverse the mighty Esker Riada roadway that bisected the heartland of his territories, to get to the ancient monastery of Clonmacnoise, but they were almost there now.

The esker traditionally divided the country into two from the days of his ancestors where north of the esker was *Leath Cuinn* or Conn's half and south of the Esker was *Leath Mogha* or Mogha's half. Seven hundred years previously it may have served as a boundary between ancient kingdoms, but today it served as the main arterial roadway between the Kingdom of Meath in the east and the Kingdom of Connaught in the west. Despite its sandy rills and ruts and the occasional boulder that blocked the way, it was a relatively simple route to move through his own territory. The alternative was to face the arduous trek through the bogs of Offaly or the vast forests that shrouded the west of his lands. Neither passage seemed optimal especially with women and children in the party.

The Esker itself was circuitous and meandered across the country like a river, but at the cost of time, Flann had considered it a gentler route for the children, attending womenfolk and servants for his soon-to-be Queen. His party totalled exactly ninety-five people. It was made up of four children, ten women, twenty stewards, labourers, advisors of various descriptions, and of course an honour guard of sixty warriors under the command of Aidan mac Fergus. They travelled carefully and peacefully, but still warily. Flann had known almost four years of peace since 871 with only the occasional raid from the Connaught men across the Shannon to contend with, but this was Ireland and bad things could always happen.

The monastery of Clonmacnoise marked the western edge of Clan Colman and Southern Ui Neill control in the region, with the wide expanse of the River Shannon providing the border with the west. The monastery itself had been built during a time of strength for the Ui Maine, one of the strongest tribes in Connaught, and they had granted the land to the founder of Clonmacnoise, Saint Ciaran, several centuries ago. Since then the Southern Ui Neill had taken control of the monastery and the surrounding territory when the Connaught men had retreated across the Shannon long ago. Mael Seachnaill his father had always demanded hostages and tribute from the Connaught men and they had always acceded to his wishes for fear of invasion. In return he had helped them fend off attacks from the Munstermen and the occasional Viking raid from the Shannon. Now the Connaught men, just like him, owed their allegiance to Aed Findliath in the north.

The thought of marriage somewhat terrified him but in truth he had yearned for the company of a good woman for some time. His first wife Gormlaith Ingen Conaing, was the sister of the former King of North Brega in east Meath, a princess of the Sil nAedo Slaine, a minor Ui Neill clan. She was a striking woman with long brown hair and uncanny humour and wit, and he had been grateful to his father for the match. Mael Seachnaill had made the marriage for Flann when he was very young to strengthen bonds between the tribes of the Southern Ui Neill at a time of tension in the region. She had borne three children over the years but the last one, his daughter Eithne, had proven too much. After a difficult birth Gormlaith had passed away. She was subsequently buried in Knowth in North Meath with her people, in the old way.

*

Although the island of Ireland was predominantly Christian, the old gods and traditions had quietly found a place buried in the new faith, especially within the tribes of the Ui Neill. Bealtaine, Brigid's day and the solstices had been integrated into the Christian calendar by the wise clergyman that had come and gone over the centuries in Ireland. Flann did not care what gods were worshipped under his rule whether it be Dagda, the Christ or the All Father of the Norse and Danes. As long as they swore him allegiance and obeyed his rule and gave tribute, he was indifferent. He had remained unmarried over the last four years, electing to wait patiently for the right political match to emerge. He had kings from all over the country and even some of the Welsh kings from across the Irish Sea looking to match a sister or a daughter with him.

For the past thirteen years since his father's submission to the Northern Ui Neill, he had kept his warriors out of the many internecine conflicts that had occasionally flared up around him, only once travelling in serious force and even that was an economic opportunity rather than a territorial or power-driven dispute. His people had thrived as a result. Massive yields in the annual crops had yielded massive crops of children in equal measure and the population of his kingdom rose and prospered. The wars in England had drawn away a lot of the power of the Dublin Vikings and his discreet family connection with Ivar the Boneless had kept Clan Colman relatively insulated. Other kings observed his quietly growing power and wanted to secure his allegiance now in a time of relative peace.

Flann knew his star was rising and understood perfectly that other kings had noticed this too. Flann saw through them all though and the matrimonial chance he had patiently been waiting for had finally arrived. Aed Findliath, the High King of Ireland, had offered the hand of his daughter Eithne in marriage to him. Why was the question though? And why now? Flann, who kept himself abreast of all political machinations in the country, could guess at the answer to both, but he refused to allow himself to leap to conclusions until after the wedding.

*

At times during the journey his son Donnchadh had his horse saddled and came to ride beside him. As they approached Clonmacnoise, Flann made sure the boy with him could see the entire monastery in all its magnificence. Donnchadh was only twelve years of age but looked as big and strong as a lad several years older. His long dark brown hair somewhat reflected his dead mother's image but the face, the build and even the attitude was all Mael Seachnaill. *Give this boy another ten years and feed him plenty of beef and venison and he would be the High King come again,* Flann thought. This was the furthest Donnchadh or any of Flann's children had ever travelled but it was important to introduce them all as quickly as possible to his new young wife Eithne, for her sake as well as theirs. Eithne in truth was far closer to Donnchadh's age than she was to Flann's and she undoubtedly would be intimidated by him, but as a princess of the Ui Neill he knew she would do her duty by her father.

The esker was noticeably reducing in height as they travelled further west toward the River Shannon and Flann recalled from memory that either over the next rise or the one after that the complex would be revealed in the morning light. Flann had travelled to Clonmacnoise perhaps a dozen times over the years and each time it had not failed to mesmerise him with its austere beauty.

"Where is it, Father?," Donnchadh enquired, peering into the middle distance with impatience.

"Take your time, son, in moments we will see it," Flann replied.

The caravan stretched back half a mile and would take some time to reach the monastery, but Flann knew he and Donnchadh would shortly witness it together. He told Aidan his captain to halt the rest of the convoy for a few moments and he beckoned his son forward. He wanted for the two of them to enjoy this moment together, seeing Clonmacnoise together for the first time, the largest Christian monastery in Ireland.

*

They cantered down the banks of the drumlin they had summited together and past a copse of pine trees. The sound of the Shannon could already be discerned as it thundered its way south toward Limerick. Another couple of hundred yards' riding revealed all. Flann didn't look at the monastery but instead glanced at his son to witness his wide-eyed reaction.

It was one of wonder. Clonmacnoise was enormous.

A massive stone wall surrounded an open area many acres wide, hugging the River Shannon close. An imperious stone tower that had been constructed fifty years ago dominated the compound, a sure defence against Viking raids. More than fifty small buildings with thatched roofs glimmered in the morning sun and hundreds of shacks, huts and other abodes were built around the outskirts of the holy grounds, so much so that you could really accuse Clonmacnoise of being a small town rather than a Christian holy place. Flann could understand it, given the regularity of Viking raids over the last fifty years; the people saw the robust stone walls and lofty tower and had retreated there for safety.

On the banks of the river more than two dozen fishing vessels, currachs and other barges were moored up. Hundreds of people were milling about between the buildings and traversing an open area that clearly served as a market square outside the front gates. Enormous flocks of sheep were corralled in various pastures and paddocks around the monastery, some shepherded by normal people while others were overseen by tonsured members of the holy brotherhood of Saint Ciaran. It gave Flann great joy to see his people, under his protection, thriving in the throes of commerce like this in times of peace. Donnchadh was amazed and visibly thrilled at the sights he saw, every one a delight to him.

"I will race you, Father, to the front gates!" he shouted before emitting a might *whoop* and he thundered down the hill toward Clonmacnoise.

Flann smiled and had no option but to follow.

It took several hours for the entire retinue to decamp and set up their quarters for their stay. The soldiers would all sleep in tents pitched to the rear of the complex and use their time constructively by training with sword and spear with the local militia. Aidan's men were the cream of Flann's armed forces and there was no harm in having them show the local militia how to fight. The commander of the local garrison was a gnarled veteran of a score of battles at the side of Flann's father Mael Seachnaill. His name was Murchu mac Diarmuid and he had lived here at Clonmacnoise for this past thirty years from the time when the barbarian Turgesius raided up the Shannon. Flann had made his way immediately to Murchu upon arrival to enquire on all comings and goings of the past year and how things sat in Clonmacnoise.

It was Murchu himself who had suggested the joint training and drills in the fields outside the walls, complaining that some of his men were as green as summer grass and had never so much as seen a proper professional soldier apart from him, never mind participated in a battle against actual warriors. Flann had agreed, deeming it wise. With that off his chest, while sharing a glass of mead with his king, Murchu divulged the news from Clonmacnoise and the surrounding territories since Flann's last visit. The river was quiet apart from Viking traders coming up the river from Limerick, selling their wares in exchange for sheep, furs and grain. Several boats also occasionally sailed from the North too, from the territories of the Breffni heading south, but they rarely if ever stopped at Clonmacnoise.

News had come his way of trouble brewing between the old King of Limerick Ceitl Flatnose and the Kings of Munster, and there had also been some Viking raids on settlements on the coast of Galway and Mayo. The only news of real note was that the Viking town of Limerick had swelled in its number of inhabitants as warriors had returned from the wars in England laden with gold and slaves. Murchu had raised the possibility of more raids up the Shannon but Flann dismissed it as unlikely without referring to his secret non-aggression pact with Ivar in Dublin. The fewer that knew about that the better it was for Clan Colman. They finished their mead and walked out to attend the mock battles to the south of the monastery. Sixty veterans under the command of Aidan mac Fergus faced off with two hundred and fifty of Clonmacnoise's finest under the command of Conchobar mac Murchu, son of the commander. Both sides were armed with wooden swords and shields and lined up twenty yards apart. Conchobar desperately tried to form them up into a semblance of a line while Aidan mac Fergus did not even have to issue a command, his men responded on instinct. The fight was one-sided and thankfully short. The men of Clonmacnoise were blitzed and battered with dozens of them lying groaning on the ground.

"Mother of Jesus," exclaimed Murchu as he stormed into his men in the aftermath.

"Lugaid, what were you and your men doing on the left flank? They carved through you like piss through snow." He belted the beaten-up and somewhat sheepish-looking sergeant on the side of his helmet.

"You think that sort of stuff would work against the men from Connaught, or the Vikings of Limerick? Un-bloody-likely!" He stormed off through his two hundred and fifty men, berating them and giving lessons simultaneously.

Flann looked over to his captain Aidan who just smiled and winked in his direction. Flann laughed and walked off in search of his children to see what mischief they were up to. The caravan from the North had not yet come and Flann had yet to gain an audience with the Abbot. There was still much to do before the sun went down.

After checking with the ladies assigned to mind his younger children and witnessing Donnchadh mingling with the boys his own age, he made his way toward the stone church to the side of the stone tower. *It is good to see Donnchadh mixing with those boys. When I die, he will have to lead them,* he thought, *they will remember how impressive he is.* At the entrance to the church one of the tonsured monks was waiting for him to escort him inside the building. There was a set of uneven steps leading up to the oaken front door of the church and a piece of hollowed-out masonry that served as a vessel for holy water for those who wished to enter. The man introduced himself as Brother Padraig and waited, staring at Flann. It took Flann a moment to gather that the holy man was waiting for him to dip his finger into the holy water and bless himself with the sign of the cross. For the sake of expediency Flann rolled his eyes and went through the motions. It seemed to placate Brother Padraig and he obsequiously opened the door for Flann to enter.

The Abbot, a man called Geroid, waited at the foot of his alter, dressed in his more exotic robes of office, and beckoned Flann to come forward with one hand while flipping his other hand to Brother Padraig, banishing the young monk from their presence. Flann's teeth ground involuntarily. He knew what the Abbot was doing. The message was clear: *You might be the King of Clan Colman, but in here you will defer to my authority.*

"Welcome, King Flann Sinna, King of Clan Colman. As a humble servant of the Lord, I welcome you to Clonmacnoise.."*Humble indeed,* thought Flann.

"How fares the monastery of Clonmacnoise and its surrounding lands, my Lord Abbot?" Flann answered with a forced smile and clapped the clergyman on the shoulder.

The Abbot grimaced as if a foul smell had passed his nostrils; the physical contact had disconcerted him, as Flann knew it would. The Abbot quickly regained his composure and ushered Flann to the rows of wooden pews arranged the length of the church.

"Let us sit, my King.." The two men sat down in the very front seat. The Abbot shifted his robe before beginning.

"King Flann, I have several matters of import to discuss with you before we go through the particulars for your marriage to Princess Eithne of the Northern Ui Neill.."

Flann inwardly winced, *here we go.*

"As you know, the Christian faith is one of charity and peace and as you can see, a viable town has been built around our humble monastery. Your man Murchu mac Diarmuid has done an admirable job in keeping both my brothers and the folk living outside of our walls safe." The Abbot steepled his fingers and appeared to gather his thoughts. "I have debated with myself on the matter and I believe it is time to station a larger garrison of your soldiers from around Meath to ensure our protection."

Flann searched around for an answer, one which would deny the Abbott but soften the blow sufficiently. Flann usually left it up to local garrisons to provide protection to the towns and villages in his territory as he did not sustain sufficient full-time soldiers to deploy them everywhere at once. While Flann wrestled internally for a suitable response, the Abbot sprung his trap.

"My brothers and I take no sides in politics in Ireland and apart from the heathen Viking savages of Limerick and Dublin, we have no enemy among the people of this Island. Recently Cathal mac Conchobar the King of Connaught has granted us land on the western bank of the Shannon and has offered to aid us financially in the building of a wooden bridge and a permanent ferry linking east with west. He has also advocated the implementing of a minor toll for commerce on the Shannon, which would of course be split three ways between you, the King of Connaught and of course the Holy Church, so as to better tend to our flock. What say you, mighty King of Meath?"

Flann froze for a second and ever so slowly, raised his eyes to meet the Abbot's. The Abbot attempted to hold his gaze but in moments quailed under Flann's stare. All arrogance and resolve fled him in the furnace of Flann Sinna's implacable visage.

The fact that he would call Flann the King of Meath made him livid. He was not and had never been King of Meath and the Abbot's attempt to curry favour had the opposite effect.

Flann began speaking quietly. "My dear Abbot, although the governance of Clonmacnoise is yours by right, your lands and autonomy are guaranteed by me, Flann Sinna, the King of Clan Colman of the Ui Neill. If you ever attempt to gain even a modicum of independence from my rule it is not the Vikings you need worry about. I will bring down a force of men from the plains of Meath and we will sack the monastery, OURSELVES!" He screamed out the last word. "I am the authority in these lands. If Cathal son of Conchobar wishes to parley deals on what is my land, he can come to me himself at Kells, Tara or Navan. But I warn you this, Abbot, you tell your... friend—" his hand shot out like lightning and he grasped the Abbot roughly by the collar, "that he should come with a host at his back or he will find himself at the bottom of Lough Owel with the Viking Turgesius."

The Abbot began to stutter and wave his hands in terror. "But, but, but, m-m-my K-King, I-I-I…"

At that moment Brother Padraig returned through a side door. "Lord Abbot, my King, the Northern Ui Neill have arrived!"

If the young monk noticed his monarch manhandling the Lord Abbot, he gave no sign before turning and leaving as he came in.

"We will discuss this later, my Lord Abbot," Flann said as he released the monk and straightened out his robes.

With a wink, a nod and a smile Flann Sinna left the firmly intimidated Abbot to regret his arrogant stupidity. If Flann Sinna wanted a bridge over the Shannon and to toll the river, he would bloody well do it himself and perhaps ravage Connaught while he was at it.

The wedding took place two days after the Ui Neill arrived. The service itself was presided over by the Lord Abbot and some of his brethren, with the senior members of the Southern Ui Neill and Northern Ui Neill contingents filling the pews inside the church. There were several notable men who attended, arriving either with the Northern Ui Neill caravan or separately with their own small group of retainers. Flannacain mac Ceallaig, cousin of Flann's first wife, arrived a day after Flann. He was a spare, lean whip of a man and haggard despite his youth. He was clearly carrying a wound of some sort to Flann's trained eye. None of the Caille Follamain had come, the true Kings of Meath, as Clan Colman and the Caille Follamain were at odds ever since their king, Donnchadh mac Aedacain, had treacherously sided with Aed Findliath to depose Flann's father many years ago. They had neither warred against each other nor come to each other's aid in the intervening years and an uneasy truce had crystallised.

From the south, Flann's notorious uncle, Cerbaill mac Dunlainge, the King of Osraige, had seen fit to attend. He was a monstrous bear of a man, a veteran of a hundred battles, and he arrived with a retinue of hard men at his back who were almost as fabled as he was: Sean mac Brian, the slayer of the King of Munster in 856, and Diarmuid mac Aguirre, a distant relation to one of the under-kings of Leinster and who allegedly killed eleven Northmen in a single battle. His uncle had been central to the political turbulence in Ireland from his seat in Osraige for twenty-five years and seemed to draw fabled warriors such as Sean and Diarmuid to him. His appearance was strange all the same; weddings were not usually high on his uncle's list of priorities, Flann thought, *perhaps there is more going on than meets the eye?* The northern contingent was no less sprinkled with nobility but with one enormous absentee. The High King himself, Aed Findliath, had not deigned to attend the wedding of his own daughter. In his stead he had sent his eldest son Domnall to walk his daughter down the aisle and to presumably speak for him.

At first when informed of this by his captain Aidan, Flann raged inwardly at the disrespect of it all, but when he took a step back from it, he perceived several interesting possibilities at this turn of events. Perhaps it was a good thing? Amongst other notables were Ceallach mac Cearnach of the Kings of Breffni, Ainbith mac Aedo, King of the Ulaid and ruler of the Dal Riadans, and Dal nAridi also; and a man that Flann had never met before, Congalach mac Finnachta, the King of Argialla. *Now what would a man whom I have never met, be doing turning up to my wedding?* he wondered. There was too much recent bad blood under the bridge for anyone from the Kings of Munster or Connaught to attend a Southern Ui Neill marriage of state. The Kings of Leinster were subject to the Caille Follamain and owed them their allegiance, and due to the uneasy standoff between the two main clans of the Southern Ui Neill, the Leinster men had sent no representative to avoid antagonising their over-king.

The relationship that Flann maintained with Ivar of Dublin was a private affair. He was forbidden to hold truck with his brother-in-law by Aed Findliath himself, and even his foray to Scotland with Ivar in 870 was kept quiet despite more than three hundred of his own warriors having gone there in the company of the Vikings. They knew what side their bread was buttered and had sworn on the old gods and the Christ, never to betray Flann to the Northern Ui Neill.

None from Dublin would be in attendance. Flann's sister Aibreann had often visited with him and his family over the years, discreetly, but with most of the noblemen of the Northern Ui Neill in attendance, Flann deemed it wise to maintain the illusion of no relationship with Dublin. He would introduce his last living sibling to his new wife in secret when the excitement had died down and his contingent had returned home to central Meath.

The service itself was beautiful and the ladies he had brought with him, plus the companions of his new Queen, had done an extraordinary job in joyously decorating the church for the ceremony. They had also co-opted some of the soldiery to erect the tent for the celebrations afterward and the whole town was invited to attend. Flann smiled to see grizzled warriors carrying garlands, hen-pecked by bustling high-born ladies. Flann barely remembered his first wedding it was that long ago, and he certainly didn't remember the guests who attended apart from the obvious few. It saddened him to think that for his beautiful and indeed dutiful young bride, it was the biggest day of her young life and yet the happiness for this coupling was of secondary importance to the politics of the union.

Aed Findliath's daughter carried a high price in loyalty and potential future conflict for all in attendance. Eithne was a surreal beauty; a daughter of Aed Finliath and his first queen Gormlaith Rapach ingen Murchada. She had died in childbirth just like Flann's first wife, in 861. Eithne possessed long red hair and clear skin and stood as tall as most of his warriors. She was gently spoken; her demeanour was very calm and she exuded nobility. She smiled often and was wonderful with his children. Donnchadh was standoffish with her initially but by the feast she had won him over, hitting him in the head with blackberries from the high table. The feast itself was wonderful with a banquet for all to plunder at their will and the mead, beer and even wine from Francia flowed freely courtesy of the King of the Ulaid who traded occasionally with neutral Norse-Gael traders from the Hebrides. A squall of rain did not dampen spirits and a massive bonfire was lit to the chagrin of the Christian monks who equated it with a nod to the gods of old. If Flann was honest with himself, it was, but he didn't care, especially after the stunt the Abbot had tried to pull earlier.

At sunset, the dancing started, and the Mead started to really flow, but Flann had commanded Aiden to oversee things in his absence; there was a serious event about to occur behind closed doors. He kissed his new wife and bid his children goodnight before meeting the eyes of the kings and princes present. They retired to a large stone cloister near the front gates of the monastery's grounds that Flann had set aside for this purpose. It was used by the monks to illuminate holy books during the day, but the easels and other paraphernalia had been removed and a large pine table had been set in their stead. There were no seats and the kings and princes present took their places, standing at intervals around the ugly piece of furniture. Some monks set some jugs on the table with mead and some cups before being dismissed by Flann. This he sensed could and would be the most important meeting of his life after the subjugation of his father by Aed Findliath.

"Why has your father consented to me wedding his daughter, Domnall? Why is your father not here himself, what am I to make of that?" Flann was abrupt and to the point deliberately.

Prince Domnall of Aileach was a large man like his father but lean and bookish. He was no coward; a veteran of a number of battles against recalcitrant chieftains and Viking raiders, and in a room like this with the men inhabiting it, Flann thought the direct route would yield the best results. To his left, his uncle crossed his arms and peered at Domnall, an arrogant sneer painted across his lips. The limping Flannacain mac Ceallaig leaned heavily and wearily on the table to his right, his wound worsening by the hour. Domnall was flanked by the Kings of Ulaid and Breffni with the King of Argialla on the right wearing a brooding indignant snarl. Domnall reached for a jug of the mead and slowly poured himself a drink. Flann could nearly taste the uncertainty that Domnall harboured. None of the men in this room were his father's enemy. In fact, most were at least nominally under his father's control, but any sign of weakness here could sow the seeds of rebellion down the track should Domnall come to power, regionally or nationally.

Flann had a secret card to play: he had learned through his brother-in-law Ivar that Aed Findliath was having terrible trouble dealing with Viking raids from the Orkneys and the Hebrides. Flann was pretty sure that all the kings here were aware at least partially of that. The real issue though was to the southeast of the Northern Ui Neill territory. Donnchadh mac Aedacain, in an unholy alliance with Vikings from Dublin, mercenaries from Leinster and the King of South Brega, Tolarg mac Ceallaig; had been ransacking Northern Brega. They had even begun to raid and pillage the Kingdom of Argialla. If you presumed to be High King of Ireland and demanded tribute from those under your control, you must be able to protect those kings. The constant battle with the Norsemen that infested the Hebrides and the Orkneys had drained some of Aed Findliath's strength and the Caille Follamain knew it. He had Domnall, and by extension the High King, over a barrel if they asked him for some sort of support. His father Mael Seachnaill had always impressed upon Flann in his youth to *never ask a question unless you already knew the answer.*

Domnall took a deep draught before speaking. "King Flann, my father has instructed me to give the hand of his most beautiful daughter in marriage, in his stead. He is confident that such a gesture will help reconcile any… ah… trouble our two clans may have had in the past, but…"

"And why is the High King himself not here to speak these words and instead sends… you?" interrupted Flann.

That drew a chuckle from his uncle Cerbaill. A flight of anger rippled Domnall's brow but he ignored the sally.

"My father is otherwise disposed, and many important issues consume his attention. Because he has taken Mael Muire, daughter of Cinead mac Alpin, to wife ten years ago, he has agreed to foster two of her nephews and their education is a priority. They are of an age with my youngest brother by Mael Muire, Niall Glundub. Civil war rages in Scotland and they are under his protection at the behest of his wife. The Vikings harass our northern coastline constantly and our armed forces are kept busy patrolling the shores of our northern kingdoms. The Great Heathen Army that has devastated the entire isle of the Britons has disbanded into allied strongholds dotted across the island and from these bases they hit all kingdoms, including ours, not under their control."

Silence reigned in the cloister but nobody was surprised by this news.

"I repeat, Prince Domnall," Flann calmly answered, "what is it you want of me and why is the High King himself not here to ask it?"

All eyes were on the Prince now and he duly crumbled.

"My father," he paused if searching for words, "is a proud man and I can admit to you nobles that he would not like to lose face in this matter. He believes, perhaps, he made a mistake in the removal of Clan Colman and the installation of the Caille Follamain and their King Donnchadh mac Aedacain, as the ruler of the Southern Ui Neill."

With that Cerbaill mac Dunlainge laughed out loud and slapped Flann on his back. It was Flannacain, the King of North Brega, who spoke next.

"My lands are the lands being raided here, Prince Domnall. Every couple of weeks our cattle are being stolen, our people are being enslaved and our men are being killed. I bent the knee to the Caille Follamain and the Northern Ui Neill, and accepted the judgement of your father, but my lands are being ravaged. My own treacherous cousins in Lath Gore have joined in the slaughter. It's true, Mael Seachnaill did business with the Vikings of Dublin, but at least when he was High King my people had peace and prosperity. Now they are at the mercy of barbarians from the south and plunderers from the southwest. I demand that you reinstate Flann Sinna son of Mael Seachnaill as King of the Southern Ui Neill or I will renounce your father as High King!"

Ceallach of Breffni roared at Flannacain and threatened to come across the table with the word traitor on his lips, but he was restrained by King Cerbaill of Osraige as easily as if he were a child.

Once settled, Ceallach shouted at Flannacain across the table, "A king who can't defend his own people is no king at all. Instead of treachery, hand the reins to your son or your brother; at least they would have the balls to face Ivar and Donnchadh in open battle!"

Shouted arguments and heated exchanges flew back and forth across the table in flurries but Flann waited until it all died down before responding.

"If your father recognises me as King of all the Southern Ui Neill, I consent to leading my forces against Donnchadh."

Domnall winced at that. "My father cannot be seen to take a side here, or Donnchadh – who is married to the daughter of the King of Connaught – may march north." He puffed himself up with pride. "We are the Northern Ui Neill, still more powerful than any three of your kingdoms combined" – Flann doubted the veracity of that but allowed him to continue undebated – "yet even our forces would be stretched thin facing the Vikings, and the forces of Connaught and North Meath also. Even if we did win, it would devastate the land. How long, I ask you, until the Eoghanchta rise up in Munster or Ceitl Flatnose, the old demon, comes raiding up the Shannon unchallenged?"

Howls of derision erupted from every corner, some were offended, some were appalled, Cerbaill just laughed as was his wont.

Flann spoke once more. "I will give you what you ask, Prince Domnall, but on certain conditions. Firstly, the old traditions must resume. The Northern and Southern Ui Neill kingdoms will alternate the High Kingship and the seat of power will always be in Tara." A weary nod of consent came from Domnall after a moment of consideration.

"Secondly, the Tailteann Fair must resume at the autumn harvest to rekindle our old alliances between north and south so as to end hostilities and build friendships amongst all of our kingdoms."

Nods of agreement came from all corners of the table and several *ayes* were muttered by the assembled kings.

"Thirdly, Ivar the Boneless is my brother by marriage, by my father's doing, not my own. If I can, I want the authority to deal with him politically rather than raise swords against his stronghold. Should we attack him and draw his warriors into battle, how long before Halfdan, Ubba, Hvitserk, or Sigurd land on our shores with thousands of berserkers to reinforce him?"

This third condition drew shouts of denial and anger from the others, but Flann patiently waited for the noise to dissipate. Common sense would prevail or so he hoped once they considered the ramifications of raising arms against Ivar of Dublin.

"These are my terms, Domnall son of Aed, will you accept them? Or shall I take my new wife home and watch from Tara as Argialla, East Meath,

Breffni, the territories of the Ulaid and the Northern Ui Neill burn?" Domnall considered all of what Flann had said. He took another gulp of Mead and nodded to himself, slamming the cup down on the table.

"I will agree with those terms, on one condition; if any sons are born to you and my sister Eithne they will become heir designates of Clan Colman and the Southern Ui Neill ahead of your eldest son."

The room went quiet. Any sons born of Flann and Eithne would be grandsons of Aed Findliath and nephews of Prince Domnall and his younger brother Niall Glundub. A quick glance right revealed what Flann had expected, Flananacan mac Ceallaig was unhappy with this condition. Donnchadh Donn as he was affectionately known – was related to the Northern Bregan kingdom through Flann's late wife, but Flannacain mac Ceallaig was as much at the mercy of this arrangement as Flann and Domnall were. It was his lands that were being ravaged.

Flann answered, "I accept."

# CHAPTER 2

# THE UNHOLY ALLIANCE
# (877)

The forces of Clan Colman moved as quietly as a host of two thousand men possibly could through the depths of the night. The weather was clement which pleased Flann as the march would not diminish his men's store of energy before the fighting. If they were discovered by some element of the enemy, it would help to have sure underfoot conditions to fight in. The host marched out of eyesight on the south bank of the River Boyne, obscured by the undergrowth and trees that stood sentinel on its banks. It had taken two weeks to summon his men from all corners of his kingdom, and they had fully assembled at Drum Samhradh some forty miles from the intended battleground. Every single one of his chieftains and minor kings had supplied men to his force, keen to see their brothers of North Brega freed and the oppression of the Caille Follamain ended. The vanguard of Flann's force was led by Uincent of Clan Cairbre, a veteran commander of men and old enemy of Donnchadh mac Aedacain himself, *a perfect choice,* Flann thought. Uincent's hatred for Donnchadh, the usurper of Clann Colman, would surely rub off on his men come the battle.

This freed up Aidan mac Fergus, Flann's cousin and general, to lead fifty scouts into the forests and hills to look ahead and report the movements of each force as they approached the intended battlefield of Slane on the banks of the Boyne. The rear of the force was led by Diarmuid mac Aguirre who represented Flann's uncle Cerbaill mac Dunlainge in the field. His uncle and his other fifteen hundred warriors of Osraige had a different role to play, a role that had been set in motion months beforehand in anticipation of this battle. For some time Cerbaill had been ravaging the lands of the Kings of Leinster, thus forcing the Leinster men to deal with him rather than supplying any aid to Flann's enemies. Diarmuid mac Aguirre, although a sworn man to Cerbaill, was originally a Leinster man and to spare him the pain of fighting against potential relatives, Cerbaill had sent him north to reinforce his nephew Flann.

The Caille Follamain had being allying with men from Leinster to plunder North Brega for more than a year, and the people were afraid to farm and instead huddled inside their chieftain's forts in fear of being slaved or massacred. This was intolerable to Flann and one way or the other there would be a reckoning. In terms of numbers, the forces available to each side were relatively even, but Flann had formulated a subtle plan so full of deception that even King Alfred the Great of the Saxons would have approved. For a couple of weeks now, Flann had conspired with Flannacain mac Ceallaig, the King of North Brega, to goad and threaten Donnchadh mac Aedacain and try and force battle upon the Caille Follamain. It had worked. Arrogant in their power, the Caille Follamain had begun gathering their forces a week after Flann had assembled his and had reached out to the Vikings of Dublin and Tolarg mac Ceallaig, the King of South Brega, for support. Flannacain had not been discreet about where he had moved his forces to, in a subtle attempt to draw Donnchadh into a fight.

Slane was the place where Flannacain, to all appearances, would make his defiant last stand against the King of the Southern Ui Neill. Aidan mac Fergus and his spies had employed riders through the night to bring word to not just Flann on the south bank of the Boyne River, but also to Flannacain mac Ceallaig, on the movements of the enemy hosts to the west and the south. The Boyne River at Slane was only seven or eight feet deep at its deepest point and therefore fordable. Flannacain wished to make Donnchadh believe that he was deploying his forces there to access an easy route of retreat if his forces were routed. It was a ruse. Unbeknownst to Donnchadh, Congalach mac Finnachta, the King of Argialla, had moved his forces to a hidden vale near the monastic town of Kells and waited for the host of the Caille Follamain to pass through. They had instructions to follow on behind, wary of any scouts and to wait until battle was joined before entering the fray. Flannacain would wait at the ford in Slane to meet Donnchadh and hold him long enough to allow reinforcements to arrive. Donnchadh's allies, the men from South Brega, would surely cross the river and attempt to hit Flannacain from the south and Aidan and his scouts had confirmed that this was exactly their intended strategy.

The enemy had no word of Flann's forces approaching from the west under cover of darkness from the undergrowth. Flann's army would wait until nearly half of the warriors loyal to the King of South Brega, Tolarg mac Ceallaig, had crossed the river before hitting them in the flank. Congalach's forces would simultaneously take the Caille Follamain from the rear in that moment, leaving their enemies with nowhere to go and nowhere to retreat. The final blow would be dealt to the forces of South Brega from an unexpected source. What Donnchadh did not realise was that his assumed ally Ivar the Boneless was not in fact an ally, he was an enemy. It made Flann laugh when he thought of Donnchadh's lack of understanding of the treachery of Vikings; *had he learned nothing from the last fifty years?* Ivar's forces would hit the men from South Brega as they forded the river and their host would be cut to pieces by the dragon-headed prows of the Vikings.

If the forces of South Brega broke, both Ivar and Flann would reinforce the position of Flannacain mac Cellaig and catch the Caille Follamain in a vice and the battle would be over. Flann was riding in the middle of his army, lost in the subtleties and intricacies of the plan when Aidan and one of his scouts rode up panting and out of breath.

"My King," Aidan gasped between great heaves of his empty lungs, "Ivar and his forces are hidden in a cove at Bru na Boinne, the ancient Celtic holy place some ten miles east of here. He eagerly awaits your presence. We must leave now though to avoid the scouts of the army of South Brega."

Flann smiled. It had been too long since he had seen with his own eyes the scourge of Francia, the leader of the Great Heathen Army and the King of Dublin. He kicked his heels into the ribs of his horse and followed Aiden eagerly. Ivar the Boneless had come.

Flann and Aidan carefully steered their mounts through the path that meandered parallel with the south of the River Boyne, silent as fieldmice and ever alert to the sound of undergrowth moving or branches breaking in the night air. They had sent their young scout, a young man named Ardal, south to watch for the approaching South Bregan army and to return to Flann's force once their approach was marked. This was Ardal's first battle and he was unknown to the Vikings of Dublin, unlike Aidan and Flann. The King felt it was wise to send him back rather than risk him being mistaken for a South Bregan scout in the darkness instead of a man of Clan Colman. Uincent of Clan Cairbre had command of the Clan Colman forces; Flann felt it was more important to make sure Ivar and his warriors kept to the plan he had devised. Flann recalled that when he had broached the plan to the Boneless, Ivar had responded somewhat petulantly, stating that every battle plan is great until the first man is killed. If Flann knew his brother-in-law's mind, he had hurt the Viking warrior's pride by not requesting any input from him. The plan was simple in a way, and with men such as Uincent and Diarmuid to lead Flann's considerable forces, he knew that his wishes would be carried out. Flann was eager to gauge the mood and the strength of Ivar's forces, *if we could bloody find them.* The river was wide, deep, dark and slow-moving at this point and emitted a low steady rumble rather than the crash of fast water against rock. There were no sounds of life except the whistling and warbling of some nocturnal birds and the wind amongst the trees. Flann rode on for a moment beside Aidan before pausing suddenly – *nocturnal birds that weren't the hoot of an owl, impossible this time of year.*

"Aidan, stop," he hissed. He listened carefully to the night. He and Aidan warily turned their mounts hither and thither on the pathway, carefully searching their surroundings for something out of place, some glint from an unsheathed weapon or the sound of a bowstring grown taut. The track they followed east was densely forested and the starlight revealed little out of the ordinary. A few yards ahead a huge boulder, some ten feet tall and the same wide, served to fork the path. The left pathway accompanied the river, the right turned to the south. *There it was again, a sound out of place.*

This time Aidan heard it too and silently drew his short sword from its scabbard. If scouts had come upon them from King Tolarg's forces, the entire battle could be undone. Flann nodded to Aidan and then to the river that flowed no less than ten feet through some brush to their left. They would take their chances in the water rather than risk capture. Aidan let out a curse under his breath and Flann glared at him. Now was not the time for errant noises.

"Something hit me in the head, my King" he rasped.

Flann himself was next to feel a sharp little blow right between his eyes. He glared left and right. *Is this some children's idea of fun,* he raged inwardly? If it was, he would discipline the boy or boys most severely. He heard a chuckle from up above them.

On the giant boulder in their path, completely unarmed but for a pile of conkers, sat Ivar the Boneless; the King of All Foreigners in Ireland. At his whistle, ten men emerged from the undergrowth that Aidan and Flann had never even realised were there, armed killers one and all. Aidan was shocked but Flann could only smile at his fabled brother-in-law. *Typical,* he thought.

"Flann of the Shannon," Ivar said in his broken Irish, "you are most welcome to my camp."

With that he somersaulted off the rock, landing on his feet like a cat. His extraordinary athleticism had clearly not diminished despite being forty years of age or beyond.

"Well met, brother-in-law," Flann said. Ivar had found Flann, not the other way around.

The Viking camp was well secluded from prying eyes, in a natural depression cut into the rising land on the south of the river. It was invisible to the casual eye for anyone marching from the south, and it also had a sandy beach on the south bank for Ivar's men to haul their longboats ashore and cast off quickly if required. Flann counted ten ships and each usually carried a complement of forty or fifty Vikings. It pleased him to know that Ivar had delivered as promised. Four or five hundred hardened fighting men were at his disposal and would almost certainly split the forces of South Brega at the ford. Flann sent Aidan to get settled around a campfire with some of Ivar's guards while he and Ivar walked toward the ships together.

"How goes it in Dublin, Ivar?" Flann ventured.

While Ivar considered his answer, Flann eyed up his brother by marriage as it had been several years since he had seen him in the flesh.

Ivar was a massive man like all his fabled brothers, huge even for a Viking. He was not slabbed in thick muscle like some of his fellow Danes and Norse that followed his command, but leaner like a greyhound. The moniker the Boneless came from his astonishing athletic ability and his ambidextrous style of fighting that made him almost unbeatable in single combat. Flann was a big man, well over six feet tall, but Ivar overtopped him by several inches. He wore his hair in a long dark braid that dangled down his back like a horse's tail. What was unusual about Ivar's hair was that he had a natural white stripe that dissected the raven black colour of the rest. He also shaved his beard which was unusual amongst the Northmen.

"All is in turmoil, Flann, with the death of my brother Olaf and most his sons in Scotland; I am now King of all the Norse and Danes in Ireland. I had to return from Britain to secure my Irish holdings as word of infighting had reached me. Ceitl Flatnose, the old bastard, was trying to exert influence upon Dublin and raise up the Norse against me. Oitir son of Auisle, my own cousin, has been taxing Waterford, Wexford and Longford without my consent. He may be the King of the Isle of Mann but he owes the Kingdom of Dublin his allegiance."

It didn't surprise Flann in the slightest to hear of the dissension amongst the Viking kingdoms of the Irish Sea. Many Irish kings seemed to believe that the Northmen were a great cohesive force and they had already maximised the extent of their power, but Flann knew this to be untrue. Indeed, they were even more factionalised than the Irish kings, and no one Viking ruler could ever claim dominion over them all. Vikings followed legend, cunning, vision and strength in that order and Ivar possessed each in abundance. He had put no fewer than four British kings to the sword and sacked a dozen cities across Britain, Francia and the Umayyad Caliphate to the south. He had participated in the sack of Paris in his early teens and could call on the allegiance of more than a dozen small Viking kingdoms. He was the son of Ragnar Lodbrok, the most notorious warlord to ever have set foot on a Viking longship. *Thank Christ Almighty that he was the youngest of Ragnar's sons,* Flann thought, *for if he was the eldest, he perhaps would have been the one who could unify them all. Francia, Britain and Ireland would have all burned.*

Flann prided himself on keeping abreast of all the comings and goings of the world outside of Ireland. His father had always explained to him that what happened in Britain especially, always echoed in Ireland. He pressed Ivar for more information, carefully though lest he offended the warrior-king or was perceived to be prying into the Viking world too much. They were as friendly as an Irish king and a Viking ruler could be, but as with all Vikings, Ivar could be as changeable as the tide.

"How fare your brothers, Ivar? When we left Dumbarton Rock those few years ago, you were not on good terms."

Ivar wearily glanced in Flann's direction. *Maybe he suspects I'm fishing.* Flann lowered his eyes, throwing a stone in feigned nonchalance into the river. The Viking lord shrugged his shoulders then and continued, his arms crossed across his broad chest.

"Ubba has joined forces once more with Guthrum and they march on Wessex, sacking and burning. Alfred has retreated into the wilderness with his forces and has had great success hitting their camps in the night. I warned Ubba that so far from London and East Anglia, he would have trouble subjugating the Saxons. Hvitserk has raised some forces and struck out on his own. He has joined the Kieven Rus to forge his own path and raids the Slavs, Bulgars and the Khazar Khaganate to the east. Halfdan has overall command in parts of Britain and has laid claim to Eastern Mercia and some of Northumbria. He wields influence in Yorvik amongst the Danes and the Saxons, and Sigurd fights with him."

Ivar stopped walking for a moment and turned to Flann.

"It's possible, Flann, that Halfdan as my oldest surviving brother may turn his gaze west to Ireland and look to gain fealty from Dublin."

Flann's heart skipped a beat. Halfdan was a fiend with a savage reputation and his presence in Ireland would only mean war. "What will you do, Ivar?" Flann enquired.

The Viking uncrossed his hands and cracked his neck and each of his fingers, both shoulders and then his back. "I will be forced to meet him in open battle."

The walked on in silence then for some time, circling the campfires on the bank.

"My brothers seem to have forgotten Olaf who was second oldest of us after Bjorn Ironside himself. He was slaughtered by Constantine in Scotland with two of his sons… with only Thorstein his youngest surviving. Harald Fairhair the Norse King has defeated Constantine in battle and ravaged his eastern coastline, but the lord of the Picts has regrouped. Thorstein licks his wounds in the Hebrides with his mother's kin possibly trying to raise another force. All the survivors from our sack of Dumbarton Rock have swelled Constantine's numbers, Flann. When I have time, I am going to try and convince my brothers to march and sail north and smash this King of the Scots once and for all and end the line of Cinead mac Alpin."

Normally, Flann would scoff at the ambitions of kings and noblemen who proclaimed mighty deeds to come and make tremendous oaths for various purposes, most of which never came to pass. But Ivar the Boneless said what he meant, and he meant what he said. The question was, should he warn the Northern Ui Neill of Ivar's plans? He would have to give it thought. The High King of Ireland was the brother-in-law of the King of Scotland after all.

As the night wore on most of Ivar's men drifted off to catch snatches of sleep before the battle in the morning. Scouts had reported intermittently to Ivar and Flann throughout the night that all forces, both enemy and ally, were approaching as predicted. Flann was a veteran warrior, but his belly fluttered at the thought of the violence to come. The Vikings on the other hand chatted amiably amongst themselves in their guttural tongue and slept like babies under their sealskin or deerskin cloaks. It astonished him how they could have such apathy toward what could result in their possible deaths. He didn't know whether it was because of a sickness in the brains that all Vikings possessed, or the fact that commanding them was perhaps the greatest Viking commander to have ever existed. Mael Seachnaill, Flann's father, had often told him about the death of Turgesius, the first true Viking lord to invade Ireland, and even when Mael Seachnaill had him tied down with rocks around his torso and thrown him into Lough Owel to drown, his last words were of defiance not of pleading or fear. These men were of the same ilk.

Three hours before dawn, one of Ivar's men approached the campfire beside which Ivar and Flann had decided to see out the night. Ivar turned to Flann after a short report.

"It has begun; the forces of Donnchadh mac Aedacain have met with the forces of Flannacain mac Ceallaig. They are exchanging bow volleys on the outskirts of the fort at Slane. The men from South Brega are three hours out from the ford of the river and your own forces are in position waiting to attack under the old man of Clan Cairbre. The men from Argialla are approaching the rear of Donnchadh's forces from the northwest and remain undetected. We will leave in a short while and come upon the force of South Bregans as they cross the river."

Some of Ivar's men began to stir as his captains spread the word throughout the camp. There was still some time before they would set sail, but the Vikings began to prepare to leave anyway. Flann witnessed some of them brew the awful mushroom concoctions they consumed from large cauldrons before battle to heighten their aggression. He saw others sharpening their axes and swords with whetstones and checking the fletching on arrows.

"I would like you to meet three lads here, brother-in-law," Ivar announced.

He flipped himself up with an impossible thrust of his body and stood beckoning three lean and long men to approach. Flann stood up and went to greet them but stopped in his tracks upon closer inspection of the trio.

"Can this be... Ivar, three of my nephews?"

The look was unmistakable. They bore some resemblance to Flann's sister Aibreann but mostly they resembled their legendary father in both countenance and mannerisms.

"Flann of the Shannon, meet Bairid my eldest, Ivar and Sichtfridh.

Each clasped the arm of Flann in the Viking way. *They are far more Viking than Irish,* he acknowledged. They exchanged some pleasantries in Irish which pleased Flann; their mother had obviously beaten some history into them on the other side of their heritage. Bairid was perhaps twenty and the other two were in their teens.

Their father issued instructions to them in their native tongue. The youngest, Sichtfridh, was deeply unhappy by the end of them but a harsh word from their father quelled any rebellious outburst. Flann looked inquisitively at his brother-in-law as to what was said. Ivar sat down again and beckoned his three sons to do the same beside him.

"Bairid and Ivar will join us in the battle, Sichtfridh will guard the camp."

The two older lads guffawed at that and Sichtfridh stormed off in disgust. Ivar shrugged between morsels of chicken.

"I won't risk all of my three oldest sons in a single battle; he will do as I command. Come, Flann of the Shannon, tell them the tale of the siege of Dumbarton Rock to raise the spirits."

The two remaining sons made themselves comfortable and settled in closer to the fire and even a few Vikings around the other fires leaned in a little closer to hear, all expectant on a tale from Ivar's past.

Most of Ivar's men were very young and green and had not been present at his many battles on British soil. Flann looked wearily across at Ivar to see if it was some trap or if there was a limit on what he could say. Ivar never met his eyes, but Flann decided that to mention the disunity of the sons of Ragnar at that point in time or even currently, would be unwise. He began the tale:

"As you know, your father and his brothers had invaded the Saxon Kingdoms over the course of several years. Indeed, some of your uncles fight there still and rule lands. Your father, in this time, personally saw to the execution of kings from Northumbria, East Anglia and Mercia. After the sack of these kingdoms,

Ivar and his brothers agreed that he would join forces with his oldest brother Olaf, as he had done many times before, and go north along the western coast on the Irish Sea. Ivar would attack the Kingdom of Strathclyde while Olaf would fight against the Pictish Scots and their king, Constantine mac Cinead."

Ivar looked up at Flann at this point and Flann decided not to mention the defeat of those forces nor the death of Olaf. It wouldn't do to speak of defeat on the eve of battle and the flicker in Ivar's eyes showed that the Viking concurred.

The two brothers were oblivious to the subliminal exchange though, riveted by the tale. Flann elected to continue:

"The stronghold of Dumbarton Rock was the capital of Strathclyde or Alt Clud as the Scottish Gaels sometimes called it; a fortress that had never been captured by force since the time of the old Roman kingdoms. Other Vikings, Saxons and even my people, the Irish, had tried to take this stronghold but none had ever succeeded…" He paused for dramatic effect. "Until your father. Your uncle Ubba was stretched thin in Mercia to the south and Northumbria to the north and needed most of the experienced men to fight for him on his campaigns. Your father decided to approach me and your dead great aunt's husband Cerbaill mac Dunlainge about reinforcing him. He convinced us to go. Ivar travelled in force with Danes, Norse and Irishmen under his command. We landed on Easter Sunday and surrounded the hill upon which the fortress sat. Three times in the first few weeks, their forces tried to break out, but we beat them back behind their walls. Allies of theirs attempted to break our blockade from land and sea, but your father's man, young Brunbolg Headtaker, smashed their naval forces and your great-uncle Cerbaill drove them off on the land, routing an army of Picts and another of Britons.

"Eventually their water and food ran out and they opened their gates and attempted to flee. Your father, your great-uncle and I shared in the plunder and a great haul of slaves was taken. We slaughtered many men. Not only was the King of Alt Clud put to death as your father broke his back over his knee, but a former under-king of Munster was found within too. He had attempted to cower with the women and for that your father had him stripped and brought back to Dublin to be sold to the Muslims of the Umayyad Caliphate."

The two brothers were enthralled at the tale and a good number of men had dropped what they were doing to listen in. All Vikings loved a tale of battle even if they had heard it a hundred times before. They had never heard it from an Irish king though, a man who had actually been there.

Flann continued: "That ended your father's campaign in Britain and ended his time at the head of the Great Heathen Army, as it was known. He left to deal with political situations in Ireland but not before having killed four British kings and selling another Irish king into slavery, doomed to pull an oar most likely for some Berber barbarian. Dumbarton Rock, an unbreakable fortress for almost a thousand years, fell to Ivar the Boneless at the cost of only forty men. That sort of victory can never be forgotten by the histories. But for my part – and your great-uncle Cerbaill's – we must remain hidden lest our over-king of the Northern Ui Neill uncover our participation."

The two lads scoffed at this with the younger Ivar saying, "Those Northern Ui Neill are soft, we have been raiding them for two sum—"

His father sharply rose from his seat and glared at his younger namesake. Ivar had never intended to allow Flann to know that. He decided to pretend not to have heard his nephew's comment and continue with further embellishments of the tale, but at that moment one of Ivar's captains approached and spoke in their own language. Flann didn't need any translation; it was time to leave. The sun was rising.

# CHAPTER 3

# THE DEATH OF
# THE KING OF ALL THE
# FOREIGNERS IN IRELAND
# (877)

The midday sun shone down on the battlefield, almost but not quite dispelling the pall of smoke, blood and death that shrouded everything. Flann's hands shook from the fighting and he felt as tired as he ever had in his life. He had seen thirty-seven winters but felt like a man twice as old. He had done very little fighting himself in reality and only had to draw his sword at the end when a force of South Bregans had tried to break back across the river after the Vikings had shattered them on the north bank. He had parried a few blows from a man with a mane of red hair who fought with desperation to get away from the Vikings, but it had been his nephew Ivar by his side that had disembowelled the man with a blow from his axe. *I have won a battle without killing a man myself,* Flann thought. He stumbled on up the hill, attempting to gather his wits about him for what must come, slaloming his way through the piled corpses of slain warriors littering the ground. Blood and viscera matted the grass and occasionally a groan of pain from a wounded man would break the unsettled silence that had endured since the end of a battle.

Here and there priests and monks attended to men lying dead on the ground and they also oversaw the digging of pits for the slain. Captured men sat in circles in silence under guard from laughing Vikings or grim-faced warriors from Clan Colman. Flann had only been informed second-hand as to what had occurred in the battle between the Caille Follamain and the forces of Flannacain mac Ceallaig and the Argialla. A captain of his had reported that once the arrow fight had died down both the Caille Follamain and the Northern Bregans marched upon each other, and battle was joined. The Caille Follamain had initially begun to drive the forces of Flannacain back through weight of numbers and would have taken victory if not for the men from Argialla arriving at their rear. The forces of Donnchadh mac Aedacain were caught then between a rock and a hard place and began to suffer heavy losses almost immediately. It had taken a few hours but eventually the men of the Caille Follamain had submitted and bent the knee, having lost over two hundred men. Their leader Donnchadh was taken uninjured and was under guard by two of the sons of Congalach mac Finnachta, the King of Argialla. Flannacain mac Ceallaig had survived the battle too, unwounded, and was taking his ease inside the walls of the fort of Slane and seeing to his men.

The battle on the banks of the river had been just as hard-fought. It had started well if imperfectly. The Viking longboats had been sighted slightly too early as the South Bregans were crossing the river and Ivar had no choice but to pick up the pace and smash into them. They broke the South Bregan host into two uneven parts like a rotten stick but the main strength of King Tolarg still stood on the south bank. Flann's own forces had struck from the west at that moment but with the majority of Tolarg's forces remaining with their king they vigorously met the men of Clan Colman amongst the trees. Flann's warriors failed in surrounding Tolarg's men and the South Bregans were able to battle their way to an ordered retreat back the way they had come. It took two hundred men of Ivar's forces under the command of Bairid Ivarsson and Brunbolg Headtaker from the river to completely break Tolarg's men, and after several hours of fighting the South Bregans finally ran from the site of the battle in disarray.

Meanwhile, Ivar and the remainder of his forces landed on the north bank of the river and gave chase to the quarter of Tolarg's men that had reached the shore. Flann and Aidan had joined this group at the rear behind the Boneless' shield wall with Ivar Ivarsson acting as a bodyguard beside them. Ivar had insisted on assigning his son as a bodyguard to Flann and Aidan on the pretext that he was unwilling to let the next High King of Ireland die under his watch with five thousand Irishmen surrounding his mere five hundred. Flann, though, was one of the few people to be able to see right through Ivar and not be blinded by his legend, and knew it was just as much to keep his son from the thick of the fighting as anything. Bairid his eldest son was the veteran of five or six raids and battles already and had earned his father's trust. Ivar Ivarsson had not even half that amount of experience and his father was unwilling to blood him in a battle with thousands of Irishmen on either side. The battle had effectively split into three at that point. Some of the forces of Ivar in concert with most of the strength of Clan Colman chased Tolarg mac Ceallaig on the south of the Boyne, the Argialla and the North Bregans fully subdued the Caille Follamain on the flat fields to the west of the fort of Slane, and Ivar and two hundred of his men faced around two thirds of that number fighting uphill to the east of the fort.

This last fight was a minor skirmish, in a relatively obscure battle for control of the Kingdom of Meath. In the annals of history Flann knew that it would barely be recorded. In the storied and blood-soaked history of the mighty Ivar the Boneless it was about as important as an alehouse brawl. And yet, Flann Sinna had witnessed Ivar the Boneless die. An arrow had taken him in the chest from a man of South Brega. He had fallen but had time to take his two swords in hand, his weapons for his final journey to the halls of Valhalla. And so passed Ivar son of Ragnar, the scourge of Francia, the leader of the Great Heathen Army and the King of all the Foreigners in Ireland. As Flann trudged up the hill to take oaths of fealty from Flannacain mac Ceallaig in the fort, his eyes were watered. He would blame the smoke of the battlefield should any of his men ask, but he knew that wasn't true. Ivar the Boneless in life had been a heathen barbarian, a slaver and a pirate, but as Viking warlords went, he was the best of them. Flannacain had joyously went to greet Flann Sinna once he had entered the fort. He roared and bawled his praises and loudly extolled his virtues as a leader, but Flann himself could only utter a few numbed sentences in praise of the courage of the warriors of North Brega in response to the men's cheers and those of their king. He agreed with Flannacain that they would have a feast tonight to celebrate the victory and praise those slain in battle in the old way. Aidan mac Fergus could see that Flann was distracted and barely aware of what was going on. He stepped in to organise the particulars with the exulting king lest Flann say something unseemly or fail in his courtesies. Flann thanked Fergus and took his leave of Flannacain before returning outside into the air and was inevitably drawn back to the side of Ivar. Even in death the great Viking warlord had a magnetic effect on men. In the battle's aftermath, both Flann's forces and the Viking forces under Bairid Ivarsson had crossed back over the Boyne to join with the main bulk of the combined armies. They had sent for the youngest son Sichtfridh and the Vikings had sailed the remaining ships upriver from their hiding place at Bru na Boinne.

A massive crowd now surrounded the pyre being built for Ivar the Boneless at the crest of the slope leading down to the river. His three sons had commanded their men to drag the largest of their ten ships up the slope to the ridge to form a base for the pyre. Ivar's fearsome captain Brunbolg had removed his armour and leather tunic and had joined in with the men, all seven feet and four hundred pounds of him, adding his enormous strength to the task. Multiple Irishmen including some of Flann's own men had offered to help drag the large ship across the land but were rebuffed. Only the Norse and Danes were allowed approach. Branches, leaves and other flammable kindling were piled inside the ship and around its base in a massive pyramidal pile. A bed was made at its summit and Ivar's remains were placed on top of it with many weapons and offerings to their strange gods laid across his corpse. A horse was killed and placed to the side of the boat to ride in Valhalla. Flann had heard that some Vikings were laid to rest inside of cairns or inside buried ships with grave goods, but Ivar had told his brothers and sons that should he fall in battle, he was to burn. He would ride the towering pillar of smoke to

Valhalla and meet his deceased brothers and father, in whose mighty company he would feast and drink in the Halls of Odin the Allfather. He would do battle in Odin's heavenly wars from this day until Ragnarok.

The three sons each carried a torch alongside Brunbolg. Bairid Ivarsson was rigid in his grief and dour in his expression. Ivar Ivarsson was clearly angry, teeth bared as if they were about to crack with the strain. Sichtfridh was weeping uncontrollably, the death of his legendary father too much to take for a young lad of such tender years. The four torch bearers had their torches lit and a dirge began in their native tongue, sombre and menacing, from the throats of the hundreds of Vikings present. At the crescendo of the Viking song, the three brothers and Brunbolg Headtaker lit the four corners of the pyre simultaneously. It took more than three hours for the fire to consume all of the combustible material. The Irish warriors who witnessed it left as the time passed, looking for food or checking on wounded friends or relatives. No Viking moved an inch. Neither did Flann or Aidan. Flann deemed it important to pay his respects at this moment as even the very wise couldn't say what the reaction of the Vikings would be if respect wasn't paid by the Irish. It was Bairid who moved first, close to sundown. He stirred as if awakening from a bad dream and unsheathed his sword and raised his shield. He strode toward the fort and all of his warriors arrayed themselves behind him as he passed. No word was spoken by any Northman as they lined up in an intimidating formation.

The Irish warriors stood back, allowing the column of Vikings to pass, which Flann deemed wise. Flann joined the march adjacent to Bairid but maintained a respectful distance. He didn't ask him where he was going, he already knew. Donnchadh mac Aedacain would not survive this day. The King of South Brega, Tolarg, had fled with the survivors of his force south, back to Lath Gore and the security of his massive hill fort there. That left Donnchadh alone as the senior commander of the enemy and Bairid would hold him responsible for the death of Ivar.

Flann knew what lay in store for Donnchadh, he would fight Ivar's son Bairid to the death. If, somehow, he prevailed against Bairid, he would then fight Ivar

Ivarsson. If he miraculously survived that fight, he would face Brunbolg or one of the other champions amongst the Vikings until he fell. He had not slain Ivar by treacherous means as the Boneless had simply died during the course of battle. For that, Donnchadh would receive the honour of a warrior's death. He would die by the sword or axe, the honour of Ivar's family demanded it. Flann's enemy Donnchadh had been tricked by Flann and his allies into a battle that they couldn't win and would pay the ultimate price, but Flann couldn't help but feel that he was still lucky to die in his manner. The sons of Ivar could have easily blood-eagled him, a gruesome form of execution where a man's lungs were pulled from his back and rested on his shoulders. Flann had witnessed the aftermath of that form of execution once in his youth and it still haunted him. Instead Donnchadh would die with a sword in his hand and a curse on his lips.

The Vikings approached the temporary stockade where Donnchadh was being held. King Congalach mac Finnachta stepped forward and met the column of Vikings twenty feet away from the wooden stakes that served as the wall of Donnchadh's cell.

"Halt, Bairid mac Ivar. I know what you intend but I must deny you. This king is answerable to me. He led two raids inside my territory and his actions have resulted in the deaths of many of the people of Argialla. It was I, Congalach son of Finnachta, who captured Donnchadh in battle and as such his life is mine."

Flann noted that Congalach did not mention the almost certain presence of Vikings alongside Donnchadh on those raids, wisely leaving it out, yet still he was impressed with Congalach's courage to step out in front of a column of furious Vikings and state his claim.

When Bairid stopped, the whole column halted too. The champion Brunbolg unsheathed his formidable battle axe from over his shoulder and clasped it in his massive paws on seeing the King of Argialla step forth. Congalach's personal guard drew their weapons also in response. Flann stepped in immediately and raised his arms to defuse the situation before the shimmering violence that was tangible in the air, boiled over and two of his allies tore themselves apart.

"King Congalach, Bairid son of Ivar, let us calm ourselves," Flann roared. "It is my wish that Bairid and his brothers get their justice this day for the death of their father. Everybody who fought today will take their share of plunder from the Caille Follomain and they will now fall under my rule. Everybody will be well satisfied with the division of spoils, King Congalach, you have my word as king. But Donnchadh mac Aedacain must die. Come forward, Bairid son of Ivar, and have your justice."

Congalach seemed mollified by these words and stood aside, and the host of Vikings roared their approval at the fight to come, clashing axes and shields together in a cacophony. A square was marked out on a patch of hard ground and Donnchadh was summoned from the stockade. There was a resigned, haggard look to his face when he emerged, but Flann could sense a sort of fatalistic determination in his enemy also, as he was handed his weapons. Hundreds of Vikings and Irishmen surrounded the square around the combatants as the two men prepared to fight. Donnchadh turned to face Flann, sword and shield in hand.

"Flann of the Shannon, I know I shall not survive this day, but you must grant me the right to speak as a fellow King of the Ui Neill."

Flann hesitated but then acquiesced with a nod. *Has he one more blow to strike before the end, physical or verbal?*

"Many years ago, I joined with Aed Findliath to remove your father from power, it is true, of that I am guilty. He hated your father's association with these heathens across from us now, whereas I was also ambitious for my Clan. I also felt that Mael Seachnaill was too open-handed with these Viking marauders and it turns out I was right. My mistake was to trust them also. All I did was for the greater good of the Caille Follamain and the Southern Ui Neill. Flann son of Mael Seachnaill, grant my soldiers their lives and the lives of their families and children and I will swear them to your rule right now."

Flann slowly nodded his head. Donnchadh bowed before him.

"My men are yours and under your protection, King Flann, I do so swear as my last act as King of the Caille Follamain."

He shook his arms loose, giving his sword an exploratory swing, and turned away from Flann and faced Bairid and the Vikings.

"As for you treacherous pagan barbarians, you are lower than the belly of a snake."

Not all of the Vikings understood Irish but the occasional man who did, hissed in anger at the insult.

"Bairid son of Ivar, you are the lesser son of greater sires. Perhaps I will slay you and your two brothers this day and erase some of the suffering that Ivar the Boneless inflicted on the Irish people by slaying most of his rotten brood. You are a pup, nothing more, and I am glad it is I, Donnchadh son of Aedacain, who has the chance to strike this blow against the Vikings, for Ireland. Beware, Congalach King of the Argialla, today you fought with these heathen monsters, but it will only be a matter of time before you will be fighting against them. Now come, Bairid son of Ivar, and join your father in the afterlife!"

At this Bairid screamed his hatred and charged the Irish king, unleashing a flurry of blows to the roar of the crowd. Donnchadh was well past his prime, with more grey than black in his beard and hair, but he had fought innumerable battles during his time. He knew what he was doing. An even more nasty inconvenience emerged for Bairid in the fight when Donnchadh changed his sword from his right to his left hand.

He was a *citeog*, a lefthander and had hidden that fact until now. Bairid would surely not have faced a warrior this experienced whose stance was unconventional. Bairid threw an endless sequence of bone-shattering blows at the old king to try and overwhelm him, but with little or no accuracy or plan. Each was easily parried by the old king. Flann recognised what Donnchadh was doing, he was hoping that the raw emotion of the fight would encourage Bairid to burn up all his energy against Donnchadh's shield and then the old man would have him as he tired. Flann threw a worried glance at the young but massive warlord Brunbolg Headtaker, catching his eye. Flann hoped that he wasn't as big an oaf as he seemed and would advise Bairid from the side of the square. *To lose one descendent of Ragnar Lodbrok was a disaster, but to lose two in a single day would be the end of Meath for sure, a pretext for invasion,* thought Flann worriedly. Brunbolg shouted some words to Bairid in his native tongue and Bairid quickly took a step back and began wearily circling the Ui Neill king. The Headtaker had clearly understood Flann's concern and had seen the same thing. *Thank Jesus Christ,* thought Flann.

Bairid moved to Donnchadh's right-hand side in a clockwise direction, wary of the left-handed strikes of the old king. The young Viking feinted forward, Donnchadh lunged, but Bairid's footwork was too sharp and suddenly he spun his way deftly behind Donnchadh. It was over. One slash of Bairid's sword and Donnchadh's head rolled free, stopping at the feet of Ivar Ivarsson. Ivar promptly spat on the decapitated head and stalked back down toward the ships, followed by the Viking forces. Flann exhaled a huge breath he did not realise he had been holding as the Vikings receded from the square, honour satisfied. With that stroke of Bairid mac Ivar, Flann Sinna was now the King of the Southern Ui Neill and the heir designate of Ireland.

# CHAPTER4

# THE HIGH KING OF IRELAND (880)

The snow fell gently on the slopes of Tara Hill as Flann strolled slowly, lost in thought, around the outside palisades of the fort. He enjoyed circling around his growing base ever since he had decided to make it the permanent headquarters for his kingdom. It was the winter solstice this evening and the weather seemed apt somehow, *perhaps a sign of good fortune.* Accompanying him were two of his hostages, one of whom led his horse and another who carried a jug of Francian wine and a goblet for Flann should he desire to quench his thirst. They served him personally but also received education with the monks at Treoit and training with sword and spear when not at his side. Both could read and write, a rare but growing talent in modern Ireland. One of the young hostages was a son of Donnchadh of the Caille Follamain who was slain several years before. His name was Aed and he was an able lad who seemed to bear no ill will toward Flann himself. At night in his cups, Flann often considered marrying him to one of his daughters when the time was right to solidify the relationship between Clan Colman and the Caille Follamain.

In the aftermath of the defeat of the Caille Follamain Flann Sinna had been very open-handed with them in an attempt to heal all wounds and resolve all grudges. Flann treated the Caille Follamain as valued allies and not as a defeated enemy. He wanted the Southern Ui Neill to act as one giant clan. He had not taxed them heavily nor allowed the Northmen and the men from Brega and Argialla to take a ludicrous sum in silver or livestock. No slaves were allowed to be taken either, which Flann remembered had irked his Viking nephews. It was the Viking way; if you won a battle the right to slave the vanquished was yours, but Flann had denied them. Flann had quickly gathered the chieftains of the Caille Follamain together in the aftermath of the Battle of Slane and made them swear their allegiance to Donnchadh's son Aed. He then had assured those same chieftains that Aed would receive his education in his court, a hostage in all but name. This was standard procedure amongst the kings of Ireland, and it didn't shock or offend the surviving leaders of the Caille Follamain. Two hundred good fighting men of theirs had been killed at the battle and Flann had sworn to help protect their lands and borders in return for their loyalty.

He made a public show of threatening the Argialla more for the benefit of the Caille Follamain than agitating a Northern Ui Neill kingdom, promising violence to them if they should think to raid south in revenge and attack his new subjects. This had the desired effect Flann wished and the Caille Follamain had been incredibly loyal to him since then. Congalach mac Finnachta the King of Argialla had died in battle the previous summer, fighting against Vikings on behalf of Aed Findliath. The new King of Argialla, Mael Padraig mac Mael Curarada, was a bookish man who at one stage had considered the religious life at the monastery in Armagh. He seemed amiable, affable, and harboured no threat or ambition to expand Argiallan land south. Only once was Flann forced to summon his warriors to stave off a raid from the men of Breffni, but they had been dealt with swiftly. In fact, Flann was glad of the fight at the time as it had united all the men under one banner to see off the Northerners. Victory was the best salve to heal all wounds between the clans. Friendships were forged amongst the men from all of Brega and the rest of Meath that day and a slew of marriages were made between the families of the lesser chieftains across Meath.

The second hostage Flann possessed was Fogartach mac Tolarg. Tolarg mac Ceallaig, his father, had escaped the Battle of Slane and had regrouped inside his fortress in Lath Gore. Flann had at the time considered marching south immediately to burn him out of his keep and have him drowned as a traitor, but when weighed up with the loss of life it would cost, he decided to demand that Tolarg's firstborn son join Flann in Tara as a hostage and foster son instead. Tolarg had agreed and Fogartach was sent to Tara on the next moon. He was a likeable young man, able and sure-footed, good with sword and spear, but Flann had made it plain to both Fogartach and his father that should the men of Lath Gore displease the King of the Southern Ui Neill, his life was forfeit. Knowing the Vikings as Flann did, he also did not really want to weaken Tolarg's military strength immediately after the Battle of Slane either. South Brega served as a buffer between Flann and the Vikings, and should a ruler rise in Dublin that was not as benevolent as his nephews, Tolarg would initially take the brunt of their assault. The Vikings had ravaged Tolarg's land on their way back to Dublin along the coast in the aftermath of the battle but had not really attacked in force since those first weeks.

The answer as to why saddened Flann. As Ivar the Boneless had predicted, Halfdan Ragnarson had sailed to Ireland at the head of a fleet to take not just Dublin but all of the Kingdoms allied to Ivar before his death. It had come to a head in the previous summer, when the fleet of Halfdan was caught from the rear besieging the Viking town of Linn that sat in the northeast corner of Flann's Kingdom. Bairid mac Ivar and his forces and those of his uncle met in a disastrous sea battle and both kings died that day. Halfdan, one of the leaders of the Great Heathen Army, and Bairid son of Ivar the Boneless, both now lay at the bottom of the Irish Sea. This had split the Vikings of Dublin. Some warriors felt that Ivar Ivarsson and Sichtfridh were too young to lead and deserted to the Kingdom of Mann or to the Danelaw in England. Others, particularly the Norse, looked to the half-Norse half-Dane son of Olaf the White to lead them. His name was Thorstein the Red and he had made his name rampaging across the lands of Scotland, plundering, slaving and reaving. He had only nominally ever paid obeisance to Ivar the Boneless himself and certainly had no respect for Flann's nephews. He used Dublin mostly as a base to launch raids and only ever wintered there. Outright violence had not yet spilled out between the Norse and Danes but it was only a matter of time, Flann felt. Unless Ivar and Sichtfridh proved themselves, Thorstein would take it all.

Flann had chosen early on not to intervene should that come to pass; his nephews must stand or fall by themselves. And besides, should Thorstein win, he would surely be weakened from the fighting and an opportunity could present itself. Perhaps then it would be time to finally bring Dublin under his control, a secret dream he had harboured since the fall of Ivar. All sixty thousand inhabitants would be his subjects and all their tribute and gold as well. If Dublin now bent the knee to Flann Sinna, all the kingdoms of the Irish Sea would have to beware. Young Fogartach tugged his sleeve, breaking Flann's train of ambitious dreams, and brought him to the present. The young Bregan pointed to the north. A long procession of people was emerging from the forest and farmland along the Slige Midluachra, the famous road to the north from Tara.

There were perhaps only fifty warriors flanking the wagons with notably several priests in attendance riding on mules. At the head of the caravan rode Domnall son of Aed, the statuesque son of the High King. Two young boys rode beside him and to his rear, a striking woman slightly past her prime but one who handled a steed very well. She carried a sword strapped to her back like a Viking warrior and a shield was slung on the flank of her horse. Flann prided himself on knowing all the names of important or powerful people in both his land and the surrounding nations that could affect his kingdom. He searched his brain for an answer. He cursed himself for his bad memory which had certainly worsened as the years progressed. And then it dawned on him. *That lady is Mael Muire ingen Cinaed, the wife of the High King.* If she was here, it could only mean one thing: Aed Findliath the High King of Ireland, Lord of the Northern Ui Neill, was dead.

*

The Bishop of Armagh approached the mound of Niall of the Nine Hostages surrounded by priests and acolytes, one of whom carried a massive crosier, the symbol of the Good Shepherd. Flann shivered as snowflakes settled on his hair and shoulders and melted through the thin full-length shroud he wore. The Liath Fail stone stood erect, now central to the Christian spectacle of an Irish king being crowned, despite its fabled past. It now represented the marriage of the history of the Irish people with the Christian faith of the land. Flann was not a religious man. He believed that God or the gods, old or new, Norse or Celt, only took care of the strong. There were people of at least three different religions living within his borders, but it didn't concern him. The Bishop and his entourage took an age to waddle through the thousands of people who crowded the walkways, doorways and even the roofs of the huts, halls and buildings, to witness the crowning of the new High King of Ireland, Flann son of Mael Seachnaill. He had time to look around and drink it all in.

Domnall, the grim-faced son of the now deceased High King, looked stoically on, his face creased with what Flann thought was worry. The impressive Queen, the Scot Mael Muire, held her arms around the two young boys to Domnall's rear. Once informed of the death of Aed Findliath, Flann had sent word to his under-kings and to Dublin, of his impending coronation and gave each several days to attend. Only Flannacain mac Ceallaig had made it in time along with some of his chieftains who had made their way to Tara anyway for the winter solstice celebrations. Immediately once Domnall had informed Flann of Aed's death formally, he had spent four days between the winter solstice and Christmas Day in isolation: fasting and praying in a gesture of humble piety to both the clergy and the people of Ireland. But that was ended and here he was ready to be crowned High King. Aiden mac Fergus, his loyal commander and friend, held the King's crown, sceptre, sword and cloak for when the ceremony reached its close. Flann knew very little Latin despite having been instructed for a time by his cousin, a Benedictine monk, but his ears perked up when he heard the occasional *Imperator Scottorum* droned or muttered by the clergymen present. It meant Emperor of the Irish in the old Roman tongue but only to an extent was it true.

In reality he controlled perhaps a quarter of the country and wielded influence and was paid homage from an area maybe half as large again if you counted the Leinstermen. He had dreamed of this day from when his father had ruled as High King and fought his wars with Munster, Leinster and Connaught, in search of fealty. His father had not succeeded. Someone somewhere always rebelled or raided or threw their lot in with the Vikings or some other mischief. Flann was determined that his reign would be different. He would unite the Northern Ui Neill and the Southern Ui Neill and would march west and south, bringing the Connaught, Leinster and Munstermen to heel. If or when the opportunity arose, he would bring the Viking kingdoms into the fold as well. *I swear it,* he silently vowed, *I will succeed where my father failed.* Aidan nudged him in the ribs. The priests had finally arrived onto the hill and he bent to receive Holy Communion from the Bishop of Armagh and make his pledges.

"Do you, Flann Sinna, accept overlordship of the People of Ireland?" the Bishop asked.

"I do."

"Do you promise to protect your people from violence and rule justly over the land?" the Bishop continued.

"I do."

"And do you take Mael Muire ingen Cinead to wife in the tradition of the Ui Neill?"

Flann looked over to his current wife Eithne sister of Domnall, but she betrayed no emotion about having to share her husband with the last wife of her father.

"I do as well," answered Flann. Mael Muire stepped forward to Flann, the Bishop and the Liath Fail stone. Each swore their marriage vows to the Bishop as was the custom and the union was blessed.

Flann had not spoken a word to her in his life. When she had arrived, he had been already cloistered away in a cell in preparation for his coronation. Now that he saw her, the transformation mesmerised him from when he had first witnessed her approach on horseback to Tara. She had arrived dressed in leathers, armed to the teeth, more akin to a Viking shieldmaiden than a Celtic princess. But now the beauty and nobility she possessed radiated from her and all he could do was admire her. She was almost of an age with him though, so the likelihood of children was negligible, but even still, he could tell that this regal lady would enhance the standing of his kingship considerably. The ceremony eventually reached its end with some prayers and Flann, in the company of both of his wives, retired to the feast hall to cheers from the people of Meath.

The feasting and celebrations continued for many days and on into the new year on the hill of Tara. The other Kings of Meath arrived with their senior advisors and immediate family sporadically, to pay their respects and swear oaths of fealty. Flann felt confident that South Meath was now completely under his control, but despite this he felt it was time to tour his entire domain from the Cenel nEoghain and the Ulaid to the north, to the Kings of Munster in the south. He would demand hostages from kingdoms that concerned him, threatening them with battle if they did not submit. Levies of cattle and other tribute would be demanded annually from the other kings around the country, a form of tax that the Irish called the Borumma.

Marriages were a valuable tool in forging alliances amongst his under-kings also; a powerful political tool. His father used to accept gifts from one king on his pilgrimages around the country and then give those very same gifts generously to the next king he visited. He would use this time to solve border disputes and other matters of law too.

The Viking world was best left alone for now as their looming civil conflict focused their attention inwardly and all Flann had to do was watch them unravel from a safe distance. It was best for the entire country to not draw their ire and perhaps unite them once more against the Irish. Every night of the celebrations, Flann had toasted his warriors and the people of Meath and from further abroad, from the high seat in his hall, but he never got too drunk or careless. He wanted to see when Domnall would make his move and return to the north. He intended to extract one last item from the King of the Northern Ui Neill. Domnall had made a critical error; he had only travelled with perhaps fifty men and that just wasn't enough to prevent Flann from doing what he wished; he was going to take both of the young lads that travelled with Mael

Muire and Domnall, as hostages. The boys had intrigued Flann and when the drink was flowing on the third night of the celebrations, Flann had approached them. He learned that both were ten years of age and they were cousins, not brothers.

The brown-haired lad was called Niall Glundub. He was a lively fearsome boy who would clearly grow into a warrior. He was the son of Aed Findliath and Mael Muire and was the heir designate of the Cenel nEoghain of the Northern Ui Neill until a son was born to Domnall. He would make a hugely valuable hostage until he came of age and Flann could shape him as he saw fit. Flann's daughter Gormlaith was almost of an age with him and would be a suitable match. The second boy was almost Niall Glundub's equal in importance. His name was Constantine mac Aed mac Cinead. He was a nephew of Mael Muire his new wife which would make him his own nephew by marriage, and he was a grandson of Cinead mac Alpin; the greatest Pictish king of all time. He was a curious boy, trusting and friendly. When Flann had tried to question him alone, Niall Glundub would butt in, fiercely protective of his cousin. When Aed, Constantine's father, had fallen in a civil war with a first cousin of their grandfather by the name of Giric the Son of Fortune, Constantine and his older brother Domnall had been whisked away under cover of darkness by men loyal to the line of Cinead mac Alpin. Their aunt Mael Muire in Ireland had taken them in, lest they become pawns or probable casualties in the internecine warfare there.

Scotland was a deadly dangerous place just now, Flann knew. Border disputes with the Bernician Saxons from the south, raids from Harald Fairhair and his Norsemen, and even attacks inland from the Vikings of Dublin and the isles, arguably made Scotland one of the most lethal places in the known world. It took a few nights more to gain the two lads' trust and get them talking. If they were to be his hostages and foster sons, they would have to get to know him. It was Niall Glundub who plucked up the courage to break the ice and ask Flann why he was called Flann Sinna or Flann of the Shannon. He had then told the boys the story.

Many years ago, as a boy younger than them, he told them, he had stowed away in the carts that supplied his father's warriors for battle. He wanted to see the fighting for himself and not be left at home. They had travelled to the Shannon where his father had confronted the King of Connaught on its bank and all the time Flann had hidden himself away. Mael Seachnaill and the Connaught King had bandied words and made threats, typical of what usually occurs when mighty men negotiate, but Flann did not understand due to his youth and took some of it personally. After one particularly vile insult or threat to his father's kingdom issued by the Connaught King, Flann had leapt from his hiding place with a stolen dagger in hand and threatened him with it. The King of Connaught had laughed while Mael Seachnaill's bodyguard had taken the boy away. The Connaught King was heard to have mocked Mael Seachnaill calling his son, a child, the defender of the Shannon, but the name stuck. Mael Seachnaill's men gave Flann his respect even as a child for this fact. They had seen that he was willing to defend the border of the Shannon against the King of Connaught, by himself, with just a dagger in hand. The tale had impressed the two boys as Flann knew it would; the dream of every young boy was to be a warrior of renown.

Some days later Domnall, who expected treachery, made his move to escape in the night. Aidan mac Fergus was waiting for him at the gate with a hundred spears. Domnall was marched back to one of the smaller halls where Flann waited beside an open fire.

"What is the meaning of this?" shouted Domnall. "You may be crowned the High King of Ireland, Flann Sinna, but make no mistake the title is more tradition than reality. If you don't release me, the north will descend upon your kingdoms and burn them out."

Flann let the storm of anger wash over him before calmly asking Domnall to sit by the fire. When Domnall would not move, Flann dismissed his guards to make Domnall more at ease. It worked and the new King of the Northern Ui Neill wearily made his way to the fire. His long dark hair and moustache lent him an exotic air and he looked more mature than his meagre thirty years. He wasn't renowned as a warrior *per se,* but his father's chieftains respected him none the less. His bravery in repelling endless Viking attacks and raids on behalf of his father had earned him admiration from the Argiallans, Ulaidians and the Breffni. He also maintained good relations with factions of the Scots, relationships and alliances that Flann now wanted for himself.

"I know you are wondering why I haven't confronted you in this manner since you arrived and have only exchanged pleasantries with you over the banquet table."

Domnall did not answer but stared into the fire.

"If I simply asked for what I am going to now take, you would have grounds to decline me in front of my kings and chieftains and I would have to accept it. That in turn would erode their respect for me and eventually I would be as ineffectual a High King as your father was."

That comment sent Domnall's nostrils flaring. He did not like to hear his father disparaged.

Flann continued, "I have respect for you, Domnall, I know you are an intelligent and educated man... a true king of the Ui Neill... and the proof of this is that you attempted to leave under cover of darkness in secret tonight. You knew what I would do, did you not?"

Domnall sulkily looked away before meeting Flann's gaze.

"You believe that holding those boys will give you power over us? I assure you, Flann Sinna, your reign will be short if you think you can control us while holding those princes captive."

Flann took a drink of wine and considered what Domnall had said before responding.

"I am going to tour around the island of Ireland, and I am going to take tribute from all my subjects. Some may oppose me, Domnall, as they did my father and yours. When I call the banners of the Northern Ui Neill I want guarantees that they, and by extension you, will obey me. I am open-handed with any spoils earned in battle, ask any of my warriors. Your northern men will quickly come to see me as fair and a profitable king to serve under. With time, when the whole country is mine, I will release my... guests...back to you. This I swear on my honour as a king of the Ui Neill. I know what is happening in Scotland currently. Mael Muire's surviving relatives do battle with this usurper Giric and should they win, I want a piece of that pie as well, through you and the boy I hold. By holding young Constantine, it is guaranteed."

Domnall grimly looked back to the fire and Flann recognised a resignation in the Northern king. He knew Flann was right.

"I have released your fifty men and retainers and they are already riding north along the Slige Midluachra unmolested many miles from here, and I will release you now to join them."

Before Domnall could go, Flann gripped his shoulder.

"I promise you, King Domnall, under my stewardship we will finally realise both mine and your father's dream; a unified Ireland."

Domnall took his leave and walked out of the hall.

*

Flann had gone to the walls to watch Domnall leave on horseback. A man of Domnall's had waited concealed in the trees a mile distant from the fort. Flann had cleared the trees around Tara for miles around to see any possible attacking force coming long before they reached the walls. In the distance he could see the two men speak on horseback, Domnall and his man. They suddenly took off as if entered in a race through the trees. Flann waited there a while before turning back toward the main halls in the centre of Tara. The palisades had been extended many times over the last couple of years to accommodate the quickly growing population. After Dublin itself, it was the biggest town now within fifty leagues. When the spring came, Flann knew he would head north first to parade his power there and take tribute. He would take armed men from each kingdom to strengthen his own forces. He would then travel to Connaught and then move south, which was always the most dangerous part of the trip for any Meathman, not just the High King. He smiled to himself; all was as he had wished. He recalled the sight of Domnall and his man sprinting away in the far distance, no doubt re-joining the bulk of his men further up the road. *So strange that he would sprint away like that,* Flann thought to himself, *so strange indeed.* A slow creeping dread ascended his spine and the hairs on his arm rose in accordance. Something was amiss, and he was damn sure he knew what.

"AAAIIIDDDAAANNN," he screamed for his commander. He sprinted for his family quarters near the centre of the gargantuan fort. He raced toward the small hall where he had placed the two princes inside with a guard, but the man lay groaning in a concussed heap on a pile of straw outside the door.

"Get up, you lug." He kicked the man on the ground, before bursting into the interior of the hall. Mael Muire awaited him, sitting on a wooden table with her feet resting on the bench beside it. She was sharpening her dagger but when she noticed Flann she sheathed it on her belt. She had reverted to the vision of the warrior shield maiden and dispensed with the womanly clothes once more.

Before Flann could raise his voice in anger Mael Muire spoke.

"My husband, I have freed the boys. My son and nephew should not be pawns for your politics. I am a princess of the great lines of Dal Riada and the Picts, lines as storied and famous as the Ui Neill of Ireland. I am all the hostage you will need, and I stay willingly and am honour-bound." Flann approached her and unsheathed his sword.

"If you ever defy me again, woman, I don't care who you are I will send you in chains to my nephews in Dublin to be sold on the slaver's block."

Flann was livid, but in him, his fury was a cold one which made it all the more menacing to his enemies. Mael Muire stood her ground bravely, but her voice betrayed her fear.

"My King, this is the first, and the last time, that I will ever betray you."

Flann, despite his fury, could not help but admire her courage. He regretted threatening her and his anger fled like a shadow from light. He wondered had it been him in her place what would he have done? The same he presumed. He apologised to her and made his exit. *Should I send men after them,* he thought. *No, I would have to split my forces in too many directions.* As he walked toward the main hall, Aidan mac Fergus arrived, breathless.

"My King, what has happened?" he asked.

"The boys have escaped but I don't mean to pursue them. My new wife has freed them," he answered. "Send for Ivar Ivarsson, send for the Kings of Brega, and send for my uncle Cerbaill mac Dunlainge and all the Leinster Kings who call me lord. Come the feast of St Brigid in the spring, we will march north."

Aidan nodded his head and queried, "To have all of the Northern kings swear fealty to you, my King?"

Flann Sinna, High King of Ireland, shook his head.

"No, Aidan, we will ravage the north and plunder Armagh. Ireland is mine to rule and no other. Domnall believes he can defy me, but he is wrong. The Northern Ui Neill will bend the knee or be destroyed."

# PART 2

## THE FORGING OF
## THE WARRIOR
## NIALL GLUNDUB

# DRAMATIS PERSONAE:

**Aed mac Conchobar** (*Aid-mac-con-co-bar*) – Prince of the province of Connaught, subject to the High King.

**Aidan mac Fergus** (*Aid-an-mac-fergus*) – Captain of the High King's guard and close confidant. Southern Ui Neill and Clan Colman warrior of repute.

**Ainfith mac Aedo** (*An-fi-mac-aido*) – Warlike king of the Ulaid, subject to the rule of the Northern Ui Neill.

**Alfred the Great** – King of the West Saxons

**Aud of the Deep Mind** (*Owd*) – Famed Viking noblewoman, wife to Ceitl Flatnose. Known for her wisdom and her abilities as a seeress.

**Becc mac Airemoin** (*Bec-mac-air-e-mo-in*) – King of the Ulaid and usurper of that crown, owes fealty to the Northern Ui Neill.

**Benandonner** (*Ben-an-don-er*) – Mythical giant slain by the hero Finn mac Cumhaill.

**Cathal mac Goll** (*Ca-hall-mac-goll*) – Veteran Cenel nEoghain warrior and sergeant.

**Ceallach mac Cearnach** (*Kyall-ach-mac-kyar-nach*) – Deceased King of the Breffni clan.

**Ceitl Flatnose** (*Ket-tel-flatnose*) – Ancient Viking King of Limerick and some of the Hebrides and Orkneys.

**Cerbaill mac Dunlainge** (*Ker-ball-mac-dun-lang-ga*) – King of Osraige and relative through marriage to the High King Flann, politically powerful.

**Charlemagne** (*Sharl-a-main*) – Deceased leader of the Holy Roman Empire, which encompassed most of the land between the Danube and the Atlantic in Europe.

**Conchobar mac Flann** (*Con-co-bar-mac-flann*) – Youngest son of the High King Flann Sinna.

**Constantine mac Aed** – Exiled Scottish prince.

**Cuchullainn** (*Coo-cull-en*) – Mythical Irish warrior, leader of the famous Red Branch Knights.

**Domnall mac Aed Findliath** (*Donal-mac-aid-find-liath*) – King of the Cenel nEoghain and the over-king of the Northern Ui Neill.

**Domnall mac Constantine** – Exiled Scottish prince.

**Donnchadh Donn mac Flann** (*Dun-na-ka-dun-mac-flan*) – Powerful king of the Caille Follamain tribe in Meath, son of the High King Flann Sinna.

**Einar Iron Knee** (*Eye-nar-iron-knee*) – Brutal Viking warlord who held some sway in Dublin.

**Eiremon the Fat** (*Air-a-mon*) – important Ulaidian chieftain.

**Eithne mac Flann** (*Eth-knee-ingen-flann*) – Meath Princess and daughter to the High King.

**Eochaid mac Cinneide** (*A-o-kaid-mac-kin-aida*) – Scottish prince and contender for the Scottish throne.

**Eolair** (*Vole-ar*) – Minor Ulaidian chieftain.

**Finn mac Cumhaill** (*Finn-mac-cool*) – Mythical Irish hero and leader of the legendary Fianna.

**Flann mac Domnall** – Cenel nEoghain prince, son of the King.

**Flann Sinna** – High King of Ireland and over-king of Meath and the Southern Ui Neill.

**Flannacain mac Ceallaig** (*Flan-na-kawn-mac-kyell-ig*) – King of North Brega and under-king of the Southern Ui Neill.

**Giric mac Roth** (*Gir-rick-mac-roth*) – Usurper of the Scottish throne. Known as the Son of Fortune.

**Gormlaith ingen Flann** (*Gorm-la-ingen-flan*) – Princess of the Southern Ui Neill and eventual wife of Niall Glundub.

**Guthrum** (*Guth-rum* ) – Powerful Danish Viking warlord.

**Harald Fairhair** – King of all Norway.

**Hastein** (*Has-tin* ) – Danish Viking warlord, active in Francia.

**Ivar the Boneless** – Deceased former King of Dublin.

**Jarl Sichtfridh** (*Jarl-sic-frith*) – Powerful Norse warlord who holds sway in Dublin, cousin of the King of Norway.

**Kjotve the Rich** (*Kyot-ve*) – Conquered Norwegian King, defeated by Harald Fairhair in battle.

**Lergus mac Cruinnen** (*Ler-gus-mac-crin-nen*) – Bishop of Kildare and ferocious Irish warrior.

**Lethlobar mac Loingsig** (*Leth-lo-bar-mac-lin-shig*) – King of the Dal nAridi, a splinter tribe of the Ulaid who owe their allegiance to the Northern Ui Neill.

**Lugaid mac Conn** (*Lug-ad-mac-con*) – Warrior of the Cenel nEoghain and Northern Ui Neill.

**Mael Craoibh** (*Male-crave*) – Known as the Black Fox and King of the Argiallans, under-king of the Northern Ui Neill. Formidable warrior.

**Mael Muire ingen Cinead** (*Male-mwir-a-ingen-cin-aid*) – Princess of Scotland and Queen of Ireland, wife of Flann Sinna.

**Mael Padraig mac Mael Curarada** (*Male-paw-rig-mac-male-coo-rarada*) – King of Argialla and under-king subservient to the Northern Ui Neill crown.

**Mael Ruanaid mac Flann** (*Male-ruin-ad-mac-flann*) – Prince of the Southern Ui Neill and heir designate to Flann Sinna.

**Mael Seachnaill mac Mael Ruanaid** (*Male-shock-nail-mac-male-ruin-ad*) – Deceased High King of Ireland and the Southern Ui Neill and father of Flann Sinna.

**Muirchertach mac Niall** (*Mwir-he-tach-mac-niall*) – Son of Niall Glundub and prince of the Northern Ui Neill.

**Niall Caille** (*Niall-keye-lya*) – Deceased former High King of Ireland and grandfather to Niall Glundub.

**Niall Glundub mac Aed Findliath** – Cenel nEoghain and Northern Ui Neill prince and general in his brother Domnall's armies.

**Niall Noigiallach** (*Niall-noi-gee-allach*) – Also known as Niall of the Nine Hostages. Semi Legendary ancestor of all Ui Neill nobility.

**Odin** – The chief god of the Norse and Danes, also known as the Allfather.

**Oengus mac Flann** (*Ong-gus-mac-flann*) – Prince of the Southern Ui Neill, son of the High King.

**Ruarc mac Ceallach** (*Roorc-mac-kyall-ach*) – Prince of the Breffni and renowned fighter.

**Sichtfridh Ivarsson** (*Sic-frith-ivar-son*) – First generation warrior of the Ui Imair, son of Ivar the Boneless. Nephew of Flann Sinna.

**Thorsten the Red** (*Thor-stin*) – Viking warlord who partially controlled Dublin, son of Olaf the White.

**Tiernan mac Seallachan** (*Tier-nan-mac-shall-a-kawn*) – King of the Breffni clan and under-king of the Northern Ui Neill.

**Tolarg mac Ceallach** (*Tol-arg-mac-kyal-ach*) – King of South Brega, subject to the King of the Southern Ui Neill. Powerful under-king whose territory bordered the Vikings of Dublin.

**Ulf Francslayer** – Viking warlord and reaver.

# CHAPTER 1

# THE SEEDS OF DISPUTE
# (885)

Niall Glundub gathered his giggling nephew Flann into his arms before releasing him to sprint after the lurchers who loped after game, flushed from the gorse.

"I half believe that when he grows up, he wants to be a hound," said his brother Domnall, the King of the Northern Ui Neill.

Niall Glundub smiled and gazed after the boisterous lad as he tripped laughing into a dishevelled heap. One of the lurchers came back around to nuzzle the boy and duly received a pat on the head for its troubles. The coursing had become a weekly jaunt into the countryside for Domnall mac Aed, his son and his half-brother Niall Glundub mac Aed. Niall knew that affairs of state often kept Domnall awake at night and impossibly busy and as a result he used this time with his son and his brother to clear his head. The grey hairs on his brother's brow had multiplied over the past few years, hinting at late nights bent over letters by candlelight. *Heavy weighs the crown*, thought Niall. Several of the kingdoms that Domnall nominally ruled over were currently in turmoil. In the Kingdom of Argialla to the southeast, civil war amongst their chieftains had erupted after the murder of their king, Mael Padraig mac Mael Curarada.

Endless skirmishes between various factions had plunged the countryside into chaos. Niall Glundub had met the former King of Argialla at his brother's court several times and had found him more akin to a clergyman than a warrior. *A singularly unimpressive man,* Niall remembered. It did not surprise him in the slightest that the Argiallans had found King Mael Padraig weak and murdered him for it and he knew his brother hadn't been taken by surprise either. Domnall had toyed with the idea of interfering in the conflict, but in the end he had decided not to. He would allow them to find their own king however violently. Domnall always included Niall Glundub in his senior policy discussions and matters of state as he had often expressed his desire for Niall to be both his and his son Flann's senior advisor and diplomat. Domnall included the two exiled Scottish princes also in these discussions and meetings; both his namesake Domnall and Constantine, Niall's closest friend. State craft was equally as important in his brother's eyes as learning the ways of the warrior.

Strangely he always used Flann Sinna, his hated rival, as an example of astute rule. Despite what his personal grievances were with the High King, Domnall was always complimentary on how Flann Sinna had the ability to unite a patchwork of other kings under his banner, despite some factions despising others. In this case Domnall decided that to make his presence felt in Argialla would have potentially united the entire kingdom against him, instead of solving the leadership dispute. In Niall's opinion from what little he had seen of the Argiallan chieftains, he concurred with his brother's decision. In the Kingdom of the Ulaid, things were not much better. Ainfith, the current over-king of the Ulaid, was struggling to quell his chieftains. One of his supporters, Eiremon the fat, had been defeated in battle by his rival Eolair in a land dispute, and in that fight Ainfith's own son and heir had taken a wound which had suppurated and killed him. Ainfith had other sons, but it was still a blow to the old king.

The situation was not all bad though, either further south or across the sea. In England, Alfred the Great had marched on London and taken the city back from the Francish Danes. He had then gifted it to his subject Kingdom of Mercia, tightening relationships with the two largest English kingdoms. Every

Dane and Norseman around the entire Irish Sea was reportedly outraged by this and clamouring for battle. All over Ireland, Norse and Danes began joining war bands in the hope of exacting vengeance on all Saxons. No one ruler had yet emerged with the strength to unite them all, except perhaps Hastein, but that pirate was occupied in the Francian heartlands. As far as Domnall was concerned, if the Danes were in Britain, then they weren't raiding his towns and villages. Dublin, the largest Viking city in the Irish sea, was in turmoil. The Norse and Danes, or the fair foreigners and the dark foreigners as they were known in Meath, were at each other's throats. The Norse currently seemed to hold sway under the half-Dane, half-Norse Thorstein the Red with the sons of Ivar appearing to be diminished in influence.

In the far North Seas, Harald Fairhair, the King of all Norway, seemed content to concentrate his efforts in Scotland against the Picts and waging internecine warfare in Norway, Denmark, Fresia and Francia. With no Viking incursions into the territories controlled under the Northern Ui Neill, Domnall and his soldiers had begun to set the region to rights. They had not seen major conflict for four years since Flann Sinna had marched north to Armagh shortly after his coronation. Not three months after being crowned, the High King had sacked and burned the monastery there and allowed his Danish allies to take hundreds of slaves. The four years of peace afforded by this relative lull in violence meant that Domnall had time to fortify his towns and encourage the economy of the north to prosper, and it had. Two Viking settlements had been captured on the northern coast and their fighters killed or taken prisoner. Their ships were burned and the remainder of the people from these settlements were given the choice of submitting to Irish rule under the Ui Neill King or beheading.

It shocked Niall Glundub how many of the Norse chose the axe. Killing captured prisoners was tasteless work that neither Niall nor his brother were ever comfortable with, but there were warriors under their command who reveled in the task, seasoned killers with no qualms. There had been a peaceful union in the years since between Irish and Norse settlers as the subjugated settlements were resettled with Irish folk. Domnall had been concerned at first but as the taxes raised on the festival of Lughnasadh accrued in his brother's coffers, his position had softened. Some of the Norse women had accepted Irish men as husbands and children were already born under Domnall's rule that were of mixed descent. The King put his arm around Niall's shoulders. He had to reach up to grasp Niall as the younger son of Aed was a good four inches taller than his brother already, despite being only sixteen years of age.

"I think the blood of Benandonner, the legendary giant that Finn mac Cumhaill fought on the Giant's Causeway, must somehow run through your veins, Niall. How did you get so massive?"

Niall shrugged his shoulders and smiled. He had reached his brother's height by the age of fourteen and had never stopped growing since.

"You are already a great fighter, Niall; you never hesitated in your first two battles and have slain four Viking warriors already."

"Five," Niall interrupted with a *harrumph*.

"Very well then, five," Donal laughed. "And I guess the berserker that came at you with the axe counts as two." They both laughed at that. Domnall's face took on a serious demeanor suddenly.

"I need you, Niall, more than you know. My son is still seven or eight years from coming of age and my other children have died either through accident or illness, God have mercy on their souls. My wife is sickly, but I love her and I won't take another woman to wife, I think. Flann is precious not just to me but to the Kingdom of the Northern Ui Neill and the Cenel nEoghain clan."

Domnall took a step back and admired Niall Glundub. He was a throwback to Cuchullainn, the historic hero himself, narrow of hip but muscular, and already he possessed the arms and shoulders of a blacksmith from hours of practicing in the yard with sword and spear. He had short cropped brown hair and went clean-shaven like his grandfather for whom he was named, Niall Caille, the first High King to meet the Vikings in Ireland, in formal battle.

"I am going to use you more and more as you get older, Niall. I have no doubt that your prowess in combat will strike respect and fear in equal measures, in both my allies and enemies."

He paused for a moment to check on his son Flann who rolled playfully in the grass with the lurchers.

"It's a thankless lot you have, Niall. You are as much a son of Aed Findliath as I am, but for unity amongst not just the Cenel nEoghain, but the entire northern Ui Neill, you must remain behind me. Every victory, even any that you win individually, must be mine, Niall," he stated. "You are of the highest noble birth, which is a great strength but also a great weakness too for the Kingdom. Your mother is a warrior princess of the Picts and now that she is married to Flann Sinna, the Southern Ui Neill may seek to divide us through her. Even the Scots might attempt to use you to gain influence in my court. I cannot have it, Niall, and it keeps me up at night how my enemies, even in our own clan, could try and use you to supplant me. My authority must be total as any weakness in my kingship will be exploited and I could end up the same as that sorry soul Mael Padraig mac Mael Curarada of Argialla."

Niall Glundub shook his head.

"I understand your position, brother. All I ask is for the opportunity to gain glory and prestige under your command and to fight at your side against the enemies of the Northern Ui Neill."

Domnall was pleased at that answer, Niall could tell. The King turned away to whistle the coursers back to his side, but a noise caught Niall Glundub's attention, and he tapped his brother on the shoulder. The sound indicated that a horse was clearly galloping toward them from around a stand of gorse bushes. Niall drew his long sword and stood on front of his brother, but when he saw who it was, he sheathed it with a smile. It was Constantine mac Aed, his cousin and friend. Niall's smile faded when he saw the look of panic on his cousin's face.

"Domnall, Niall, the town of Doire is being raided by Viking corsairs. A messenger has ridden all morning to get word to us. They ask for help."

"How many enemies?" Domnall asked.

"Some two longboats, perhaps eighty men, but the townsfolk were unprepared and have fled to the hills."

Domnall pondered his words for a moment before beckoning Constantine down from the horse.

"Niall, Constantine, you will go on foot to the fort at Aileach. You will move all of the women and children into the stone keep. I will leave fifty men there awaiting your command and also my son Flann. Defend the wooden palisades of the town itself in case of attack. Guard my heir with your lives."

"Domnall, I should be at your side fighting these raiders, I am already the best fighter you have," Niall interrupted.

"NO," shouted Domnall, "I will take Constantine's horse back and his cousin Domnall and I will lead my forces to Doire to relieve the townsfolk and drive off these pirates. You must defend Aileach in my absence and protect my son Niall. You must!"

With a disappointed and resigned nod, Niall answered, "Yes, my King, as you command."

Domnall galloped away leaving Niall Glundub, his cousin, his son and two lurcher hounds behind him.

It took Niall Glundub forty minutes to repair to the fort and another ten minutes for him to issue the commands instructing the women, children and elderly to retire to the stone keep at its centre. The entire settlement was encompassed by stout timber walls with a planked walkway across the top. Niall had been left with perhaps fifteen seasoned warriors and another thirty-five green boys, most of whom were visibly disappointed not to have been included in the force led by the two Domnalls to the east. Niall Glundub did not allow his face to betray the same emotion as the young men left behind, even if truthfully deep down he felt the same. He was a prince of the Ui Neill and it was his duty to not just follow orders but also to portray an air of confidence and command to inspire his men. It was his first opportunity to hold outright command in any case. Now was not the time to be perceived by the veterans or the thirty-five youths as petulant.

He commanded Constantine and five of the seasoned men to man the stone keep as a rearguard, in case enemies got past Glundub and his other men. They would also use archery to put down any Vikings who breached the outer walls. It was extremely unlikely, but it was not beyond the realms of possibility that the marauders may have feinted at Doire and would try and sack Aileach and ravage the lands around. When all was in place and ready, he joined his men on top of the wall over the front gate. The palisades were surrounded by a deep dry moat filled with sharpened wooden spikes, but at the large oak gates there was a permanent wooden bridge that spanned it. At the top of the wall waiting for him was his third in command after himself and Constantine, Cathal mac Goll, who handed Niall his spear and shield. It felt strange for Niall to command much older men such as Cathal, but he felt that he had earned the man's respect by besting him multiple times in sparring and fighting alongside him against Viking raiders over the last year.

"All is in readiness, Prince Niall," he rasped. "I would guess this is just a raid and the King will see these pagans off."

Niall mostly agreed with his sentiment but refused to believe that the danger had passed. Vikings had tricked his brother and his father before and were certainly not devoid of cunning when it came to warfare. It was perhaps a two-hour ride between the walls of the fort of Aileach of the Cenel nEoghain, and the town of Doire on the banks of the Foyle River.

An hour of watchful time passed and yielded no suspicious noises or movements betraying a hidden body of men approaching. Of the forty-odd men that manned the palisades, perhaps twenty of them were armed with bows. Sheaves of arrows were left at intervals along the walkway for easy usage by the defenders. At strategic points, particularly at the front gate, Niall had piles of stones and rubble ready for his men to rain down on any enemy who wished to breach the gate. Although there was only one way in or out on the entire circumference of the palisade, there was a hidden tunnel beneath the stone keep itself that led to a secluded copse of trees a few hundred feet away to the north. If Aileach was ever to fall and be sacked, the weakest would use this tunnel to escape and Niall had left instructions for that very eventuality. Glundub's grandfather Niall Caille had had it dug out forty years ago for just such a day. Whatever happened, Flann mac Domnall must live. All was as ready as Niall Glundub could make it. If the invading force from the river was as small as it was reported, he mused, his brother would have routed them by now and perhaps would be on their way back already.

Another hour passed and vigilance began to waver in Niall's soldiers. Their initial watchful intensity drained away in the late afternoon sun. They were beginning to joke with each other, their attention wandering, but Niall and Cathal mac Goll issued a few rebukes and warned them to concentrate. The land in front of the gate was flat except for a succession of drumlin hills to the southeast and a small wood of pine trees to the northeast. The road to Doire lay between these two landmarks. Something about the shadows in the trees did not look right to Niall. They were slightly off from the umpteenth time he had scanned them for movement. He glanced over to Cathal mac Goll to see if he had also sensed something and his heart sank. Cathal's shoulders had slumped at that very moment when following Niall's gaze.

"We are under attack, my Prince; there is a force of Vikings in the trees. They have played your brother false."

And sure as day, men began emerging from cover armed with axe and shield. The men on the wall went quiet, all humour withered from them and silence ruled. The force pouring from the small wood numbered around two hundred Vikings and they were led by a giant chieftain wielding two axes. For the first time in Niall Glundub's short military career, he felt unsure if he would win the coming fight.

The sheer arrogance of the Vikings galled Niall as they approached. They sauntered toward the fort as if they were coming to trade in the summer markets and not to sack the settlement and enslave or murder the people there. On approaching arrow range, they formed up into one of their famed shield walls and moved forward phalanx-like, as Niall and Constantine's monk teachers had described to them when reading of old Roman military tactics. On Niall's order, Cathal signaled for the archers to let fly. Only one Viking fell when a lucky arrow found a gap in the shields and pierced his throat. Another warrior took a wound in his bicep on the left-hand side of the shield wall but simply pulled the arrow out of the wound and tossed it on the ground in a worrying display of toughness. With fifty feet left to go before they reached the wall, their shield wall was bristling like a hedgehog with the amount of arrows festooning it. They paused momentarily and in a seamless sequence of coordination, opened windows from within the shield wall for their own archers to fire. Two of Niall's men fell to his left, one killed instantly having been shot through the eye, the other dying noisily as the arrow pierced his lung and knocked him back twelve feet onto the ground, breaking his spine.

The shield wall split then, and two groups of fifty Vikings went right and left respectively, looking for weak spots on the wall to scale with rope. The core group of warriors sprinted toward the gate in a column with shields raised over their heads. A fallen trunk of an ash tree was carried between them having been shaped into a crude battering ram. Around twenty archers peppered the palisades with arrows in an attempt to keep the heads down of any men brave enough to hurl rocks from above. Niall grasped a short spear and hurled it at the front man carrying the ram. It took him above his beltline and he tumbled to the ground howling, tripping a few of the men behind him. The ram became imbalanced and was dropped. It landed on the wounded man, killing him instantly and broke the leg of the man behind him also. It took a minute for the Vikings to drag the dead man and the stricken man out of the way and this allowed a moment of reprieve for the archers on the wall to pepper the attackers. Several Vikings were slain or crippled with accurate shots including a number of the archers who had no more shield wall to hunker behind. A minute later and the Vikings had reached the gate.

Niall felt the first ram blow through the wooden walkway as it slammed into the gates. His men hurled dozens of stones down upon the Vikings. Most thudded harmlessly on upraised shields and rebounded away but the occasional one brained a Viking or broke an arm or shoulder. *We should have had pitch and fire ready,* Niall Glundub cursed himself. He would have doused the marauders from above and burned them to hell at this point. Niall looked over to his left a hundred feet from his vantage point where ten of his men were slashing at Vikings trying to scale the walls. High-pitched screams from several hundred feet to his right meant that one or more of the Vikings had succeeded and had scaled the walls and were in amongst the folk who elected to defend their homes rather than retreat to the stone keep. *Constantine and his archers will have to deal with them,* he thought.

The booming outside stopped momentarily, to Niall's surprise, and a shrill female voice began wailing the same words again and again:

"WHOEVER IS IN COMMAND, COME TO THE GATE. I ULF FRANCSLAYER, OF THE LINE OF HALFDAN THE BLACK, SWEAR THAT MY MEN WILL NOT SHOOT."

The woman repeated this again and again. A glance over the wooden palisade showed Niall that the Vikings had indeed retreated thirty feet and reformed their shield wall. It pleased Niall to witness that it was not just the archers who had ceased shooting and re-joined the formation, but the survivors of the flanking attacks had been repulsed and had re-joined the main force too. At least twenty of the Vikings were killed or incapacitated and, judging by the returning men, another score had been lost trying to traverse the spike-filled moat and scale the walls.

"How many men have we left, Cathal?" Niall whispered.

"Perhaps thirty. Glundub, if they come at us again we can't hold them. We will have to retreat to the stone walls of the inner keep and allow them to sack the town." That annoyed Niall massively and a dogged resolve rose in him.

"I will try and buy some time with these heathens. We have to believe that every moment they are delayed brings my brother closer. If they are caught beneath the walls of the fort they are finished."

Niall rose slowly to his full height in an attempt to impress the Vikings and glowered down at them. The woman who was screaming out the same sentence again and again went silent. The poor wretch was a girl of perhaps Niall's age but was leashed by a chain around the neck which was in turn clasped in the massive fist of the most brutal-looking Viking Niall Glundub had ever seen. Only a Viking of such prodigious size and savagery would possess the hubris to call himself the Francslayer. The chieftain shook the chain violently and spoke a few soft sentences to the girl. She nodded her head and addressed Niall Glundub.

"TELL YOUR LEADER, BOY, THAT IF YOU OPEN THE GATES TO US

WE WILL NOT SLAUGHTER EVERY PERSON AND WILL TAKE ONLY ONE IN TEN AS SLAVES. IF YOU DON'T, I WILL PULL OUT YOUR LEADER'S GUTS AND MAKE HIM EAT THEM."

The words sounded absurd to Niall coming from this bedraggled slip of a girl. Niall addressed them all, knowing that the girl would translate.

"I AM IN COMMAND HERE. I AM NIALL GLUNDUB MAC AED FINDLIATH MAC NIALL CAILLE. LEAVE THESE WALLS OR PREPARE TO MEET YOUR HEATHEN GODS IN THE AFTERLIFE."

The girl tentatively translated the words for the warlord and he laughed along with the rest of his men. Niall could see that this chieftain was not going to be browbeaten with words and only strength of arms and superior force would see him off. Niall saw a chance here.

He whispered to Cathal, "Quietly gather the remaining men and retreat to the keep. Go immediately."

Cathal grabbed his arm. "What are you going to do, Glundub?"

Niall scratched his chin. "I am going to challenge this Ulf Francslayer to single combat. If he wins, well, nothing has changed and we will have wasted minutes. If I win, I am going to sprint away as only a champion of the Tailteann Fair can do!"

Niall had gained some notoriety recently with his victory in the footraces held at the Tailteann Fair the year previously. He was the quickest in the land but he doubted that would help him here, but it served as something to say to placate Cathal mac Goll.

Cathal was still about to argue but Niall stopped him with a single word, "Go."

He turned his attention back to the Viking chieftain.

"ULF FRANCSLAYER, I CHALLENGE YOU TO SINGLE COMBAT. MY MEN AND PEOPLE ARE GOING TO RETREAT TO THE CENTRAL KEEP. IF YOU WIN, THE TOWN IS FREE FOR THE SACKING AND ANYTHING THEREIN IS YOURS. BUT IF YOU LOSE, YOUR MEN MUST LEAVE."

The captive woman translated for the Vikings and they banged axe and shield together. Some of them clearly approved of this new development. Ulf

Francslayer briefly seemed perturbed, but the cheers of his men encouraged him to nod his head in agreement. A minor Viking chieftain like this could only lead through strength. Any challenge by an outsider must be answered, or he would look weak. He beckoned Niall down from the rampart.

They would fight.

Moments later Niall had Cathal open the gate and once he'd slipped quietly out, the gate was barred behind him. He was on his own now, victory or death. He had a dagger tied to his calf, two swords crossed at his back and a short spear and shield. The Francslayer used two axes, one in each hand, but was festooned with other daggers around the great furs and mail he wore. He even had a dagger carved from the antler of a deer strapped to his leg. At six feet six and fourteen stone Niall Glundub was two inches the bigger man, but he was heavily outweighed by the Viking warrior. Out of the corner of his eye Niall could see that to the right there was a slight alleyway of escape to the south of the fort. The Vikings had fanned out in a semi-circle with only a few onlookers manning the far left. There and then, he determined that should he prove the better fighter he would chance his luck there and sprint for the hills. Niall could see that it wasn't just Ulf Francslayer that was very confident in victory but his men as well. They were wagering with each other, *probably on how quickly I die,* thought Niall. Ulf himself wore a crude iron helm and heavy linked mail with boiled leather beneath it. His furs were matted and filthy and he possessed a beard that nearly reached his navel. *He might be big and powerful, but he is older and less mobile and that is how I will beat him,* thought Niall.

Without warning the giant Viking attacked. He roared and rained down axe blows. Niall retreated carefully from the strokes, parrying each with his round shield. He could tell the Francslayer favoured his right side and deliberately moved to his own right to stay out of his reach. Impatiently the Viking lashed with both axes at once against Niall's shield and the Irish prince pounced with his short spear, piercing the thick left thigh of the Viking. Ulf roared in pain and slashed at the spear, breaking the shaft of the weapon in two. Niall moved back a couple of feet while Ulf ripped the spearhead from his leg and cast it aside. Niall drew the first of his swords from its scabbard. Again Ulf began to attack but this time he began to vary it, mixing in low blows with head shots, forcing Niall to parry with the sword as well as the shield. Sweat was drizzling down Niall's brow and was beginning to impair his vision. The Francslayer was the hardest and most dangerous fighter he had ever faced in battle or in the training yard. He was relentless.

One particular blow reduced Niall's shield to kindling and he had to parry the second axe with his sword. Ulf anticipating this, kicked Niall in the chest and sent him sprawling onto the muddy ground. The Vikings unanimously roared their approval, clearly enjoying the spectacle. Niall heard an unexpected shout of encouragement. It was Cathal, who was still at the wall in defiance of his command. *At least someone will witness my death,* Niall thought in a moment of morbidity. He rolled up to his feet and drew his second sword, determined that if this was to be his death then he would make it such a death as to be worthy of the Ui Neill. With his shield in pieces and his spear shattered Niall decided that defence was no longer an option. He lunged forward and for the first time in the fight decided to put the Francslayer on the back foot. The exuberance of youth flowed through Niall and his veins sang in the violence. This was what life was about; at that moment he neither cared whether he lived or died. Only the fight mattered.

The chieftain staggered after a flurry of blows at one point. Niall assumed it was a slip but when he did it again moments later, he quickly realised that Ulf was feeling the pace. The blood was in the water. The wound in his thigh had weakened Ulf and now he was purely deflecting blows from Niall's swords without looking for a chance to attack. *I have him,* Niall exulted inside. He feinted with a thrust from his left-hand sword and Ulf tried to block, falling for the trick. The fighter of three minutes previously would not have bought it, but this was a tiring man in front of Niall, with a seriously wounded leg. Niall reached in with his right-hand sword and pierced the Francslyer's chest. It was a killing blow Niall knew, but the Viking just stood there staring at the several feet of steel in mute surprise. Niall sent his second sword plunging through the Viking's heart and Ulf collapsed to his knees, blood vomiting from his mouth. With a flourish Niall freed his dagger from his calf and sent it down through both the chieftain's helmet and skull, and Ulf the Francslayer toppled like a poleaxed horse.

The Vikings surrounding the fighters stood momentarily in stunned silence, seeing their Chieftain felled by this Irish youth. Niall considered making a run for it but something about the situation was odd. He stepped back from the twitching corpse of Ulf Francslayer and sheathed his swords. At last, one of the Vikings stepped forward. *Glundub Drengr,* he uttered in his tongue, before removing a golden torque from his forearm and throwing it down at Niall's feet. Dozens of their warriors followed suit. *Glundub Drengr* was repeated again and again and small treasures were cast to the ground. Some didn't bother with that and just stalked off shaking their heads and muttering to themselves back toward the trees in groups of five or ten. The last group to leave threw the enslaved woman to the ground beside Niall and spoke a rapid-fire sentence before departing with a final respectful nod. The woman, with tears in her eyes, looked up to Niall Glundub and spoke.

"They say that you have vanquished them. They have taken enough plunder from hitting all of the communities from here to the river. One of those villages was mine. The loss of their leader to a *Drengr* is a sign from their gods Heimdall and Thor that they should leave this place untouched."

Niall Glundub, shattered from the fight, sat down beside her and began to remove her chains.

"What is a *Drengr*?" he asked.

"It has no real meaning in Irish but the closest would be *Honoured One* or *Honoured Enemy*," the girl whispered.

It was dark when the two Domnalls returned with their men. They had driven the Vikings back to the river, the raiders having retreated almost immediately without a fight. Domnall knew it instantly then to be a feint. He had left a hundred men in Doire to fortify the town but had travelled with all speed back to the capital of the Cenel nEoghain, inland. He arrived to see the bodies of the dead Vikings being burned and the corpses of more than fifteen of his warriors laid out on the ground. He rode ahead of his men to the stone keep.

"Where is my son?" he shouted, and the boy fled down the steps into his arms.

His wife was helped from the keep and greeted her husband and King with tears in her eyes. He turned to his younger brother, the prince Niall Glundub, and embraced him in a fierce hug. Niall winced, gasping in pain from the blow struck by the boot of the Viking chieftain, but endured the embrace anyway.

"Brother, you have saved our clan and my family." He looked over to the Scottish prince by Niall's side. "And you, Scottish prince, Constantine mac Aed, if ever you require anything that is within my power to give, it is yours."

Constantine bowed graciously. "Thank you, my King, but this was Niall Glundub's victory, all honour and praise should be his."

Domnall turned back to his brother then and begged him to recount every detail of the battle from memory. Niall recounted the details as best he could; the deployment of his men, the number of the Vikings attacking, the leader of that force and of course the single combat against him. Domnall appraised his brother then, standing back and looking searchingly at him.

"I said earlier this day that you would be a great warrior one day. I was wrong. You are already a great warrior today. To defeat a Viking raiding party with four times your number and then to slay their chieftain in single combat is a thing we haven't seen since the days of Finn mac Cumhaill and the Fianna."

At that moment, more than four hundred warriors entered the front gate of the town as Domnall had ridden ahead to ascertain the fate of his family. Niall and Domnall could see some of the remaining warriors who had fought with Niall Glundub on the walls of the fort embrace their brothers, fathers, uncles, cousins and friends and describe what had happened. Niall could see Cathal Mac Goll gesticulating wildly and pointing at him on the steps of the stone fort a hundred feet away. The roars rose to the heavens, a cacophony of cheers.

"KING DOMNALL" could be heard amongst chants of "UI NEILL" and "CENEL nEOGHAIN," but by the time they reached the central keep they were all shouting one name, raising their spears in victory.

"GLUNDUB, GLUNDUB, GLUNDUB!"

Domnall glared over in the direction of his brother, but Niall didn't see him or the concern and naked jealous fury in the King's glare. He just raised his sword to salute the victorious warriors of the Northern Ui Neill.

# CHAPTER 2

# THE BATTLE OF PILGRIM
# (888)

Smoke rose on the horizon as Niall Glundub and his hundred retainers approached Tara from the north along the Slige Midluachra road. He glanced across at his cousin Constantine mac Aed to see what his cousin's expression would be, witnessing the scattered carnage that lay between them and the capital of the land. Only the two princes were mounted amongst the column of armed men, and their seats afforded them the first view of the evidence of violence before their soldiers. The trees for miles around Tara had been cleared for arable farmland several years ago and the deforestation also allowed the defenders of Tara to witness the approach of any enemy without surprise. As the vision of the land before Tara appeared to the rank-and-file warriors emerging from the wooded flanks of the Slige Midluachra, shocked gasps escaped from stunned lips. The scene of devastation was horrendous to behold for even the most hardened man. Along the road, overturned carts, dead livestock and the occasional body of a despoiled and brutalised farmer lay heaped on the verge. Thick black flies rose in clouds away from the rotting flesh that lay everywhere as the warriors passed. Even women and children had not evaded the massacre.

The Viking forces under Thorstein the Red, the Norse-Dane de facto ruler of Dublin, had utterly ravaged the land around Tara. They had gone elsewhere for the moment, thankfully allowing an unchallenged approach for Niall's men. Glundub knew what was happening: the Vikings wished to draw Flann Sinna the High King out from behind his walls and into battle, goading him through atrocity. Flann Sinna had no doubt decided to wait for sufficient reinforcements to arrive before marching out and vanquishing Thorstein, but so far, he clearly felt he did not have enough men to deal with the Northmen. Thorstein was supported by a Norwegian sea king called Einar Iron Knee, a fierce barbarian who had plundered the Scottish coast for a decade and held sway in parts of the Hebrides. Flann Sinna had sent a messenger to Niall's brother's court, demanding reinforcements quickly. All available strength the Northern Ui Neill harboured was to be dispatched to assist the High King in his hour of need. For more than a year, Niall Glundub and his brother Domnall mac Aed had not been on good terms. Glundub did as he was commanded always, but Domnall grew ever more jealous as time passed. The men of the Northern Ui Neill and the Cenel nEoghain were torn between their King and their war-leader in battle, Niall Glundub. Even when Niall tried to diminish his own victories and achievements and funnel the glory to his brother, it seemed to grow his reputation further. The last straw came when some chieftains of the Breffni had requested that Niall Glundub, not the King of the Northern Ui Neill, lead forces to their borders with Connaught and help them drive off the men of the west.

Flann, Domnall's young son and heir, was growing and learning, but he was some way off being able to command men or serve as an effective advisor to the King. Every time Domnall was forced to seek Niall's council or required his military prowess to settle a dispute, resentment grew within him. Instead of viewing Niall as a valuable asset, he overtly suspected and even publicly accused his brother of attempting to usurp his authority. It had almost become intolerable for Niall too and a reckoning was coming between the pair, he knew. It saddened Niall to see their relationship depreciate so much as Niall had no ambitions for the crown, but neither he nor the Scottish princes, Domnall and

Constantine, could convince the King otherwise. A week past, it had almost come as a reprieve when the messenger from Tara had breathlessly arrived and explained the predicament that the Southern Ui Neill were in. Domnall's first reaction was to laugh and shout expletives at the messenger. He repeatedly pointed out the irony of the fact that Flann Sinna had forced his father Aed Findliath to marry his sister Eithne to him, to secure his help many years before. He gleefully pointed out that the shoe was now on the other foot and he should demand some similar concession from the High King. It took the intersession of Prince Domnall of the Picts stepping forward and volunteering to lead men down for the sake of his aunt and for the King's own nieces and nephews by Eithne, to interrupt the King's vengeful gloating over the strife the Southern Ui Neill found themselves in.

The King had then reluctantly and begrudgingly come to his senses but had decided to only allow one hundred men go south and not under Prince Domnall's command. He insisted that he would not risk the prince of the Picts in a minor scuffle like this, despite the fact that the messenger had indicated the significant strength of the Viking host. He decided to send Niall Glundub instead. Constantine had requested permission to join Glundub as his second in command. The King was reluctant at first but caved eventually on the prince's insistence. On the journey down to Tara the two princes had discussed the King's decision thoroughly.

Constantine was a direct young man and never shied away from a hard truth.

"Niall, it is an unlosable situation for your brother," he said. "Should the Vikings prevail, you could certainly die or be taken captive which would suit your brother. All of the men he sends with us are young and mostly unproven, so he doesn't deplete his strength if the Vikings defeat Flann Sinna. By sending a hundred men, he sends the High King a message and it is this: Domnall knows that he is weak and only nominally sends an arbitrary number of men to support him; he offends without disobeying him completely. If Flann Sinna perceives this as a slap in the face – which he will, I might add – you will bear the brunt of the High King's anger as a prince of the Ui Neill. He may even take you hostage, Niall, and Domnall will not care a bit if he does. He will give lip service and emote false outrage but will welcome your absence. No matter what happens here, Niall Glundub, it's good for Domnall."

Flann and Constantine approached the *Rath na Riogh*, the Enclosure of the Kings, once their men had been quartered. Tara was effectively a town now, far larger from what Niall recalled as a young boy. The old King of the Southern Ui Neill, Mael Seachnaill, had only used Tara as a ceremonial defensive fort and only held court there at political meetings and festivals. Flann Sinna had turned it into his capital, a fearsome bastion of strength from which on a good day you could see into the mountains of the Ulaid and the Leinster men, at its summit. Tara was packed as thousands of farmers and labourers had fled there with their families, crowded in to shelter under the King's protection. Fear and desperation were rife. The Vikings had chosen the time of harvest to hit the surrounding hinterland of South Meath, a cruel blow to the chieftains of the Southern Ui Neill. Without a harvest a hard winter would hurt the people of Meath.

"Flann Sinna must march out and meet his foes or there will be no more land or people to protect. He is no king if he refuses to come out and face Thorstein. He may have to march before he feels that he has the numerical upper hand," Constantine whispered conspiratorially to Niall under his breath.

It wouldn't go well if any of Flann Sinna's men overheard two foreign princes discussing the predicament the Southern Ui Neill faced. As they approached the gates of the Kings' enclosure, a familiar figure was waiting for them. Mael Muire ingen Cinead, Princess of the Picts and Queen of Ireland, stood with arms folded, smiling from ear to ear. There was more silver in her long dark hair than Niall remembered but she looked strong and fit to fight. She had always eschewed the traditional dress of female royalty in favour of leather armour, riding boots and a steel sword strapped across her back.

Niall remembered asking her, years ago, why it was that she dressed like a male warrior. She had answered that all Pictish Gaelic women had learned in the last century that *even those without a means to defend themselves could die by the Viking axe anyway*. As long as he had known his mother, she had always been unapologetically armed. She embraced her nephew Constantine first and pinched his face, embarrassing the prince who looked around furtively to see if the men under their command had witnessed his aunt squeeze his quickly reddening cheeks. She then turned to Niall Glundub to admire him. Her son was massive, towering over her by a foot. Despite being only eighteen years old, he was as broad and as muscular as any men around. His short brown hair framed his clean-shaven face in a style unusual for an Irish warrior. Most Irish warriors normally kept a beard or moustache with braided long hair.

"Niall Glundub, in the flesh," she whispered. "I had heard rumour of your rise to power in the north but also the ill feeling between you and the King."

Niall noted that she didn't refer to Domnall as his brother.

"Hello, Mother," Niall answered and grabbed her into a great big bear hug. "You still look like you could best me in a fight."

She laughed and punched him in the arm. *She still hits hard,* Niall thought in surprise.

"We haven't much time, Niall. I wanted to catch you before you two approached the High King. There are things you must know." She paused before drawing the two princes closer. "The King and his eldest son Donnchadh Donn are not on speaking terms. Donnchadh has never forgiven his father for passing him over as his heir on the agreement made with your father Aed Findliath long ago. He has publicly sworn to the Bishop that his heir will be Mael Ruanaid and after that Oengus, your twin nephews born to your sister Eithne. She retired to a religious life on the King's marriage to me. Donnchadh sits now as the head of the Caille Follamain since marrying the old king's eldest daughter. He has become powerful in his own right and stirs trouble in the west and north of Meath."

Niall Glundub was aware of the agreement reached many years ago by Aed Findliath his father and Flann Sinna, but he had not realised how badly the relationship had degenerated between the High King and his eldest son.

"Flann Sinna is getting older now too, he relies a lot on my advice and that of his chief warriors. He is almost fifty years of age and sometimes… he forgets…" The Queen trailed off then and Flann could detect sorrow from her.

"He is still knowledgeable and extremely clever, Niall, do not try and deceive him. That would be dangerous for you. He is very prideful and demands respect. I am told that you have brought only one hundred men, but I have already explained to him that this was Domnall's doing and not yours," she said. "We have almost the numbers to challenge these savages now and I expect the High King to move before dawn and try and catch them unawares. They are camped near the Gabhra River, the place where Finn mac Cumhaill and the Fianna met their end. The farmers call it by the name, Pilgrim."

A shadow crossed her face then. "Son, nephew, this is a fight that Flann Sinna could lose. I have no doubt that Domnall would welcome this as the High Kingship would pass to him should Flann Sinna die or be seriously wounded. Even better would be if you were killed also, Niall. I have heard of these two Viking captains. Thorstein is a Norse raider of great infamy, also a cousin of the sons of Ivar, but many times more vicious. His ally, the Iron Knee, is a feral predator known for strapping two spikes to his knees and gutting his foes in close combat. These two warriors are formidable."

A small boy ran from the gates of the Kings' fort up ahead and weaved his way between the buildings and the crowded street and leapt into the arms of the Queen. With a smile she introduced the boy to the two princes.

"Niall, Constantine, this is Conchobar mac Flann, our youngest son. This is your brother Niall."

"I am pleased to meet you, Conchobar," Niall said while playfully grabbing the handsome little chap in the old warrior's grip in greeting.

"Who are you?" the young boy answered shyly before burying his face into his mother's neck.

"My name is Niall Glundub mac Aed Findliath, your older brother."

Niall and Constantine stood patiently at the foot of the throne of Flann Sinna some minutes later.

"ONE HUNDRED MEN!" the High King shouted, apoplectic with rage. "If you survive this battle with Thorstein and the scum who follow him, you can tell your brother that he is next!"

Neither Niall nor Constantine responded and cast their eyes down, conscious of the advice offered to them by the Queen.

"The effrontery of Domnall in this matter is too much; the Kingdom of Ireland is at stake. My kingdom. What's your name again?" the King impatiently demanded of Niall.

"Niall Glundub mac Aed Findliath, my King," he answered.

"Aye, I remember now. You are the man who killed that maniac Ulf Francslayer a few years ago aren't you? Yes, you did my nephews in Dublin a service there," the King mused. "And what's your name again?" He impatiently waved at the Pictish Prince.

"I am Constantine mac Aed mac Cinead of Scotland, as I have said already, my King."

Flann Sinna charged off his dais to grab the Pictish prince by the throat. Before Glundub could intercede, Flann Sinna's guards had drawn swords. His captain of the guard warned Niall Glundub when he reached for his own swords, "Just try it, boy, and I will cut you down here and now."

The Queen's voice rang like a bell over the clamour before violence erupted.

"Calm yourself, Aidan mac Fergus, my son meant no offence. My King, release my nephew. These two are proven warriors and you will need every man who can bear steel against the Vikings."

The High King released Constantine and shoved him away. "Do not be insolent with me, Scotsman, or I will send you back in pieces to your kin."

The hall went quiet as the King returned to his seat on the dais and the guards all resumed their stations. Niall Glundub, his ego pricked, stared at the captain Aidan mac Fergus who stared right back.

"I don't care who you are, boy, I will cut you in half if you so much as look at the King in a way I don't like." Niall elected not to respond and looked away.

"We have one hundred men from the Northern Ui Neill, two hundred from Connaught under the command of Prince Aed mac Conchobar and five hundred from all of Brega. We make eighteen hundred when combined with my own guard. Both Donnchadh Donn and Cerbaill mac Dunlainge have men in the field now harrying the flanks of this Viking horde, but they number perhaps only two hundred. The warrior Bishop of Kildare, Lergus mac Cruinnen, fights alongside Cerbaill's Osraigans with a small force of Leinster men. Cerbaill has given what men he could, but Donnchadh Donn has withheld from me every bit as much as Domnall has. He has not deigned to show his face himself to defend Tara. My own flesh and blood," he railed.

Flann Sinna turned to Mael Muire. "What say you, my Queen?"

Mael Muire stepped forward. "We must go now, husband, with the forces we have assembled. If we do not meet them in battle, this one legion of Vikings could end life as we know it in Meath."

A murmur of consent echoed around the hall among the twenty or so guards and nobility present. It was their families and friends in the path of this horde after all. The King paused for a moment and nodded.

"My twin sons, Mael Ruanaid and Oengus, will lead our forces in the line. They are younger than you, Glundub, but they will represent the High King in the field. I will command from the rear."

The King stood regal and strong, unbowed by the weight of years, and faced the people in his hall.

"MEN OF MEATH AND THE COUNTRY OF IRELAND; MARCH WITH ME NOW AND WE WILL SEND THESE HEATHENS INTO THE ABYSS!" he shouted.

As one every man in the hall roared in approval. The King turned to Constantine and Niall Glundub, delaying them from leaving with the rest of his men.

"My Queen has requested that you two will remain beside my captain and me. I have agreed. You will protect me and bring me back to Tara should the battle go ill," the King commanded out of earshot.

*Wise not to contemplate the possibility of defeat in front of his men,* thought Niall Glundub. The two princes knew better than to argue and went to prepare both themselves and their men.

*

The two forces opposed each other across the valley of the River Gabhra in the early morning light. The Vikings had formed a massive shield wall, hundreds of feet across and many men deep. Niall Glundub admitted to himself that he had never felt as scared. He had never witnessed such a force in his young life, and he couldn't help but fear the worst. *How can we defeat so many Northmen?*

A quick glance across to Constantine his cousin revealed that the Pictish prince was as terrified as he was. Constantine had gone pale, and his shield arm shook. Niall nudged him to snap him out of it. They had men to show example to after all. The High King Flann Sinna stood several yards ahead of the line formed by the Irish forces. It impressed Niall, the courage the High King showed, to stand in front of his army to challenge the Viking horde opposing him. A parley would occur, Niall knew, before battle could be joined. It was an Irish custom, but in pitched battles, the Vikings were known to honour the tradition also. News had reached the High King that the full might of Meath was being assembled by some of his under-kings and a cousin, but it would take some time to assemble and march from Kells to Tara. The damage done by Thorstein's army could well be irreversible if they went unchallenged for much longer. Flann intended to drive the Northmen into the path of this auxiliary force and thus have them destroyed, or at least do sufficient damage to them that they would have to retreat.

Due to the ancient traditions of the Ui Neill, a High King must remain unblemished and Flann Sinna, ever cautious with his power, was conscious of that. He would be forced to abdicate on the loss of an eye, ear, disfiguring facial scar or loss of limb and so before formal battle was joined, Flann would retreat to the rear. Both Constantine and Niall would then join the King with his captain Aidan mac Fergus from a preselected vantage point, with young boys running messages between the King and his sons and captains in the thick of the battle. All that separated these two forces was fifty feet of ground on the green plain, on the banks of the Gabhra.

The morning was clear and cold and even the wildlife held its breath. Five Vikings stepped out of the shield wall. Thorstein the Red and the Iron Knee were recognisable as one had a cascading waterfall of red hair flowing down his back from under his helm, and the Iron Knee was bristled like a hedgehog with iron spikes, the largest of which extruded grotesquely from each knee. The three other men were unknown, but Niall Glundub guessed that given their youth, they must be sons of both men. Flann Sinna stood alone. The discussion that took place was out of earshot and no one on the Irish side could hear. Niall knew that the King could speak some of the tongue of the Norse and Danes and that Thorstein, at least, could speak some Irish.

"What are they saying?" Constantine asked Niall nervously.

Niall shrugged his shoulders and looked on. *It doesn't matter.* There was no way out, no matter how much Constantine mac Aed may have wished it. There would be a battle this day. At length, the High King and his Viking counterparts walked back to their respective battlelines. Thorstein the Red held up his axe as he reached his lines and a cacophony of shouts from the Vikings arose. Their battle chant began.

"TYR! TYR! TYR!"

And then it changed to what sounded like ODIN A YOR ALLA!

The High King Flann Sinna raised his own sword in the air and a massive cry of UI NEILL AND IRELAND went up from the Irish.

With a signal from the High King the boom of the bodhran drums began to thunder through the air. The hairs rose on Niall Glundub's arms as he mentally braced himself to face the Vikings. He had fought many Norse raiders in his life already and had even battled his own tribesmen in internal disputes, but this was different. All around him men gathered themselves, howling threats and challenges at the Vikings and prayers to the Christ God and the gods of old. Some stood rock-still infused with quiet determination, others clashed their weapons while screaming at the Norse, others looked like they were ready to turn and run with piss stains visible on their trousers. Niall Glundub couldn't help but feel invigorated, alive amongst an army of Irish and ready to do battle with the greatest of enemies. To stand with an army of Irish warriors in the face of such a horde of evil barbarians, it felt like righteousness, and then he remembered that he had been ordered to retreat to the rear with the King once hostilities began, and that hurt him. His two younger nephews would be in the line. He wanted to face these fiends and it quietly sickened him that many men would die this day while he protected Flann Sinna at the rear. The shield wall of the Vikings parted in the middle then and around a hundred warriors came forth, armed with axes and wearing absolutely nothing.

"They have berserkers," the King muttered when he reached them.

Mael Ruinaid, the Prince of the Southern Ui Neill, stepped out from the Irish line, threw down his shield and turned to his men.

"*FAUGH A BALLAGH!*" he screamed, the old Irish battle cry where the heroes of old would ask their warriors to clear the way, to cleave a path through their enemies. The berserkers were a special breed of Viking warrior that imbibed pagan concoctions of mushrooms that made them furious and capable of enduring wounds that would kill a normal man. They would form the vanguard for the Northmen. Mael Ruinaid took his sword, picked up his shield and charged by himself straight at the berserkers. This act of insane courage fired the Irish and they charged behind him, sprinting downhill toward the river. Niall Glundub joined the King on a knoll to see the battle. Constantine and Glundub flanked Flann Sinna and Aidan mac Fergus stood in front, weapons drawn.

"What does their chant mean, King Flann?" asked Constantine.

The King answered, "It means Odin will take you. Odin will take you all."

Within half an hour, the battle looked lost to Glundub; men were fleeing everywhere. Cores of veterans were trying to retreat in order as a unit one step at a time through the trees, but to do so was grueling and men were dying for it. The Bishop of Kildare had been killed in the centre of the left flank when a Norwegian berserker had split his head in two with a battle axe. To see the holy man fall had shattered morale and the Irish had given ground before the Norse. Iron Knee and his sons had advanced then and began turning their forces inward to outflank the Irish host. Flann Sinna had sent both Constantine mac Aed and his captain Aidan mac Fergus down to the battlefield to take some men and try and stiffen them, but it had only slowed the Norse momentarily. *If Iron Knee gets round the back of Flann's forces, the entire Irish army will probably perish,* Niall thought.

Tara itself lay only two miles to the south but a small wood lay between the battlefield on the banks of the Gabhra and the great deforested clearing around the enormous fort. The King had decided to call the retreat when he heard that his uncle and great friend Cerbaill mac Dunlainge had taken a serious wound and had fallen. If either of his own sons fell now, or Prince Aed of Connaught, or even King Tolarg mac Ceallach of South Brega, this defeat would turn into a rout. The battle was lost.

"Niall, sound the horn. Two blasts. All of the captains and kings know what that means," the King commanded.

Niall Glundub put his lips to the ox horn and blew two long echoing blasts. Immediately the army began to retreat before the shield wall.

"Take me back to the fortress, Niall Glundub, we must retreat and ready the archers to cover our forces." The King screamed his fury.

"CURSE THEM. I SHOULD HAVE MARCHED ON DUBLIN YEARS AGO AND BURNED IT OUT ON IVAR'S DEATH!" he roared. "We should have waited Prince Niall, until all of my armies were ready."

Niall didn't know how to respond but ushered Flann Sinna back through the trees. In minutes, the battle was out of sight. Even the sounds of five thousand men slaughtering each other became dim and dull as Niall Glundub and the King passed through the trees. They burst into sunlight at the south of the wood and into the open and the two men began jogging back toward the Hill of Tara. It was a thousand yards at this point to the fort. The archers on the palisades had a range of around fifty yards, Niall knew, and to keep the High King safe he had to get him at least that close to the walls if not behind them.

With five hundred yards to go the sound of shouting emerged from the left of the woods. It was a small group of five Vikings, led by one of the warriors who had met with Flann Sinna at the centre of the battlefield. A son of Iron Knee it looked like. They pointed up the hill toward Niall and the King and began sprinting.

"Run, my King, you must make the walls. I will try and hold them." Niall Glundub realised what had happened. When Iron Knee had collapsed the left flank of the Irish, he had sent some of his best warriors under one of his sons to try and capture or murder the High King. In his arrogance, the High King had left the horses inside Tara and his entire host was on foot. He had no option but to run. The Vikings were only two hundred yards away now and closing, and Flann Sinna was past his prime and flagging. A small stream lay within two hundred yards of the fort and there was a single small wooden walkway across it.

"My King, I will hold them here. Get to the walls and command our rearguard." Flann Sinna turned and sized up Niall.

"You are a man of honour, Glundub. Your mother always spoke highly and proudly of you from afar. Now I know you to be the man she says you are."

The King pointed to the right. Some of the Irish forces were emerging from the trees. It was a footrace.

"Our men come. If you can hold them, Glundub, until our forces reach you, you will have saved Tara and the High King." The King turned and ran.

Niall knew it wasn't cowardice that forced Flann Sinna to run. He ran because he must. No High King had ever fallen in battle to a foreign invader and both Flann Sinna and Niall Glundub were equally determined that it would not happen today. Niall took his short spear in hand. He hurled it at the five Vikings racing toward the footbridge only forty feet away now. The spear took a warrior full in the face and exploded his head like an overripe fruit. The other four did not slow down for a second, desperate to get through Glundub and to the King. Niall thought about perhaps fighting with sword and shield but when he weighed it up in his mind, he elected to go with two swords. With a scream the four Vikings reached him in a staggered sprint and time slowed down. Each second was like an age and Glundub could see every move as if he was playing chess with Constantine.

Slash and the lead Viking fell. Parry and stab, and the second was ran through, a foot of steel emerging from his back. A spin out of range in combination with a backhanded swipe of his other sword and a headless Norseman toppled to the ground. *One man left*, thought Niall, *the son of Iron Knee*. He was not covered in spikes like his gruesome sire but around his waist he possessed chains with impaled and dangling skulls. Lives he had taken no doubt, grizzly trophies of his martial prowess. He was armed with axe and shield to Niall's paired swords. The two clashed. Instantly Niall triumphantly realised that this Viking prince was no match for him. Glundub when fighting with paired swords he knew, was like a walking whirlwind of destruction and in no time at all the Viking's shield had been splintered and his axe hand had been severed at the wrist. The Viking had time to spit in defiance before Niall punched his left-hand sword up through his chin and out through the top of his head.

The warriors from Connaught were the first of the Irish warriors to arrive seconds later. They had witnessed the astonishing feat of skill and murder exhibited by Glundub from distance and each touched three fingers to their forehead in respect, in the old way. There were perhaps fifty of them but amongst them they carried the body of Aed son of Conchobar. He was a bloody mess, but his shock of blond hair made him recognisable to Glundub. As the minutes wore on, the bedraggled Irish forces began arriving at the footbridge. Niall Glundub commanded the uninjured men to stay with him and form up a line at the small river. The last men to arrive were commanded by Aiden mac Fergus and Constantine mac Aed who led five hundred men in an ordered retreat. Niall could see Viking warriors shouting at them from the trees, but they did not attempt to pursue or advance toward the Hill of Tara.

Constantine looked as weary as Niall had ever seen him when he arrived. He almost sagged into his arms and Glundub sent him on up the road to the fort. *He is no use to me here,* thought Niall. He stood watch for an hour with his ragtag rearguard and apart from the occasional wounded survivor staggering up the road or, in one or two cases, crawling toward Tara, nobody came. The Vikings had had their fill of battle for the day. In his head Niall had counted the remaining Irish forces as they retreated. Flann Sinna and his two sons had survived but almost three hundred men had been killed. Two under-kings of the High King had been slain in battle, in Cerbaill mac Dunlainge the old warrior, and the old enemy of Flann Sinna and now ally, Tolarg mac Ceallach. Tolarg's body was only recovered a day later, having been hacked to bloody bits and without his head. Bishop Lergus mac Cruinnen, the warrior of Kildare, had been slain by a Viking axe and Aed mac Conchobar, the Prince of Connaught, had also succumbed to his wounds. Niall's heart sank; the biggest battle he had ever fought in had been a catastrophic defeat and he had only played a peripheral part, protecting the King and defending him from pursuit. The Battle of Pilgrim had been an unmitigated disaster. The Irish had suffered a horrendous defeat to the Norse of Thorstein the Red and Einar Iron Knee. *A sad day for Ireland,* he thought.

It took two more days for the full assembled forces of Flann Sinna to arrive at Tara, but the Vikings had travelled south via the River Boyne and then the coast, to avoid possible ambush on the road to Dublin. The Kingdom of Meath and South Brega in particular, had been ravaged. The High King refused to see anyone apart from his wife and his captain Aidan mac Fergus. Even worse news emerged when several wounded Viking prisoners revealed that the King's own nephew, Sichtfridh son of Ivar the Boneless, had been slain in single combat by a son of the Iron Knee a month prior to their invasion. *I wonder was this son of the Iron Knee the man I slew on the bridge*, thought Niall, but he could not really bring himself to care. Nephew of the High King or not, Sichtfridh was as much of a pirate and slaver as Thorstein the Red and was not deserving of his pity. Seventy-five men had survived of the contingent that Niall and Constantine had brought from the north and after several days' rest, they were sent back north once more under the command of a fine young soldier named Lugaid mac Conn.

Constantine had decided to stay with Niall for now. Glundub was glad of his cousin's decision. The battle had done something to Constantine, Niall had noticed. He was quiet and introspective, staring into space with his drink in his hand, only speaking when spoken to and uncaring of the goings on around him. Niall had heard his brother Domnall speak of it sometimes, a certain battle affliction that can befall some men who have witnessed shocking violence in war. Selfishly, Niall had been glad of Constantine's presence, as apart from his mother, Niall was on his own. Word had spread around the town of his deeds in defence of the King, slaying five Vikings on the bridge by himself. The Connaught men who had witnessed the fight from distance had told other soldiers in the barracks and they in turn had told their friends and families around Tara and so the legend of Niall Glundub grew, even amongst the Southern Ui Neill.

On the fifth day after the battle, Niall Glundub was finally summoned to the King's presence. When Niall arrived, the hall was empty apart from three armed guards, his mother and the High King himself. A large fire was burning in the hearth and the King sat brooding in his chair staring at the flames. He nursed a cup of mead in his hands. Mael Muire, Niall's mother, used a discreet nod of her head to indicate that he should sit on the other chair by the fire. Niall carefully sat down, a little unsure of himself and not knowing what to expect. The two men sat in silence for many moments before the King shuddered and turned his face from the fire to Niall.

"Glundub, you have done a great service to me. Had the Vikings taken me alive, in fifty years the people of Meath would have been speaking the tongue of the light and dark foreigners." The King shrugged disconsolately before continuing.

"As it is, Brega and all of Meath have suffered great loss of life. I am going to have to send out my own guard to help rescue what is left of the harvest so that my people do not starve."

He took a drink from his cup. *He looks old and tired, every bit of his fifty-odd years,* thought Niall.

"What you have done, Glundub, must be rewarded. But your brother is a disloyal treacherous dog not deserving of the Ui Neill lineage."

The King grabbed Niall's wrist, staring intently into his eyes. "He sent you down here hoping for one or the other, or even both of us to die against Thorstein and the Iron Knee. When I gather my strength, I am going to march upon him, Niall, and I want you to join me or at least stand aside."

A shiver ran down Niall's back. The wrong word here would ensure trouble.

"King Flann Sinna, I am a man of the Northern Ui Neill. I may not be in my brother's good graces, but I will not disobey a command, to whatever end. I am a warrior first and a prince second. It is not my place to question my brother, but only to follow his orders."

The illustrious High King of Ireland pondered Niall Glundub's words, stroking his beard.

"My spies tell me that should you rise up now, even at eighteen years of age against your brother, at least half of the Northern Ui Neill would choose you over Domnall. Some of the Dal nAridi under-kings would join you as well. I am going to bind you to the Southern Ui Neill from this moment onward, Niall Glundub. You will marry my daughter Gormlaith."

Niall was in shock. He was surprised firstly that Flann Sinna had spies in his brother's court, but the issue of marriage had struck him like the blow of an axe.

"Come forward, daughter, from the shadows there," the King commanded. A hooded female silhouette stepped from an alcove and revealed her beauty by the firelight. All of Niall Glundub's concerns melted away. He met his mother's eyes and there was a glint there; *it was her notion as much as her husband's*.

# CHAPTER 3

# THE SACK OF NORTH MEATH BY DOMNALL MAC AED (889)

A southerly summer breeze blew in the night air, warming Niall Glundub, his wife and his newborn son Muirchertach. They had taken a walk around the outside of the palisades of the fort of Aileach to try and soothe their child asleep. The hustle and bustle of the thriving town inside and around the fort made it difficult for the child to rest, but they had discovered that walks at night succeeded where patience failed.

"Muirchertach mac Niall, he will surely be a great warrior, Gormlaith," Niall said to his wife, "the grandson of two high kings of Ireland and the great grandson of the most famous King of the Picts. He must be destined for greatness."

Gormlaith raised an eyebrow. "Perhaps he is destined for the monastery to be a brother of the holy faith?"

Niall went pale before Gormlaith burst out laughing, to his relief.

"No, I agree husband, he is immaculately bred for battle and leadership."

Gormlaith ingen Flann was a tall, graceful woman possessed of wicked humour. She never took any situation seriously and constantly played tricks on Niall Glundub. When tensions ran high between him and King Domnall, she was always able to defuse the situation deftly. Even Domnall's son Flann thought she was great fun and he often sought her advice being bereft of a mother of his own. The King though saw her as an invader, an avatar of Flann Sinna's will transplanted into his court. From the first day he had met Gormlaith, the King had treated her with suspicion and ice-cold courtesy. Niall knew that the union had made Domnall furious, having his brother married to the High King's daughter without his permission. In a way he was right to be vexed with this turn of events. As a Prince of the Northern Ui Neill, it was Domnall's job to secure a suitable bride for Niall Glundub and despite his young age, many of the northern kings had paraded daughters before the King for his perusal. That choice was taken away from Domnall now by Flann Sinna and the marriage had been witnessed before the Bishop of Clonmacnoise and God himself; therefore, it could not be annulled.

Niall was eternally grateful for that as he was smitten with Gormlaith. He had broached the idea of perhaps building his own fort in Ui Neill territory away from his brother, maybe even close to the coast or the rivers as a deterrent against raiders from the sea. His brother had actually considered it, the first real piece of alignment they had had in years apart from when discussing battle strategy and political machinations in the country. Looking at Gormlaith and his young son, Niall would happily disappear into obscurity and farm the land or something similar, only fighting his brother's wars when called upon. A slight drop of temperature on the breeze made him shiver; reminding him that in Ireland nothing was permanent and the shifting tides of politics everywhere around the Irish Sea was mercurial at best. It didn't do well to dream of future pleasantries.

With their son sound asleep in Gormlaith's arms they re-entered the stout timber palisade surrounding the town and stone fort. After the attack of Ulf Francslayer and his Norsemen, Domnall had revamped the entire defensive arrangement of the capital of the Cenel nEoghain. The moat had been deepened and broadened. The walls had been made higher. When Glundub had told Domnall of what Flann Sinna had built at Tara, the King felt he had to duplicate. The expanded fortress drew people to the town from as far as Breffni, Ulaid and Argialla. They had decided to make their homes here under Domnall's protection. Several years of civil war had weakened the other three Northern Ui Neill kingdoms although in the last six months Niall admitted that situation had improved.

The noise of barter and trade echoed around the town as Niall and his family made their way to his small living quarters adjoining the King's hall. Blacksmiths hammered on anvils and the fishmongers cried their daily catch. Children played freely despite it being dark and cooking fires brightened the walkways, casting shadows on the walls of the many buildings. A runner approached Niall Glundub from around a corner.

"What is it?" he demanded brusquely. Despite being only nineteen his achievements intimidated old and young alike, along with his freakish size and strength.

"Prince Niall, the King and his advisors request your presence in the main hall."

With that the boy fled. Gormlaith and their son retired to their own abode while Niall continued to the King's hall which sat outside the stone fort in the middle of the town. He encountered Constantine mac Aed waiting there for him.

"What's happening?" Niall asked.

"All of the Kings of the Northern Ui Neill have arrived secretly today, cloaked and hooded with only a few bodyguards apiece," Constantine answered. Niall wondered uneasily what that could mean.

"I believe your brother means to war upon someone, Glundub, the question is who?"

*There can only be one answer,* Niall thought, *he means to devastate the Kingdom of Meath.*

A massive fire drove all the gloom and shadow from Domnall's hall. A squat set of abnormally large benches and tables dominated the middle of the floor. Around the top table sat Niall Glundub, the two Scottish princes, Domnall and Constantine, and the four most powerful Kings of the Northern Ui Neill.

Jugs of water and mead had been placed on the table with stacks of goblets for the nobles to use. All servants and soldiers alike were banished from the room. King Domnall's giant ornate throne from the dais had been dragged down to the head of the table. *That's petty and looks insecure,* thought Glundub, *everybody knows that Domnall is the King without that sort of chicanery to reinforce his authority.* Every single thing that Domnall did bothered Niall Glundub lately and he now truly dreaded being in his presence.

Niall sat as far as he could from his brother at the distant end of the table, flanked by his two cousins. The first man to the right-hand side of King Domnall was Tiernan mac Seallachan the King of Breffni, a weaselish man almost as uninspiring as his late cousin Ceallach mac Cearnach. He was already in his late thirties, almost of an age with King Domnall, and was a close supporter of him. Niall had heard that he had a teenage son called Ruarc who was a far more formidable man already and would make a fine king compared to his barely adequate father. To the right of him was Mael Craoibh or the Black Fox as he was known, the winner of the internecine battles that had plagued Argialla for several years. He was a brutal monster of a man and had won his kingship through strength of arms. Niall had fought beside him on occasion, and each had a grudging respect for the other. On the other side of the table to Domnall's left sat the two most powerful kings to the east. Becc mac Airemoin of Ulaid, and Lethlobar mac Loingsig, the king of the Dal nAridi tribe. Becc had usurped the kingship in Ulaid from the old King Ainfith with the help of Lethlobar, and when the time was right had reciprocated the coup, placing the Kingdom of Dal nAridi firmly in Lethlobar's lap.

It was King Domnall who began. "I have summoned you here for a single purpose. I wish to invade Meath and the Kingdom of the Southern Ui Neill. Their defeat at the hands of Thorstein the Red and the berserker known as the Iron Knee last year, has significantly hurt the High King and his allies."

The King was interrupted by the Black Fox. "King Domnall, with respect, my lands border Flann Sinna's. If we do this thing there will be retribution. He will devastate my lands first. I fought at the Battle of Slane many years ago and he made his threat plain. If we of the Argialla ever came south, Flann of the

Shannon would raise an army and destroy us, root and branch."

King Domnall rose himself up to his full height.

"I am the King of the Northern Ui Neill, my star is on the rise and his is on the wane. Between us here, we have the strength to dissuade him from retaliation."

The Black Fox harrumphed and sat back, arms folded, clearly not placated or convinced.

Domnall continued. "At the full moon in three weeks, we will each meet at Armagh with five hundred men and march south through Argialla and into Meath. We will take any and all livestock we encounter, take any crops the people of Meath may have gathered and seize any gold and silver. Any who stand in our way will be killed. We will keep marching south until Flann Sinna comes to meet us. He is weak, my Kings, we may be able to extract tribute from the High King himself from behind his walls, if we can get there before he raises a large enough force to meet us."

Lethlobar the King of the Dal nAridi scratched his chin and queried Domnall, "We know that Flann Sinna still has connections with some of the dark foreigners in Dublin. What if Flann Sinna sends them up the River Creggan at the Viking town of Linn and cuts us off from our retreat? The Danes are formidable, King Domnall, and no Danes fought at the Battle of Pilgrim which means their strength is not spent like Flann Sinna's, is that not true, Prince Niall?" He turned to Niall.

Glundub, surprised at being consulted here in the presence of his brother, responded while thinking, *The King will hate that.*

"That is true, any Danes present were connected to Thorstein the Red and not to the Ui Imair, the name the Irish peasant folk have now given the descendants of Ivar the Boneless. Thorstein the Red has been killed and will threaten the land no more. Is this true, brother?" Niall asked King Domnall.

"That is true, Glundub. My sources tell me that the demonic Iron Knee has had Thorstein murdered and now shares power over the Norse with a cousin of Harald Fairhair. He goes by the name of Jarl Sichtfridh. The Norse are no friends of Flann Sinna and the Danes are losing the civil war for Dublin. I believe that at least two of the sons of Ivar are still alive and there are multiple very young grandsons, but it is the Norse who have the upper hand in Dublin. The dark foreigners are in no position to help Flann Sinna." With that, King Domnall sat back satisfied.

The Black Fox questioned the King again: "What of the Vikings of Limerick, my King? If we bring our best warriors south would we not open up Breffni and the Ui Neill to raids from the Shannon?"

Domnall answered," It won't be an issue, Black Fox. Ceitl Flatnose, the old bastard, has finally died. For a Viking like him to have lived so long after as many battles as he has fought in, is frankly astonishing. He has died in his bed at the age of eighty. His wife Aud of the Deep Mind, who actually ran Limerick for the Flatnose in his dotage, has fled to Iceland with the son of her son-in-law Thorstein the Red, for fear of the Iron Knee coming south and destroying Limerick. Limerick will be no threat."

The next question came from a surprising source – Prince Domnall of the Picts stood up.

"King Domnall, my correspondence with my kin has revealed that Harald Fairhair is now the king of the entirety of Norway. He has defeated Kjotve the Rich in a great sea battle and now controls everything from the North of Norway to parts of Francia. Even the Danes and the Francish descendants of Charlemagne fear him. He will be looking to reward his loyal supporters by leading raids for plunder and slaves. Should you move your best forces south, you will leave your entire northern coast vulnerable to Norse reavers."

King Domnall shook his head in denial. "Harald Fairhair is no threat to us yet. There is low hanging fruit for him elsewhere in Frisia, Francia and the Scottish coast. Let him raid Scotland as he wishes, he is no threat to us here yet. Besides we will have returned in six weeks from Meath."

Prince Domnall sat back into his chair. He looked pale and anaemic.

*That was a mistake,* thought Niall Glundub, *you are basically acknowledging that the prince's land is fair game to the Norse and not worth a thought, a terrible lack of empathy.*

The King continued, oblivious to the slight he had issued to the Scottish princes.

"There is another reason why the Danes of Dublin will not bother coming to Flann Sinna's aid as they did almost ten years ago when they sacked Armagh; King Guthrum the Danish King of East Anglia has died. Every Danish warlord worth his salt will be looking to assume his mantle. They will be much too busy to help old Flann Sinna against us."

He steepled his fingers and looked each king in the eye and asked, "Are we all in agreement then, my Kings, that at the full moon we will assemble at Armagh and raid south?"

Nods of agreement and several *ayes* went around the table from the four under-kings. Prince Domnall said nothing, stewing in anger or perhaps contemplating the fate of his homeland.

Constantine mac Aed raised his voice. "King Domnall, I would like to stay here with Niall Glundub to guard your lands while you go south, as I assume with the prince married to the High King's daughter, you will not expect him to fight in this case?"

King Domnall smiled arrogantly. "My brother will not just fight, he will do his duty to the Northern Ui Neill and lead my vanguard wherever the fighting is thickest!"

Niall Glundub's heart sank. He weighed up every possible response and the consequences for each and ended up remaining mute. As he left the hall with his cousins and the under-kings, he went straight to his quarters. He had to tell his wife the dreadful news that if it came to it, he may have to kill her own father in battle. There was no other choice.

The weeks passed rapidly for Niall in preparing both himself and the Northern Ui Neill soldiery. He had drilled the men under his command relentlessly as much to take his mind off the possibility of fighting his wife's father, as getting the men ready for battle. When the three weeks had elapsed, all forces were assembled in good order at the monastery at Armagh. It was a formidable host, the largest gathering of Northern Ui Neill fighters since Aed Findliath had warred against the Vikings of Limerick and the Munstermen.

Niall Glundub would usually exult at being part of such a host like he did at the Battle of Pilgrim, but the dread he felt was unshakeable. It was a betrayal of his wife, his son and his word of honour. In Ireland, brother often fought and killed brother and by extension fighting against a father-in-law should not have resulted in the slightest hesitation for him, but Niall did not feel that this fight was justified. Glundub fought in battles to ensure the superiority of the Cenel nEoghain over all the Northern Ui Neill Kingdoms, he fought against Viking marauders to defend his lands and he had even fought on behalf of the High King himself against an army of foreigners on behalf of the entire island of Ireland. This potential war, though, was driven purely by his brother's greed and opportunism. It was dishonourable. He understood that wars like this had been fought since time immemorial, but he felt that he was above it. What did the farmers and villagers of Meath ever do to Domnall to draw his wrath? It made Niall Glundub feel dirty and no better than the Norse or Danes.

The two Scottish princes had remained at Aileach with Domnall's chief of his household guard, Cathal mac Goll. Prince Flann, Domnall's young son, was left in their care. The leaders of this force were the five major kings of the North and each commanded a faction of several hundred men. His brother, being the King of the Cenel nEoghain and the Northern Ui Neill, controlled the largest part of the army and Glundub himself was a captain under that command. Many of the nobility were mounted but Niall preferred lately to march with the men. He made a point of suffering whatever the men were suffering, enduring what they endured and fighting with them where the fighting was thickest. *It is what inspires loyalty and respect.* The only other king who even bothered to spend time with the rank and file was the Black Fox. The King of the Argialla was only loosely what could be considered nobility having seized his title by strength of arms, *but hadn't all great lines started like that?* thought Niall.

On the fifth day south from Armagh they exited Argiallan territory and entered the Kingdom of Meath. The first few villages had no warning. The forces of the Northern Ui Neill fell on them at the break of dawn. Very few villagers were killed but the few warriors they had were quickly subdued. Glundub had witnessed the Black Fox execute two of his own men for attempting to rape the daughter of a blacksmith. Glundub had given him the three fingers to the forehead in respect and the Black Fox reciprocated. *At least there are two who lead who are not devoid of honour,* thought Niall.

The army had travelled with dozens of wagons and young lads to drive cattle and whatever plunder was seized back north to be distributed. King Becc and King Lethlobar wished to enslave the villages or at least put them to the sword, but Niall had interceded and even drew his weapons on one occasion to prevent it.

"The first of your men to lay a hand on these people dies," he had warned them.

The pair of Ulaidian kings had hurled abuse at Glundub but the Black Fox had backed him up.

"Are you Irish men or Viking scum to enslave your own people?" he had shouted.

The pair had slunk off, no doubt to complain to King Domnall. Their kingdoms were newly won and they were won mostly through treachery, Niall knew. They wanted to pillage the Kingdom of Meath for everything to unite their forces under them, through lavishing their men with spoils. Cattle, gold, wheat and women were all promised, Niall guessed, but his brother for all of his faults did not condone the murder or enslavement of Irish people for profit in most cases. That was the very thing that both Domnall and their father Aed Findliath had hated the Vikings for in the first place.

Several days later they had hit another large village but failed to stop some men escaping south. Niall was quietly pleased by this development as Flann Sinna would now surely come in force having been made aware of the Northern Ui Neill host approaching. Niall craved fair battle, not this overwhelming of simple people and the theft of their livelihoods. On the eleventh day of ranging hither and thither and seizing all the crops and cattle of the people of Meath, Flann Sinna had come, waiting on the banks of the Uisce Dubh, the Blackwater River. His forces were significant and there was another nasty surprise waiting. The army of the Caille Follamain had been roused in defence of Meath also, their banners standing clear and bright in the summer wind. It could only mean that Donnchadh Donn, the estranged son of the High King Flann Sinna, had made common cause with his father to defend Meath and fight the Northern Ui Neill.

Flann Sinna, Donnchadh Donn and the old King of North Brega, Flannacain mac Ceallaig, had all brazenly crossed the river with no guards and stood in the hastily erected tent of King Domnall. His brother, the four northern under-kings and Niall Glundub himself represented the Northern Ui Neill. The air was tense as Domnall and Flann Sinna stared at each other. It was the obsequious King of Breffni, Tiernan mac Seallachan, who broke the silence.

"Flann Sinna, we demand that you pay us tribute to each of our kingdoms in order for us to leave. We dema—"

Flann Sinna shouted in interruption, "SILENCE, WORM, YOU ARE NOTHING TO ME AND HAVE NO RIGHT TO SPEAK HERE!" He turned to Domnall and asked, "By what right do you lead the Northern Ui Neill against your rightful High King? Why are you here, King Domnall, if that is what you are, a king?"

The King of Breffni was about to respond but Flann Sinna merely pointed his finger and silenced him without ever taking his eyes from Domnall.

Niall Glundub could only admire Flann of the Shannon. There was a reason that this man had led the Southern Ui Neill for almost twenty years. The absolute unshakeable confidence in himself to cross the river to parley with the Northern Ui Neill without fear of capture was brazen, but when Glundub considered the size of the host that they had managed to summon in just four or five days, maybe the old High King had a right to be dismissive of the risk of capture.

"Flann Sinna, you were defeated by the Norse last year at the Battle of Pilgrim. You no longer have the strength to contain the forces of the Northern Ui Neill. We will allow you to keep the title of High King until your death, then that title passes to me, but you and your kings will pay tribute to me from this time forward." Domnall paused. "Or we will cross this river and end the Kingdom of Meath."

Flann Sinna laughed derisively. "My scouts tell me that you have sent your spoils north. That was unwise, Domnall. You have no way to feed your army for long, you must return home or starve in weeks. These are our lands and you and your forces will leech from them no longer."

At that point Donnchadh Donn interceded. He had stood an obvious and uncomfortable distance from his father throughout the verbal exchanges. *Things aren't yet set to rights between them,* thought Niall. Donnchadh Donn pointed at the Black Fox.

"You were warned many years ago by my father never to cross in force into Meath with all the rest of the Argiallans. My chieftains all remember you, Black Fox, as a captain who came upon the rear of their forces like the cowardly curs you are. If it comes to battle, I will capture you alive, bring you back to Kells, and have you whipped to death for the amusement of my people."

The Black Fox responded, "Come draw swords then, Donnchadh Donn. Prove your worth as a warrior because it looks to me that you are nothing more than a spoilt brat still sulking from your father's rejection of you."

Shouts and roars erupted but Niall Glundub stepped into the middle.

"THERE WILL BE NO VIOLENCE HERE," he shouted, and the tent quieted down.

The High King addressed him directly. "Niall Glundub, nobody here can naysay your courage as a warrior and your honour as a prince of the Ui Neill. If this comes to swords, will you fight against me, your own father by marriage, and the kingdom of which your mother is Queen? Or will you lower yourself to treachery like these two Kings of the Ulaid and this rodent of the Breffni?"

The three kings in question began to shout in outrage at the insults thrown, but the High King continued regardless.

"I cannot in good conscious ever allow the title of High King to go to the Northern Ui Neill ever again after this betrayal, King Domnall. There must be consequences. Only my line of the Southern Ui Neill will have this right henceforth. You have proven the Cenel nEoghain are unworthy. So will you, Niall Glundub, take up arms against me and mine unprovoked?"

Uproar was unleashed in the tent as the eight kings present hurled insults and threats at each other but when Niall Glundub, who dwarfed them all, raised up his hand, they all quieted. He looked at his brother and then back at the High King.

"I will not fight."

He turned around and left the tent.

# CHAPTER 4

# THE FATE OF NIALL GLUNDUB, NEW YEAR'S DAY (890)

Niall Glundub paced his home, hands clasped behind his back and deep in thought. He had been imprisoned there since returning from the tense stand-off with Flann Sinna's army on the banks of the Blackwater River. Only his wife and child were allowed to visit him freely under guard. All other visitors required express permission from the King himself. The march back to Aileach had taken a week. Niall Glundub had immediately been taken captive by his brother on the insistence of most of the Northern Kings. Only the Black Fox of Argialla had objected. Domnall his brother had not spoken to him at all throughout the journey back and had waited to pass judgement in his hall in Aileach.

"My brother, you have disgraced me for the last time, and now you have put me in the most terrible position. I must decide your fate. You have undermined me not just in front of Flann Sinna, who make no mistake is my enemy now, but in front of my own kings."

He had levelled that accusation once the two brothers had the central hall in Aileach to themselves. Niall Glundub had decided not to say anything in his defence. There were only a handful of guards in the hall with the brothers, but those men were older and completely loyal to Domnall, and any words said in his defence would have fallen on deaf ears. They would only have inflamed his brother's rage.

"How long, Glundub, before the Ulaid or the Black Fox rise against me? How long before they abandon their loyalty to the Northern Ui Neill and ally themselves to Flann Sinna or pursue independence? Your actions, Niall, although you wanted to prevent violence, will no doubt cause deaths here in the north instead. I am more convinced than ever that you never possessed the capacity for rule. There is no doubt about your capacity as a warrior, but you lack the ability to make dishonourable choices for the greater good of your own people. You think you are strong, but you are actually weak."

The King had risen from his throne and began circling Niall Glundub but at a wary distance.

"Niall Noigiallach, Niall of the Nine Hostages as the Southern Ui Neill call him, the ancestor of us all, would be ashamed of us. He conquered the Ulaid, the Breffni and the Kings of Meath and Connaught. The rulers of the entire northern half of our country are descended from him to one degree or another. Even the Ulaid, although they like to claim descent from Cuchulainn and the Red Branch Knights, have married our sisters and daughters for more than five hundred years. You have given Flann Sinna the excuse to ensure that his line will now dominate for decades, perhaps hundreds of years to come."

The King grabbed Niall by the collar of his tunic. "Do you know what you have done, Glundub? DO YOU?" he screamed.

Niall felt he had no option but to respond.

"I did what I felt was right, Domnall. I am married now whether you like it or not. My own mother sits as Queen of the Southern Ui Neill. I could not fight them for a dishonourable reason. I never stood in your way though, I just would not have fought myself."

Domnall barked out a sharp laugh. "Don't be so naïve, Glundub. Once all those kings saw us disagree publicly, they instantly would have lost respect for Northern Ui Neill authority. This is what Flann Sinna wanted. Whether you like it or not you are Flann Sinna's pawn. There will be bloodshed at some point, Glundub, caused by your actions in that damned tent."

The King wearily slumped back down on his throne.

"What you don't understand, Niall, is that my under-kings would have raided Meath anyway without my leave. I had to act, Niall. Do you think for one second a vulture like Becc mac Airemoin would not have plundered Meath anyway, to pay off his supporters? I would have ended up having to defend the Ulaid from Flann Sinna no matter what. At least with my way we would have projected unity and strength at a time when Flann Sinna was weak and probably barely keeping control of his own kings."

Domnall sighed and looked earnestly at Niall.

"We have never seen eye to eye, Niall, and despite yourself you undermine my rule with your very existence. I don't hate you, Glundub, but you are a stone in my shoe. The soldiers, indeed, all the people, love you. I still love you. You are their defender and their champion. But I am the King. For now, I confine you to your own house until I can decide what to do."

He had dismissed Niall then and had left him in his house to contemplate his fate for almost three months as winter encroached. The Samhain festival and Christmas had come and gone, and only the Scottish princes, and his wife and child, had come to see him. The first visit from anybody apart from his immediate family and cousins arrived at sundown on New Year's Day, when a hooded and cloaked figure slipped through an open window and not through the guarded front door of his abode. Momentarily Niall thought it was a hired killer out to get him but discounted that as unlikely. The most likely person to want him dead was Domnall and all he would have to do is summon him and have him beheaded. The person was too slight anyway. Glundub couldn't hide his shock on discovering it was a woman when she folded back her hood. And it wasn't just any woman. It was his mother.

Niall stood, arms folded, in the centre of his small house, bemused at seeing his mother, who was armed to the teeth as usual, standing before him.

"Mother, how are you here? How did you pass the guards undetected?"

Mael Muire laughed and unstrapped her sword before taking a seat.

"You forget that I lived here for many years, Niall. I can move around unseen if I wish." She pointed to another chair and beckoned Niall Glundub to sit.

"What you did on the banks of the Blackwater was brave and honourable, but stupid, Niall. But your brother has also been idiotic and careless. His attack has forged a partial if temporary reconciliation between Donnchadh Donn and Flann Sinna. By attacking through Argialla it meant that Domnall's host came into Meath through the territory of the Caille Follamain. It was their lands that he devastated. The High King has acknowledged Donnchadh Donn as third in line for outright Kingship of the Southern Ui Neill now on the back of this. The enemy of my enemy is my friend. It did not completely mend all bridges but it somewhat mollified Donnchadh Donn for now. He is a powerful warrior and commander in his own right."

Niall thought about what she said momentarily before responding.

"Will Flann Sinna march north with his full strength to fight Domnall? Perhaps Domnall would have me freed to defend our people?"

Mael Muire shook her head. "I still have friends here in Domnall's court. You are either to be executed or banished. Domnall is leaning toward execution."

Niall turned away disgusted. All the battles that he had fought and all the times that he had risked his life for the Northern Ui Neill would count for nothing it would seem.

"There is something afoot though and I may be able to sway him toward another solution. Be ready, Niall. If this plan fails, I will not allow you to be slain. If the plan I have in mind goes awry, I have secreted a few warriors loyal to me around Domnall's hall and we will cut our way out to freedom through the escape tunnel at the back of the stone fort and I have horses waiting in the countryside."

Niall nodded and braced himself as hope stirred within him once more. He determined there and then that he would not submit meekly to the executioner's axe.

"News has come to me from Scotland," his mother continued. "I have informed your cousins and they have a plan to use this to their advantage to bring you with them back home. My brother-in-law Eochaid is summoning his forces to face off against the usurper Giric mac Roth, the Son of Fortune, and he means to place my nephew Domnall mac Constantine as King of all the Picts. The Ulaid want you dead, Niall, and will find ways to discount this development in Domnall's mind, but we intend to hit him with this news in front of his whole court and give your enemies no time to respond. We believe Domnall would agree to your banishment if we suggest that you leave for Scotland on the morning tide with the princes."

*Yes*, Niall thought to himself, *this could work.*

"If your enemies in the Ulaid overrule Domnall's sense and call for bloodshed, by God, we will give it to them and buy you time to flee south. They hate you for what happened on the road to Meath. Strangely, the Black Fox of the Argialla has privately offered to grant you refuge if it comes to violence. It was he who sent swift word south to Tara. The news from Scotland only reached the princes' ears today through me, but we haven't yet told King Domnall."

Niall explored the plan in his mind. It all seemed sound.

"Should we not hold off until the Ulaid and the other kings return home from the Christmas feasts after the sixth of January?"

Mael Muire shook her head. "It has to be tonight, Niall, because the King has announced that your fate will be decided in a couple of hours. You are to be summoned to face his judgement."

She squeezed his hand and exited stealthily the way she had come in.

*

Domnall's hall in Aileach was cavernous and it backed onto the inner stone keep. It had high wooden rafters, thatched with reeds, and a broad stone fireplace cut into the south wall. Niall Glundub stood alone, head down, with his wrists chained in the centre of the hall. It was packed inside as the people of Aileach had piled in to witness the fate of their champion. From out of the corner of his eye Niall recognised several faces. In deep discussion with the King on the dais were Becc mac Airemoin and Lethlobar mac Loingsig, the treacherous and ambitious kings of the Ulaid. To one side stood Mael Craoibh the Back Fox, who gave him the most imperceptible of nods. *Good,* thought Niall, *a man of honour exists in this hall.* His mother was only several feet to his right. She had sleeved a dagger that he could see and God knew how much of an arsenal was strapped invisibly on her person. When they met eyes, she delicately nodded to various corners of the hall, indicating where she had deployed men loyal to her. The two Scottish princes stood behind Niall. Constantine whispered then in his ear.

"Say nothing, Glundub, and this won't come to violence. Your wife and son are already hidden away. They are safe."

Niall nodded and awaited his brother's judgement. At length, Domnall took his ease on his throne and a soldier thudded the butt of his spear on the ground three times to silence the crowd.

The King spoke. "Niall Glundub, you have treasonously disobeyed your King's command and as a result the interests of the Northern Ui Neill have been damaged. Have you anything to say in your defence before I, King Domnall mac Aed, pass sentence?"

The crowd went quiet in anticipation.

"No, brother. If I was in the same position again, I would make the same decision."

The volume of the crowd's murmuring went up slightly. Clearly some had expected some spite and vitriol from Glundub, or perhaps some thought that he would fall on his knees and beg forgiveness. He did neither. *They clearly don't know me.*

"Very well then," Domnall answered. "As King of the Northern Ui Neill, I sentence you to die."

The crowd became unruly as the decision proved unpopular amongst most of the attendees. Prince Domnall of Scotland seized the moment to stand forward.

"MY KING! PLEASE, MY KING, ALLOW ME TO SPEAK," he shouted.

A nod from the King resulted in that same soldier's spear being smashed into the ground for silence. The crowd quieted.

"Word has come to my cousin and me from our aunt, Queen Mael Muire."

At that, Mael Muire stood forward, withdrew her hood and bowed to the King who was clearly shocked with this development. Her presence to this point had clearly been unknown to him. Prince Domnall continued.

"The Son of Fortune, Giric mac Roth, the usurper of my family's throne, has made alliances with Norse war bands loyal to Harald Fairhair the King of Norway. Our uncle Eochaid has sent messages through our aunt requesting our return to do battle with him and seek his overthrow for the good of Scotland. We will be returning to Dunkeld at once where we will march to Fortriu and destroy him or be destroyed in the attempt. We beg you to allow Niall Glundub to accompany us. You have sentenced him to die and so we have learned what his life is worth here. Let him join us, his cousins, to perhaps die in battle against the Son of Fortune and his Viking allies. And if he were to survive, let him be banished to serve as a captain in our armies to defend Scotland from now until the end of his life."

The room exploded with shouts from all quarters. Niall could see the two Ulaidian kings attempting to dissuade Domnall from any rash action amidst the din and chaos. It was Domnall's ten-year-old son Flann who sealed Glundub's fate. He ran up to the dais from where he had hidden in the crowd and pleadingly grabbed his father.

"Please, Father," he begged, "let Niall Glundub go, he is my uncle, and I don't want to see him die."

The child's desperate appeal had visibly moved his brother. Domnall called for silence once more.

"Noble sons of Scotland, go forth with our hopes for victory. I agree to allow the Glundub, our most decorated warrior, to leave with you. He is yours."

He turned to Niall. "You are banished forthwith from the Kingdom of the Northern Ui Neill, all land, titles and rank have been stripped from you. Leave my presence at once… and good fortune in Scotland, my brother."

With a flowing twirl of his royal cloak King Domnall retreated from the hall with his son. Niall Glundub released a huge breath that he didn't realise he had been holding. He was free to go. As the two Kings of Ulaid walked past, he couldn't help himself.

"Pray you never face me on the battlefield," he said, "because you will not survive the encounter."

# PART 3

## THE BIRTH OF
## THE TRUE KINGDOM
## OF SCOTLAND
## UNDER
## CONSTANTINE
## THE GREAT

# DRAMATIS PERSONAE:

**Aethelfled of Mercia** (*A-thel-fled*) – Saxon Queen of Mercia and daughter of the King of Wessex.

**Aileen – Queen of Scotland**, wife to Domnall mac Constantine. Of highland stock.

**Aimlaib Ivarsson** (*Am-layb-ivarson*) – Young Ui Imair warlord, slain in the civil wars in Dublin.

**Alfonso III – King of Spain**, at war with the Umayyad Caliphate in Al Andalus.

**Alfred the Great** – King of the West Saxons.

**Anarawd ap Rhodri** (*An-a-rawd-ap-Rod-ree*) – Militaristic Welsh King of Gwynedd the strongest Welsh petty kingdom, son of Rhodri the Great.

**Bjorn Ragnarsson** (*Byorn-ragnar-son*) – Eldest son of Ragnar Lodbrok also known as Bjorn Ironside, fearsome Viking warlord and explorer.

**Ceitl Flatnose** (*Ket-tel-flatnose*) – Deceased Viking King of Limerick and some of the Hebrides and Orkneys.

**Cerbaill mac Dunlainge** (*Ker-ball-mac-dun-lang-ga*) – Deceased politically powerful Irish king of Osraige.

**Charlemagne** (*Sharl-a-main*) – Deceased leader of the Holy Roman Empire, which encompassed most of the land between the Danube and the Atlantic in Europe.

**Cinead mac Alpin** (*Kin-aid-mac-alpin*) – Long-deceased King of Scotland.

**Constantine mac Aed** – Scottish prince, advisor and general for Domnall mac Constantine his cousin.

**Cuchulainn** (*Coo-cull-en*) – Mythical Irish warrior, leader of the famous Red Branch Knights.

**Domnall mac Constantine** – Scottish Prince and contender for the Scottish throne.

**Dungaill mac Giric** (*Dun-gall-mac-giric*) – Prince of Fortriu, son of the Son of Fortune.

**Dyfnwal ap Eochaid** (*Dif-nwal-ap-a-o-cad*) – Prince of Strathclyde and supporter of the grandsons of Cinead.

**Eadwulf** (*Aid-wolf*) – King of Bernicia and candidate for rulership over all of Northumbria.

**Eorl Thororim** (*Thor-or-rim*) – Norse nobleman and henchman of Harald Fairhair.

**Edward the Elder** – Prince of Wessex and general in the Saxon armies.

**Eochaid mac Rhun** (*A-o-cad-mac-roon*) – King of Strathclyde, uncle through marriage of Constantine and Domnall.

**Erik Haraldsson** – Also known as Erik Bloodaxe. Fearsome Viking marauder and raider, young son of the King of Norway.

**Evir ingen Giric** – Daughter of Giric, Son of Fortune. Married to one of the Viking leaders of the Danelaw.

**Finn mac Cumhaill** (*Finn-mac-cool*) – Mythical Irish hero and leader of the legendary Fianna.

**Flann Sinna** – High King of Ireland and over-king of Meath and the Southern Ui Neill.

**Giric mac Roth** (*Gir-rick-mac-roth*) – Usurper of the Scottish throne and King of Fortriu. Known as the Son of Fortune.

**Grinnar** – Norse-Gael warrior, sworn to Eorl Torr-Einarr.

**Gudrod Skirja Haraldsdottir** (*Good-rod-skir-ya-haralds-dot-tir*) – Norwegian princess who married Ivar Ivarsson and was the mother of a generation of the

Ui Imair leadership in Dublin.

**Guthrum** (*Guth -rum*) – Powerful Danish Viking warlord.

**Halfdan Haraldsson** (*Half-dan-haraldson*) – Also known as Halfdan Longlegs. Norse Viking warlord and son of the King of Norway.

**Harald Fairhair** – King of all Norway.

**Hastein** (*Has-tin* ) – Danish Viking warlord, active in Francia.

**Ingamundr Bairidsson** (*Ing-ga-munder-ba-rid-son*) – Formidable Ui Imair warlord, grandson of Ivar the Boneless.

**Ivar Ivarsson** – Ui Imair warlord who ruled parts of Dublin and the Irish Sea. Son-in-law of Harald Fairhair and son of Ivar the Boneless.

**Ivar the Boneless** – Deceased former King of Dublin.

**Mael Muire ingen Cinead** (*Male-mwir-a-ingen-cin-aid*) – Princess of Scotland and Queen of Ireland, wife of Flann Sinna.

**Muirchertach mac Niall** (*Mwir-her-tach-mac-niall*) – Son of Niall Glundub and prince of the Northern Ui Neill.

**Niall Glundub mac Aed Findliath** – Exiled Northern Ui Neill Irish prince. Fierce warrior and general under his cousin Domnall's command.

**Ragnall Ivarsson** (*Rag-nal-ivarson*) – Extremely young Ui Imair warlord. Grandson of both Ivar the Boneless and Harald Fairhair and a grand nephew of High King Flann Sinna.

**Ragnar Lodbrok** (*Ragnar-lod-brok*) – Long-deceased legendary Viking sea king and ravager, ancestor of multiple Viking warlords.

**Rhodri the Great** (*Rod-ree*) – Famous Welsh King, who made his name fighting both Vikings and Saxons.

**Rollo the Walker** – Expelled Scandinavian chieftain, warlord in the Hebrides and West Scotland.

**Sigurd the Mighty** – Famous Norse Viking warlord.

**Sihtric Ivarsson** (*Sit-rick-ivarson*) – Young Ui Imair warlord, slain in the civil wars in Dublin.

**Snorri of Lincoln** – Viking eorl who partially ruled Lincoln in the Five Boroughs. Son in law of Giric of Fortriu.

**St Brendan the Navigator** – Legendary deceased Gaelic saint and explorer.

**St Columba** (*Col-umba*) – Famous Irish Christian saint, long-deceased.

**Tadg mac Conchobar** (*Tie-g-mac-con-co-bar*) – King of the province of Connaught in Ireland.

**Torff Einarr Rognvoldarsson** (*Torf-eye-nar-rog-vol-dar-son*) – Norse warlord expelled from Norway and partial ruler of the Hebrides and parts of the Western Scottish coast.

**Turgesius** (*Tur-geese-e-us*) Deceased Viking warlord, brother of Ragnar Lodbrok and founder of the city of Dublin.

**Wulfhere** – Archbishop of Yorvik in Northumbria. Politically important clergyman.

# CHAPTER 1

# THE DEFEAT OF GIRIC, THE SON OF FORTUNE (890)

Constantine mac Aed trembled on the floor of his tent. A rough woollen blanket served as his mattress and another covered him from head to toe to drive off the chill of the dawn. He now served as second in command of his brother's army on the death of his uncle Eochaid, and the thought filled him with dread. His uncle had been well past fifty and had never been a robust man even in his youth. The long march from Dunkeld to Fortriu in the north had finished him utterly. The idea of battle filled Constantine with a rampant dread that he could not shake. He had never revelled in the glory of it, unlike his vaunted cousins Domnall and Niall Glundub, but had never dared voice his dislike of it lest he lose the respect of the men under his command.

He had fought in six minor skirmishes in Ireland on behalf of the king of the Northern Ui Neill, Domnall mac Aed, but it was the Battle of Pilgrim at Tara that haunted him every waking moment. His mind constantly raced back to the slaughter he had witnessed, the sheer murderous brutality of the Norse that day and the butchery that unfolded on the plains of Meath. The nightmares were relentless and never seemed to recede. He was tortured nightly as he relived the gut-wrenching terror of that battle again and again and again. He found that he required strong drink before retiring to his bed for any sort of sleep and in his waking hours he hated being on his own. He much preferred to be in the company of Niall Glundub and his wife or his elder cousin Domnall the King, as it took his mind off the abhorrent violence of that faithful day. His hands sometimes shook for no reason when he was on his own and his concentration sometimes deserted him, his thoughts morphing into some anguished daydream.

In the middle of the night, he would come roaring awake reaching for his weapons, with his heart hammering in his chest. The only person he felt that he could confide in was Niall Glundub, but he simply didn't understand what Constantine was going through. His Ui Neill cousin was a warrior born and relished battle, or if he didn't, he hid it so well that Constantine couldn't tell. Most men were at least apprehensive on the eve of battle, Constantine knew, but for him the effects were not just mental but physical as well.

In truth, once the fighting commenced Constantine never hesitated or suffered from this accursed affliction and had killed a dozen men at least. His woes approached him when he was on his own, in the silence and the dark. Domnall his cousin relied upon Constantine for advice both politically and tactically, in that respect Constantine knew that he was superior to both the King and Niall Glundub. With sword and shield he was just barely more than competent, far short of the abilities of his heroic cousins; but in strategy, politics, and logistics he was a level above. Their uncle by marriage, Eochaid mac Rhun, had been hesitant to move straight away on the prince's return from Ireland and had advocated fortifying their stronghold in Dunkeld, but Constantine had convinced Domnall otherwise. A surprise attack he felt would yield the greatest result particularly if Giric had little time to summon his Norse allies. That move, Constantine felt, would ensure that Domnall's forces would outnumber Giric's by two to one.

Eochaid the King of Strathclyde was a good man but timid, married to another aunt of both Constantine's and Domnall's. He had perhaps only two thousand men at his disposal due to the attrition of constant warfare with the

Vikings of Dublin, the Isle of Mann and the Hebrides. He had committed only eight hundred to this fight, leaving more than half of his army at home to defend his coastline. It angered Domnall at first, but Constantine had reminded his cousin that should the battle go badly versus Giric, they had a base to retreat to in their uncle's stronghold.

Scotland was a beautiful land particularly in the spring, but severe when travelling cross-country. When Eochaid had passed away, his son Dyfnwal had sent his father's remains back with an honour guard of twenty men and had proceeded with the remainder of the forces of Strathclyde under his command. The men of Strathclyde had not suffered hugely under Giric, but they could not afford another enemy, this time on their eastern border, as well as Saxons to the south, and Vikings to the north and from the sea. When the forces of Strathclyde were combined with all the men gathered from the Pictish under-kings of central Scotland, they numbered almost four thousand warriors. They had assembled their full military strength at Dunkeld and had begun the arduous march on Easter Monday. Giric mac Roth, or the Son of Fortune as he was known, had his capital in the coastal town of Lumphanon. It was a large settlement that dominated the local hinterland but was designed with defence from the sea in mind rather than the land. It possessed a wooden palisade and an earthen ditch but with the forces King Domnall was bringing to bear, these would prove little obstacle if it had to be stormed.

Constantine had impressed upon his warlike cousins, to their satisfaction, that if Giric offered battle it would be on the plains outside the wall. If Giric decided to sit behind his walls, the town would quickly begin to starve as the sea would not yield enough food to feed the people. *He might yield and offer himself up,* thought Constantine, *or more likely he would make his escape by sea if he couldn't rally sufficient force to withstand Domnall.*

It had taken three weeks to move their full army north to Fortriu and when they arrived, they had split their forces on the two roads to the south and to the west into the Highlands. King Domnall had taken command of the southern part of their forces with their cousin Dyfnwal of Strathclyde as his second in command and Constantine himself had taken command of the western part with Niall Glundub serving as his right-hand man.

Constantine emerged from his tent into the dawn light, reliving every aspect of the last several months in his mind. All possible outcomes of the coming days rolled around his head like a storm, but always the lingering dread of battle hung there like the sword of Damocles. Glundub was waiting for him at the quartermaster's wagons where the men received their bowl of stew and their heel of bread to break their fast. Constantine had always admired Glundub's willingness to endure the same hardships when warring as his men, and in his own first command he had deemed it prudent to replicate his esteemed cousin. As the fat quartermaster handed them their breakfast, Glundub asked Constantine how he had slept.

"Like always," he had responded with a weary sigh.

With food in hand, the two cousins began the inspection of their camp. It was located within a mile of the fortress at Lumphanon and the palisades of the town were just visible in the distance. There were very few trees still standing in the area due to their having been chopped for lumber in aeons passed. The road was flanked by small hills covered in gorse and wildflowers, and rocky outcroppings covered in moss and grass. Both men were pleased to see that the latrine pit was almost completely gouged out of the rocky soil and the few horses they had for pulling wagons were set cropping grass as far away as possible from the town. The men's tents were erected in orderly rows and sharpened stakes were placed at the side of the camp facing Giric's stronghold. At all times Constantine had squads of scouts patrolling the hills around with numerous sets of eyeballs always facing the town lest Giric attempted one of his famous subterfuges. King Domnall on Constantine's urging had set up his camp identically. At several points during the day, Domnall had sent men toward the main gates of the town, but they were repelled by archery from the ramparts. Domnall and Glundub were eager to see what strength Giric possessed.

By the size of the town, Constantine estimated the upper range of the populace at around six thousand and from that he inferred that Giric would only have perhaps a third of that, at best, of actual warriors. The scouts had reported that there were no longboats in the harbour which meant that none of Giric's Norse allies were likely present either. *If he offers us battle, we will win,* Constantine thought. When Giric himself arrived on horseback to Constantine's camp with a peace banner three hours later, it was apparent that the Son of Fortune had reached the same conclusion. *There will be no battle amongst Scottish men today,* thought Constantine with relief, *we have enemies enough.*

Giric mac Roth sat across from Niall Glundub and Constantine in the tent with a resigned look upon his face. He had a large red moustache that drooped down either side of his mouth and a shaggy shock of red and grey hair that cascaded down his back like the tail of a horse. He wore the traditional Scottish tartan kilt draped across his shoulder with a tunic beneath it. He was perhaps in his early forties, but he was still robust and brawny around the shoulders. He had come to the camp unarmed and had no cloak either in defiance of the brisk Scottish spring weather. *This is a hard man and no coward either,* thought Constantine.

He had controlled eastern Scotland for ten years but the people loyal to the line of Cinead had always chafed under his control. When he began hiring Norse and Danish mercenaries to devastate Scottish clans who defied him, it was probably the beginning of the end for Giric and opened the door for the two princes' return. He leaned forward on the wooden chair with his elbows rested on his knees, facing Constantine. The prince had not bothered with guards for two reasons. He wanted to show Giric strength, that he was unafraid of him, and the second reason was with his cousin Glundub there, there was little chance the Son of Fortune would survive any attempted escape. *No,* he thought, *there will be a reckoning between him and King Domnall, Glundub will fillet him if he backs out now.* Niall Glundub broke the silence by speaking to Giric.

"You are going to have to be very fortunate as your name suggests, to survive your encounter with King Domnall when he arrives, Giric. Allying yourself with Vikings to plunder your own kin; if you did that in the land of the Northern Ui Neill, you would be tied down with stones and thrown into the nearest river."

Giric looked at the formidable Irishman, his pride pricked. "You know nothing at all about Scotland, you impudent pup. Who are you anyway?"

Glundub stood forward. "I am Niall Glundub mac Aed Findliath, Prince of the Northern Ui Neill. If the King wants your head to leave your shoulders, Giric, I will be volunteering for the task."

Giric sprang from his chair bristling, facing Glundub eyeball to eyeball. Constantine considered intervening but decided to allow whatever would transpire to transpire. Something shifted in Glundub's eyes and Constantine saw the slightest hint of submission and fear in Giric's demeanour. The Son of Fortune sat back down in his chair and stared back at Constantine.

"You are Constantine the Prince of Dunkeld, aren't you? I prefer to speak with you and your cousin rather than this Irish thug," Giric said, nodding at Glundub.

A clamour of horns erupted then from outside. Constantine smiled; *The King comes to deal with this traitor.*

Domnall arrived in the tent. *Kinghood suits him,* thought Constantine. At twenty-four years of age, he was in the prime of his life. He wore riding boots that reached to his knee with a tartan kilt. His shield was slung on his back and his jewelled sword lay in its scabbard at his hip. In the crook of his arm, he carried the massive, feathered half helm he wore, an heirloom of their mutual grandfather, Cinead mac Alpin. A servant laid out some chairs to sit upon, but Giric spoke before a third chair could be placed before him.

"This is a meeting of Scottish nobility; this Irishman has no place here."

Constantine could see Glundub's face darken at this insult, but Domnall placed an arm on Niall's shoulder and gently asked him to leave. Constantine approved. *Best not to antagonise Giric if there is a peace to be won.* Domnall extended his legs before him and stretched out his muscles. Once Glundub and the servant exited he began speaking.

"Giric mac Roth, my army has travelled north to Fortriu and its capital Lumphanon to retake the Kingship of Scotland for the line of Alpin. You have decided wisely to not give us battle and have elected to surrender to us unarmed. Do you accept my overlordship of Scotland?"

Giric sat back and smiled. He played with his moustache, twirling it between thumb and forefinger before responding.

"King Domnall, before we get to that let's speak a little bit about what is going on here. It is true, I am in your power, but I can still make life difficult for you." He nodded at Constantine.

"My spies told me that it was the cunning of your cousin here that has allowed you to land on my doorstep with an army of four thousand before I had time to raise any significant force to oppose you. You have no power by sea though and I can send out boats to rally all the chieftains of Fortriu, Moray and Caithness to relieve the siege. But there is a reason that I won't."

Giric leaned forward conspiratorially. "Believe it or not, I want what's best for Scotland, our entire country, even if it means my life. We need to be unified under one flag to endure the storm that's coming."

Constantine was taken aback by this and probed him further.

"Why is it that you used Viking mercenaries to raid and subdue Pictland and the Highlands and into Caithness? Scottish men died because of your ambition, Son of Fortune!"

Giric had the good grace to look abashed when Constantine mentioned the Viking raiders. He straightened up in his seat and spoke.

"Twenty years ago, you lads were still just boys and weren't privy to what was happening in Scotland at the time. Domnall, your father Constantine was indecisive and weak and Constantine, your father Aed was a drunk. I had to step in. The Orkneys, the Hebrides and most of what was the northern Dal Riadan kingdom of old had been colonised by Norsemen. Some of these settlers were simple farmers, traders and fishermen but others were reavers and raiders, near as bad as Olaf and Ivar of the Great Heathen Army. Under the rule of your respective fathers, Scotland fell under the sway of these Norse. Our people suffered. I had to seize power."

Constantine had heard so little about his father growing up that it stunned him to hear of him in this manner, a weak and ineffective ruler in the face of the Vikings. Constantine could see with a glance that Domnall was thinking the same. Giric continued.

"I was able to force some of your under-kings to bend the knee to me and pay tribute, men whose faces I recognise now amongst your army in passing. Fortriu is mine always and I had my own kin's support. The chieftains of Caithness took some convincing but eventually I brought them to heel with minimum casualties. The Highlanders were a problem. Heathen savages near as bad as the Vikings in places, but they are Scottish after all. But then the news came to me last year, the great struggle in Norway had finished and Harald Fairhair was the victor. What is worse is that many of the factions that opposed him have fled Norway and have settled in the Norse towns in the Hebrides and the Western Coast and islands. I hear from some allies of mine that Fairhair and his young sons Halfdan Longlegs and his youngest the Bloodaxe, are moving against the Geats, the Swedes and the Danes. The question is, King Domnall, Prince Constantine, how long before they turn their gaze upon us? If we the Scots are not united under one rule, we will fall before Fairhair one by one."

Constantine considered all of what Giric said. He had not been aware of Harald Fairhair's current machinations, but it had crossed his mind before that there would be little to stop the Norse King or any of his allies invading Scotland. Domnall spoke next.

"By working with Norse fighters to subdue Pictland, the Highlands and Caithness, you have given our people a taste of what is coming from the Norse. Fire and blood and slavery."

Giric reacted angrily. "I never allowed the Norse under my command to take free Scotsmen as slaves; they were a means to an end, the rapid submission of Scotland to my rule. These mercenaries were paid in gold, weapons and furs. I even had to marry my second daughter Evir to a Dane named Snorri of Lincoln, to secure his hundred men to fight against the damned Highlanders. The only reason that I had to resort to hiring mercenaries is that time is of the essence. Harald Fairhair is coming, King Domnall, make no mistake. I have beggared Fortriu to pay this scum, to force my other kinsmen from around Scotland to bend the knee. Fortriu and Moray are the nearest Scottish lands to Norway, it will be my friends and family that will meet the Vikings first."

Domnall nodded solemnly and took in all that he said.

"I am inclined to believe you, King Giric. Your intentions were indeed noble, I believe, but it cannot be denied that you killed other Scots in battle in alliance with Vikings. That is undeniable."

"Look around you, King Domnall," Giric pleaded, "the Vikings are here to stay. In Caithness, the Hebrides and the Western coast, Norse marries Scot and Scot marries Norse. There will be no way to drive them out fully ever again. For centuries to come I foresee Scottish Norsemen farming the land and being loyal subjects to the Scottish crown. The question will be, is Scotland a free independent country which accepts foreigners as its subjects if they wish to settle and adopt our customs and laws? Or will we be a subject people to Harald Fairhair and the Kings of Norway forever until we become just another conquered province within his realm? And I have worse news for you as well. His eldest daughter Gudrod Skirja married Ivar son of Ivar the Boneless of Dublin, almost twenty years ago. The tales of the conquests across the entire Irish Sea of the Ui Imair, as the Irish call them, have reached my ears, the ravaging and pillaging of the sons and grandsons of Ivar the Boneless. These barbarians are Harald's grandchildren and there is nothing surer than that they will do his bidding. If you think Fortriu is in danger alone, you are wrong; Strathclyde and Pictland will face the same evils too. Mark my words. So leave me now, King Domnall and Prince Constantine, and decide my fate. I have said my piece and the reasons for my actions."

Domnall stirred after a few moments and withdrew with Constantine but not before sending the fearsome Glundub to guard Giric first.

"What do you think?" asked Domnall as the pair walked through the camp. They had dismissed any guards so that no deliberations could be overheard by the rank and file and misconstrued. There were hard decisions to be made.

"I believe he is sincere, Domnall," Constantine answered, "he no more wants to shed Scottish blood than we do. Our under-kings will not accept his reasons and will demand his death. We have to be seen as stern and strong or you will have rebellion to deal with in the coming years. On the other hand, if we hang him or we take his head, we will always have trouble with the people of Fortriu. We need to find a solution that is both strict and simultaneously merciful."

They walked on, pondering the fate of the King of Fortriu together in silence. The evening air was cold and chilly and dark clouds gathered overhead. *Every choice has consequences,* thought Constantine. He knew that Glundub would advocate having Giric's head off in a heartbeat and to send it back to the people of Lumphanon, not before pissing on it first; but that would gain no friends behind those walls and in the surrounding countryside. The matter had to be decided quickly too as their forces had roughly three more weeks of food remaining to them before they would have to start foraging the land.

"He is right about one thing, Domnall," said Constantine, "Scotland has to be truly united to withstand the years to come. How can you call yourself truly the King of Scotland if you barely control a half of our land?"

Domnall nodded worriedly. "It is not just the Norse and the Norse-Gaels from Dublin and the Irish Sea that concern me, Constantine. To the south we have the Saxons in Bernicia who constantly probe our southern lands. The death of Guthrum in East Anglia has drawn the attention of every jarl and eorl from Yorvik to the five boroughs, south. In this chaos the Northumbrians of Bernicia are growing more powerful and ambitious. Alfred waxes strong in Wessex as the power of the Danelaw wanes and I have no doubt that both he and his puppet kingdom in Mercia, wish to extend their influence north. I will never yield to a Saxon king no more than I would a Norse one."

"The biggest threat right now is Harald Fairhair, Domnall," answered Constantine. "Giric mac Roth is not wrong about that. We must be united, all the clans of Scotland under one banner: your banner to be precise."

The King agreed with a nod and walked ahead with his hands clasped firmly behind his back, deep in thought. Constantine prayed that Domnall could find the wisdom to unlock the correct path to proceed. *Prayed,* thought Constantine. *Perhaps a solution presents itself.* He raced after his cousin to tell him what he had in mind.

\*

Three days after Giric's surrender, the two hosts faced each other at the gates of the town of Lumphanon. Domnall's forces outnumbered the army of Fortriu by almost two to one, but it didn't matter. The thousands of men in attendance were there to witness an event rather than take part in a battle. Constantine's sleep had been torturous the previous night, and at one point his screams had roused a manservant who had entered his tent to wake him. Constantine had not bothered to go back to sleep after that and had awaited the dawn, exhaustion clouding his mind.

The two armies formed a sort of ellipse around the five men who stood at its centre. Constantine was one, King Domnall was two, a kneeling and shrouded Giric mac Roth was three, his son Dungaill was four and the Bishop of Fortriu made the fifth with his giant crosier in hand. Giric had agreed to the stipulations laid down by King Domnall and a peace had been forged. Giric had agreed to Constantine's suggestion of leaving on pilgrimage to Rome on behalf of the whole of Scotland. In that way, Giric could prove his selfless intentions by sacrificing himself on a mission to the Vatican to secure the Pope's blessings in Scotland's ongoing wars with the Norse. His kingship would pass to his eldest son Dungaill, who seemed a capable young man to Constantine. Fortriu would pay tribute to Dunkeld and their armed might would be Domnall's to command in defence of Scotland against any foreign power.

The coastal fortress of Dunnottar to the south would be manned at all times by a garrison of five hundred soldiers each, from both Fortriu and Pictland, as it stood in a perfect position to defend against threats from both the sea and the Saxons and Danes to the south. Once all of these decrees had been proclaimed by both Giric and King Domnall, the Bishop had given his holy blessings to Giric mac Roth and the former King of Fortriu began his march to the coast to take ship to Francia and on to Rome. The men of Fortriu formed a corridor for him to walk through with their spears joined in a triangle above their heads in respect. And so passed Giric mac Roth mac Dungaill, Lord of Fortriu and the Son of Fortune. When Giric had passed out of sight, the first act of his son was to place the Crown of Alba upon the head of Domnall mac Constantine mac Cinead. Domnall had knelt before the newly crowned King of Fortriu and accepted the simple golden circular crown that Cinead mac Alpin had worn many decades before in his wars with Viking warlords such as Ceitl Flatnose, Ragnar Lodrok and Torgesius. When he arose, he did so as King of Scotland to thunderous roars of approval from the Picts and the men of Fortriu and Strathclyde. The line of Cinead mac Alpin, the first King of Scotland, had been restored. *And not a single drop of Scottish blood had been spilled to achieve that,* thought Constantine.

There was a celebration that night both inside and outside the walls of Lumphanon. Revelry and celebration erupted around the town as the men exulted in not having to die in battle fighting their own kin. All was right with Scotland in that moment and yet Constantine did not sleep easy in the night once more. In fact, he barely slept at all, his blood-filled dreams reverberating with the sound of weapons clashing and the screams of dying men. These were only remnants of the savage past, he hoped, but deep down he knew they were as likely to be a portent of the future.

# CHAPTER 2

# THE SUBMISSION OF
# THE NORSE-GAELS TO
# KING DOMNALL
# (893)

Constantine rose from his bed dishevelled and distraught, the fleeting horror of his nightmares ever so slowly evaporating away. He put on his undergarments, kilt, tunic, and riding boots. His brother had told him to appear at his court in the centre of Dunkeld by midday as there was a duo of distinguished guests due to appear. Aethelfled, daughter of Alfred, the newly crowned Lady of Mercia. had approached by sea and landed in Strathclyde with a company of men. They were quickly approaching by the western road and would arrive shortly. In her company though was a man of rare renown, Anarawd ap Rhodri, with his own company of soldiers. He was perhaps the greatest Viking fighter of the age, the eldest son of Rhodri the Great and the king of the largest Welsh Kingdom of Gwynedd. Constantine knew that it would have taken them weeks to get here and with rumours of war in the Saxon Kingdoms to the south, they could only be travelling this far north for one reason: alliance. News travelled slowly between north and south and it was only through word of mouth from traders and the occasional displaced refugee that information generally reached the ears of Constantine and his cousin, the King. Even then it was occasionally spurious.

Two years previously a story had reached the court in Dunkeld that a ninety-five feet long naked woman had washed up dead on the shores of Strathclyde. The court had found this news humorous at the time and Glundub had even suggested that they send investigators to try and recruit any kin she may have had, to guffaws from Domnall's advisors. Constantine hated this sort of nonsense though as the day could come when news of a real threat might arrive, and they may not believe it. The rumours swirling around the conflict to the south had been too many to ignore however. A great war was taking place across Mercia and the Welsh kingdoms, of that there could be no doubt in Constantine's opinion. There were too many unconnected sources saying the same thing. Francian, Norse-Gael, and Irish traders all had stories to tell of Alfred's Saxon armies fighting Vikings across the land. Hundreds of refugees had been heading north to the kingdoms of Strathclyde for several months with all their belongings to try and set up lives for themselves in the Scottish kingdoms. They spilled garbled tails of monstrous Danes and allied Norse ravaging the countryside, seizing crops, livestock, women, and gold.

The one name that was present in every story was Hastein, a name that inspired fear from the Mediterranean Sea to the Orkney Islands. He was a man older even than Flann Sinna the High King of Ireland, but even in his dotage, his savagery had not abated. In his early days, he had made his name sacking Muslim cities in Al-Andalus alongside the long-dead reaver, Bjorn Ironside. He had not been part of the Great Heathen Army that had ravaged the Saxon world as he had used his wealth to set up camp in Francia. For thirty years he had ransacked towns and cities along the Francian river systems, sometimes even being hired as a mercenary by one side or the other in the internecine conflicts that racked the remnants of Charlemagne's old territories. When Guthrum the Danish King of East Anglia died several years ago, numerous Viking warlords had vied for supremacy of the Danelaw and the eastern seaboard, but it was Hastein who had emerged victorious. He and his forces had been pillaging up and down the Thames and now were raiding on the Severn, but the word was that a combined Mercian, Wessexian and Welsh army had the venerable warlord penned up in the old Roman fortress of Chester. Perhaps they felt that with King Domnall's help, and that of his cousin Dyfnwal of Strathclyde, Hastein and his force of Danes and Norse would be eradicated for good.

Constantine walked outside into the brisk Scottish morning and searched for Niall Glundub. It always lifted his spirits to see his formidable Irish cousin. He could usually be found in the training yard with his young son Muirchertach. His wife Gormlaith, the daughter of Flann Sinna, was heavily pregnant with their second child and usually stayed close to the hearth out of the worst of the Scottish weather. The clash of blunted and wooden weapons drew Constantine to the southeast corner of the training yard and as he suspected, Glundub and his son were there.

The Irish prince was on his knees with a blunted dagger in his hand while his three-year-old feebly battered at him with a wooden branch shaped into a tiny sword of proportionate size to his frame. Every now and again Glundub would allow a blow to land and would roll onto the ground in feigned throes of death to gales of laughter from the young boy, but even the sight of fake weapons in the hands of those he loved bothered Constantine and the old familiar demons rose quickly in the back of his thoughts, of blood and slaughter on the fields of Meath. Glundub looked up.

"You look like death, cousin. What has happened?"

Constantine shook himself out of his gloomy reverie and asked his cousin to accompany him to breakfast. They escorted young Muirchertach back to his mother rather than have him accompany them to the main hall of Domnall's court. Dunkeld itself sat on the River Tay and was named after the old Roman name for the settlement, the fort of the Caledonians. The name had stuck over the centuries despite it changing hands from ruler to ruler, and tribe to tribe. Its holy church and grounds were twinned with the famous monastery in Kells, in the territory of the Southern Ui Neill in Ireland, and between them they preserved numerous holy relics of Saint Columba. Because of the relics, the town saw many visitors come and commerce was an inevitable and positive side effect. It had wide wooden walls and even sections of it that were made of piled stone. When the two cousins entered the hall where the morning's food was being served, they immediately noticed that there were many strangers present with even stranger accents. None wore kilts or the tartan patterns of the Pictish men, all preferring to wear woollen trousers and surcoats with mail over that. The King was not present yet on the dais so Constantine and Glundub chose a secluded spot in the corner and called a serving girl over to provide them with some of the day's fare.

Once they had taken their fill the two cousins began to discuss the upcoming day's events.

"These Welsh soldiers look a fearsome lot," said Glundub under his breath.

Constantine nodded. "They have been battling the Ui Imair and the other Kings of Dublin for almost fifty years. Their warriors are tried and blooded."

The Welsh soldiers were different to the Mercian Saxons they accompanied. They were more uncouth and savage in appearance and each wore a red tunic under their armour. Their Celtic ancestry was apparent in their faces and in the way they kept their hair and beards. In truth, Constantine knew, they had more in common with the Scots and Irish than they had with the Saxons and yet they often allied with them.

"This Queen I have heard is a noted general and diplomat, Niall," said Constantine. "She is effectively Alfred the Great with womanly parts. I hope that Domnall does not underestimate her."

Niall scoffed at the suggestion. "What could a woman possibly say or do to force a king to obey her whims, especially Domnall with how bull-headed he is?"

Constantine crinkled up his nose in disgust and threw a stray pea that had rolled free of their empty plates and onto the bench, striking his cousin in the middle of his forehead.

"Don't be so naïve, Glundub. Your own mother Mael Muire even now would batter you in a fight."

Constantine looked sheepish and laughed. "Besides," Constantine continued, "old King Aethelred is well past sixty and in bad health. He is older than Queen Aethelfled's father. Who do you think actually rules Mercia in all but name, Niall? Think, you great lummox."

He threw a second pea which unerringly found the target on the Irishman's forehead.

"What do you think of the Welsh King Anarawd?" asked Niall. "I have never met the man."

Constantine answered, "By all accounts, he is his father's son. Rhodri the Great was an incredible warrior who kept the Kingdom of Gwynedd free and independent for decades while all the great Saxon kingdoms fell to the sons of Ragnar. When Rhodri died fifteen years ago Anarawd continued where his father left off. He has defied the Kings of Dublin, repelling attacks from Danes and Norse and the slaver Kingdom of Mann that sits off his coast. He is so fearsome that the Vikings ignore his coastline and go further south to raid, to the weaker Welsh kingdoms or the Cornwallians. Glundub, I have no doubt that this Anarawd and his father in the centuries to come will be held by the Welsh in the same regard as Cuchullain and Finn mac Cumhaill are by you Irish."

Glundub nodded his head in admiration. *He always appreciates the tales of great warriors*, Constantine thought.

"And yet they come to Domnall's court looking for assistance against Hastein?" Niall answered thoughtfully.

Constantine nodded in agreement with the rhetorical question posed by his cousin. *And I am not so sure Domnall should lend any to them*, he thought.

When the two men had finished their breakfast, they had decided to find the King himself as he had not yet graced the hall with his presence. After enquiring with some of his guards they found him sitting out on the banks of the River Tay. He had a fishing rod beside himself on the grass and looked peaceful but deep in thought. He turned his head at their approach.

"Constantine, Glundub, I knew the calm couldn't last. I assume you are here to advise me on how to treat with our guests. I have asked the Bishop to look into his records. It is the first time a non-Scottish king or queen has visited Dunkeld in over a century."

Niall Glundub remained standing, but Constantine sat down beside his cousin. He knew that sometimes Domnall could be rash with his decision making and prideful when he made a bad choice, following through out of spite. He would have to be tactful with him. In the past battle season, Domnall had not waited for reinforcements to see off a Norse raiding party on the village of Bowra north of Dunnottar as Constantine had advised; he had charged in with his household guard outnumbered two to one. He had taken a blow from a Viking mace on the shoulder that had never recovered properly due to his impetuousness and lack of patience. His guards had started calling him *Dasachtach* or the mad, due to his propensity to charge in headfirst. Constantine knew that the King was more like Glundub in temperament than himself, which could be a liability as much as an asset in both war and politics, and Constantine always tried to present alternative options to the King rather than the direct approach that both Glundub and Domnall favoured in all things.

"Domnall, I know you have guessed the purpose as to why we have been graced with such noble visitors." Domnall stared at him bemused.

"Of course, Constantine, we aren't all as smart as you but even a blind man could see their intentions." That drew a snort of suppressed mirth from Glundub. "They want our help against Hastein to the south and I am of the mind to give it to them."

Constantine nodded. *It's as I suspected, my cousin itches for a chance to destroy the Vikings.*

"Perhaps, Domnall, you would consider a few... *alternative...* options."

The King was about to respond but Constantine elaborated before his cousin could speak over the top of him.

"Let us say we send three or four thousand men south with Aethelfled and Anarawd and we fight Hastein at Chester. It is true that we could rid the world of one of the main suppliers of Saxon and Breton-Celt slaves to the empires of the Muslims and the black men of the Aifric. But at what cost, my King? Alfred the Great did not gain his title by being tentative, naive or lacking in ambition. If he wins, he will gain influence into the Danelaw and East Anglia. He controls

Mercia through his daughter. If he rids himself of Hastein cheaply with our assistance, we will have the most powerful Saxon king right on our borders. How long before he looks further north into Strathclyde and our lands because we both know that he has designs on Northumbria already!"

Domnall nodded his head, staring into the middle distance across the water of the river.

*He at least is considering my words,* thought Constantine.

"We also have our own borders to consider, Domnall. Harald Fairhair and his two most warlike sons, Halfdan Longlegs and the Bloodaxe, will look to Scotland as a source of revenue and slaves. Any Norse that have fled Fairhair's wrath will be hunted and forced to yield or die, and there are numerous peaceful settlements of Norse-Gaels in our lands already. Perhaps we don't have soldiers to spare to fight Alfred's wars for him? And what if Hastein wins? The Saxons will have to adjust their ambitions heavily and we will not have to ever look south in fear of a host of men with Alfred's banners above them. Hastein will surely take so many losses even in victory that he will be barely able to defend his new lands and his lands in Francia. All we would have to contend with, Domnall, is Harald Fairhair and the Kingdoms of Dublin and Mann."

Domnall stood up from the grass of the bank and straightened out his tunic and kilt.

"Any ideas from you, Glundub? What would you do if you were King of Scotland?"

The Irish warlord shrugged his shoulders nonchalantly.

"The Vikings are the number one priority. If there is a chance to destroy Hastein and break Danish autonomy on the island, we should take it. And if Alfred, his daughter, or the Welsh try and come north we will destroy them too."

Constantine grimaced. *Of course he would say that.*

The King parted from them saying, "I will think on all you two have said, cousins, and I will inform you, Aethelfled and this Welsh King of my decision at noon."

*

The main hall at Dunkeld had been laid out with a long oak bench with five chairs set around it. All of the servants and the usual inhabitants of the court had been dismissed and the five kings, queens and princes present had left their arms at the door. They had begun with small talk over a platter of cheeses and meats that had been laid out for them. Constantine was pleased to hear his cousin probe gently on the situation occurring down south in an oblique manner. Despite being a Saxon, Queen Aethelfled had a decent grasp of the Gaelic tongue spoken throughout Ireland and Scotland, and when Glundub had complimented her on it she had disclosed that it had been an Irish monk at the court of her father who had taught her. The Welsh tongue was similar enough to the Scottish and Irish versions of it that both Constantine and his two cousins could hold a conversation with the Welsh King reasonably well also.

Aethelfled wore a conservative gown typical of a noble lady of the Saxon courts with gentle colours and lace on her sleeves but Constantine instantly saw it for what it was, a ruse designed to disarm any political opponent and infuse them with arrogance. Her eyes blazed with a piercing intelligence and Constantine could see that this lady was an avatar of Alfred's will and not the meek maiden she tried to portray. Constantine had warned both of his cousins on this matter beforehand and prayed dearly that they would remain unmoved by her delicate suggestions.

The Welsh King Anarawd was cut from a different cloth. He was a bull of a man, perhaps in his early thirties, direct and abrupt, yet not uncourteous. It was clear immediately that it was the Queen who carried the authority here and the Welsh King seemed content to let her steer the conversation. Constantine did not think it impossible that the Welsh King was simply a pawn employed by Aethelfled and deployed to impress upon Domnall the fact that there were men out there every bit as mighty as Glundub that the Saxons could call upon. Inevitably the company ran out of inane things to say to each other, and it was the Queen who began the real conversation, a proposal for alliance to end the predations of Hastein the Dane.

"King Domnall and Princes, both my lord husband and my father the King of Wessex are elderly men and were unable to travel. Instead, they have sent King Anarawd and me north to treat with you in good faith. Know that I know their minds and speak with their full authority."

*There is no doubt of that, especially for her husband's part, an empty vessel at best,* thought Constantine grimly.

"The barbarian Hastein has for almost two years been raiding the Kingdoms of Wessex and Mercia but he has overstretched himself. My brother Edward the Elder has already inflicted a defeat upon his forces at the Battle of Farnham. We captured two of his sons and several other members of his close family. Hastein subsequently sued for peace and as a condition he accepted that his two sons would be baptised in the name of God. My husband stood as godfather for one and my father the other. He immediately showed why no Vikings can be trusted. He reneged upon his agreement and rallied more forces from both East Anglia, the five boroughs and from Yorvik. My father, my husband and the Welsh Kings under the command of King Anarawd have fought a series of skirmishes with Hastein and now surround his current fortress at Chester. To starve him out will take eight months and great expense and he can partially resupply by sea. We need more men to force the issue and storm the fort. Your men to be precise."

It was Domnall who answered. "Tell me, Queen Aethelfled, how is it that you reached out to Scotland and not to Northumbria or the Kings of Ireland? Flann Sinna is mighty and controls much of the island of Ireland. We are only a newly formed kingdom and in a precarious position with our proximity to the Kingdom of Mann and indeed Harald Fairhair himself. How is this to Scotland's benefit?"

The hint of a smile crossed the Queen's face. "The Northumbrians are too weak. They are scattered, divided and leaderless. They would be as likely to fight for Hastein as on our side."

Constantine thought he caught a glimmer of anger there momentarily, and it dawned upon him why. *It's likely that they have sent envoys to Northumbria but have been rebuffed,* he thought; *King Eadwulf fears Alfred's ambition as much as I do.*

The Queen continued, "Flann Sinna is a fearsome king I admit. But his grip on his kingdoms is not as secure as he thinks it is. The Kings of Munster chafe under his control as the Eoghanachta still believe the High Kingship has resided too long in the hands of the Ui Neill. There is dissention between his under-kings and even some of his sons are not as loyal as they should be. Further north, I am sure you are aware, Prince Niall," she nodded at Glundub, "the Northern Ui Neill fought a battle against the Ulaid to bring them to heel, on the shores of Lough Neagh."

Glundub sat up ramrod straight and King Domnall shifted uncomfortably.

Neither said anything but Constantine knew that someone as sharp as the Queen would have picked up on the fact that that news was unknown to the three cousins.

"Flann Sinna still has connections to the Ui Imair of Dublin. That makes him untrustworthy in our eyes. We have sent an envoy to him to warn him to back off and give no aid to Hastein or the Ui Imair should they come to the old warlord's aid, and he agreed. Should he prove treacherous though, my father has vowed that we will sail across the Irish Sea and burn Tara to the ground once he has dealt with the Danes. The Ui Imair princes only hold the south of Dublin from the Norse but hold sway with a lot of the Leinster Kings to the south who owe them fealty."

The Queen took a breath before steepling her fingers.

"No, King Domnall, it is only you that we can trust with this responsibility. This island belongs to the Saxons, Bretons and Gaels. It is time for the Danes and Norse to bend to our collective will. The defeat of Hastein will prove the catalyst. What say you, King Domnall?"

He sat back and stared at the ceiling for a moment and turned to meet the Saxon Queen's stare. Constantine was nervous: *This could go either way.*

"King Anarawd, Queen Aethelfled, I am afraid that I cannot agree to reinforcing you in your battle with the Danes. You would weaken my forces too much destroying Hastein, leaving my newly united Scottish kingdom at the mercy of the Norse, the Northumbrians or whoever else. I do wish you well in the wars to come and my prayers will go with you as you vanquish Hastein.

Should the battle go ill, you and your family are welcome to retreat to Dunkeld under my protection."

The Welsh King shrugged his shoulders, snorted in derision, and stormed from the hall disgustedly but the Queen rose to her full height, her veil of courtesy and geniality disappearing on the spot.

"Heed me well, King Domnall. This was a chance to unify against a foreign invader for the good of the entire island. Hastein will be defeated with or without you. Make no mistake, my father and my lord husband will take your decision badly. The next enemy you may face could be Saxon and not Norse as a result. My father will take all the Saxon kingdoms eventually and if you do not reconsider this act of betrayal, your new kingdom will be brought into the fold as well by hook or by crook. We will then decide what is best for Scotland."

Furious, Domnall rose in response, his knuckles whitening on the table.

"Keep your forked tongue behind your teeth, Queen Aethelfled. How dare you threaten me in my own hall? When last I looked it was I, Domnall, who was King of Scotland and not your father."

A little bit of anger drained out of him then and he sat back down.

"I don't underestimate Hastein's ability to make war, he will not go down without a fight and I don't underestimate your father's ambition for this island. You are Queen of Mercia but we both know that it is your father's mailed fist that fills your silk glove. I must do what is best for Scotland with the resources at my disposal. I do not rule out alliance in the future, but at this moment, surrounded by the Vikings of Dublin, Mann and Norway, I must look to my own defences."

The Queen twirled her skirts and threw one last withering look at the three cousins before retiring from the hall. Within moments, the sound of galloping horses indicated the prompt retreat of the Saxon and Welsh party from Scotland, *for now at least,* thought Constantine.

A knock rattled on the thick wooden doors of the hall immediately on the Saxon and Welsh departure and the head of a servant peered around the corner, leaving little time for the three cousins to digest what had just occurred.

"Your Highness, there are three guests here requiring an audience that I believe you may wish to entertain."

Constantine thought Domnall might refuse to give the three cousins time to discuss the political ramifications for Scotland, but the look on the servant's face portrayed a sort of fear and dread that his cousin could not ignore. Domnall told the manservant to disarm them whoever they were and then allow them to enter.

The three men filled the doorway, and Constantine's blood froze in shocked surprise. Domnall's face went pale, while Glundub, who had taken a drink of water from a goblet, spluttered in shock and spilled the liquid on his tunic. The three men were enormous, the largest standing almost seven feet in height. They were no Scotsmen, Irishmen or Saxons standing before them, they were Vikings through and through. They approached in a spear tip shape and stood at the far end of Domnall's table. Glundub rose rapidly to his feet, desperately searching for weapons, but the leader of the three held his hand up in a sign of peace.

"Please wait, Glundub *Drengr*, word has reached us of your prowess. We three know who you are as much as we know of the King and his cousin. We only wish to talk peacefully and have no wish for conflict."

*What is going on here?* thought Constantine as Glundub warily took his seat once more. The leader of the trio of Vikings carefully and smoothly pulled out a chair and sat gracefully down, defying his size. His two companions remained standing behind him, arms crossed. The seated Viking had long brown hair and a thick beard with spiralled tattoos swirling across his neck. The man standing to his left wore a leather studded jerkin, sleeveless with the same tattoos rolling down his bare arms. He looked similar to the seated speaker – *he must be some kin,* assumed Constantine. The seven feet tall giant had a massive shock of long un-braided black hair that reached his navel and down his back. He was massively muscled and scarred on both face and forearm, which spoke of a warrior familiar with violence and its consequences. The seated man began.

"My name is Torff Einarr Rognvoldarsson. The man to my left is Sigurd the Mighty, my uncle, and the other is Rollo the Walker, my cousin. My mother is

Irish, so I am very familiar with your tongue. She was a daughter of the Irish King Cerbaill mac Dunlainge who died in battle against the Norse and Danes of Dublin."

Glundub nodded in response. "I was there that day. I fought with your grandfather, a brave man who died fighting against your own kin. What side were you on I wonder?"

The Norseman spread his hands in a conciliatory manner. "I don't deny that my kin have fought against the Irish for generations, the Scots as well. But I am a Norse-Gael. I have taken the Christ as my god, my mother's faith. I live on Shetland in my fortress of Jarlshof. It is I who control all the lands from the Shetlands and the Hebrides down south to your own kingdoms. I am the jarl since I came of age and took the mantle from my uncle Sigurd to my left."

The older Viking's eyes lit up on hearing his name, but Constantine could tell he understood little if anything of what was being said.

"I speak for all the eorls and jarls of the Norse-Gaels."

Constantine could see that Domnall was agitated but intrigued by this. It was widely known that the Norse, Dal Riadans and Picts had mixed and mingled further north to form a distinct nation to all intents and purposes. The sea and the mountains lay between the lands of Scotland and the Norse-Gael but trading for furs, weapons and pottery did occur.

"Why are you here, Jarl Torf Einarr? I have just entertained guests who would see my kingdom burn to the ground for speaking with the likes of you."

The young jarl didn't disagree with the King's question. Nodding sagely, he answered, "Even as far north as where our people live, we have heard of the great Mercian queen and the more warlike of my eorls have regularly clashed with the Welsh. Word of this Anarawd has reached my ears, a fearsome warrior of great repute. We three hid until they left before revealing ourselves. Conflict is not our purpose. We wish to make an alliance."

"What sort of an alliance do you suggest? Trade, military or both?" asked Glundub.

Constantine could see the look of excited glee in the corner of Domnall's eye. If Domnall could secure his borders to the north, or perhaps even begin to bring these Norse-Gaels into the fold, it would strengthen his kingdom immeasurably. The young jarl answered, "All of the above."

Over the next hour the jarl explained what had been occurring in the North Seas over the last few years. Harald Fairhair and his young sons had routed their opponents in Norway and the losers of that conflict had sought refuge west in the Orkneys, the Hebrides and the Western Isles and coast. He told the sorry tale of his companion and cousin, Rollo the Walker, who had watched as his whole family was butchered by Erik Bloodaxe, Fairhair's maniacal teenage son, and how he had barely escaped with his life. For almost two hundred years there had been Norse settling in those northern lands, the jarl told them, mixing and living peacefully with the Scots there and forging a unique culture. Fairhair had tried to wield influence across the North Sea through a proxy overlord in Ceitl Flatnose of Limerick, but when the Flatnose had passed away of extreme old age, Torf Einarr's father Rognvold had overthrown Fairhair's puppets and freed the island kingdom from Norway's nominal control. But now that Fairhair had destroyed his enemies and sent his defeated foes fleeing, he was turning his attention west and south. He explained that the Orkney Islands had already fallen back under Fairhair's control and Halfdan Longlegs, his son, was using it as a base to raid as far south as London and Francia.

There was a dour cast to his features when he described what Halfdan Longlegs had done to his father Rognvold by trapping him and sixty of his warriors in a Christian church and burned it down around them as a sacrifice to Odin. At length, he impressed upon them the reality that Harald Fairhair would conquer each Norse-Gael settlement, one by one, until he controlled the seas from Ireland to the Kingdom of the Rus. He went into detail on how the Norse-Gael had sort of formed their own culture similar yet different to their Norwegian cousins. The language most in use there was what was called *Norn*, a pidgin hybrid of Gaelic and Norse. Most of the people there were followers of the Christ with only very few newer settlers keeping the old gods, but even then, Christ now appeared in the pantheon as strong as Thor or maybe Heimdall. He outlined the issues faced by his people with the encroaching power from the east and the cloud of fear his people lived with, wondering would today be the day that a hundred longboats would appear on their shore to enslave the women and children and slaughter the men?

None of the three cousins bothered to interrupt as the jarl weaved his epic tale on the history and politics of his people. He didn't shirk from the reality that although many of his people farmed, fished and traded goods up and down the Irish Sea, many occasionally dared to raid the kingdoms of Ireland, Wales and Strathclyde. And then he arrived at the purpose of his visit. He, Jarl Torff Einarr Rognvaldarson, would bend the knee to Domnall King of All Scots and pay him tribute on each summer solstice. But only in return for a promise of protection from the advances of Harald Fairhair and his savage sons. Should Harald Fairhair attack any of the other Scottish kingdoms, the Norse-Gael of the Scottish Isles would provide men to fight the Norse to King Domnall and a navy to transport them. No Norse-Gael or newly arrived Norsemen would ever raid another Scottish kingdom without sanction from the King of Scotland himself from this day forward.

At the end, Domnall negotiated a few finer details and the administration of what would effectively become the newest kingdom to join the nation of Scotland, and the three Vikings bent the knee and swore allegiance. Constantine approved. *It was exactly as King Giric had said several years ago,* he thought, *the choices were stark but simple; bring these Norse-Gaels into the fold under the banner of a united Scotland or face them amongst the armies of Harald Fairhair.*

# CHAPTER 3

# THE BATTLE OF SEIL
# (899)

Constantine wistfully stared into the blue skies around the Isle of Seil and dreamed of a more peaceful time. Scotland had thankfully earned a temporary peace by staying clear of the Saxon defeat of Hastein and consolidated their strength. Constantine and his cousins had hoped for a time of quiet and plenty for their kingdom, but that idyllic concept would now be inevitably shattered on this small westerly island. Seil was only split from the mainland by a stretch of muddy sea water that retreated and shrunk when the tide was out. Torr Einarr had insisted that the channel had never gone dry in living memory, and at its narrowest point the Norse-Gael community that inhabited the island had built a bridge made of stout timber and stone linking it to the mainland.

The island itself was little more than a thousand hectares but it was dominated by the small hill the native people called *Meall Chaise*. Before the Norse had arrived and intermingled with the native Picts, the island had a couple of Gaelic names; one was Innisibsolian and the other was Hinba, the supposed home of the historic explorer, Saint Brendan the Navigator. The Norse had turned it into a thriving little trading port, selling pottery, quarried slate and wool to other Norse-Gael settlements, the communities in the Hebrides and the northern coasts of Ireland and Strathclyde. A strong timber fort stood on the flank of *Meall Chaise* and a small town had grown up around it and down to the small wooden pier that served as a dock for ships on the coastline.

At the centre of the fort stood an ancient broch, one of the impressive stone defensive towers that had been inherited by the Scots and Norse-Gael from an older and mysterious long-dead culture. It dominated the island and could be seen from almost any vantage point on Seil. It was three weeks since Torr Einarr had come breathless to Domnall's court begging for military support from his High King and Domnall had honoured his word to his new subjects: he would come in force to their defence.

The King had mobilised a thousand men in the space of a week and had sent them northwest over the mountains under the command of Constantine and Glundub. It had taken a week to reach Seil and their force of men had made camp on the mainland coastline beside a freshwater stream that flowed down from the highlands. Glundub and Constantine had quartered in the fort for no other reason than to be closer to the battle decisions being made by the Norse-Gaels. On the arduous trek through the mountains Constantine had harboured hope that perhaps there would be no need to fight a battle and had insisted on Domnall preparing a *Geld*, which was effectively the Dane and Norse equivalent of a bribe to avoid conflict with them. This form of bribery had worked all around the Irish Sea in the past. But Torr Einarr, who had accompanied them, had blown Constantine's hopes away when he explained what had happened over the last month and what he and his uncle intended to make happen in the next few weeks. They fully intended to pick a fight. A massive fleet of Norse Vikings had been sacking and burning Norse-Gael settlements all the way down through the Hebrides and were edging ever southward.

Worse news then followed;it emerged that a smaller fleet from the Kingdom of Dublin had reinforced the Norse fleet, increasing their strength to roughly ninety longboats packed full of warriors. Traders pulling into Seil had told the story of how and why the Vikings of Dublin were joining with the Norse fleet.

Allegedly, Harald Fairhair had sent one of his henchmen, Eorl Thororim, to Dublin to help his son-in-law, Ivar son of Ivar, in his fight with Eorl Sichfrith, and the warlord known as the Iron Knee and their Irish allies. The Iron Knee had been killed in the fighting by Ragnall of the Ui Imair, but two men of the line of Ivar the Boneless had been slain in battle also: Aimlaib and Sihtric. Only Ivar son of Ivar survived from his legendary father's original brood, but there were at least ten surviving grandsons descended from the Boneless in existence, many of whom were already reavers and plunderers of renown despite their youth. In exchange for Fairhair's distant backing, the Norse King had demanded their alliance when subjugating the Hebrides and West Scotland and here they were. It was one great fleet designed to bring the entirety of the Norse-Gael Kingdom of the Isles under the control of the Kingdom of Norway and the Kingdom of Dublin. When the three Viking leaders had heard who was in outright command of this Norse fleet, Constantine had known on the spot that only one decision would be made and that was to give them battle. No peace or surrender would be entertained. Fairhair had not entrusted command to Thororim the Eorl nor Ivar, Ragnall or Ingamundr of Dublin. The leader of this army of Vikings was Halfdan of the Longlegs, Fairhair's eldest surviving son. Torr Einarr, Sigurd the Mighty and Rollo the Walker were of one mind: with the help of Constantine and his forces they would draw this fleet to the Isle of Seil, trap them and destroy them, decapitating Norse and Ui Imair authority in the Irish and North Seas with one fell stroke.

The plan was a complex one but each of the commanders had deemed it sound. Each would take charge of a subset of their forces to achieve a certain objective. They were probably going to be outnumbered but with the right strategy they were confident that they could destroy their enemies piecemeal, or at least bloody them so badly that they would have no option but to retreat. The first part of their forces would have the unenviable task of baiting the trap. Twenty longboats each with a complement of thirty men would be sent out into the sea to draw Halfdan's forces in. The easiest place to land longboats on the island was on the dock on the body of water facing the mainland which suited the plan perfectly. Their job was to skirmish with the vanguard boats of

Halfdan's fleet and turn tail and flee back to the island to draw them into the channel. There was a chance that the Norse leadership would suspect a trap, but the hope was that twenty ships would be considered just few enough to make Halfdan believe that they could smash through any potential trap regardless.

This force of men would be led by Sigurd the Mighty. He had slain many allies of Harald Fairhair in the Norse civil wars, and the other leaders felt that his presence alone would invite chase from the Norse fleet. His role was a sacrificial one; his body of men would not come out of this unscathed. Torr Einarr would lead the best men they could muster from the island itself and he would deploy dozens of archers on the shore and meet the Norse and Dublin men as they landed. Rollo the Walker would wait on the bridge that linked the island to the mainland, raising the central wooden part of the bridge up to allow the surviving ships of Sigurd's fleet to flee or at least come ashore at a safe location, and then lower and hold the bridge against pursuers. Constantine and Glundub's warriors would be deployed upon the shoreline of the mainland and would launch arrow after arrow into the Norse fleet and harass their armada. If a significant number of Vikings came ashore on the mainland, they were to engage them and drive them back into the water. If they landed in strength upon the island to engage Torr Einarr, the Scots would join with Rollo's men upon the bridge and flank the Norse landing on the stony beach.

Within two hours of that meeting, Sigurd's ships had set sail in the direction of the Hebrides, the estimated last known location of Halfdan's fleet, seeking to engage them. Nobody could guess with certainty when friendly and hopefully enemy sails would be sighted on the horizon. The remaining four commanders, Glundub, Rollo, Torr Einarr and Constantine, would each take six-hour watches and command early lookouts from vantage points on the coast. Men would be drilled incessantly with shield, axe and sword, and archery butts were erected for practice. Stockpiles of arrows, stones and even caches of food and water were set down in likely places of action upon both the island and the mainland.

The last job was to send all the elderly, women and children up into the hills to a hidden valley with a small band of warriors to protect them; if the fight went ill, at least their people would survive. Constantine was impressed to see many of the women among the Norse-Gaels taking up arms to fight alongside their fathers, brothers, husbands and sons.

Over the next three days the monotony of incessant preparation and training began to wear thin on Constantine. Every man jack in his army had been drilled thoroughly and knew exactly what was about to occur, but it concerned Constantine that carelessness could potentially set in amongst the rank and file through boredom. On the evening of the fourth day, rough shaking by Niall Glundub's hand awoke Constantine to the moment he had dreaded for years; in defence of the nation of Scotland, Constantine mac Aed would have to bear arms against Viking warriors.

The battle itself began at dusk and went on into the night. Constantine had initially fretted about being unsighted in the gloom, but the blazing fires aboard torched longships and burned dwellings on the island leading up to the fort, had bathed the entire breadth of the battlefield in a luminous glow. This was different to Constantine's last battle on the plains of Meath. Here, multiple fronts were separated by roughly two miles between the bridge, the island and the shoreline he commanded, whereas in Meath the two sides had collided in a tidal wave of steel and blood and fury. Most of his command was comprised of archers upon the shoreline peppering the Norse longboats as they entered the seawater channel of the island and the mainland, setting fire to any that they could. He also had auxiliary units of specialist veteran Scotsmen at his disposal and he occasionally sent them forward when groups of Vikings landed on the wrong shore in confusion or looked to flee in some of the burning ships. He sat on his horse on a lofty vantage point overlooking the water, Rollo's bridge and the island, but the smoke and distance made it hard to perceive what was occurring at the furthest reaches of the battle. Beside him he had two bodyguards and a group of young fit Norse-Gael lads whose job it was to relay messages to his various sergeants deployed across the mainland shore.

When combat commenced, he felt in a way disassociated from his body, as if it was some other man that looked like him barking commands. He was enveloped in the sounds and smells and sights of disorganised chaos that was the battlefield. Hours blurred together. He vaguely remembered half of the Norse ships turning and fleeing the way they came. He barely recalled ordering his men down to the bridge to support Rollo the Walker in the vicious melee that was taking place with the trapped Vikings on the bridge and either shore. He had a vague recollection of commanding his men forward onto the island and coming up on the flanks of the Norse as they fought upon the hill against Torr Einarr and his best men. The only thing he vividly remembered was the sight of the Norse attackers running for their lives and diving into the water after dropping their weapons and discarding their mail shirts. And then the dawn light rose on the horizon and quiet enveloped the battlefield. Constantine collapsed onto his backside, releasing his short sword and shield from numbed arms, leaden with fatigue. Moans of the dying could be heard at the edge of his awareness and a deep ringing in his ears made his head hurt. He saw Rollo the Walker stride past with his warriors, bloodied and battered but triumphant. He was a foot taller and wider than most men on the battlefield and he waded through the debris and corpses on his way to the fort, like a giant amidst children. Constantine could see why men were drawn to him. *I would dread to face him,* he thought.

A shout from the south lifted Constantine's heart: Niall Glundub the mighty Irish fighter had survived. With a savage grin on his face, he plopped down beside Constantine and draped his arm around his shoulders.

"What a fight that was, cousin," he gasped, still struggling for breath. "I caught Thororim on the shore two hundred feet from the bridge and ran him through. He will trouble the Norse-Gaels of Scotland no more."

Constantine didn't bother to reply. He abhorred violence, if truth be told, and even when hearing of a savage like Thororim being cut down by his cousin, he could only ponder on the worst possible outcome. What if Glundub had missed his stroke and Thororim had taken his head? Or what if a patch of blood-stained grass had caused Glundub to lose his footing, as even one as mighty as him could be easily slain by a lucky warrior who would usually have no chance in a straight-up fight? His mind was always drawn to the bigger picture and the worst-case scenario. This was a notable defeat for Harald

Fairhair and would, he knew, enrage the Norse King. Constantine envisaged that retribution would not be long in coming.

As the morning progressed, Constantine tried to use his time constructively. He checked with his sergeants to see how fared his men until he got a clear picture of the losses incurred. Of the thousand he had brought with him, only thirty-five had been killed with the same again wounded, and most of those were lost in the savage melee that had swirled on the bridge around the giant, Rollo the Walker.

The Norse-Gaels under Torr Einarr had endured losses of roughly double that and Rollo had taken around the same, but the biggest loss of life had occurred on the water. A dozen ships had been captured or sunk and roughly two hundred men had been dispatched, including Sigurd the Mighty, whose ship had been caught and boarded by dragon-headed boats from Dublin. Some of the survivors had witnessed his death at the hands of the Ui Imair. He was a warrior of singular renown and his loss, Constantine knew, would hurt the entire community of the Kingdom of the Isles. If Harald came in force again, they could no longer look to Sigurd to defend them, *and those responsibilities would at least partially fall under Domnall's banner now,* thought Constantine.

The casualties amongst the Norse and Ui Imair fleet had been significant, the piles of prone corpses lying broken on the shore and floating in the water giving truth to the tales of slaughter reverberating amongst the Scottish and Norse-Gael soldiery. There were sixteen longboats burned and sunk in the water between the mainland and the island and Torr Einarr had already instructed teams of men to pull them onto land to clear the small harbour. Once the battle had gone against the Norse, they had made their escape back the way they had come. The Norse and Dublin Vikings had been harassed by arrows as they retreated until they were far enough out to sea and out of range.

Constantine made himself busy all day, overseeing work being done to repair Rollo's bridge and the piling of Viking corpses for burning. He also liaised with the clergy of the island for the burial of his own casualties in a newly consecrated graveyard. He took his food and drink on the hoof, never resting until his men had completed their tasks and had been properly quartered and fed. At dusk, Glundub and Constantine were summoned by one of Torr Einarr's captains to the main fort on the island.

When they arrived, they saw hundreds of the Norse-Gael soldiers standing around in a circle, facing a hastily erected wooden stage with two pillars standing on it five feet across from each other, with leather straps nailed to their summits. Every third or fourth warrior carried a burning torch. Constantine had tried to pry the truth of what was happening from Rollo, but the giant Viking had so little Gaelic that it was impossible to decipher. The two cousins found a small wolfish-looking soldier named Grinnar, who informed them what was about to occur. Halfdan Longlegs had apparently led the vanguard of the Norse himself and had been knocked unconscious from the glancing blow of an axe. He had been captured by Torr Einarr's men and brought here at the conclusion of the battle. Rollo and Torr Einarr had then consulted with some of the other senior men on what to do with the Norse prince. Several had advocated selling him back to his father for a massive ransom which Harald Fairhair would surely pay for his eldest surviving son. Others advised that holding him prisoner indefinitely would be the wisest course of action as it would force Fairhair to stay his hand and not seek retribution for this defeat, although Grinnar noted that the supporters for this course of action had failed to explain how this decision would stop the Ui Imair from raiding north, as they were only nominally allied to Norway.

Rollo and Torr Einarr had overruled them all; they mutually agreed that Halfdan, son of Harald, must die. The massacre of Rollo the Walker's family in Norway by Halfdan's young but notorious brother Erik Bloodaxe, and the burning alive of Torr Einarr's father in the church, had to be answered with blood. Halfdan Longlegs was a prince of noble birth and there were only a couple of ways of taking his life that would be acceptable to the Norse gods. In the end, Rollo and Torr Einarr decided to perform the ancient rite of execution known as the blood eagle upon the Norse prince. The soldier Grinnar was about to explain what this entailed but at that moment the ceremony began and Glundub and Constantine stood back to witness it for themselves.

It started eerily with a drum booming out in the night and only the crackle of the flames challenged its eminence as the island held its breath. The drum thudded out a slow and steady beat that felt to Constantine as if it originated from the centre of the earth. First to emerge onto the wooden stage was the Norse prince Halfdan Longlegs, not chained or restrained in any way. He was a whip of a man, a towering six-footer with a long-braided moustache that reached down past his neck. He slowly removed his tunic as calmly as if preparing for his bed. His face betrayed no fear or rush or anger. His torso was heavily tattooed and rippled with muscle. He knelt on the stage between the two polls and extended his arms out from his shoulders and gripped the dangling leather straps. Rollo and Torr Einarr appeared on the stage next. Each was bare-chested and armed with daggers and axes that gleamed in the light of the torches.

Torr Einarr was a big man almost of a height with Glundub but compared to Rollo the Walker, he seemed a child. Boom… Boom… Boom. The drums continued to pound with five second intervals between each strike. Constantine's heart was hammering in his chest as if he was on the brink of some great calamity that he could not escape from. The Walker strode in front of Halfdan and offered him a small wooden stick, but the prince slowly shook his head. It dawned on Constantine what it was for; it was for Halfdan to bite down upon during the ordeal to come. Simultaneously Torr Einarr wrapped the leather straps around Hafdan's wrists and drew them tight. There would be no escape from the stage for Halfdan. Rollo and Torr Einarr took position behind the kneeling prince and then it began in earnest. Torr Einarr took his dagger and carved a bloody red line down the prince's back and out and around in the shape of a butterfly. Constantine and Glundub had an angle which afforded them a line of sight of both the wounds being inflicted and the face of the victim. When the entire bloody line was completed, the skin was torn from the back with a sickening rip and left hanging from each side of the kneeling man's back. No sound came from the hundreds of onlookers, and astonishingly none from the victim either. The only sign of awareness that the prince was registering the pain of the mutilation happening to him was a slight widening of his eyes. The hair on Constantine's arms stood on end as he witnessed the atrocity on front of him. Glundub had his arms crossed, his mouth turned down grimly, but he stoically endured it. *How can he be so calm?*

The next part was even more brutal. Both Rollo and Torr Einarr took turns in breaking individual ribs in the prince's back. Each blow was accompanied by a sharp snap of the bone breaking, and each bone was pulled back away from Halfdan's spine. Each axe strike drowned out the drums momentarily but from the surrounding warriors watching on, no sound came. The victim impossibly endured this barbarism stoically.

The stage now resembled an abattoir with blood and gore spattered everywhere. *He must surely die now,* thought Constantine, but it wasn't finished. Rollo and Torr Einarr each reached into Hafdan's back and pulled a lung out and placed it almost gently upon his broad shoulders, and so the blood eagle was revealed in all its savage glory. The two executioners jumped off the stage and knelt before Halfdan and held vigil until he passed. Boom... Boom... Boom, went the drums. Constantine felt faint. It was some minutes before the light passed from the eyes of the victim, and so died Halfdan, son of Harald Fairhair, in silence and in acceptance, in the ways of the old gods. The Viking way.

# CHAPTER 4

# THE REVENGE OF
# HARALD FAIRHAIR,
# LORD OF ALL THE NORSE
# (900)

Constantine woke screaming, with tears streaming down his face. But as consciousness gathered itself the dreadful nightmares faded, and he could not recall what had affected him so badly. He cursed himself for his weakness. Fists hammered on the door from some concerned man servant, but Constantine shouted out that he was fine and sent him on his way. *I can't let anybody see me like this,* he thought. At twenty-nine years of age, he felt that he should be mature enough, that he shouldn't be afflicted like this and yet he was. This… malaise… hit him in unusual ways.

Over the past number of years his cousin Domnall had floated the idea of marriage to Constantine, but he always found a way to avoid agreeing to it. He had invented numerous excuses to fob off his cousin, but the truth was he feared sharing his life with another person lest they witness the cursed mind illness that he carried with him. Glundub was the only person he trusted with this secret shame, but the Irishman did not understand. Niall had suggested he see the bishop and take confession, but Constantine didn't see how the pious bleating of a clergyman could cure his problem. Glundub, and Domnall to a lesser extent, seemed to be able to take battle and violence in their stride; in Niall's case he positively embraced it. But Constantine was cut from a different cloth. He enjoyed peace, reading, hunting in the hills and fishing in the stream. He loved to see his people going about their lives in Dunkeld trading their wares and seeing children playing and running breathless through the streets. The endless violence weighed on him and dwelling on it affected him in his mind, waking or sleeping. He shook himself off and dressed warmly for despite it being spring, there was a bite to the wind.

The winter of 899 had been one of the coldest and harshest in living memory and had carried into the year of Our Lord, 900. Word had reached his cousin's court that the savagery of the winter was the main reason for the death of the Saxon King, Alfred the Great. He had passed away after a long battle with illness and already civil war was brewing amongst the Saxons for the throne. Edward his eldest son, Constantine assumed, would be the victor but the Danes were supporting another candidate, a son of Alfred's brother, who was more sympathetic to their cause. *It will boil down to who Aethelfled the Queen of Mercia backs,* thought Constantine. The winter of 899 and early 900 had been brutal across Europe as well, taking many of the old and infirm, including numerous names of note. The Pope had died in his sleep leaving a void in Rome, with the Germanic and Francian rulers vying to place their own men on the holy seat. In Ireland, rumour had it that one of the kings of Connaught had caught consumption and passed as well. Wulfhere the Archbishop of York had died of an illness too, a famous warrior-priest who had fought both with and against the Danes on occasion. Again, Constantine cursed himself for always dwelling on death and morbid trains of thought and made his way to Domnall's main hall at a brisk pace to clear his head. On entering through a side door, he bumped into Domnall's wife Aileen. She was a highland princess of the mountains and Domnall had made the marriage to bind the unruly Highlanders to his will. It was a political match made a year ago but to Constantine's delight she was both beautiful and intelligent and a perfect consort and queen for his cousin. She was heavily pregnant and glowing and the monks that Domnall had invited to Dunkeld to oversee her care assured the King that she was due to give birth in the next few weeks.

"Good morning, Constantine, how are you?" she asked amicably.

"Absolutely outstanding," he lied.

As she left the hall Constantine approached his cousin who was reading scrolls on the dais. Domnall smiled on seeing his cousin.

"Come have a look at this parchment, Constantine, it arrived with traders this morning from the river."

Constantine took it and read it. It was written in Latin and was a call to arms for all Christian kings to send soldiers to reinforce Alfonso III of Spain in his battles with the Berbers and Arabs of the Umayyad Caliphate of Al Andalus. He had won several battles already and was slowly driving the Muslims from the north of that land. Constantine knew Domnall's mind on these issues and they both concurred that for Scotland's best interests to be served it was wise to stay out of events like these. The doors exploded inward at that moment and Constantine dropped the scroll to the floor. It was Niall Glundub.

"Domnall, Constantine, the stronghold of Dunnottar on the coast is under siege."

Domnall stood up from his throne. "BY WHOM?" he shouted.

"By Harald Fairhair, Erik Bloodaxe and the Ui Imair. Domnall, Scotland has been invaded."

Domnall strode across the yard shouting for his horse and weapons. Constantine chased after him, pleading against his decision.

"*Please,* Domnall, do not do this. This is rash."

Domnall had been apoplectic with rage on the news that the Norse had laid siege to Dunnottar. The people of the surrounding settlements had all fled to the fort once the Norse sails were sighted and the commander there had taken them in according to the messenger.

The news had been a day old on arriving as the distance between Dunkeld and Dunnottar was around seventy miles. Domnall had decided to rouse the garrison immediately and sent riders at full speed out to Caithness, Moray, Strathclyde, the Kingdom of the Isles and Fortriu, to send men immediately to Dunkeld. On horseback, at breakneck speed, word could reach most lands under Domnall's control within a few days. Domnall would march on the hour with the five hundred or so men he had at his disposal and hoped to take the Norse in the rear as they surrounded the fort. He had commanded both Constantine and Glundub to wait four days for reinforcements to come and then they must march with whatever strength was mustered. Constantine had disagreed wholeheartedly with Domnall and even Glundub, who was usually eager for battle, voiced his reservations. Constantine stated that they should wait a week or more and assemble the entire military strength of Scotland before moving against Fairhair but Domnall was deaf to reason. Niall had pointed out that the fort at Dunnottar, out on the promontory, was as formidable a fortress as any in the country and the Norse would struggle to take it by force. Domnall's response was to remind Niall that at one time the same was thought of the fortress at Dumbarton Rock until Ivar the Boneless sacked it, slaughtered the men and sold the women and children to the Arabs and the blue men of the Aifric, notorious slavers all.

Constantine could only grind his teeth in frustration as Domnall marshalled his men. There was nothing he could do. Glundub could only shrug his shoulders and shake his head. The moniker the soldiers had given the king, *the mad* or *Dasachtach,* seemed well earned when Domnall acted like this. As the men formed up with all of the supplies and wagons they could muster, Domnall mounted his horse and turned to his two cousins.

"On the fourth day you must march, obey me in this."

All the two cousins could do was tap their three fingers to their foreheads in obedience and watch as the King galloped out through the gates of Dunkeld. Constantine turned around to begin preparations of supplies for the force that would assemble in the allotted days. He saw Queen Aileen standing on the stone steps of Domnall's hall, holding her enlarged belly protectively with a deeply worried frown on her face. *And she is right to be worried,* thought Constantine, *Domnall should have waited for more men.*

Four days passed glacially slowly for Constantine. He slept little and kept himself busy by preparing the logistics for the army being assembled. Cartloads of grain and food were gathered outside the walls with coverings to keep them dry. As the men began to gather at the end of the second day, he had Glundub drill them with sword and spear. The first chieftains and their complements of men to arrive were from the surrounding areas in Pictland and from up into the Highlands. On the fourth day Constantine was glad to see Torr Einarr, King of the Isles and the Norse-Gaels, arrive with four hundred men, having arrived by longboat and raced over land. When he asked where Rollo the Walker was, Torr Einarr informed him that he had gone south in the winter to the wars in Francia to make his fortune with a hundred young unmarried men. *A terrible loss for us in the fights to come,* thought Constantine.

Later, on the fourth day, Dyfnwal their cousin arrived with seven hundred seasoned veterans from Strathclyde. That brought their number up to two and a half thousand men. *Will this be enough to break the lines of the Norse?* wondered Constantine. It wouldn't matter anyway as the orders were set in stone; they must march at daybreak. Constantine had left instructions with Queen Aileen that if more soldiers came, they were to stay in Dunkeld to reinforce it.

That night he plied himself with strong drink with Glundub and the other commanders and for once thankfully enjoyed a full night's sleep, nightmare free. The weather the next morning was warm and mild and pleased Constantine as it was more conducive to making good time on the march. The food wagons would follow on behind but if all went well, Constantine thought that at a brisk pace his army could reach the coast by nightfall. He had toyed with the idea of perhaps camping maybe fifteen miles away from the fortress and arriving fresh the next morning to engage the Norse and reinforce Domnall *if he is still alive.* But he decided against that plan as he knew that every second delayed would cost Scottish lives. They made good time over the first six hours and stopped at noon to water and feed the men and pack animals. Constantine used the time to question Torr Einarr on what and who they would be facing.

"Tell me, Torr Einarr, what do you know of the leaders of these Norse?" he asked the rugged chieftain.

"Well, Harald Fairhair is arguably the greatest king the Norse have ever seen.

His ruthlessness is only matched by his ambition. He is shrewd and cautious but calculating. My worry is that his vast experience may have allowed him to anticipate what Domnall would do and he may have planned accordingly. Why hit a fortress like Dunnottar, Constantine? There were far easier targets to attack on the coast. Why didn't he war against Lumphanon on the coast of Fortriu, a bigger target but easier to attack?"

This point of view alarmed Constantine. He had not had time to consider what was actually occurring. *What was Harald Fairhair doing?* There was a bad feeling growing in his gut, something was very wrong here.

"Tell me about this son of his, the one they call the Bloodaxe."

A dark shadow crossed over Torr Einarr's face as he considered the Norse prince.

"He is a savage and a fiend. He killed one of his own brothers in single combat which earned him the title Bloodaxe. He is a monster. He has been raiding since he was eleven years of age and at seventeen, he has fought in dozens of battles. All he cares about is piling skulls in front of Odin's throne. Everywhere he turns towns are sacked, women are raped and murdered, and children are enslaved. Should we be defeated and the Norse win Scotland, the entire country will drown in blood. At times I regret killing Halfdan Longlegs as that act made Erik Bloodaxe the heir to Fairhair's kingdom, and he is far more diabolical than his elder brother ever was."

Glundub had joined them at this point and the description of the Bloodaxe had riveted him as much as it had appalled Constantine.

"He's seventeen years of age you say, a child," answered Glundub. "I have slain dozens of Vikings and their berserker captains, and you tell me to fear this boy?" He shook his head in denial. "If this Bloodaxe faces me he will fall before me like all the rest."

Constantine could see that Torr Einarr wasn't wholly convinced by Glundub's reasoning.

"Tell me about the Ui Imair then? Who leads them, Torr Einarr?"

He laughed. "Good Question. The shifting sands of politics in Dublin are tumultuous at best. The Ui Imair are slowly growing again in prominence. Ivar son of Ivar the Boneless is married, as you know, to Harald Fairhair's eldest daughter, and that gives all of his sons legitimacy amongst the Danes and Norse as they are technically both. Potentially they could permanently unite them which would be bad for all of us. Even my own people have reverence for these famous Vikings. They are the sons and grandsons of Ivar the Boneless and he of course was the son of Ragnar Lodbrok, the legendary Viking who sacked Paris sixty years ago. Everywhere they go, they draw young men to their banners. The men you have to fear most are Ivar himself and maybe his first son also called Ivar. But in the last year a younger son has come to prominence, a young sea king called Ragnall. I've met him once. He is an impressive young man; a swaggering bully who walks into every hall like it belongs to him. He is the Boneless reincarnated by all accounts, even looks like him. Another of them to fear is Ingamundr, the last surviving son of Bairid, Ivar the Boneless' oldest son who was slain in battle by his uncle Halfdan years ago."

Both Constantine and Glundub were enthralled. Niall was all but licking his lips at the thought of facing such men of renown but all the tale did for Constantine was to dismay him and fill him with dread and fear. As they resumed the march minutes later, all Constantine could do was think on the rhetorical questions posed by Torr Einarr on King Harald. And every possible answer Constantine could think of was bad.

*

Nearing nightfall, as the host approached Dunnottar, Constantine's bowels were shaking. His mouth was dry and he felt physically ill. Every step forward toward the Norse engulfed him with so much dread that he could hardly breathe. Even with two and half thousand men surrounding him he felt naked and alone and at the mercy of the Bloodaxe or these Ui Imair princes. Torr Einarr and the Glundub looked implacable and confident and it mystified Constantine how this could be so. *Do they not feel fear?* He could see the men all around them look to the Norse-Gael chieftain and the Irish prince and draw courage from them. It shamed Constantine that he did not, nor could not, project the same arrogant charisma and surety that they could. With a mile to go they were halted by their advance scouts, still out of sight of the fort. It was quickly getting dark, so Torr Einarr instructed the host to begin lighting their brands and torches.

As the head scout approached, Constantine could tell instantly something was horrifyingly wrong. The scout was in no hurry and his eyes were downcast. The vanguard made way for the man and allowed him to pass through to where he stood. Glundub called a halt to the march. Constantine summoned himself, steeling his heart for the worst.

In a wavering voice he asked the scout, "Has the fortress been taken?"

The man slowly shook his head. "No, my lord, the fortress yet withstands the siege."

Constantine trembled; there was more to come he knew.

"King Domnall's relieving force was defeated."

A great clamour of shouts and angry outbursts erupted from the surrounding soldiery as they listened in. Constantine silenced them with a raised hand.

"And what of the King?" he asked.

"I don't know, my lord, but the other scouts and I feel that all were either slain or captured."

A cacophony of outrage exploded from the rank and file but a few sharp commands from Glundub stilled them to silence. All Constantine could do was pray that Domnall had escaped or perhaps had been taken prisoner. *Maybe we could ransom him back,* he pondered.

"What is the strength of the Norse host and how in your opinion was Domnall's vanguard defeated?" Constantine asked.

"They have at least two thousand men and many longboats in the sea off the coast. They haven't bothered to ram the gates or use siege equipment and looked content to just sit outside Dunnottar out of arrow range."

Constantine thought back to Torr Einarr's premonition of Harald's intentions. He could even guess what happened next.

"My lord, I think that the Norse concealed a large part of their force in some woods a mile away from the fortress and deployed less than half their men to the gate. When the King saw that they were not as numerous as feared, he must have charged them and fallen for the ruse. They formed a shield wall and once King Domnall was fully committed to battle, the concealed auxiliary force emerged from the trees and hit King Domnall from the rear."

There was silence now amongst the soldiers as each one contemplated the inevitable.

"They were caught between the hammer and the anvil, my lord."

Glundub cursed and threw his shield to the ground in dismay. Torr Einarr could only shake his head in disgust. There was a lump in Constantine's throat as he knew now that he must discover the condition of his cousin the King and thus treat with the Vikings. *Fairhair knew we would come*, thought Constantine, *he never intended to take Dunnottar. He wanted to draw Domnall to him.*

*

The captains of both forces stood their ground on the ragged patch of loamy soil several hundred yards from the fortress of Dunnottar. More than twenty torches had been planted into the ground in a rough square to allow each side to take each other's measure. Each host of men stood well back from the meeting of the leaders and maintained silence. Constantine had left Dyfnwal of Strathclyde back to command the Scottish and Norse-Gael army with orders that on the first sign of treachery they were to charge and drive the Norse over the cliffs and back to the sea.

Accompanying him were Niall Glundub, fully armed and armoured, and Tor Einarr, who was fluent in the Norse tongue and could translate Constantine's words so that they could understand. Three Vikings stood across from them. The one in the centre was the eldest by far and Constantine presumed the leader. He was perhaps in his late forties or early fifties and possessed a long beard that reached his chest of striking blond hair. *Harald Fairhair I presume,* acknowledged Constantine. He wore no crown but held a helmet under one arm and leaned forward on a deadly looking and well-maintained axe. To his left stood a youthful giant with a formidable two-handed battle-axe slung across his shoulders. He had a shock of fiery orange hair shaped into a crest on his otherwise shaven head. He had one foot perched on what looked to be a treasure chest which seemed odd to Constantine. *Do they intend to pay us or us them?* thought Constantine confusedly.

The third Viking prowled like a predatory cat, never standing still. He was young, lean and tall with a strange white stripe of hair running vertically through the middle of his head. Torr Einarr in Norse introduced the three leaders of the Scottish side. The stripe-haired young Viking spoke next for the Vikings. Niall Glundub and Constantine shared a momentary look of surprise when he spoke in fluent Irish-accented Gaelic. *Ui Imair,* thought Constantine.

"I am Ragnall son of Ivar son of Ivar the Boneless of Dublin, and I will translate," he said. "Our leader in the middle is Harald Fairhair, King of all Norway and the North Sea and my grandfather. The man to the right is my uncle, even though we are the same age. He is Erik Bloodaxe."

Constantine was staggered how young Erik Bloodaxe and Ragnall of the Ui Imair were. Both were teenagers yet commanded massive authority amongst the Vikings. *How had they amassed such experience for Vikings so young?* Constantine immediately got to the point.

"Where is our King, Domnall mac Constantine mac Cinead?"

There was a brief exchange in Norse between the Viking Ragnall and the King, before the Bloodaxe shrugged his shoulders with a smile and lifted his foot off the box. Ragnall opened the lid of the chest and reached in. He plucked the severed head of Domnall by the hair and threw it on the ground at Constantine's feet.

"Here's your King," Ragnall laughed.

Glundub drew his swords and leapt forward and the Bloodaxe did the same.

A great sigh went up from the two armies only several hundred feet apart as the shocking turn of events registered. Ragnall smiled at Torr Einarr and reached for his axe. All of this happened in a split second. *It must be now,* thought Constantine, *or thousands of men will die.*

"WAAAAIIIIIIIIIIIIIIITTTTT!" he screamed as loud as he could.

It worked. Barely. The Bloodaxe and Glundub took a step back from each other and sheathed their weapons. Ragnall Ui Imair strutted back behind the Norse King Fairhair laughing, but thankfully away from Torr Einarr.

Constantine could see that Glundub was barely restraining himself from slaughtering these three Viking nobles where they stood. The Bloodaxe looked like someone's death waiting for a place to happen.

"Torr Einarr, translate for me before this turns to further bloodshed."

The Norse-Gael chieftain nodded angrily, staring at the cocky Ui Imair prince.

"King Harald Fairhair, you will vacate our lands immediately with your warriors and never return. You have murdered our King and the price of this is death. If any of your warriors are captured on Scottish soil ever again, we will be forced to put them to the sword. You will release any prisoners you may have under guard, and you will lift the siege of the fort of Dunnottar. We have forces massing at Dunkeld and in a week, we will outnumber you ten to one. If you do not meet these terms, we will give you battle again and again until your invading army is destroyed. What say you?"

Torr Einarr's words in the strange Norse tongue washed over Constantine but he could see that Harald Fairhair was considering what he said. Fairhair began talking to Ragnall of Dublin at length and when he had concluded, the Dublin Viking begun speaking in Gaelic on his behalf.

"Last year, you and your Norse-Gael allies killed my eldest son and now I return the favour; your King has been slain. My son the Bloodaxe cleaved his head from his shoulders. If it is any consolation, he died well. I have nothing against you or your country but I, as King of Norway and all the Norse-controlled kingdoms, must answer any threat to my power. You killed my son; I killed your King and massacred his soldiers in revenge. His own arrogance and stupidity cost him his life. Do not threaten me with your tales of soldiers. I have heard of you, Constantine mac Aed, the whisperer in the ear of your betters, a mouse among the rushes, the lesser son of greater sires. My warriors are hardened veterans and would smash your army no matter the size. But worry not, I accept your terms and will depart; I came for vengeance, not to conquer your lands... for now." The strutting Ui Imair prince smiled enigmatically at them before turning and walking back to the Viking army. The Norse King followed.

The Bloodaxe waited a moment, spat in the direction of Glundub and pointed menacingly at the Irish warrior before walking away too. All that was left was the severed head of King Domnall mac Constantine mac Cinead on the grass and the three commanders of the Scottish army left contemplating a terrible series of events for Scotland.

The march back to Dunkeld passed like a blur for Constantine. He could feel the anger amongst his commanders, especially Glundub. The Irish prince was penning up his rage and funnelling it into a mute and impenetrable stare into the middle distance. The Norse had completely abandoned Scotland in less than two hours; they were such master sailors that even the stygian darkness of night couldn't deter them from the water. *We need a navy,* mused Constantine. They had located Domnall's remains amongst the dead close to the gate of the fortress and had taken both his head and body back for burial at Dunkeld. When the fortress had opened its gates the thousands of people inside had cheered wildly for their saviours but that had just sickened Constantine further. Torr Einarr had advised that he should be crowned king on the spot lest the sons of Giric or others rise and reach for independence or overlordship of Scotland upon Domnall's death. Constantine had agreed. *There can be no indecision or lack of clarity on the line of succession, or we will have civil war on our hands like the Saxons to the south.*

He was pronounced King of the Picts, Gaels, and all of Scotland in front of thousands of people and each of his chieftains came forward to swear oaths of fealty. Although Torr Einarr and Glundub were furious with what had occurred, Constantine could tell that the rank and file soldiery were exultant. They would not now have to face two thousand howling berserkers at the fortress of Dunnottar. They would get to sow their crops, bounce their children on their knees and see their wives again. Domnall was a tremendous loss for Scotland but if Constantine was honest, he had ignored wise council yet again and this time he had paid the ultimate price. *It was damned selfish,* thought Constantine, *Domnall leaves a young wife and an unborn son behind.* Domnall's death would have other ramifications, Constantine knew. He would have to take his forces around the entirety of Scotland as a show of strength. Peace and prosperity were all Constantine wanted for his Kingdom, but it was imperative that he be able to strike some fear in his subjects too. They had to believe that if he wanted, he could play the part of the warrior every bit as much as Domnall or Niall Glundub.

He knew he would always have Strathclyde, Pictland and the Highlanders due to the fact that he would name Domnall's unborn son as his heir. He would have to intimidate the men from Fortriu and Moray into obedience, but the threat of Harald Fairhair should be enough to keep them in line. Torr Einarr was a problem though, he could sense that the Norse-Gael chieftain felt that Constantine had capitulated in front of Fairhair and that prancing peacock Ragnall, the Ui Imair warlord. The Northmen were a strange breed of people and reputation meant everything to them. Constantine could tell that Torr Einar felt that Domnall, and by extension Constantine, had shamed Scotland over this debacle. *I will have to win him over again.* Caithness was under the control of no particular line of kings, and it was every strong man for himself, but again, as with Fortriu, Constantine hoped that the threat of the Norse would keep them in line. He was now King and whether he liked it or not, he would have to now consider marrying. There was a plethora of choices before him but he knew that whomever he chose must be beneficial to Scotland. Perhaps a daughter of Flann Sinna the Irish King? But the fact that the Irish Sea stood between them lessened its appeal. It was the most dangerous body of water in the world and wolves patrolled it and controlled it. *A daughter of one of the Northumbrian Kings could suffice,* he considered, *as it would put another ally between Scotland and the Danes and Saxons to the south.*

The army took two and a half days to return to Dunkeld, double the time it took to reach Dunnottar. On the way home, sections of the army had peeled off from the column to return to their own lands rather than go to Dunkeld. Constantine as King thanked each of them for their bravery and courage in coming to the aid of their country, even if they were not required to fight. When the column reached Dunkeld and marched through the gates there was huge celebration. Women flew into the arms of their menfolk in sheer delight at seeing them return home alive. News of what had transpired had not yet filtered through the town and Domnall's death had not tempered the emotions of the people. Constantine could almost hear the teeth grinding inside Glundub's granite jaw as he probably felt that these people should not be celebrating the return of their menfolk but should be mourning the death of their brave King. Constantine knew better, they meant no ill. Not every man or woman was as fearless as Niall Glundub, a six-foot-six eighteen-stone giant who could lift a cart off its back axle with his bare hands. Normal people were afraid and disgusted at the thought of battle. The sheer terror of sending their loved ones out to face Norse marauders took courage alone, never mind having to actually face them.

Constantine knew. He was one of those people. Glundub was far removed from them though. Niall was forged in battle, bred for a single purpose, to end the lives of Viking barbarians. Leaving his deliberations behind him, Constantine asked one of the man servants to fetch Domnall's remains and bring them to the central church. He walked there slowly, playing with words inside his head. Tears came to his eyes, and he paused to wipe them away. *How can I face this woman? How can I tell Aileen her husband, my cousin, is no more and her son will grow up fatherless?* He hadn't realised but Glundub had followed in his footsteps. The big Irishman met his eyes and nodded. He didn't have to speak; he knew the enormity of what he must do and acknowledged the bravery that Constantine must show right at this moment. There were many types of courage. Glundub had endless amounts of it on the battlefield, but this was an emotional courage with which the Irishman was unfamiliar. Constantine could see the relief in Glundub's eyes that it was Constantine who would do this thing. He loved Niall Glundub at that moment. He knew his formidable Irish cousin would rather face a thousand Erik Bloodaxes than walk into that church, and then they were there.

The church was dark inside with only a few candles piercing the gloom and the Queen was on her knees praying at the altar. Constantine approached with Glundub behind him but halted six feet away. The Queen turned around and looked at Constantine. He held her eyes but couldn't find the words, they evaporated on his tongue. But she could see. She raised her eyebrows and recognition flooded across her oval face. Pure grief poured from her as she held her full belly with her unborn son.

"Oh no, oh no, oh no," she repeated, again and again and again.

# PART 4

## THE EMERGENCE OF THE WARLORD RAGNALL UI IMAIR

# DRAMATIS PERSONAE:

**Abdullah Ibn Muhammad** (*Ab-dul-lah-ib-in-Muhammad*) – Emir and ruler of all of Muslim Al Andalus and some of North Africa.

**Aethelfled of Mercia** (*A-thel-fled*) – Saxon Queen of Mercia and daughter of the deceased King of Wessex.

**Aethelwold** (*A-thel-wold*) – Saxon prince and contender for the throne of Wessex.

**Amir Ibn Hafsun** (*Am-meer-ib-in-haf-soon*) – Umayyad nobleman and slave trader from the Islamic city of Cordoba.

**Amlaib Ivarsson** (*Am-layb-ivarson*) – Son of the King of Dublin. Notorious Viking warrior and older brother of Ragnall of the Ui Imair.

**Anarawd ap Rhodri** (*An-a-rawd-ap-rod-ree*) – Militaristic Welsh King of Gwynedd the strongest Welsh petty kingdom, son of Rhodri the Great.

**Arpad** – Hungarian steppe warlord who conquered huge swathes of eastern Europe.

**Augaire mac Aililla** (*Aw-gair-a-mac-al-lila*) – Ferocious young Irish warlord and bother-in-law to the Ui Imair princes.

**Auisle Ragnarsson** (*Ow-shla-rag-nar-son*) – Long-deceased son of Ragnar Lodbrok.

**Bairid Oitirsson** (*Bar-rid-oh-tier-son*) – Called Bairid mac Oitir by the Irish, distant kin to the Ui Imair as his grandfather Auisle was brother to Ivar the Boneless. Ruler of the powerful Kingdom of Mann in the Irish Sea.

**Bodil Ivarsdottir** (*Bow-dil-ivars-dot-tir*) – Ui Imair Princess, married to Augaire mac Aililla – Prince of the Ui Dunlainge; a powerful Leinster tribe.

**Brunbolg Headtaker** (*Brun-bulg-head-taker*) – Physically gigantic Viking warlord, subject to the influence of the Ui Imair.

**Ceolred of Chester** – Saxon ealdorman in charge of Chester.

**Cerbaill mac Muirecain** (*Ker-ball-mac-mwir-a-kawn*) – Powerful King of Leinster but subject to Flann Sinna's overlordship.

**Cinead mac Alpin** (*Kin-aid-mac-alpin*) – Long-deceased King of Scotland.

**Cnut** (*Can-noot*) – Danish ruler of Northumbria and political player in the region.

**Conall mac Finn** – Minor regional Irish ruler in North Leinster.

**Domnall mac Aed** – Over-king of the Northern Ui Neill, brother of Niall Glundub.

**Domnall mac Constantine** – Known by some as Domnall Dasachtach the former King of Scotland, slain in battle with the Norse.

**Dyabbi Cisse** (*Dee-yabee-see-say*) – Wealthy Ghanaian nobleman and slave trader, emissary of the rulers of the West African Ghanaian kingdom.

**Eorl Sichtfridh** (*Sict-frith*) – Partial Viking ruler in Dublin, major powerbroker in the Irish Sea.

**Edward the Elder** – Saxon prince and contender for the throne of Wessex.

**Eowils of Yorvik** (*Eow-ils*) – Joint King of Yorvik and much of Northumbria.

**Erik Amlaibsson** (*Erik-am-laybson*) – Ui Imair prince and nephew of Ivar the King of Dublin.

**Erik Haraldsson** – Also known as Erik Bloodaxe. Fearsome Viking marauder and raider, young son of the King of Norway.

**Estrid Ivarsdottir** (*Es-trid-ivars-dot-tir*) – Ui Imair Princess, married to a minor Irish King, Conall mac Finn.

**Faelan mac Muiredaig** (*Fail-on-mac-mwir-edeg*) – King of Leinster and renowned fighter.

**Flann Sinna** – High King of Ireland and over-king of Meath and the Southern Ui Neill.

**Fogartach mac Tolarg** (*Fo-gar-tach-mac-tol-arg*) – King of South Brega, under-king of the Southern Ui Neill.

**Frode the Clever** – Minor Norse-Gael jarl who ruled the town of Linn on the east coast of Ireland.

**Garangr Sichfridthsson** (*Gar-rang-gar-sic-frith-son*) – Ui Imair prince and nephew of the King of Dublin.

**Godfrith Ivarsson** (*God-frith-ivarson*) – Twin brother of Sihtric, the youngest sons of Ivar, King of Dublin and brother to Ragnall.

**Grimnir** (*Grim-near*) – Ui Imair Norse-Gael warrior.

**Gudrod Skirja Haraldsdottir** (*Good-rod-skir-ya-haralds-dot-tir*) – Norwegian princess who married Ivar Ivarsson and was the mother and aunt to a generation of the Ui Imair leadership in Dublin.

**Gunnar Sihtricsson** (*Gun-nar-sit-rick-son*) – Ui Imair prince and nephew of the King of Dublin.

**Halfdan of Yorvik** (*Half-dan*) – Joint King of Yorvik and much of Northumbria.

**Hastein** (*Has-tin*) – Ancient Danish Viking warlord, active in Francia and Britain.

**Hywel nDa ap Rhodri** (*Hew-will-da-ap-rod-ree*) – Notorious Welsh warlord, known by the Welsh as "The Good".

**Idwal ap Anarawd** (*Id-wal-ap-an-ar-awd*) – Welsh prince and war leader.

**Ingamundr Bairidsson** (*Ing-ga-munder-ba-rid-son*) – Formidable Ui Imair warlord, grandson of Ivar the Boneless.

**Ingvarr of Yorvik** (*Ing-var*) – Joint King of Yorvik and much of Northumbria.

**Iron Knee** – Deceased savage Viking warlord, former ruler in Dublin, enemy of both the kings of Meath and the Ui Imair.

**Ivar Ivarsson** – King of Dublin and leader of the Ui Imair.

**Ivar Ivarsson** – Ui Imair prince and third generation of the notorious clan to bear the name Ivar, son of the King of Dublin and older brother to Ragnall.

**Ivar the Boneless** – Deceased Viking warlord and King of Dublin. Primogenitor of the Ui Imair dynasty.

**Jormungand** – Ancient mythological demon of the Norse pantheon.

**Leo of Tripoli** – Renegade Greek naval commander who fought for the Abbasid Caliphate.

**Loki** – Major deity of the Scandinavian pantheon.

**Louis the Child** – King of East Francia and parts of Germania.

**Lubb Ibn Muhhamad** (*Lubb-ib-in-Muhammad*) – Powerful Umayyad general.

**Luitpold the Bavarian** – Prince Regent of Bavaria, Germanic warlord.

**Mael Finnia mac Flannacain** (*Male-fin-knee-a-mac-flan-na-kawn*) – Warlike King of Brega in Meath, under-king to the Southern Ui Neill.

**Magan Majan** (*Mag-an-maj-an*) – Overlord of the Ghanaian province of Takrur, extraordinarily wealthy nobleman and procurer of slave stock.

**Niall Glundub mac Aed Findliath** – Exiled Northern Ui Neill Irish prince. Fierce warrior and general under his cousin Constantine's command.

**Odin** – The chief god of the Norse and Danes, also known as the Allfather.

**Olaf the White** – Much older half-brother of Ivar the Boneless and Joint King of Dublin. Long since slain in battle in Scotland.

**Olga Ingvarrsdottir** (*Ol-ga-ing-vars-dottir*) – Viking noblewoman, daughter of one of the joint kings in Yorvik. Married to Godfrith of Dublin.

**Ragnall Ivarsson** (*Rag-nal-ivarson*) – Ui Imair prince and famous Viking raider despite his youth.

**Ragnar Lodbrok** (*Ragnar-lod-brok*) – Long-deceased legendary Viking sea king and ravager, ancestor of multiple Viking warlords.

**Rollo the Walker** – Notorious Viking warlord who plagued the Francian river systems.

**Sigurd the Mighty** – Famous Norse Viking warlord. Slain in battle against Ragnall Ui Imair off the coast of West Scotland.

**Sihtric Ivarsson** (*Si-tric-ivarson*) – Twin brother of Godfrith, the youngest sons of Ivar King of Dublin and brother to Ragnall.

# CHAPTER 1

## THE FALL OF VIKING DUBLIN (902)

Ragnall Ivarsson of the Ui Imair closed his eyes and inhaled a calming breath of familiar sea air on the docks of Dublin. Seagulls fluttered in the breeze and the sound of the Irish Sea drowned the noises coming from the hustle and bustle of the city. *It's great to be home.* The weather was reasonably clement, and all the fishermen were crying their catch on both sides of the river. As he made his way to the centre of the city from where his men had tied up his longboat on the Liffey, Ragnall could see that Dublin was thriving. It was a massive city, the only settlement that truly could be called a city on the island of Ireland and depending on what time of the year it was, hosted as many as sixty thousand people. Danish blacksmiths, Irish farmers, Francian traders and spice and silk merchants from the Mediterranean Sea, all jostled shoulder to shoulder and traded what they could.

Ragnall had a busy day ahead of him. He had just returned from four weeks at sea from a successful raid on the Saxon coastline. His father Ivar had commanded him to hit the coast of Somerset and they had taken many slaves. His father, brothers and cousins were all fighting in the Danelaw in the Saxon civil war and Ragnall had been commanded to harry the west of Wessex to make Edward the Elder think twice before leaving his lands undefended. Aethelwold's revolt against his cousin the elected King of Wessex continued apace with no side yet looking likely to achieve outright victory any time soon. The Danes and Saxons of East Anglia and the Danelaw had backed Aethelwold and with the help of his Viking allies, the usurper looked like he could potentially win. The Saxon kingdoms were a maelstrom and both Ivar son of Ivar and all his sons and nephews were taking full advantage. Ingamundr Bairidsson, Ragnall's notorious cousin, was raiding and pillaging up and down the Severn River which served to dampen Queen Aethelfled's commitment to fully reinforcing her brother Edward. How could she leave a warrior as formidable as Ingamundr devastating Mercia behind her after all? Ragnall's father and brothers, Ivar and Amlaib, were ravaging all the villages and forts along the river systems throughout Wessex.

Ragnall, as the youngest warleader, had been given the task of harassing the Summerset coast south of the Welsh Kingdoms with strict instructions to take as many slaves as he could. Through Ragnall, his father was monetarily hedging his bets with his young son's raids, for even if the civil war turned against their puppet Aethelwold, Ragnall would loot and plunder enough for all of them. No matter what, it would be financially worthwhile. His younger cousins Erik, Gunnar and Garangr each served under seasoned captains within his own command, making their first forays into the Irish Sea as Vikings. It pleased Ragnall that he had his own command even if it was only ten longboats in strength. When his father had told him what he was to do, away from the main strength of the Vikings of Dublin, he could tell at the time that his brothers and cousins felt that it was an insult. His father was always hard on him, but Ragnall never knew if it was because he looked exactly like his famous grandfather Ivar the Boneless, or because he went with men instead of women, or perhaps the fact that he had already been part of several famous battles on the winning side and in ways his own fame had surpassed his father's reputation already. Perhaps it was simply fear, he chuckled to himself; he was the best fighter of the Ui Imair after all. He had taken the heads of Sigurd the Mighty and the Iron Knee to prove it. What other Viking could claim to have killed two fabled warlords before they had turned eighteen years of age? *Ragnall Ui Imair was a name that commanded fear and respect from Norway to Limerick and everywhere in between.*

The hall of his parents lay on the south side of the River Liffey high up on a prominent hill overlooking the water and city. Dublin was truly enormous. It was a massive source of wealth for not just the Vikings, but the Irish who traded with them in the hinterlands. His father had made several brilliant moves politically that made Dublin the city it was. By marrying Gudrod Skirja, the daughter of Harald Fairhair, he had unified the Danes and Norse in the city to such an extent that when Ragnall killed the Iron Knee, there were few calls for vengeance. Even Eorl Sichtfridh, the joint Norse ruler with the Iron Knee, had conceded that with his former ally out of the picture, there could be an enduring peace. The Eorl had ceded control of Dublin to Ivar, in exchange for a part of the taxes collected from trade and mostly served now simply as an advisor to the Ui Imair. All Sichtfridh's sons had died in battle in the intervening years, and he had acknowledged Ivar Ivarsson as the one who would inherit all, once he passed on. Dublin would be unified.

When Ivar and Gudrod Skirja started to have many sons and daughters, with both Norse and Dane heritage, it had further united the city. The inhabitants were no longer Norse and Dane, they were now just the Vikings, the foreigners, or Norse-Gaels of Dublin. The Irish for twenty years had called them by a different title and this one had spread far and wide across the Irish Sea; all the Vikings of Dublin were simply called the Ui Imair. Ragnall's father had not finished there. He had married both of his daughters to Irish kings to keep them from encroaching on his territory. Both had come with massive dowries. Estrid, Ragnall's older sister, was married to a chieftain of Cuala, Conall mac Finn, and the other, Bodil, was married to a young up-and-coming prince of Leinster called Augaire mac Aililla of the Ui Dunlainge. It was Ragnall who had arranged that latter marriage the year before as he was very familiar with the lands and people of the Ui Dunlainge of Leinster. He regularly visited with his sister to check on her welfare but there was an ulterior motive as well. Augaire mac Aililla had a brother who lived in his shadow. A quiet and considerate young man who was destined for the monastery, but to Ragnall he was a special friend. When Ragnall went on raids it was not frowned upon to take women by force, it was positively encouraged. But he was never attracted to women in that way and only saw captured women as chattels for the slaver's block rather than targets to be ravished on a raid.

It had been a confusing time for him as he grew to manhood. He had told his mother and sisters first and they had never cared and just wished for his happiness. It was not illegal in the Viking world to go with men, but it was certainly deemed unusual and dangerous if you could not produce any heirs. Ragnall didn't care; he had many brothers who he knew would go on to have loads of sons of their own. When he told his brothers and cousins, they had also shrugged their shoulders indifferently. His father though was nonplussed and warned him that fathering children was a responsibility for a Viking. His father impressed upon him that to live his life eschewing women for the company of men, he would have to absolutely excel as a fighter or Viking warriors would not respect him. But that was no problem for Ragnall. He was six foot four and bore the inherited white stripe of hair that occasionally turned up in the line of the Ui Imair. He was ambidextrous and could fight evenly with either hand, which was a terrible surprise for any foe he faced. His joints were extraordinarily flexible, and he was capable of amazing feats of acrobatics. He had mastered axe, bow, sword and spear and had earned renown in every battle he fought. Men followed him because he always brought them the three things every Viking warrior wanted above all others: victory, wealth and reputation.

His father's hall was long and wide and dominated all the hundreds of dwellings that surrounded it on that section of the river. As Ragnall's brothers had grown older and his sisters had married, they had moved out, but he had remained quartered at home. He had never longed for a hall of his own and much preferred the freedom of his longboat. All that remained at home were Ragnall, his parents and his youngest brothers who were twins. They were between nine and ten years of age and looked up to all their older siblings, hoping one day soon that they could take to the seas and live the Viking way. Ragnall entered through the large wooden double doors of the hall and although there was a fire in the central pit and a pot bubbling away, neither the twins nor his mother were inside. He moved to a small door at the back and stepped outside once again. His mother had set up a large Viking loom out in the light and was intricately weaving patterns for a new blanket. His brothers were fighting with miniature shields and wooden swords. They were energetically battering at each other, laughing all the time, but as identical twins each were so accustomed to each other's footwork that neither could gain an advantage. Ragnall snuck up upon them and tackled the two to the earth.

"RAAAAGGGNAALLLLL!" they shouted in delight and wrestled with him upon the ground.

After a minute Ragnall submitted to the two twins and the trio picked themselves up and dusted themselves off. His mother looked on beaming but allowed him a few more moments with his twin brothers. He unlaced a sack that he had set down before he playfully ambushed his brothers and unveiled the presents he had for them. They were two small steel curved Saracen swords. He handed one to each boy to ooohs and aaahs as they examined them. They had known weapons all their young lives, but they had never seen the carved scimitar blades of the warriors of Al Andalus. His mother finally interceded at that point as the twins began clashing their new swords together in feigned battle.

"Be careful, you two," their mother warned them. She turned to Ragnall. "It is great to see you again my son, I prayed to Odin for your safe return."

Ragnall laughed "What Saxon could ever hope to kill me? Godfrith and Sihtric would give me a better fight."

His mother laughed and guided him inside and sat with him by the fire. He told her all about the raid, the slaves taken, which men had been wounded and any other plunder that they had seized. His mother in her youth had been a shield maiden and fought beside her famous father and brothers. She was Harald Fairhair's eldest child and had married Ivar Ivarsson at fifteen. Their son Ivar had been born soon after that and Gudrod Skirja had settled for a sedentary life in Dublin raising their children, while her husband went on campaign every raiding season. They spoke together for several hours during which the morning turned to afternoon. At length, Ragnall knew that it was time to take his leave. His slave stocks were corralled down close to the docks in stockades under guard by some of his warriors. They would have to be fed and watered but the inherent cost of keeping this stock around he hoped wouldn't hang over him for too long. Representatives of two of the Ui Imair's biggest customers were quartered in halls down near the main docks of the city. For three generations, the Vikings of Dublin had funded their city and warriors from selling slaves to both the Islamic Caliphate in Al Andalus and several of the biggest independent kingdoms of the Aifric, and many powerful and wealthy kings had permanent representatives present in the city.

He bid his mother and brothers farewell and made his way down through the town. It was only a short five-minute walk from his parents' hall to the slaver's block on the dock. The streets were wide and bustling with people still. Several groups of men nodded at him in recognition and respect as he walked past. From what he was told by the older Vikings who remembered, he bore such a striking resemblance to his grandfather Ivar the Boneless that some of the more superstitious among them felt that Ragnall was a reincarnation. He used to laugh at that idea with his cousin Ingamundr, as if Ivar the Boneless shared the same sexual proclivities as Ragnall, there would have been no such thing as the Ui Imair.

As Ragnall turned the final bend toward the slaver's block on the pier he was glad to see that his young cousin Garangr had taken the initiative and begun leading up the slaves, six at a time, to the block. The first six were all mature women who were either too old to breed children or flawed in some way and would not make much money. These lots were quickly sold to the highest bidder. The two main competitors for the chattels were two men he recognised. The first was the Arab Vizier, Amir Ibn Hafsun, a senior diplomat and procurer of slaves for the Most Holy Emir of Cordoba, Abdullah Ibn Muhammad. The Emir and his Vizier had a voracious appetite for female slaves to work as both cooks and cleaners, but also to add as concubines to either the Emir's own harem or those of his brothers, cousins or friends. These women, Ragnall knew, could expect a life of luxury compared to a hard life working on Saxon farms which was the contradiction faced by the captured slaves. Occasionally Amir Ibn Hafsun would work freelance and supply some of the other Islamic kingdoms far to the east who all admired the strange pale flesh and light-coloured hair of some of the women of northwest Europe. He controlled a small fleet of four boats manned by eunuch sailors, with eunuch Slavic soldiers providing security. Several of them accompanied the Vizier now, wrapped up in pelts and furs to protect them from the Irish cold. The sails of the Vizier's ships carried the same sickle-shaped sign of the Muslims and the arms of his master and were easy to spot. Ragnall saw four tied up on the docks a few hundred feet away. *This is good,* thought Ragnall, *he will be wanting to pack his holds full of slaves this early in the battle season so he can make another run later in the summer.*

The second major customer that Ragnall acknowledged with a nod was the mighty nobleman and warrior of the Ghanaian Kingdoms on the west coast of the Aifric, Dyabbi Cisse. He had ebony skin as dark as coal and his soldiers all shared the same look. He was one of several sons of Magan Majan, the current overlord of the province of Takrur. They were an incredibly wealthy nation who gathered their riches through the mining of gold and salt. What they required were numerous young boys and girls to wield pickaxes and climb into small dark crevices to chip wealth from the rock. Occasionally they would compete with the Arab representatives for some women the Dublin Vikings might capture, but only if they were of incredible beauty or noble birth. The few men that survived to land on Dublin's slave blocks were usually gelded and sold to the Umayyad as strong backs for various tasks. Other buyers occasionally frequented the blocks from the Viking world but compared to these two exotic customers, they just didn't have the wealth to compete for the most valuable of stock.

The crowd was heaving today, Ragnall noticed. Lots of slaves were produced to the block, quickly inspected, and then bid for, before being herded onto the ships of the buyers. He was surprised to see that the crowd did not dissipate even after the first twenty lots were sold. There were many faces present that Ragnall did not recognise.

Most of the warriors of Dublin were away on campaign with Ragnall's father and so the city was guarded and policed mostly from amongst the young and untested and the old, all commanded by a few seasoned men. His mother and Eorl Sichtfridh usually sat in judgement late in the evening in the main hall on any pressing matters that affected the city of Dublin, but in terms of authority that was about all there was. A particularly beautiful young woman with blonde hair appeared in the next lot which caught everyone's eye. Ragnall ushered her gently to the front of the block away from the other five in her lot and signalled to the two heavy hitters to begin. Thirty dirham from the Ghanaian was doubled by the Arab Vizier, the Ghanaian nobleman considered for a moment before raising the price by another ten. The Arab shouted something derogatory to the Ghanaian and immediately bid another ten for the girl. The Ghanaian, affronted by the arrogance of the Arab, raised the price by another thirty. Both the Kingdoms of the Aifric and the Caliphates of the Islamic world had voracious appetites for Celtic and Saxon slaves, but sometimes they were so greedy and intent on a particular asset that Ragnall had to laugh. *There are another ten thousand girls waiting to be raided just like her and these greedy idiots want to beggar themselves over her.*

In the end the Ghanaian won the bidding war for this beautiful girl for a colossal sum of one hundred and twenty-five dirham. In disgust the Arab Vizier slunk away and instructed one of his underlings to bid on his behalf for the remaining stock, his pride severely dented. Ragnall knew that the Vizier had to hit a certain quota of slaves on each journey north lest he face reprimand by his master, so he could not afford to blow all of his coin on a single piece of stock unless he knew her great beauty would mesmerise one of the royal houses. That would not be a sure thing though. The Islamic world was an enormous place, but the Arabic tribes saw themselves as kings of it. A Francian wine merchant had explained this to him. There were black Africans and Berbers from the Aifric, Nubians and Egyptians, Turkic and Bulgar nomads and Persians who all called Allah their God, but the Arabs always considered themselves above the others. After all, their godling Muhammad had come from Arab stock. A Ghanaian nobleman outbidding the Vizier for a slave was a slap in the face to the Arab Vizier. Ragnall didn't care though; they were just customers to him, enriching his father's Kingdom and by extension, the city of Dublin. When finally, the last lot of slaves, a group of young boys, were sold and paid for and packed away on the ships, Ragnall had his men count the gold and then sent a few reliable warriors to accompany it up to the main hall. All his warriors that had raided with him took their cut as well and Ragnall sent them on their way with his compliments on a raid well conducted. They would spend two weeks with their wives and families and then they would take to the seas once more, but this time to sail up the Severn River to support his cousin Ingamundr in his distractionary raids on Wessex and Mercia.

Evening was falling rapidly, and grey clouds were gathering above the Dublin skies, but Ragnall had this feeling that something was amiss. *Why is it so damn busy?* He looked around trying to identify people he knew but that was virtually impossible in a city this size. He started walking again up toward the hall of his parents and stood in the main thoroughfare looking around in a circle. A pair of flat-topped wagons almost ran over his foot and he hopped out of the way in annoyance at the carelessness of it. The two men leading it were hooded and issued an apology in Irish and continued on their way toward the docks. When Ragnar looked around more studiously, he saw that a lot of people were hooded as if bracing for bad weather, but the skies were iron-grey. There was no rain yet. *There were a lot of men around,* he thought, on both sides of the river too from his memory of sailing into port, way more than there should be at this time of the year with the bulk of their warriors on campaign. A glint of metal caught his eye on one of the wagons that had nearly run him over, from just beneath the furs piled inside it. He saw another trio of men, hooded as well, meet with the two leading the wagons and the five spoke furtively together.

*Oh no,* Ragnall thought, *surely not, not today.*

He slowly drew his two axes from his belt and walked back toward them, a certainty growing in him that something was appallingly wrong. One of the men reached into the back wagon and pulled away the furs and unveiled dozens of weapons lying on its floor. Ragnall was now jogging and when the others reached in and began pulling weapons too, Ragnall was sprinting. The men were pulling back their hoods and discarding their cloaks when Ragnall hit them. He plunged his right-hand axe through the spine of the first man and decapitated the second with a blow from his left hand. He kicked the third back into the dirt to give himself room to split the skull of the fourth. The fifth attempted to free a dagger from his breeches but Ragnall split him from sternum to groin and his intestines spilled out on the earth. He died noisily and the ordinary people of Dublin finally registered that something was awry. There were men dying before them on the street, they must be under attack. Ragnall chopped the right hand off the man he had kicked to the ground and put his axe to his throat.

"ARE WE UNDER ATTACK?" he screamed at the injured man who was groaning in agony beneath him.

Before he received an answer from him a thunderous horn call echoed across the city and it was answered by another and another and another. Silence descended momentarily and then the screams started. He buried his axe in the man's face. *The Irish are within the walls.*

Ragnall knew time was of the essence. If these Irish had any tactical sense, they would make straight for his parents' hall and make prisoners of any of the Ui Imair nobility there. He sprinted up the streets toward his family's abode. He saw Norse-Gael Dublin people slowly come to their senses and pick up arms to defend themselves, but it was obvious to Ragnall that it would be too late. The dregs of the warriors remaining in Dublin, apart from his own men, were only capable of perhaps defending the walls; but against a horde of Irish warriors out for blood, they were badly outmatched. He still couldn't believe it. No Irish army had ever taken the city of Dublin, but it was happening here and now.

They had not only picked the most opportune time to attack with more than six thousand of Dublin's warriors abroad, but they had also managed to sneak an unknown quantity of men through the walls and wooden palisades through subterfuge, bribery and probably murder. Ragnall's fury got the better of him on multiple occasions and he rushed to intercept the occasional Irish attacker racing past. He slew three or four before he got to his parents' front door but to his horror, he saw that it had been splintered and kicked in already. *The Irish have been here.*

A shudder associated with an unfamiliar emotion crept over him, it was fear. Both of his axes were bloody and his mail was covered with mud and gore. It made the grip on the hafts of his axes less than solid. On entering he found a piece of cloth and wiped both handles down. The room was dark, so he opened the doors fully to let the maximum of the evening's daylight in to illuminate the hall. It was a bloodbath. There were two Viking warriors dead on the ground, one with his throat slit and another who had the top portion of his head caved in, with his brains on the rushes. And then there came the worst sight of all. His mother, sword in hand and with a snarl on her lips, lay with a dagger buried in her breast that had impaled her to the main wooden bench. There were two Irishmen dead on the floor too. Neither of Ragnall's twin brothers were amongst the slain. Ragnall's fury rose inside of him like a volcano. *These Irish will pay,* he fumed, *this is an outright brazen attack on Dublin, the sheer hubris of these Irishmen to take Dublin like this.* He shouted loudly and swore that by Thor's hammer, he would have vengeance on the Irish. A whimper from behind a pile of chopped logs caught his attention. He ran toward the sound and looked behind the wood. It was his brother Godfrith. The boy leapt into Ragnall's arms, shaking with terror. He was just a young child and had witnessed his mother being slaughtered. Godfrith whispered into Ragnall's ear between sobs, "They have taken Sihtric, they have taken Sihtric." Ragnall picked up his terrified young brother and ran for the exit.

The city was in chaos. Ragnall could see people being massacred, women being raped and children being butchered like sheep by crazed Irish warriors. The priority for Ragnall was to get his scared young brother Godfrith out to sea in the hands of his cousins and then try and find out the fate of Sihtric. He prayed to Odin that the boy was captured and taken hostage rather than killed but the blood was up in the Irish warriors that he had seen and all they seemed concerned with for now was the sack of the city rather than the wellbeing of captives. Twice he had to put Godfrith down to cut down a handful of Irish warriors who stood in his path. He towered above them as the Irish were of Celtic heritage and usually a good bit shorter than any Viking, especially a towering Ui Imair nobleman like himself. When he encountered cadres of warriors that he was not sure that he could defeat, he took the side streets to evade them. He knew Dublin better than any Irishman ever could and easily avoided them. He could see even from distance that many Vikings and Norse-Gaels were jumping onto their longboats and fleeing the massacre, which gladdened his heart.

*How has it come to this?* he wondered. Most of the people of Dublin had some Irish in them, including himself, as the wife of his grandfather Ivar the Boneless was a sister of Flann Sinna, their High King. His father was clearly wrong in his assumption that the Kingdom of Dublin was on good terms with the Irish kingdoms that surrounded them. *When I find out who is responsible for this, I will come back with every Viking I can find and put every man and woman to the sword and sell their children to the slave mines of the Ghanaians,* he swore. He passed several of the minor market squares on his way to the docks and he could see that hundreds or maybe even thousands of the people of Dublin were being herded under guard. *At least here the massacre has ceased, and they are content to take prisoners.*

He paused to listen to the Irish captains bawling over the din and he could make out what they were saying. They were shouting to the mass of subdued Dublin people that the city was taken and if the people did not resist, they would not be harmed. He ground his teeth in frustration when he heard the proclamations of these criers shouting that they were actually freeing the Norse-Gael and Irish residents of the city from the tyranny of the Ui Imair and that under the High Kingship of Flann Sinna, they would prosper under just rule. *Lies,* seethed Ragnall, *the Ui Imair made this city what it is!* He couldn't listen to this filth anymore and moved on with Godfrith in his arms. The boy was heavy, so he eventually had to put him down. Once on the ground Godfrith surprisingly pulled his sleeve and asked Ragnall for a dagger to fight.

He explained that he and Sihtric had hidden the Saracen swords that Ragnall had given them, so their mother would not confiscate them. Ragnall could see the focused determination appearing on his brother's face despite his fear. Tears almost welled in Ragnall's eyes and he had to look away at the shocking bravery being shown by the boy. *Ui Imair to the bone this one, our mother would be proud.* The two brothers jogged downhill through the back alleys to the River Liffey.

At length, Ragnall and Godfrith reached the docks. The bodies of Irish warriors and Vikings littered the ground but Garangr, Ragnall's young cousin, held the docks still.

"Hurry, Ragnall," he shouted, "Dublin has all but fallen. They have subdued the city on both banks of the river. Already three hundred boats have cast off with thousands of our people."

Ragnall nodded. *A large portion of our strength has been preserved and whatever has been taken from us, can always be taken back.* He loaded his brother onto one of the remaining longboats and told Garangr to leave one last boat under guard with ten men and to round up another twenty of the remaining warriors; they were going back into the city to try and rescue Sihtric or at least ascertain his fate. All other boats were to leave immediately and reconvene the next morning off the eastern shore of Lambay Island. Apart from the Dal nAridi tribe of the Ulaid, the Irish were not a sea power, and he knew the people of Dublin would be safe from the attackers on the water. Once the twenty men were assembled, Ragnall led them west down the banks of the river in search of Sihtric. The sounds of violence were dying down now around the city and the conflict was almost done. Dublin was firmly under Irish control. Smoky clouds had gathered above several buildings that had been fired in the chaos.

Ragnall noticed that at every street front, cadres of Irish warriors had assembled to witness his twenty warriors jog past but they did not try to advance and just stared after them. Street after street they crossed, they were marked but not challenged by any band of Irish fighters. Ragnall slowed to a walk and then stopped. It dawned on him; *they know we are coming.* Between the quickly darkening evening and the pall of smoke, visibility was much reduced, but Ragnall could make out a shadow emerging ahead of them along the main thoroughfare that flanked the Liffey. His warriors fanned out in a circle to protect him as finally the Irish soldiers made a move to encroach upon them. The shadow in the smoke was not one person but several.

The first two to emerge from the gloom were his younger brother Sihtric, who was deeply distressed and scared, and an elderly but powerfully built grey-haired man. The man's arm was firmly wrapped around Sihtric's shoulder. *This man is familiar to me,* thought Ragnall. It was Flann Sinna, the High King of Ireland and the head of the Southern Ui Neill. The hairs stood up on his arm and his Viking blood stirred. *I am related to this man. If I cut him down now before his men get to me, I will go down forever in the sagas as the Viking who put the High King of Ireland to the sword.* That ambition withered away when his sister Bodil emerged from the smoke as well, Ragnall's nephew in her arms. She stared at Ragnall pleadingly and he inferred from that look that the wrong word could see three members of the Ui Imair slain in less than a minute. He sheathed his axes and on his nod his men did the same. Three other men emerged to stand beside Bodil, Sihtric and the High King. Ragnall knew them all. They were his treacherous brother-in-law Augaire mac Aililla; Mael Finnia mac Flannacain King of Brega, neighbour of Dublin to the north; and Cerbaill mac Muirecain, the King of Leinster to the south. All served as under-kings to Flann Sinna. It was the High King who spoke first.

"Ragnall Ivarsson, grandnephew. I want you to not speak but listen. If you utter a single word or you or your men make one threatening move, your young brother will have to die here and now, blood ties to me or not. You and your men will then follow him to Valhalla shortly afterward."

Ragnall trembled with rage, he could only nod.

"Dublin is an independent kingdom no more, Ragnall. The city will pay obeisance and tribute to me like all the rest from this day forward. I will now protect these people, not the Ui Imair. You have my word that I will not brutalise them, subjugate them or enslave them. Mine is the Christian way, not the Viking or Muslim way. You will carry word to your father, my nephew, that

I will keep his son Sihtric as hostage as his bond of good conduct. The kings of Leinster have two of his sisters. Their husbands love them dearly, but they will pay the ultimate price also if Ivar disobeys me. Sihtric will be raised in my hall and receive an education worthy of an Irish nobleman. He will come to no harm as long as the Ui Imair leadership troubles us no more."

The old king paused momentarily and pulled his iron-grey hair from his weather-beaten face.

"Ultimately, Ragnall, the rule of Dublin is mine now. The days of the Ui Imair enslaving Irish people are over. Peace will reign and the people of Dublin will be free. Except for the more notable barbarians and the Ui Imair nobles amongst your ranks, the rest of the Norse-Gael are still free to come and go and visit loved ones or even trade, but I will tax everybody and reinforce the city against counterattack. Cerbaill mac Muirecain will oversee the administration of Dublin on my behalf, from this day forward. It saddens me to be forced to usurp people of my own blood, but the Irish can no longer endure Viking tyranny. The Ui Imair will no longer rule this city. I will."

His mother dead, his brother and sisters effectively taken captive, Ragnall could summon no adequate response. He turned his back on Dublin and sailed out of the estuary of the Liffey an hour later. *The Ui Imair will return,* he vowed. *Flann Sinna will pay.*

# CHAPTER 2

## THE CONFRONTATION WITH AETHELFLED OF MERCIA (903)

Summer was on the horizon, shedding the grip of yet another harsh spring, one which Ragnall Ui Imair would never forget. His people had suffered on their exodus from Dublin. Almost a hundred had died of either hunger or disease, overwintering on the banks of the River Mersey. The river divided the lands of Northumbria and Mercia in Britain. Through the summer, autumn and winter of 902 and the spring of 903, the Ui Imair and the six thousand people who had deserted Dublin with them had searched for a temporary new home. Everywhere they appeared they were rejected, turned away and in the case of the Welsh Kingdom of Gwynned, given battle and militarily opposed. Ragnall looked around the new longfort that they had created. It consisted of hundreds of boats lashed together on the banks that served as a makeshift settlement to overwinter in, a ramshackle construction compared to their home of Dublin. He twisted the fishing rod in his hands in rage at the thought of how far the Ui Imair had fallen. The mere fact that Ragnall Ivarsson, one of the most famous Vikings of the entire Viking world had been reduced to fishing for his supper boiled him.

He thought back to their expulsion in depth. Ragnall had sent fast ships to his father and cousin and kept his people together at Lambay Island off the coast of Dublin for a couple of weeks, immediately after fleeing Dublin. They were only a few miles from their former home, but it might as well have been a thousand. Most of the people of Dublin remained where they were which further annoyed him but when he contemplated their decision he understood why. For the average Norse-Gael trader or blacksmith, it made little difference whether it was the Ui Imair who they paid their taxes to or the Irish Ui Neill or Ui Dunlainge. It was just another king to bend the knee to after all, their roots were dug deep, and life just ambled on for them. Most of the actual Viking warriors of Dublin were among the ships that did escape but with the entire city of Dublin effectively under Irish rule and the threat of massacre of their friends and families ever present, they were as hamstrung by events as Ragnall was.

Three weeks later, the retinues of both his father and his cousin arrived off Lambay. Ivar Ivarsson rightly concluded that their people could not just linger off the coast of Lambay Island indefinitely. He decided to go north initially with the entire fleet, to the Norse-Gael town of Linn on the northeast coast of Ireland. They were allowed to dock temporarily and land, but the town was too small to accommodate them all and the ruler of the town, Frode the Clever, had begged them to leave. He had explained his political situation to Ragnall's father. The town of Linn sat between the kingdoms of the Ulaid to the north and the Bregans to the south and their situation was always precarious. In fact, Frode paid both kingdoms off with tithes of fish and steel to preserve their autonomy. Ivar knew that he could take the town if he wished but what purpose would it serve except to provoke war with the Ui Neill or the Ulaid and result in more death among his people? They had reluctantly moved on.

Ragnall threw down his fishing rod in disgust thinking back on that. He had started a small fire crackling beside him, but its heat was as nothing to the anger he harboured about what had happened next. Desperately searching for a safe port in the Irish storm that had consumed them, the Ui Imair and their thousands of retainers had descended on the Kingdom of Mann. The little island was a thriving Viking port sitting in the centre of the Irish Sea, immune to attack from Irish, Saxon or Welsh aggressors. It was ruled by a cousin of Ragnall's father, a Viking called Bairid Oitirsson. The Ui Imair fleet had not even been allowed to dock near the main fort as Bairid was a suspicious and cautious ruler.

His grandfather Auisle was yet another son of Ragnar Lodbrok, but many years ago, Ragnall's grandfather Ivar in alliance with another uncle, Olaf the White, had defeated Auisle in battle and killed him. Auisle was their half-brother and even two generations later, it had not been forgotten by his descendants. Bairid Oitirsson was a cousin of the Ui Imair but all he would offer them was some resupply and a few days' safe harbour from the elements. He had then informed Ivar that if they stayed even one moment longer than that, he would fire their ships and enslave them all. Humiliated, Ragnall's father had to retreat from Bairid's hall. Ragnall had not been present for the meeting, but his cousin Ingamundr had recounted the tale to him. Had Ragnall been there he knew his temper would have gotten the better of him and he would have cut down the King of Mann in his own hall. *Probably a wise decision by my father,* he acknowledged. His father and brothers had often chastised Ragnall for his temper, but he just couldn't help it. He felt a constant need to prove himself and had slain many men in single combat over perceived slights. Any little thing could set him off: defiance from men under his command, insults stemming from his preference of going with men rather than women or insults to his family or friends; each could potentially result in death by Ragnall's hand. The red mist would descend and that would be that, he just could not stop himself.

The worst for the expelled Ui Imair had yet to come though. Ingamundr had hatched a plan where they would try to take the island of Angelsea from the Welsh Kingdom of Gwynedd. He advocated hitting them hard and fast and by surprise. The Kingdom of Gwynedd was large, but Ingamundr felt that if they could take control of the island of Anglesea from King Anarawd and his warrior son Idwal, they could cut it away from the mainland portion of Gwynedd indefinitely. Nobody could match the Ui Imair at sea after all. It was approaching winter, which Ingamundr had felt would catch the Welsh even more off guard as it fell well outside the regular battle season. Ragnall had landed with a force of eight hundred warriors on the far side of the island and had been given a day to get to the walls of Anarawd's capital Abberfraw on the southeast, while Ingamundr, his father and the others had sailed around to attack the town directly. The assault had turned into an unmitigated disaster though and evolved into a humbling rout for the Ui Imair. There was a reason that none of the Vikings warlords of the Irish Sea ever bothered to attack this particular Welsh kingdom as they were a shrewd and militaristic people. Be it the Romans, the Saxons or the Vikings, none had been able to subdue the men from Gwynedd fully and this King Anarawd had allegedly never lost a single battle.

Ingamundr's sails had been spotted off the shore before it was optimal, and the Welsh had instantly lit a series of bonfires on the hills which were answered on the mainland several miles away. Ragnall's father had attempted a raid there twenty years previously and had remembered the layout of the town, but there was a nasty surprise waiting: King Anarawd had heavily fortified it since. Massive stone walls and timber palisades surrounded it and on the sight of Viking sails all the people had sought refuge within. Unwilling to gamble Viking lives, Ivar and Ingamundr had elected to lay siege to the town with Ragnall penning them in from the land. The Welsh were well provisioned. Within a week, a significant force of men had arrived on the mainland side of Gwynedd under the banner of the King of Seisyllwg, Anarawd's relative Hywel nDa "The Good". Ingamundr and Ragnall's father had furiously debated on whether to storm the town and defeat Anarawd or else continue the search for refuge elsewhere. Pragmatism won out in the end, to Ragnall's disgust. He shook his head in frustration thinking back on the decision; *we could have won that fight, sacked the town and cut Hywel nDa's force to pieces as they crossed the channel.*

Ragnall stoked his small fire once more and considered the security of their new settlement. The Mersey River was of course the unofficial border between the north of the Saxon Kingdom of Mercia and the southwest of the mishmash of people with different heritages that made up the Kingdom of Northumbria. It was currently ruled by a Dane called Cnut who had converted to worshiping the Christ instead of the Norse gods and through this heresy now had the authority to rule over Saxon, Dane and Norse alike. Even Edward the Elder had frequently acknowledged his sovereignty rather than name him as a foreign temporary occupier. It made Ragnall laugh; *Cnut is about as much of a Christian as I am.* The Saxon king was right though. In Northumbria, Dane married Saxon who married Gael who married Norse. There were no real demarcations of nationalities, they were just Northumbrians. *It was a bit like Dublin in that regard,* thought Ragnall wistfully.

The site on the Mersey and all along the coast north of there was chosen for a place to overwinter for astute political reasons. Especially in winter and springtime, word of news travelled glacially slow and the Ui Imair would be well entrenched before Aethelfled of Mercia or Cnut of Yorvik even knew they were there. Or at least that was the hope. It bought the Ui Imair time to settle and regroup. There were old men, children and pregnant women in their fleet who needed shelter and comfort in the hard times of the year; they could not live long at sea. Word had come to Ivar Ivarsson's ears that the civil war in Wessex had finally concluded recently. The forces of King Edward the Elder and his allies from Kent and Mercia had actually suffered a terrible defeat to the Danes of East Anglia and the Danelaw, but the pretender Aethelwold had been killed by a stray arrow in the fighting, thus making the civil war moot. There was only one viable candidate standing of note and that was Edward the Elder. Despite losing the battle, he had won the war by default. The fact that could not be denied though was that the armies of Wessex and Mercia were surely severely weakened by this and would look to consolidate rather than march north and throw the stranded Ui Imair back into the sea. It was only a matter of time though, Ragnall knew, before either Cnut or Aethelfled would get wind of the presence of the Ui Imair and would demand explanation or worse.

The winter had been hard and the spring had not been easy. People had died, but as summer approached Ragnall could see that they were far more secure. The particular region of Northumbria to the north of their many new longforts, on the river and the coast, had been mostly depopulated by the constant warfare it had endured over the last fifty years. The area was known as Cumbria and was largely empty. Because of the Great Heathen Army, the warlord Hastein, the Norse and the Ui Imair themselves, the people of the region had been captured, killed or driven away to safer lands. Yet there were still a few hardy forts and communities there who were willing to trade with the people under the Ui Imair's control. The longforts had been extended, reinforced, and remade with more permanency in the last few months. Babies that had been born in the depths of winter now grew big and fat and healthy. Trees had been cleared away and those who knew how to farm began to sow crops. Even traders from Mann and Dublin began to appear to trade and some even to settle with their families, looking at the land the Ui Imair had claimed as maiden territory to be made their own.

Many of the Dublin immigrants, former subjects of the Ui Imair, had a most interesting story to tell that had gladdened the heart of Ragnall and his brothers. Apparently, the treacherous Irish chieftain Mael Finnia mac Flannacain, one of the leaders of the Irish force that had expelled the Ui Imair from Dublin, had met a violent end on the plains of Meath. A civil war had erupted between the northern and southern factions of the kingdoms of Brega. Flann Sinna the High King could not intercede lest he was perceived as showing favouritism to one side or the other. His former hostage and now ally, the under-king Fogartach mac Tolarg, had slain Mael Finnia in single combat. When Ragnall had heard of that bastard's death he had exulted inside and only wished he had been there to swing the final axe blow himself. It made Ragnall wonder, *the Irish can never remain peaceful for long, and they are as likely to fight each other as they are to fight us.* The politics of Ireland were ever changing, Ragnall observed, and it was this chaos that would surely provide an opportunity for the Ui Imair to reclaim their homeland in the future. *Who knows,* he thought, *Flann Sinna is an ancient man. If he dies, Ireland will descend into madness. There is no one there of his calibre to replace him.*

As the day slowly passed, Ragnall surprisingly succeeded in catching some fish. Despite his ability to end the lives of warriors who opposed him, his ability to do the same to fish had diminished over the years. As dusk descended his young brother Godfrith joined him and they shared some of his catch, roasted over his fire. Every opportunity he had, he took Godfrith under his wing and taught him everything he knew about the Viking way. They practised with axe, shield and sword. They constantly worked on the boy's archery too as Ragnall was determined to bring him on any future raids. It was true that Godfrith was still too weak to fight against grown men but back from the shield wall, his arrows could kill just as easily as Ragnall's axes. He taught the boy about how to handle a longboat, fix sails and gauge the wind and stars. Most importantly, he taught Godfrith how to conduct himself as a warrior of the Ui Imair. In quiet moments Ragnall couldn't help but think of Godfrith's twin brother Sihtric and how he was faring in the court of Flann Sinna.

*You take what you have the strength to keep. Your word is ironclad. You fight and die with no fear and should you fall, you will prepare yourself to meet Odin eye to eye.* These were the ways of the Ui Imair and indeed all Vikings; and that is what he taught Godfrith.

Their father Ivar had less and less time to teach Godfrith these ways and Ragnall felt responsible. At times, he was angry with his father as Ragnall felt that Ivar had made a litany of bad decisions. *He should never have got involved in the Saxon civil war, he should never have been so arrogant as to believe that the Irish would be docile and placated with a few marriages and he also should not have abandoned the siege of Anarawd's Kingdom in Wales.*

As dusk descended to darkness, a message was sent to Ragnall to attend his father, brothers, cousins and the other warriors of note in the main hall of the newly constructed longfort. His father would take the council of his senior men on what their next move would be. There was no need for Godfrith to appear due to his youth, and he left Ragnall to attend his father in the hall alone. When Ragnall arrived, he could see that his father had in fact dismissed all of the others apart from Ingamundr. *The decision has been made already,* Ragnall privately fumed, *yet another calamity no doubt.*

"Ragnall," his father addressed him, "I have a task for you to the south. I need you to go to Tamworth, the capital of Mercia. You are going to treat with Aethelfled and agree a peace."

Ragnall was disgusted. "Father, do you take me for some vizier or politician? I am a warrior of the Ui Imair. I take what I have the strength to keep."

Ivar allowed Ragnall's anger to wash over him. He looked exhausted, grey in the face and uncertain of himself.

"Ingamundr will have to do the same, Ragnall. He must treat with Cnut in Yorvik. We must have peace, Ragnall, at least temporarily. If the armies of Mercia or Northumbria march upon our new longforts in the next six months, it could be the end of the Ui Imair."

Ragnall was still not swayed by his father's appeal.

"What is to stop Aethelfled mounting my head on a spear when I appear? Ingamundr, you know that Cnut has betrayed our gods and follows the Christ too. You are as likely to have your head adorning a spear as I am!"

His cousin looked almost as dejected as Ragnall's father.

"Your father has it true in my opinion. We must have a peace. We must try."

His father interjected then. "I have asked the holy Gothi to prepare a sacrifice, a *blot* to Odin in your honour. We will appease the gods before you travel and will have their help on this matter." All Ragnall could do was agree.

\*

Three days later, the moon was full and the holy Gothi had all in readiness for the sacrifice. There was to be one slave each sacrificed in honour of both Ragnall and Ingamundr for their respective trips to the south and the east. A wooden and stone altar had been built and consecrated to Odin and the Gothi had prepared themselves, using magic herbs and mushrooms to help commune with the spirits that served the old gods. The two sacrifices had been carefully chosen to reflect what Ingamundr and Ragnall had to achieve. A Northumbrian priest, who was used usually to take care of livestock and who taught some of the children various languages and histories, was chosen as the sacrifice most meaningful to Ingamundr's journey east. A beautiful young Mercian female slave was chosen as the sacrifice deemed most appealing to the gods for Ragnall's cause. At the appointed hour, the Christian priest and the young woman were dragged in chains and subdued on the altar. The woman kicked and screamed her defiance while the priest just mumbled his own prayers to his Christ god. Ingamundr and Ragnall stepped forward from the crowd and knelt before the altar at the crescendo of the Gothi's chants to Odin. Two of the Gothi approached the two sacrifices while the other holy men held them down. Two ornate daggers were ever so calmly drawn across the throats of both sacrifices and they quickly bled out and died upon the altar. A wooden bowl was used to catch the blood of each and both Ingamundr and Ragnall ceremonially dipped their fingers into the lifeblood and marked their foreheads and chests. They each then took a drink of the sacrificial blood to link the fortune of their upcoming diplomatic missions to the will of Odin and his mighty pantheon.

Ivar Ivarsson, the king of the Ui Imair, stepped forward and gave his blessing to both Imgamundr and Ragnall, two of the mightiest warriors of the Ui Imair. He invoked Odin, Thor and Heimdall to bless their journey and bring peace to their people. Even Loki, the trickster god was acknowledged due to his skill in the sagas with the spoken word. Ragnall knew that they had done all they could; it was up to him now to strike a deal with probably the most powerful commander in the Saxon world – Aethelfled of Mercia.

Ragnall set out the next morning with no more than a small retinue of handpicked warriors, but he also insisted that his brother Godfrith accompany him south. That was the price he put forward to his father in exchange for his compliance. They could not risk the water, neither around the coast past the Welsh Kingdoms, nor down the Mersey. They simply crossed the river and went on foot, disguised as traders. It wouldn't do to appear at the court of Aethelfled in any way that could be construed as menacing.

The first couple of days went quietly with no difficulties. The weather was excellent and proved no obstacle to their six-man party as they made their way south. They stayed off the beaten track where possible and when they stopped for food and to sleep, they chose discreet locations, invisible to casual travellers on the road. The warriors that Ragnall took with him were not the Ui Imair's finest as both he and his father agreed that if Aethelfled elected to put the group to the sword for a lifetime of pillaging Mercia, it wouldn't damage the Ui Imair too much. He had a simple mandate: come to a non-aggression pact with Aethelfled whatever the cost. They reached her capital on the afternoon of the fourth day. They slipped in unnoticed through the gates of Tamworth with nary a glance from the guards on duty. Ragnall had been concerned that a group of Vikings would stand out like a sore thumb but straight away he could see bands of Danish traders from the Danelaw across Mercia's eastern border, plying their wares and giving their custom to the dozens of stalls that lined the streets. They fitted right in.

Tamworth, although large and with numerous stone walls and structures, was not even close to the size of Dublin and in five minutes they stood outside her main hall. Ragnall had been raiding in the Saxon lands since he was eleven years of age and knew their tongue very well. In hallowed antiquity the Saxons, Norse and Dane he knew, probably shared some common ancestor, the evidence being that many of the words for things were shared. He left one man back at an inn close to the gates in case the audience went catastrophically badly. He was a quirky young man by the name of Grimnir and his job was to get back to Ragnall's father immediately with the news of whatever outcome occurred here today, so his father could plan accordingly. Grimnir was also extremely quick and if push came to shove, Ragnall had confidence in him to get out of Tamworth and outrace any potential pursuers.

When Ragnall announced himself to the seneschal of Athelfled's court and requested an audience with the Queen, the man instantly summoned the guards and Ragnall and his men were searched for weapons. They had been wise enough to leave all their arms with Grimnir. They even searched Godfrith, who found it quite amusing, being a lad of all of ten years of age. *If they fear the likes of Godfrith perhaps we should look to give these Mercians battle,* Ragnall thought wickedly. When their time came to treat with the Queen, only Ragnall and Godfrith were granted entry to the main hall through the inner doors. The Queen sat on an elaborately carved throne with an austere young girl standing beside her and a small brown-haired young lad standing slightly back and behind her, *wards I assume,* thought Ragnall. Her court withdrew from the brothers giving them distance, and it pleased him to see that his presence caused them all a degree of discomfort when he was announced as Ragnall, a prince of the Ui Imair. An empty throne sat to the right of her own throne. Everybody knew that that throne would remain permanently empty as Athelfled's husband was in his dotage and his wits had scattered.

There was no doubt about who was in charge.

Ragnall stood smirking, awaiting the Queen's address. Godfrith stood still beside him, quiet and subdued in a room full of hostile people. The Queen stepped down off the dais and approached Ragnall. She was a tall and regal woman who carried an air of authority and confidence like a shroud. Ragnall could not help but be impressed. The Queen slowly circled around Ragnall as if weighing him up like a prized bull in the market. Having completed a circuit of him, she finally broke the silence. She spoke in Gaelic which caught Ragnall by surprise.

"Ragnall Ui Imair, the young warrior of the Norse-Gaels of Dublin. To what do I owe this pleasure?"

Before Ragnall could form a response she continued, making her question rhetorical.

"Could it be that for the first time in fifty years, it is your people that require a reprieve from mine?"

Ragnall did not answer. The Queen was speaking in a gentle and amicable tone, but he felt that he was on rotten ice here. One misplaced word or threat and Mercia would move north and destroy the Ui Imair and he and Godfrith's lives would be forfeit on the spot.

The Queen continued, "I have heard of you, Ragnall Ivarsson, the latest barbarian to be produced from that particular piratical line. Had my late father dealt with your heathen grandfather properly many years ago, we wouldn't be having this conversation at all, would we?"

Ragnall could not help but smirk again at that, but the Queen caught it from the corner of her eye and metamorphosed into the shrieking Valkyrie his father had warned him about.

"YOU INSOLENT CHILD," she screamed, "YOU DARE SMIRK AT ME IN MY OWN COURT? YOU ARE NOTHING BUT A SWAGGERING THUG AND I HAVE MASSACRED WHOLE ARMIES OF YOUR ILK. I SHOULD HANG YOU RIGHT NOW FOR THE CRIMES YOU YOURSELF HAVE COMMITTED AGAINST MY PEOPLE AND WAIT FOR YOUR FATHER TO GROVEL AT MY FEET."

She took an intake of breath and calmed herself and changed back into the regal queen that he had witnessed when he had first entered her hall. *I should never have smirked at her,* he thought ruefully.

"Ragnall Ui Imair, I will allow you one minute with which to speak. Say what your father has commanded you to say and offer and I will then decide whether or not to stretch your neck from the nearest hanging tree. Speak!"

Ragnall pondered what he would or should say, weighing up all the factors at play in his mind before committing himself to a course of action. Only the truth would suffice with a woman as formidable as Athelfled, he decided. *Odin, Loki, be with me here and now,* he prayed silently.

"Queen Aethelfled, my brother and I have come as envoys of peace. You no doubt have heard that we have been defeated in Dublin and in Wales, and in desperation we have had no option but to form a colony on the north bank of the Mersey River and on up the coast of Northumbria and Cumbria. We are officially in Northumbrian territory, but because of my father's respect for you and the greatness of your country, I have been sent to show our peaceful intent and that we at least nominally would be willing to pay you tribute in exchange for no aggression."

He could see that Aethelfled had anticipated what he had come to offer but he decided that it wouldn't do to allow her to believe that she could just walk over his father in any negotiation.

He continued, "We have been defeated, that is true. But the Irish caught us unaware in Dublin and the Welsh were able to withstand our siege. We have lost almost none of our military potency. I implore you, Queen Aethelfled, to accept my offer of peace. Should you come north with the Mercian army it is possible that you will defeat us and drive us off, but we will make you bleed. My brothers and cousins will not rest until they claim vengeance for your attack. If our negotiations fail here today, it could well mean the end of the line of Ivar the Boneless. But I swear to Odin that Mercia will burn alongside Ui Imair if you attempt to try us."

He had not intended to be so forceful as thousands of lives were at stake, but his pride was spiked, and his old flaw of intemperance came to the fore. On the other hand, he was glad to do away with intrigue and negotiation; his position, and by extension the entirety of the Ui Imair's position, was laid bare. The Queen said nothing momentarily but then laughed.

"You know, I am impressed, Ragnall son of Ivar. It is rare a man with a reputation such as yours actually lives up to it, but here you are with your striped hair and sheer strutting arrogance, dictating to me what will or will not happen. My nephew Aethelstan on the dais had predicted exactly what would happen here and what way you would act, Ragnall. But here it is. I accept your offer of peace on the following terms."

She paused for dramatic effect, but Ragnall inwardly was breathing a sigh of relief. The worst had passed. He had earned the peace that his father required.

"Every summer solstice, your father will deliver a tenth of all of your goods to my ealdorman at the town of Chester. You will not raid any of my land or the lands that my brother, Edward of Wessex, controls. And when I summon your father to battle, should I require it, he will martial his forces to fight under my banner. With these terms, I accept the presence of the Ui Imair on my northern border and swear never to wage war against them as long as they hold true to these terms. Are they acceptable to you, Ragnall Ivarsson?"

Ragnall nodded his ahead ruefully. "I accept." *My father Ivar and my cousin Ingamundr fighting for the Saxons? Never, but let her dream.*

# CHAPTER 3

# THE MASSACRE AT DUNKELD (904)

The fire roared in the hearth of Ivar Ivarsson's longfort and spread its tendrils of heat everywhere within its walls; still Ragnall Ui Imair felt cold. An intangible sense of foreboding and dread sent shivers up his spine that no fire could eradicate. Rows of benches sat on either side of his father's hall and all the senior captains of the Ui Imair sat supping ale and eating red meat off the bone. Ragnall and his cousin Ingamundr stood either side of his father, who himself sat on a wooden seat draped in wolf pelts. Below them stood Ragnall's fearsome young Norse uncle, the bane of the Francians, Geats and Danes alike; Erik Haraldsson, the Bloodaxe. He stood taller than any of the Ui Imair and his huge crest of red hair made him appear even bigger. His famous two-handed battleaxe was strapped to his back with a coil of leather and multiple knives and swords were attached to his person. He stood with arms folded and sported a conceited sneer etched across his features, but Ragnall could sense the rage and anger that always bubbled beneath the berserker's skin. Ragnall could see that all the men in the hall respected the Bloodaxe and rightly so, after all he had won multiple battles already despite being only nineteen years of age, the same age as Ragnall. He was the personification of murder, the absolute epitome of a

Viking Berserker. *My uncle will never die in his bed of old age,* thought Ragnall, *he will carve a bloody path across Midgard until he meets someone much like himself, and then he will fall.*

Ragnall had fought by Erik's side on multiple raids and in one or two pitched battles as well, but he could never bring himself to admire him like his father's other warriors did. The Bloodaxe was a butcher of men pure and simple. He was as mean as a rabid wolf and would go out of his way to inflict pain on enemy warriors and innocent bystanders alike; he cared not where the blood flowed from just as long as it flowed. The body count that Ragnall alone had witnessed the Bloodaxe reaping was astonishing. He went at the head of his father Harald Fairhair's armies, committing atrocity after atrocity in the name of the gods; Ragnall could not bring himself to admire that sort of appetite for destruction. Ragnall, Ingamundr and his father Ivar, fought for the betterment and protection of their people and their honour. They fought for wealth, land and respect whereas all the Bloodaxe wished to do was pile skulls at the feet of Odin. And now here he was in Cumbria, the deserted province of Northumbria that the Ui Imair now called home, at the hall of his father. The warriors packed into the hall were quiet and leaned forward in anticipation. The presence of a berserker prince like this in a longfort of the Ui Imair could only mean one thing, and that was war.

"Ivar, my father commands that you assist us in destroying the holy places of the Scots. The line of Cinead mac Alpin has stood in our path for too long and now he wants to end them. We seek vengeance for my brother. You must help us."

The Bloodaxe spat the words out as if they were a task in and of itself with little or no acknowledgment that he was addressing arguably the most powerful sea king of the Irish Sea.

"Let me remind you, Ivar, that you allowed a rabble of Irishmen to take your city and kill my sister and for that my father and I feel that you owe recompense to not just us, but to the gods as well."

Ragnall straightened, bristling at that remark, but his father gripped him by the arm in restraint and shot him a warning look. The insult was levelled in such a direct and unvarnished manner that Ragnall's blood began to boil and he couldn't help imagining what it would feel like to bury his axe in the Bloodaxe's face, uncle or no. His father defused the situation as best he could.

"Erik, your sister was my wife, the mother of my sons. We both loved her. Flann Sinna and his commanders will pay in blood, already one of his under-king's bones litter the plains of Meath, Mael Finnia mac Flannacain."

The Bloodaxe laughed in contempt. "Not by your hand though, Ivar. Was it? And now we hear that one of your own sons stands at the right hand of the Ui Neill king, learning from him, and that he even held Flann Sinna's standard at the battle of Kells, where the High King defeated his own son Donnchadh Donn. How can a son of the Ui Imair fight beside the very king who took his city and disgraced his father? I know why, because you and all your kin are mongrels and half-breeds bred in with Irish scum. My father wasted his time trying to breed some nobility back into your ragged line by marrying my sister to you!"

At that the hall erupted in anger. Ragnall could bear it no longer and leapt from the dais to face the Bloodaxe.

"COME FACE ME, ERIK," he screamed, "AND BE READY TO MEET ODIN LONG BEFORE YOU INTENDED."

The Bloodaxe laughed. "If you try and face me, Ragnall, I will pluck out your heart and eat it."

The Bloodaxe's own few retainers had weapons drawn now also to meet the Ui Imair Vikings in the hall, most of whom had some Irish heritage in their lineage.

Ingamundr stepped forward before the assembly dissolved into violence and bellowed, "SHEATHE YOUR WEAPONS!"

The anger slowly drained from the room and every warrior retreated to their seat or place of standing stiffly, in unresolved outrage, but they fell in as commanded none the less. Ivar spoke again.

"Be calm, Erik Bloodaxe. We know you are a formidable warrior and you feel the loss of my wife as do my sons and I."

*Very clever,* thought Ragnall, *he placates this brute with compliments while appealing to whatever little reason he may possess.*

"It is true that we were driven out of Dublin, Erik, but it was through treachery and not in open battle. We were never defeated in the field. At any time, I could launch, assault and retake Dublin, but Flann Sinna and some of the savages under his command, like Fogartach mac Tolarg or Augaire mac Aililla, would butcher our innocent people. Surely in your wisdom you can understand that, Erik?"

Ragnall could see that at least some of these words were beginning to register in the blood-soaked mind of the Bloodaxe.

His father continued, "I thank you for news of my son though, Erik. I have fought on the side of Flann Sinna before, many years ago. Although he is an opportunistic and ambitious politician, he would never resort to outright murder at a whim and he is related to Sihtric by blood. My son will learn from his side, of that there can be no doubt, and I can only pray to Odin and Thor that he remembers that he is Viking and not Irish. For now, it is out of my control."

Erik nodded at that in sage agreement. Despite being a murderer, Ragnall knew that Erik believed that he always did the work of the gods and to hear the pantheon invoked by his father would have no doubt pleased the Bloodaxe.

Ivar leaned forward in his chair conspiratorially, "In fact, Erik, when the time comes, I hope that you would join us and help us reclaim Dublin for the Viking world?"

Mollified, the savage Norse prince finally remembered where he was. "It would be my honour as a Viking to help the Ui Imair retake Dublin from the Irish, I will bathe my axe in Irish blood." He slammed his fist into his chest, his giant red-haired crest shivering with the blow.

"Erik, tell us of your and your father's plan to defeat the Scottish. What does King Harald intend and what would he have of the Ui Imair?"

At length the Bloodaxe went into detail on the proposed attack. On the first full moon after Easter Sunday, the combined forces of the Norse and the Ui Imair would invade Scotland unannounced. The Bloodaxe would lead a force to the ancient fort of Scone. He would consecrate the stone of destiny to the Norse pantheon with a sacrifice, the stone where Cinead mac Alpin and both of his grandsons had officially been crowned by the Christian faith. He would then taunt King Constantine to emerge from Dunkeld, ten miles to the north on the River Tay, and draw out his forces. When this Scottish army came to meet the Bloodaxe on land, the Ui Imair would sweep in and take the town of Dunkeld itself from the river, take the precious Christian artefacts belonging to St Columba and put the town to the torch. Both the Norse and Ui Imair would ensure that any nobles encountered were to be put to death, especially Constantine, his wife, the Irishman Glundub and any under-kings present. The rest of the people could be enslaved or dealt with in any way Ivar saw fit as compensation for taking part in the assault. Any spoils taken would be the property of Ivar's Vikings as well. The plan was a simple one and after several moments Ivar of the Ui Imair accepted his part in the plan and the celebrations began. The Norwegians and the Ui Imair would join forces once more to attempt to end the Scots, once and for all.

Later that night, long after Erik Bloodaxe and his retainers had left the hall, Ragnall raised his concerns about the attack with his father and his cousin Ingamundr.

"Father, cousin, this is effectively the same trick we used to defeat Constantine's predecessor, Domnall Dasachtach, the mad. I have a suspicion that it will not work again. Constantine mac Aed is by all accounts a far shrewder king than Domnall was. If he doesn't take the bait or anticipates what the Bloodaxe intends, we could be caught beneath the walls of Dunkeld and slaughtered."

Ingamundr looked perturbed by the suggestion, but his father disagreed.

"Ragnall, even if you are right, what do you suggest we do? We cannot defy the King of Norway or we could soon find ourselves facing his armies across the battlefield instead of Constantine's. We do not possess the military might to face Harald and his son in battle. Even if this plan was folly, we must do our best to execute it. We will make sure that we have routes of escape from Dunkeld if we are outmanoeuvred or overwhelmed. That I swear, son."

Ingamundr was, surprisingly, next to try and dissuade the King.

"Uncle, we have two sound offers on the table to fight for coin. Valid excuses for fending off King Harald and the Bloodaxe. Luitpold the Bavarian and Louis the Child are assembling a massive force of Germans to take on the Hungarians under Arpad, upon the Danube. We would take thousands of slaves and many treasures for easy work, cutting apart steppe riders as they tried to cross the river. We would be enriching our people for little risk while having a valid excuse for not fighting with the Bloodaxe against Constantine or his general, the Drengr, Niall Glundub of the Ui Neill."

The King looked disconcerted by the suggestion, but Ragnall could see that he was at least mentally considering it.

Ingamundr spoke on. "Amir Ibn Hafsun, the Vizier of the Ummayad Caliphate, a good customer of Ragnall's, has proposed another alliance for us to consider. He has indirectly received word of the impending invasion of the city of Thessalonica by the Abbasid warlord, Leo of Tripoli. The Abbasids will pay any captain his weight in silver and a slave for each man in his crew, to help ferry their Saracen warriors onto Byzantine land. Uncle, we would not even have to fight and we would still be as rich as the black-skinned men of the Aifric!"

Ivar sat back in his chair and weighed up the suggestions while Ragnall and Ingamundr waited upon his decision. After several moments he answered his son and nephew.

"You are both right of course, but the bigger picture must be considered. If we did not fight with the Bloodaxe after he has come himself to this hall, there is nothing surer than that he would come here with his father's forces next. It is rumoured that they command almost a thousand longboats. If we do not do this thing, the Bloodaxe will come for us. He will blood eagle every single one of our family down to the smallest child and enslave or murder everybody else. He would then invade Dublin and burn the city to the ground out of spite. I wouldn't put it past him to attack the lands of the Southern Ui Neill and put Flann Sinna to the sword, just so he can kill Sihtric, a twelve-year-old boy."

Ivar shook his head. "No, we must do what is best for our people, irrespective of the opportunities in the Mediterranean and on the Danube. We will fight for the Bloodaxe and sack and burn the town of Dunkeld." *Or die in the attempt,* thought Ragnall.

*

It took three weeks for the Ui Imair to assemble all the warriors required and have them fitted out for the journey around the entire island of Britain. Ivar had decided that the Ui Imair would send two thousand warriors north around Scotland to meet with the equal-sized fleet of the Bloodaxe. They were to meet before Easter Sunday on a small island off the coast of Moray and from there; they would begin their approach up the estuary of the River Tay toward Scone and Dunkeld. Both settlements sat on the River Tay but the river itself meandered in a huge bow to the northeast of Scone. It was hoped that when the Bloodaxe announced his presence to the Scots by taking the fort at Scone, Constantine's army would march south across land to scatter the forces of the Norse prince, by the shortest route. That would allow the Ui Imair to sweep in from the river behind them and hit Dunkeld by surprise.

The Ui Imair army would be made up mostly of older warriors, especially ones with sons to replace them. The younger warriors, the next generation, would be left behind under the command of Ragnall's cousin Gunnar, son of Ivar's brother Sichtfridth who was killed years ago in the Dublin civil wars. Ivar would lead the Ui Imair with his sons Amlaib, Ivar the younger and of course Ragnall himself. Their cousins Ingamundr and Garangr would also set sail and command sections of the fleet. Garangr would be given the responsibility of holding the rearguard and protecting the ships on the river. Ragnall had persuaded his father to allow Godfrith to at least accompany Garangr on the boats with his bow, as it would prove valuable experience for the young Viking. Ivar had agreed and Godfrith was brought. It would be his first battle at twelve years of age, the same age that Ragnall had been on his first raid.

The weather was windy and wet on the way north around Scotland. They had to sail out of sight of land off the Strathclyde coast, so their fleet was not spotted and their presence was not relayed to Constantine, inland at Dunkeld.

They only encountered two fishing skiffs on the sea, both of which they scuttled, and their crews were put to the sword. A week into their voyage, they made the mistake of stopping on an uninhabited island to gather fresh water and meat, but it was unfortunately not as uninhabited as they first thought. A handful of Norse-Gael Scots had spotted them and sprinted away, back toward the far side of the island. Ivar had sent men to chase but the runners had horses and escaped their Ui Imair pursuers easily. They were still several days away from the island off the coast of Moray and time was of the essence. Ragnall's father had weighed it up and deemed it unlikely that word would get back to Dunkeld by the time the town was already under attack if the gods were good, and it was likely that these humble fishermen or whoever they were perhaps would believe that this fleet was attacking somewhere further north and had no intention to circle the island and then sail south to Moray.

On finally reaching the North Sea, the Ui Imair fleet discarded the need for sailing out of sight of land and simply followed the coast southward as the chances of news outrunning their fleet approaching would be negligible before they landed at Dunkeld. On the morning of Easter Sunday, they anchored off the nominated spit of rock, several miles off the coast of Moray, and joined the waiting fleet of the Bloodaxe. The Ui Imair fleet was composed of fifty ships, the Bloodaxe's Norse fleet was of similar size.

In the afternoon, the Norse longboats led out and the fleet sailed down the coastline. By morning of the next day, the Norse and Ui Imair parted ways as the Bloodaxe's many ships landed on a large cove near Scone and disgorged their complement of warriors onto land. Ivar's fleet continued north upon the river for another ten miles, following the loop of the stream. Ragnall's father sent out two scouts on foot whose job it was to report on the Scottish forces as they marched south to meet the Bloodaxe. Once the Scots had been marked, the Ui Imair would row and sail up the river as if Jormungand the World Serpent himself was in pursuit of them. Ragnall didn't like the way the attack was preceding at all. There were too many variables for him. How many soldiers would Constantine have at his disposal? Who was in command of the Scottish forces at the town? None of the Ui Imair had ever set foot in Dunkeld either and they did not know the layout. What if the Bloodaxe should somehow lose and the Scottish victors cut the Ui Imair off from the sea? They were too far committed now, Ragnall knew, there would be no turning back. The Ui Imair fleet lay idle for two whole days until finally the scouts returned. Constantine was marching south in some force to face the Bloodaxe. It was time.

*

Upon landing on the sandy beach and the dock at Dunkeld, Ragnall felt that nagging sense of dread that he had endured when Erik had first broached this plan to his father. The people had long deserted the outlying homesteads that sprawled between the river and the walls of the town. The absence of people was not really what bothered Ragnall – but the fact that anything of value had also been removed from sight, brought back within the walls or otherwise hidden, was alarmingly noteworthy. It was as if the attack was fully expected. It made sense that the King would have removed his small folk back inside his walls on word of the Bloodaxe's arrival, but the town here at Dunkeld was ominously quiet. Fifteen hundred Vikings had approached the town while five hundred were left to guard the ships under the command of Garangr. Godfrith was safely ensconced amongst Garangr's command to keep the boy safe. On approaching the walls of the town, Ragnall saw that the ground before the walls of Dunkeld was completely cleared of obstacles. There was no cover available for Ivar's men to approach under, turning the land before Dunkeld into a murderous gauntlet. Even several hundred feet distant, it was apparent that the twenty-feet-tall walls were crowded with archers and warriors, far more numerous than was optimal in Ragnall's eyes.

Braziers were lit every thirty feet on the parapet and the wooden gate that stood in the entrance arch looked as formidable as any Ragnall had ever seen in his short life, a brutal thing of spiked metal and savagery. To storm this fortress, Ragnall knew at once, would cost hundreds of lives at the least. Orders were issued to the ranks and they formed up tightly, ready to deploy the shield wall. A party of fifty men were kept back guarding several thick tree trunks that would serve as rams when the time came. Sixty feet from the gates, the arrows began to rain down upon the Vikings. No men were killed in the initial volleys, but several were wounded, being hit on the arm or thigh. The scouts that his father had sent around the walls confirmed the worst; the entire fortress, and it was a fortress, was defended heavily by archers and warriors armed with rocks and other missiles.

Ivar eventually ordered his men forward. Under the cover of their shields the Ui Imair approached the fearsome gates of Dunkeld and the rams were carried amongst the ranks to the front, obscured from the men on the wall. The archers were told to remain in pairs at the back with a shield bearer and given orders to keep the Scottish archer's heads down on the parapet. All Ragnall himself could do was keep his own head down and his shield overhead, as he was positioned in the thick of the throng of Vikings. All he could hear, see or smell were the men beside him. He could vaguely discern the boom of the first wooden ram as it smashed into the wooden doors and the clang of rocks and other objects bouncing from Viking shields. Now and again, a scream or curse of a Viking warrior being hit from above or a Scottish defender falling to his death alleviated the monotony, but other than that all Ragnall could focus upon was preserving himself from damage from above, while waiting for the gates to yield.

Suddenly a strange horn was sounded to the west of the gates and was answered to the east as well, back toward the river. Ragnall did not think anything of it. He was well within the ranks with his shield raised and even if he wanted to take a look he couldn't. Soon after, worrying noises began to supplant what was happening at the gate, the occasional scream and the rising burble of chatter and confusion amongst the ranks. Eventually he found himself being jostled as the ranks astonishingly broke apart fully, in a shocking development. He was exposed. In moments, the entire Ui Imair host was breaking. Ragnall desperately searched around for his father, but he was nowhere to be seen. What was occurring quickly revealed itself in all of its horror to Ragnall. Not one but two different smaller armies of Scotsmen had come upon the Ui Imair underneath the walls of the town. One faction had emerged from the trees to the northeast while another force had come from the south. The southern element of the Scottish forces looked battered, but they still numbered close to a thousand men, *the remnants of the host that met Erik Bloodaxe at Scone,* Ragnall realised in alarm.

A cry of shocked surprise rose from the warriors between Ragnall and the gates of Dunkeld. In the confusion he had not noticed that arrow fall had ceased from the walls and the garrison had sallied out from the gates at sight of the Vikings' retreat. A roaring monster with two swords led them from the front and began cutting down fleeing Vikings at will. The Ui Imair were attacked from three sides. Ragnall shouted for the men around him to form up into a shield wall but it was useless, the Scottish were amongst them in a disordered brawl. As all the men broke around him, Ragnall could only do the same and sprint for the longboats.

The mile long race to the boats was the most chaotic thing Ragnall Ui Imair had ever endured in his young life. The butchery on either side was phenomenal, the small wooden houses that lined the pathways down to the Vikings ships turning into little islands of calm in a sea of violence. Groups of Vikings turned in twos and threes to face the howling mob of Scottish warriors as they rolled down the slope toward the river in pursuit of the Vikings, but all were quickly overwhelmed and slaughtered. With two hundred feet to go, Ragnall could see that his cousin Garangr had used his initiative and formed a four-hundred-man shield wall and arrayed the archers behind it ready to unleash arrows at the Scottish pursuers. Ragnall sprinted for all he was worth. To stop and turn was to die as the Scottish tidal wave flooded through the houses and street ways. The three Scottish hosts, from the south, northeast and the town itself, had combined into one ungainly horde now and the Vikings were being scythed down like wheat. Finally, Ragnall made it to his cousin's shield wall and passed through it. Before he collapsed onto the muddy ground in exhaustion, he roared at the archers to release their arrows.

"LOOOOOSSEEEEE."

The archers unleashed death on the Scottish warriors just as they smashed into Garangr's shield wall. The noise was deafening as sword met axe. Despite the Viking shield wall being badly outnumbered, they held firm before the

Scotsmen's charge. Ragnall, while gulping in air, looked around in despair at the remnants of the failed assault on Dunkeld. Perhaps half of the Vikings had survived the rout and made it back past Garangr's shield wall. Once the other Vikings who had survived the retreat gathered their breath, they joined Garangr's men and added their weight to the fight with the Scots. Ragnall went looking for his brothers and father. He spotted Godfrith with the archers, loosing arrow after arrow over the heads of the shield wall and into the Scots. At this range, with the density of the battle on front of them, it was almost impossible to miss and Ragnall thought grimly that the Viking archers would be reaping a heavy toll on the vengeful Scots. He saw his cousin Ingamundr, who had taken control of the Viking forces from Garangr, barking commands and directing his remaining forces where they were most required; either to strengthen the shield wall replacing fallen warriors, or to reinforce the flanks so that the Scots could not get round the side of the Vikings and surround them. *If the Scots envelop us we will be massacred,* thought Ragnall worriedly. He could not see his other brothers, Ivar the Younger or Amlaib. His father was nowhere to be seen yet either. Ragnall, once he had gathered his own breath, waded into the shield wall and immersed himself in the butchery of the fight. He lost himself in the moment and the joy of battle.

Slash, hack, parry, stab; on and on and on.

Eventually, the shouts and the pressure of battle eased and in the space of a few moments the Scots had disengaged back a hundred feet away from the shield wall and from the horrendous toll the Viking archers had taken upon their numbers. Hundreds of corpses littered the ground between the two forces and dozens lay groaning and dying noisily, searching for severed limbs or grossly trying to stuff intestines back into savage stomach wounds. The slaughter had been immense.

The Viking archers had stopped shooting as they were well out of range of the Scots. At that moment, the monstrous two-handed swordsman that had led the sortie from Dunkeld stepped forward with a wounded captive ahead of the thousands of remaining Scottish soldiers. Ragnall's heart sank when he saw who the captive was that was being dragged before the Ui Imair. It was Ivar

Ivarsson, his father. He had lost an arm below the elbow, was barely conscious and pale from blood loss. The giant warrior forced Ivar to his knees before him. He pointed one bloodied sword down the hill toward the Ui Imair forces for several seconds before taking a step back and sending his second sword whistling through the air. All it took was a single blow to take the head of the last surviving son of Ivar the Boneless. Ragnall, enraged by the death of his father, made himself ready to charge back up the hill to cut down this dual-armed fiend, but Ingamundr roared, "STAY YOUR HANDS, VIKINGS OF DUBLIN!"

Silence reigned across the battlefield as the head of the King of the Ui Imair rolled and bobbled grotesquely on its way down toward the Viking forces. It came to rest in the churned-up mud twenty feet from the shield wall in a lake of blood and offal. A victory cry went up from the Scots.

"Glundub! Glundub! Glundub!"

*The day is lost,* thought Ragnall. Ingamundr ordered a careful retreat to the boats under the cover of the archers lest the Scots tried to attack them, but it never came to pass. The Ui Imair fled back down the River Tay as quickly as their boats could sail. Out in the safety of the North Sea the grievous tally was tabulated of Ui Imair dead. Almost five hundred men had died before the walls of Dunkeld, smashed by the forces of Constantine and his pet Irish warlord, Glundub the *Drengr*.

The Bloodaxe's forces had been victorious against the initial army sent south by Constantine to relieve Scone, but he had allowed a significant faction to retreat unscathed back to Dunkeld. It was this force that had effectively broken the Ui Imair. The Scots, predicting some sort of deception as Ragnall had feared, had kept a force in reserve outside of the walls of their capital, hidden in the trees. The fishermen they had failed to catch on the Kingdom of the Western Isles a week previously, had most likely warned Constantine of their approach. Ragnall's brothers Amlaib and Ivar the Younger never returned from the walls of Dunkeld, the retreat was too panicked to retrieve the corpses of the slain and their fate was unknown, but they were presumed slain. Most likely they would be burned as heathens by the Christian clergymen of the Scots, unknown and unremembered for all time.

It was not their deaths that saddened Ragnall as Vikings longed for death in battle, but the fact that they would gain no renown now having been cut down in a massacre beneath the walls of Dunkeld. Ragnall's cousin Erik, the last son of his uncle Amlaib, another son of the Boneless, was also cut down in the retreat. The most grievous blow of all though was the death of Ragnall's father, executed by the ruthless prince of the Northern Ui Neill, Niall Glundub. Either Ragnall himself or Ingamundr would have to lead the Ui Imair now, to protect and rule the people. *The single worst day in the history of the Ui Imair,* Ragnall thought. *Can it get any worse than this?*

# CHAPTER 4

# THE BETRAYAL AT CHESTER
# (907)

The prow of Ragnall's ship smashed through the waves of the Irish Sea, scything through the water like a knife through butter. He had not lost a single ship on his latest voyage south and his holds were packed with all sorts of luxurious goods from Francia, Al Andalus and further afield. He had spent the autumn of 906 fighting for the Warlord Rollo the Walker on the Seine in the ceaseless civil wars there as the various Francish nobles fought like dogs over the remnants of Charlemagne's great domain. There was always work available for Viking war bands such as Ragnall's in the waterways of Europe. They had taken slaves and plunder there and sailed south during the winter toward the great Caliphate and offloaded much of their cargo in exchange for golden dirham and spices from the Mediterranean. The remainder of their slaves were offloaded to the Berbers of North Africa in exchange for great golden and silver nuggets the size of clenched fists. His fleet saw out the worst of late winter and early spring in a small Viking settlement roughly affiliated with the Ui Imair, off the coast of Cornwall. Once spring had arrived properly and the Thunder God had taken his foot completely from the throat of all seafaring people, Ragnall and his thirty ships had resumed their trek north to Ingamundr's new base on the estuary of the River Ribble.

Ingamundr had assumed the position of de facto ruler of the Ui Imair, with Ragnall serving as his general, admiral and advisor on all military matters. Ingamundr ruled from his newest longfort on the banks of the Ribble away from Queen Aethelfled's influence, while the job of raiding, fighting and trade negotiation fell under Ragnall's remit. It suited Ragnall's nature. He was ever restless and drawn to the sea, as were the core of his young warriors. His many successes had drawn the youngest Viking generation to him and every battle season they flocked to Ragnall's banners immediately upon receiving their arm rings, their rite of passage, from Ingamundr. It was not just the youth of the Ui Imair who followed him: young warriors came to Cumbria from all over the Viking world to fight for him. Fighters from the Danelaw, Northumbria, the Western Isles of Scotland and even the Viking towns at Mann, Linn and Limerick, flocked to him.

Godfrith his younger brother sailed everywhere that Ragnall went. At fourteen years of age Godfrith was the size of a regular eighteen-year-old and his arms and legs were corded with muscle. He had slain his first man in hand-to-hand combat during this battle season when he split the head of an Asturias man-at-arms, on a raid in the north of Al Andalus. The death of Lubb Ibn Muhammad the Umayyad general had turned the north of Al Andalus into a maelstrom of war and there were many easy targets for Ragnall and his forces to plunder. There had been a few setbacks over the years such as the exodus from Dublin and the defeat to the Scots at Dunkeld, but the Ui Imair had returned to their former strength and even the most conservative of Ingamundr's retainers were looking back confidently to Ireland with ambitious eyes.

Word had reached the halls of the Ui Imair of the chaos occurring in Ireland. Flann Sinna, despite his advanced years, campaigned every summer, proving his strength to his under-kings and reinforcing his will. In 905, he had subdued the Leinster men under Faelan mac Muiredaig and Ragnall's own brother-in-law Augaire mac Aililla, who had the temerity to request support from Ingamundr and his Vikings. Ingamundr had laughed the Leinster prince out of the hall considering the treachery that he had committed in Dublin in

902. In the previous year, Flann Sinna had laid waste to the North of the lands of Munster in an attempt to goad the Eoghanachta into battle, and even forced tribute from the Viking port at Limerick. A familiar young Norse-Gael man by the name of Sihtric was gaining repute as a warrior and executioner at the side of the old High King, and despite the anger Ragnall and Ingamundr felt at Sihtric's capture, they could not help but feel pride too. Their brother and cousin, an incredible young warrior of the Ui Imair, was carving a bloody path through the Irish despite serving at the side of their enemy Flann Sinna. Even in this, Sihtric was doing them all honour. Stranger news had emerged from the North of Ireland too. The only living son and heir of Domnall mac Aed, the King of the Northern Ui Neill, had taken an arrow in a border dispute with the men of Connaught and had been killed instantly. The under-kings of the north had forced Domnall to reach out to his estranged brother, the warlord Niall Glundub, to return from Scotland to become his heir. Civil war had almost broken out amongst them immediately but the leaders of the Cenel nEoghain, the chief tribe of the Northern Ui Neill, had interceded. Every time Ragnall heard the name of Niall Glundub he swore to the gods that he would slay him in vengeance for the death of his father on that faithful day three years previously.

On the approach down the Ribble estuary, Ragnall saw that the artificial harbour and the north bank of the river were packed with longboats and other ships. There were hundreds of people plying their trade and going about their day peacefully and Ragnall sensed that there was no threat. *What has happened while I was away?* he wondered. Godfrith pointed out a few unusual flags and sails on several of the longboats that intrigued Ragnall. Something big was afoot and Ragnall knew that whatever it was, he wanted to be a part of it. When Ragnall's ship docked, he left the coordination of the fleet coming ashore to Godfrith and instructed a few of his captains to take the plunder to the storeroom at the back of Ingamundr's hall. The closer he got to the main hall the more raucous the noise became. The crowd was so large that many Vikings were spilling outside the hall, tankards and horns of ale in hand. Ragnall was shocked to see groups of boisterous Irishmen, discernible by their accent and looks, loitering around the hall as well. It was not unusual for foreign traders to dock at Viking longforts and villages all along the Cumbrian and Northumbrian coast, but the Irish were infrequent guests due to the current political climate.

A quick glance inside the cavernous hall revealed to Ragnall that Ingamundr had not yet appeared on the dais, or his cousins Garangr or Gunnar. He quietly made his way around to the back of the hall to the rear exit that led to Ingamundr's living quarters. He slipped in to find his three cousins in deep discussion. All three turned at the noise of the door closing, and they each reached to embrace him.

"It's great to see you, Ragnall," said Ingamundr and he kissed him on the forehead.

"How were the raids, cousin?" asked Garangr.

"The best raids we have had for years, I have sacks full of spices, gold and Muslim money. I even have a few choice slaves for your household, Ingamundr. Godfrith and my lads are docking and will carry the loot in for you within the hour." Gunnar clapped him on the shoulder and rubbed his hands in glee.

Ragnall looked inquisitively at Ingamundr. "What is happening here? The hall is packed awaiting you. Something is up, cousin, tell me so that I can at least pretend I knew the plan." He laughed. When his three cousins did not laugh with him, he knew that something was wrong.

"Sit down here, Ragnall," Ingamundr asked while Garangr got a chair for each of them. "I will fill you in on all that has transpired in the last six months while you were raiding."

His cousin then outlined what had occurred in detail to Ragnall and it wasn't good. The Ui Imair had been called to fight on behalf of Queen Aethelfled of Mercia in the autumn against the Welsh. The campaign involved very little fighting and was purely a minor border dispute between Anarawd ap Rhodri and the Mercians. Aethelfled had kept all the plunder they had won in the fighting and in an even crueller twist, had used this newfound wealth to reinforce the burh at Chester, the old Roman fort that stood on the border between Mercia and Ingamundr's newly forged Kingdom. Building was nearly complete and now it stood menacingly within a day's march of many of Ingamundr's villages and longforts, a stark reminder that the Ui Imair were never safe with Aethelfled on their border and only existed at her whim.

After the Christmas festival, the newly installed Ealdorman of Chester, a worm named Ceolred, had appeared in Ingamundr's hall and demanded a tripling of the tribute required by Aethelfled to ensure peace between the Ui Imair and Mercia. He claimed that the Queen required money and food to sustain her wars to the east with the Five Boroughs of the Danelaw. His last demand was even more onerous. The Queen requested that one in every three boys that came of age annually must report to Tamworth to be conscripted and trained in the fyrd of Mercia. Ingamundr had ruefully admitted to stepping down off his dais, disembowelling the Ealdorman and feeding him his bloody intestines as he died. Garangr had unhelpfully interrupted the tale at that point to mention that Ceolred had choked to death on his own bowls long before the stomach wound killed him. Ingamundr had immediately sent envoys that very night to kingdoms that could be potentially friendly to his cause in search of alliance, as war was now a certainty.

The first warriors to answer the call were Viking warriors from the Danelaw and as far away as Francia, the most famous of whom was a former compatriot of their grandfather, Brunbolg the Headtaker. Brunbolg had allegedly been a victim of politics in Francia. Rollo the Walker had exiled the giant Viking as Brunbolg had raped an aunt of Charles the Simple, the King of West Francia, and sold a royal cousin into slavery to the Caliphate of Cordoba. Rollo was pushing for political recognition from the Lords of Francia, but a man like Brunbolg at his side only created enmity and suspicion; and now the giant found himself here, once more serving the Ui Imair. For Brunbolg, it was either flee or swing from a noose to placate the Francians, to further Rollo's cause. The choice was simple. Some of the other figures that Ingamundr named present outside in the hall were just as surprising to Ragnall.

The three brothers who now controlled Yorvik and most of Northumbria, had agreed to an alliance: Ingvarr, Eowils and Halfdan. For years they had been battling the Mercians for land and influence in the Danelaw and had never moved against the Ui Imair. To seal the pact, Ingamundr had agreed on a marriage alliance between Godfrith and Ingvarr's eldest daughter Olga. Ragnall and his three cousins had laughed at that and joked about who was going to tell the young Viking what had been agreed on his behalf. The last two allies were the most puzzling to Ragnall. Two Irish noblemen had sailed across from Leinster to offer allegiance in exchange for possible alliance in the internecine conflicts in Ireland. They were of course Faelan mac Muiredaig, a King of Leinster, and the prince of the Ui Dunlainge, Augaire mac Aililla. Ragnall had recoiled at this news. He had never forgotten the smug and arrogant sneer his brother-in-law had worn on the docks of Dublin five years ago when Flann Sinna had taken the city and banished the Ui Imair. His father Ivar had given this treacherous snake Ragnall's sister in marriage and he had been repaid only with villainy and malice.

When they had finished, Ragnall sat back and exhaled a breath. A lot had happened in just a few months, but in a way he was glad, as it had quietly irked Ragnall for years having to bend the knee to Aethelfled. Her demands were unconscionable and would require answering the Viking way and Ragnall looked forward to reminding the Mercian queen that the Ui Imair would never be slaves to her will nor subjects of her ever-growing kingdom. There was no way out apart from violence, Ingamundr had ensured that when he had choked the ealdorman Ceolred with his own intestines. All Ragnall could do was shrug his shoulders and smile as he joined his three cousins out in the main hall as Ingamundr addressed his allies and captains.

Garangr quieted the hall with three blows from the handle of his axe on the floor. The noise and banter subsided and Ingamundr addressed the entire room.

"I, Ingamundr, the Lord of the Ui Imair, will lead an attack upon Mercia. We can accept the tyranny of Aethelfled no more."

A huge roar erupted from the crowd and Ragnall could even see dislodged motes of dust floating down from the thatch due to the volume.

"The witch of Mercia has presumed too much and for this she must answer. She has tried to tax us into starvation, she wants to make slaves of our young men and boys, and she wants to send them back against our own kinsmen in the Danelaw. Are we going to stand for this?" he asked the crowd.

A roar of "NNOOOOOO!" echoed around the walls.

"Our brothers from Yorvik, Ingvarr, Eowils and Halfdan, have contended with the will of Mercia for many years and now with a betrothal of marriage of Ingvarr's daughter Olga and my cousin Godfrith, we are bound in blood to the same fate."

The men of Yorvik cheered, pounding axe to shield and raising horns of ale in toast.

"To you Warlords of Francia, Fresia, Denmark, Norway and the Western Isles of Scotland, I say to you – come with me and give the Mercians battle and I swear to you that you will have all of the wealth of the Saxons, and if you fall, I will give you a death in battle worthy of notice by the Valkyries!"

A cacophonous shout arose from all corners of the hall at Ingamundr's promise. *He has won them all over,* thought Ragnall.

"To my Irish friends from the Kingdom of Leinster; we have opposed each other and been at odds over the years." This statement was met with silence and a few *ayes* from the crowd of both Viking and Irish attendees in the hall. "But let bygones be bygones. Let us forge an alliance anew against a more dangerous power for our mutual security, and I swear you shall have the eternal gratitude and potential alliance of the Ui Imair!"

The Irish in the crowd roared their approval. Ragnall noticed that Faelan mac Muiredaig had raised his ale in acknowledgement to the hall, but Augaire mac Aililla had mutely stood, head down with arms folded. *I will need to watch him,* Ragnall decided, *with friends like him, who needs enemies? Never trust an Irishman.*

"On the fortnight, we will set sail before Aethelfled has time to call her banners. With luck, word has not reached her yet of the death of her ealdorman, nor our intentions. If we can take Chester, we will destroy her power in the north of Mercia for good."

Another rapturous cheer raised the rafters at that proclamation.

"Brunbolg," and the giant Viking stepped forward upon being addressed, "you will lead our forces from the land to the north."

The monstrous Viking punched his chest with his ham-sized fist in obedience.

"Faelan mac Muiredaig, you will land your men at the bridge that joins the burh with Mercia across the River Dee. You will hold this bridge against reinforcement from Mercia when Aethelfled raises her levies. Your kinsman Augaire mac Aililla, you have said, will sail back across the sea briefly to gather more men to supplement the four hundred you have with you and will meet us on the full moon."

The two Irishmen nodded and Augaire immediately turned and left the hall. Ragnall could not help but be suspicious of the Ui Dunlainge prince and gazed after him wonderingly as he left. *We are trusting this snake with too much.*

"My cousins and I will assault the burh directly and take it. I will not risk your lives unnecessarily and as it was I who started this fight, the Ui Imair will take the brunt of their military might. But know this, we are men of honour and we will share the spoils of victory fairly!"

The entire room roared in a deafening shout of exultation.

"Now let us seal our alliance with a night of celebration!"

Ragnall's heart rose at the sight of all these men ready for battle and walked out to find his brother Godfrith to console him. *He has been engaged to be married after all,* laughed Ragnall.

*

It took two weeks for Ingamundr's fleet to set sail, but they made great time once on the water. In a single day they had landed on the shore of the fortress of Chester upon the River Dee. Ragnall was instantly dismayed to find that somehow word of their arrival had reached the Mercians as the burh was already heavily fortified and manned. The massive stone walls were roughly two miles in circumference, twenty feet tall and even thirty feet in height in places. At each corner stood sturdily erected buttresses with murder holes and crenellations for archers to hide behind and loose arrows upon their foes. The front gate was wooden and some of the walls that sat around it were made of timber as well, enormously thick but still not as robust as stone. It was the only bit of good news that Ragnall could grasp on his first view of the Mercians' formidable defences. The stone works had obviously not been completed in time. The wooden front gate was constructed with an internal secondary wall inside the first with walkways which then linked with the existing masonry on either side. *It will be death to storm that citadel,* thought Ragnall worriedly, *but we may have no choice.*

The boats carrying the Vikings up the River Dee were pulled up on the bank on the north side of the River and the Viking host began making this temporary site defensible, with wooden stakes and traps. The Irish contingent were deployed on the south bank and made their way to the bridge that linked Mercia to the Saxons' formidable fortress on the north shore. *They should have built the burh on the south bank,* Ragnall felt, *but who knows what the Romans envisioned, perhaps their enemies at that time lay to the south and west?* The nearest fordable point on the river was way inland and it would take a day and a half for them to reach Chester and relieve it. Garangr and Godfrith had command of the ships anchored on the water itself. Their role was a flexible one. They were to reinforce the Irish if they looked to be in trouble on the bridge or to support the Ui Imair at the walls of the burh itself; and in a worst-case scenario they were to cover the retreat of Ingamundr's force if they were defeated, however unlikely. Ingamundr and Ragnall used the first few hours back on land to inspect their various positions.

The front gate was besieged by more than a thousand Vikings who were well out of arrow range. They had archers amidst them if the defenders of the burh attempted to sally forth. Garangr and Godfrith were ever watchful and patrolled the water like wolves, scanning both banks of the river. The Leinster men on the bridge were deployed and Ragnall quickly realised that Augaire mac Aililla was not present, but his kinsman Faelan mac Muiredaig had received word by fast ship and rider that he was en route with more men than just this four hundred and would hopefully arrive before Aethelfled's armies appeared. Brunbolg was as fearsome a berserker as any in the Viking world and the two cousins left him to his own devices commanding the disparate war bands at the north wall of the fortress. Any Saxon that tried Brunbolg would surely die as had all before them. Before the day was out, the camps were erected and men were rotated, fed and rested. The next day the assault would begin.

*

The dawn broke with the sound of Viking and Irish warriors breaking their fast, but Ingamundr and Ragnall ignored them and headed to the gate. They shouted for someone to approach the battlements that could treat with them with authority on Queen Aethelfled's behalf. Moments passed with no response before a single figure stood between the wooden crenellations above the gate. In the morning light the figure stood helmed and mailed and just stared down at the two cousins for minutes before ever so slowly discarding the helm. A long braid of light brown hair fell down across a woman's face and shoulders. Ragnall was stunned. Ingamundr just looked confused and looked at Ragnall.

"Aethelfled," is all Ragnall could say to his cousin.

The Queen regally stared down at the two Ui Imair commanders.

"By what right do you invade my lands, after in the light of Jesus Christ our lord I had peacefully allowed you heathens to live upon my border?," she shouted down.

Ragnall could see that Ingamundr was surprised to learn that she spoke an Irish dialect of Gaelic very well. While he was recovering from that surprise, Ragnall responded.

"You have taxed our people into oblivion. You have sent our warriors to fight your battles against the Welsh while you enriched yourself off the plunder, and now you want to steal our young men and conscript them into your own Saxon armies. We were desperate five years ago, but now we are strong. Those lands were uninhabited when we landed first and if anything, sat under the rule of the Kings of Yorvik who are now our allies. As far as we are concerned, you have no authority to dictate to us on anything and when this fort falls, which it will, Mercia will never again threaten the rights and lands of the Ui Imair."

Aethelfled laughed a great boisterous guffaw before answering.

"I landed here two days ago with my vanguard of four hundred Saxon warriors, expert killers of Vikings all. I had a garrison of five hundred men here already. I am surrounded by twenty-feet-tall stone walls with enough food and water to withstand six months of a siege. My ealdormen are raising the fyrd and in days they will be here to wash the Ui Imair away. My brother will be here in a moon's turn with the entire army of Wessex, and I will still be standing despite what you may think. I have learned that you disembowelled my dear friend Ceolred of Tamworth and fed his corpse to your dogs. Make no mistake, if I capture you or any of your captains, you can expect the same. Now I am tired of talking. Come and try my walls if you wish to die by the thousand, otherwise withdraw like the heathen cowardly savages that you are."

At that she turned and disappeared. Ragnall stood there momentarily considering all of what she said while Ingamundr just stared after her, his teeth grinding in rage to find the Queen herself manning the walls with most of her elite soldiery.

"How did she get here so fast, Ragnall?" he asked in frustration. "How is it that Aethelfled herself is here and not in Tamworth? How does she know the manner of her man's death by my hand? I know that word travels faster in the spring than the winter, but surely not that quickly?"

Ingamundr was furious and confused but Ragnall had no real answers for him.

"We must take the castle, Ragnall. We have the strength to keep any reinforcements at bay. Her battlements are not complete. We can take her; we must take her."

Within the hour, the Vikings were ready. The holy Gothi had anointed the warriors with the blood of a bull sacrificed in their honour and the shield wall approached steadily in a phalanx to the gate. Hundreds of archers exchanged arrows from the ground and from between the crenellations. The first of the rams were brought forward, covered by linked shields, and the front men slammed the felled tree into the gates. Even above the roars of the men the boom emanating from the ram meeting the gate dominated.

Ragnall and Ingamundr stood back at the rear directing the Viking forces, ensuring that the siege went smoothly. They sent men around intermittently to try the walls with ropes and salvos of arrows, trying to gain the summit.

They had no real belief that any of these men would succeed but with two miles of wall to cover, the tactic would spread the Saxons thin. A couple of young runners were used to carry messages between the Irish on the bridge, the Vikings on the river and those with Brunbolg. The Headtaker had dozens of scaling ladders with him as well as men with ropes and grapnel hooks, but in the first hour he had no success and had settled for trading arrows with the defenders. *It will be at the front gate where this is decided,* Ragnall knew.

As the hours passed the battering continued at the gate and Ragnall could see with satisfaction that the massive doorways were in fact beginning to splinter, but they had lost thirty men already to rocks and arrows. The biggest cheer came when a Saxon warrior attempted to pour a cauldron of boiling mead on top of the warriors at the gate, got pierced with an arrow and dropped it, thus frying himself with his own weapon. Ragnall could not cheer though as the method of the Saxon soldier's demise would occur upon the Ui Imair many more times before the end of the battle, he was sure; a truly gruesome way to die. As the afternoon turned to evening, they rolled out the first and second rams to the side and introduced their third. The wounded were dragged away to safety to be treated by the Gothi and the women. Ingamundr deliberately held his best warriors back, for when the gates cracked open, they would be required to be fresh to meet the Saxons head-on. Ragnall was given the job of overall command as Ingamundr deemed himself responsible for this fight and reserved the right to be the first warrior through the breach to meet the foe. A half hour before dark, the Vikings lit hundreds of fires and torches to see as they had no intention of breaking off the assault. And then just before dusk fell, the gates, with an audible snap, were broken. It had taken hundreds of blows, but they finally swung inward, shattered from the pounding of the rams. The exhausted men who wielded the ram fled from the archers on the wall and Ingamundr raised his axe, and his elite retinue screamed their prayers to Odin.

"May the Allfather be with you, cousin, I will summon Brunbolg to the gate to reinforce you," said Ragnall.

Ingamundr and two hundred of his elite sprinted toward the gate. A great cry went up from all Viking lips as the Ui Imair charged Chester with

Ingamundr at the tip of the spear. The broken gate revealed to Ragnall that the second gate behind it looked incomplete, but something struck him as being off; it was almost too enticing. Why would Athelfled's carpenters complete the outer gate before the inner gate in a temporary section of the wall like this? The wood was ten inches thick in places, sturdy and very robust as hours of ramming had proven. There was skill amongst the Queen's carpenters. This was a grievous oversight. *Or was it?* thought Ragnall in alarm.

Ingamundr and his vanguard poured through the gate at that moment, while the rest of the Ui Imair forces gathered themselves together to enter the town behind a shield wall in support. A loud horn blast echoed across the river behind Ragnall. *What is happening?* he thought. The raging, tumultuous sound of men charging turned Ragnall's head to the river behind him three hundred feet away. The Irish had sickeningly stood aside on the sudden arrival of the Saxons and at their head stood Augaire mac Aililla. *He has betrayed us again,* thought Ragnall furiously. Hundreds of Saxon warriors poured across the bridge. Simultaneously there was a loud bang from the burh. Aethelfled had played a trick. A cast-iron portcullis, such as Ragnall had witnessed in Francia, slammed down, trapping Ingamundr and his vanguard within the walls of Chester.

Ragnall was momentarily frozen between rage at the betrayal by the Irish and the mortal danger Ingamundr and his elite forces were in. The portcullis was small, but it would take massive effort to raise it, especially if archers were shooting from above and behind murder holes. Ragnall shouted at his cousin Gunnar to form a shield wall to face the Saxon reinforcements from the river.

"You have to hold until I can save Ingamundr!" he screamed. "The Irish have betrayed us and Aethelfled has Ingamundr cut off inside the walls. Brunbolg and I will try and save him. You must hold, Gunnar. If they get around you, me, Brunbolg, Ingamundr – we're all dead men!"

His cousin nodded grimly and roared his orders. A thousand Vikings formed up in a wall and prepared to meet the Saxons and Irish. Ragnall sprinted toward the walls, risking the archers as Brunbolg appeared running around the corner with hundreds of his men, shields placed above their heads to deflect rocks and other detritus from braining them. They met eyes and Ragnall knew that he didn't need to explain; a veteran warrior like Brunbolg knew exactly what was happening. They slammed into the inner portcullis. Through the squared gaps in the steel, Ragnall witnessed the horrors that his cousin Ingamundr faced. The buildings were linked with planks of wood and on every roof dozens of men were armed with boiling mead and oil. Rocks and arrows rained down on the Viking warriors amongst the streets, and dozens of Vikings were being massacred by the minute.

Brunbolg pushed his way forward. He had iron-grey hair down to his knees and a beard to match, betraying his age, but at seven feet and four hundred pounds he was the only man who could realistically do the job of raising the iron portcullis. Massive muscles bunched and inch by inch the iron moved upward. Other men reached in to help and in seconds the contraption was wedged open with some of the splintered timber from the smashed outer gates. Ragnall sprinted into the town. In seconds he was upon the Saxons who had surrounded the Ui Imair vanguard. The few survivors of this force were making their last stand with Ingamundr. Ragnall, in a fury, hacked and slashed and gutted several Saxons in his path, but it was not until Brunbolg himself smashed his way through the surrounding Saxons that they could relieve Imgamundr. The Saxons retreated despite outnumbering the Ui Imair and allowed Ragnall and Brunbolg to gather around the shattered remnants of Ingamundr's elite. They found their King. He was barely alive. Arrows had pierced him in the thigh and the midriff. He had taken a sword wound in the lung and blood was leaking from his mouth. Half of his face had been flensed by a glancing blow from a Mercian sword. Ragnall gathered him under one shoulder, and they retreated as fast as they could.

It only took minutes to reach the ships but to Ragnall it felt like days. The fire and the dark and the confusion all around, battled for supremacy in his concentration. All order and semblance of precision were gone from the Viking formations. It was every warrior for himself. If it wasn't for Garangr yet again forming a second shield wall at the ships and Godfrith and his archers feathering hundreds of Saxons and Irish, Ragnall was sure that none would have survived this day. Ragnall delivered his cousin into the care of the Gothi and turned back to re-enter the fray. Gunnar's men were retreating through this shield wall from the ferocity of the Saxons and Irish that had crossed the bridge, and some took up bows to try and help keep them at bay. Ragnall joined the shield wall, determined that if this was to be the end of the Ui Imair, he would make such an end that Odin himself would honour them in Valhalla forever. But it never came to pass. Godfrith and his archers had laid down such a withering hail of arrows that the Saxons had no choice but to retreat as their losses mounted and allow the Ui Imair and their allies to retreat up the estuary of the River Dee and out to sea. Ragnall cradled his dying cousin Ingamundr's head in his lap. One look from the Gothi told him that Ingamundr was finished. His eyes flickered open momentarily as the oarsmen furiously rowed away from the accursed Saxon fort.

"Ragnall," he whispered, "revenge me. We were betrayed by the Irish. Aethelfled, Glundub, Constantine, Augaire, they all must suffer. Don't let the Ui Imair perish. Protect our people."

With a last sigh the light of life fled from his eyes. And so perished Ingamundr, son of Bairid, grandson of Ivar the Boneless, the King of the Ui Imair; slain in battle with Aethelfled of Mercia. Ragnall knew the gods would honour a warrior as honourable and formidable as Ingamundr of Dublin, but when he met the eyes of his grieving brother Godfrith all he felt was despair.

# PART 5

## THE SHAPING OF SIHTRIC UI IMAIR, THE SCOURGE OF IRELAND

# DRAMATIS PERSONAE:

**Aed Findliath** (*Aid-fin-lee-at*) – Long-deceased King of the Cenel nEoghain and the Northern Ui Neill. Son of Niall Caille and father of Niall Glundub.

**Aethelfled of Mercia** (*A-thel-fled*) – Saxon Queen of Mercia and sister of the King of Wessex.

**Aethelstan** (*A-thel-stan*) – Young Saxon prince and Mercian commander.

**Agmund** – Saxon ealdorman of Northumbria.

**Aidan mac Fergus** – Head of Flann Sinna's guard and distant cousin from a cadet branch of Clan Colman.

**Alan of Brittany** – Warlike king of Celtic Brittany.

**Aililla mac Eogan** (*Al-lila-mac-ao-gon*) – Influential Leinster under-king, father of Augaire.

**Amalgaid mac Congalach** (*Amal-gad-mac-con-gal-ach*) – Ambitious nobleman of North Brega.

**Amir Ibn Hafsun** (*Am-meer-ib-in-haf-soon*) – Umayyad nobleman and slave trader from the Islamic city of Cordoba.

**Amlaib Ivarsson** (*Am-layb-ivarson*) – Brother of Sihtric, killed in battle in Scotland in 904.

**Anlaf the Swarthy** – Norse-Saxon Northumbrian nobleman, enemy of Mercia and Wessex.

**Augaire mac Aililla** (*Aw-gair-a-mac-al-lila*) – Ferocious young Irish warlord and bother-in-law to the Ui Imair princes.

**Bairid Oitirsson** (*Bar-rid-oh-tier-son*) – Called Bairid mac Oitir by the Irish, distant kin to the Ui Imair as his grandfather Auisle was brother to Ivar the Boneless. Ruler of the powerful Kingdom of Mann in the Irish Sea.

**Becc** – Grandson of Lethlobar of the powerful Dal nAridi tribe of the Ulaid.

**Benesing the Bulky** (*Ben-nes-sing*) – Minor Viking chieftain, sworn to the rulers of Yorvik, loosely allied with the Ui Imair also.

**Black Fox** – Deceased warrior king of Argialla.

**Brigid** – Major Irish Celtic god of the old pantheon.

**Brunbolg Headtaker** (*Brun-bulg-head-taker*) – Physically gigantic Viking warlord, subject to the influence of the Ui Imair.

**Cathal mac Conchobar** (*Ca-hal-mac-con-co-bar*) – Over-king of all Connaught, subservient to the High King Flann Sinna of Meath.

**Ceallach mac Cerbaill** (*Kyal-ach-mac-ker-ball*) – King of Osraige, subservient to the High King Flann Sinna.

**Ceitl Flatnose** (*Ket-tel-flatnose*) – Deceased Viking King of Limerick and some of the Hebrides and Orkneys.

**Cerbaill mac Dunlainge** (*Ker-ball-mac-dun-lang-ga*) – Long-deceased former King of Osraige.

**Cerbaill mac Muirecain** (*Ker-ball-mac-mwir-a-kawn*) – Powerful King of Leinster but subject to Flann Sinna's overlordship.

**Cleirchen mac Murchadh** (*Clerk-ken-mac-murk-ka*) – Rebellious Connaught under-king.

**Conaille mac Muirteimne** (*Co-nal-mac-mwir-tem-ne*) – Minor chieftain whose lands straddle the border between the Ulaid and North Brega.

**Conchobar mac Flann** (*Con-co-bar-mac-flann*) – Youngest son of the High King Flann Sinna.

**Constantine mac Aed** – Over-king of all Scotland.

**Cormac mac Cuilennain** (*Cor-mac-mac-cul-in-ann*) – Powerful King of the Eoghanachta tribes and over-king of Munster.

**Cuchulainn** (*Coo-cull-en*) – Mythical Irish warrior, leader of the famous Red Branch Knights.

**Dagda** – Chief of the old Irish Celtic pantheon.

**Diarmuid** – Legendary figure who stole the Princess Grainne from the grasp of the hero Finn mac Cumhaill.

**Domnall mac Aed** (*Donal-mac-aid*) – Eldest son of Aed Findliath and leader of the Cenel nEoghain, joint ruler with Niall Glundub of the Northern Ui Neill.

**Donnchadh Donn mac Flann** (*Dun-na-ka-dun-mac-flan-sinna*) – Powerful king of the Caille Follamain tribe in Meath, estranged son of the High King Flann Sinna.

**Dub Sinna mac Eilge** (*Dub-sinna-mac-el-ga*) – Rebellious King of Mag Itha, an under-king of the Northern Ui Neill.

**Dyabbi Cisse** (*Dee-yabee-see-say*) – Wealthy Ghanaian nobleman and slave trader, emissary of the rulers of the West African Ghanaian kingdom.

**Eadwulf** (*Aid-wolf*) – Saxon Noblemen of Northumbria.

**Eowils of Yorvik** (*Eow-ils*) – Joint King of Yorvik and much of Northumbria.

**Finn mac Cumhaill** (*Finn-mac-cool*) – Mythical Irish hero and leader of the legendary Fianna.

**Finnegas** (*Fin-e-gas*) – Wise seer Flann Sinna met in his youth.

**Flaithbertach mac Inmainen** (*Fla-her-tach-mac-in-main-in*) – Munster nobleman and chief advisor to the Eoghanachta king, Cormac mac Cuilennain.

**Flann mac Tighernain** (*Flan-mac-tier-nan*) – Opportunistic King of Breffni, sworn to the Northern Ui Neill.

**Flann Sinna** – High King of Ireland and over-king of Meath and the Southern Ui Neill.

**Fogartach mac Suibne** (*Fo-gar-tach-mac-soob-na*) – King of Kerry and under-king to the Eoghanachta of Munster.

**Fogartach mac Tolarg** (*Fo-gar-tach-mac-tol-arg*) – King of South Brega, under-king of the Southern Ui Neill.

**Garangr Sichfridthsson** (*Gar-rang-gar-sic-frith-son*) – Ui Imair prince and Viking warlord, operating in Northumbria.

**Godfrith Ivarsson** (*God-frith-ivarson*) – Twin brother of Sihtric, the youngest sons of Ivar the former King of Dublin and brother to Ragnall.

**Grainne** (*Graw-nya*) – Fabled princess who left Finn mac Cumhaill to run away with Diarmuid.

**Guthferth** – Saxon Ealdorman of Northumbria and enemy of Mercia and Wessex.

**Guthrum** – Danish Viking ruler in the Danelaw and enemy of Alfred the Great.

**Halfdan of Yorvik** (*Half-dan*) – Joint King of Yorvik and much of Northumbria.

**Halfdan Ragnarsson** – Long-deceased Viking leader of the Great Heathen Army, elder half-brother of Ivar the Boneless.

**Harald Fairhair** – King of all Norway.

**Ingamundr Bairidsson** (*Ing-ga-munder-bar-rid-son*) – Formidable Ui Imair warlord, grandson of Ivar the Boneless.

**Ingvarr of Yorvik** (*Ing-var*) – Joint King of Yorvik and much of Northumbria.

**Inneirge mac Mael Teimin** (*In-er-ge-mac-male-tem-in*) – Minor North Bregan chieftain.

**Ivar Ivarsson** – Deceased older brother of Sihtric, killed in battle with the Scots in 904.

**Ivar the Boneless** – Long-deceased former King of Dublin and a legendary son of Ragnar Lodbrok.

**Jotunn** (*Joe-ton*) – Mythological Norse giant demon creature.

**Lugh** (*Loo*) – Major god of the old Irish Celtic pantheon.

**Mael Mithig mac Flannacain** (*Male-mit-tig-mac-flan-na-cawn*) – Powerful Southern Ui Neill under-king of North Brega.

**Mael Muire ingen Cinead** (*Male-mwir-a-ingen-cin-aid*) – Princess of Scotland and Queen of Ireland, wife of Flann Sinna.

**Mael Ograi mac Congalach** (*Male-og-ree-mac-con-gal-ach*) – Rebellious Bregan chieftain.

**Mael Ruanaid mac Flann** (*Male-ruin-ad-mac-flann*) – Prince of the Southern Ui Neill and heir to Flann Sinna.

**Mael Seachnaill mac Mael Ruanaid** (*Male-shock-nail-mac-male-ruin-ad*) – Deceased High King of Ireland and the Southern Ui Neill and father of Flann Sinna.

**Maol Craobh** (*Male-crave*) – Known as the son of the Black Fox, warlike leader of the Argiallan clans and tribes, sworn to the Northern Ui Neill.

**Muirchertach mac Niall** (*Mwir-her-tach-mac-niall*) – Formidable young son of Niall Glundub and Prince of the Northern Ui Neill and the Cenel nEoghain. His reputation as a warrior was such that the people of the north called him the "Hector" of Ireland.

**Niall Glundub mac Aed Findliath** – Newly returned Northern Ui Neill Joint King and powerful general.

**Niall Noigiallach** (*Niall-noi-gee-allach*) – Also known as Niall of the Nine Hostages. Semi Legendary ancestor of all Ui Neill nobility.

**Odin** – The chief god of the Norse and Danes, also known as the Allfather.

**Oengus mac Flann** (*Ong-gus-mac-flann*) – Prince of the Southern Ui Neill, son of the High King and heir designate of all Ireland.

**Other** (*Oh-ter*) – Powerful Danish-Saxon Northumbrian eorl.

**Osferth** – Saxon ealdorman of Northumbria and enemy of Mercia and Wessex.

**Othulf** (*Oh-thulf*) – Saxon Ealdorman of Northumbria and enemy of Mercia and Wessex.

**Padraig of Clonard** (*Paw-rig*) – Head bishop of the monastery at Clonard in Meath. Affectionately known as Paudi by the High King.

**Ragnall Ivarsson** (*Rag-nal-ivarson*) – Leader of the Ui Imair.

**Scurf** – Powerful Danish-Saxon Northumbrian eorl.

**Sihtric Ivarsson** (*Si-tric-ivarson*) – Twin brother of Godfrith, the youngest sons of Ivar former King of Dublin and brother to Ragnall. Bodyguard to the High King of Ireland, Flann Sinna. Known as "The Scourge" by the enemies of the High King.

**Sochlachlann** (*Soc-lock-lan*) – Minor chieftain who ruled lands bordering Connaught and Meath. Friend and distant cousin of the High King.

**Tadg mac Cathal** (*Tieg-mac-ca-hal*) – Prince of Connaught.

**Thunferth** (*Thun-ferth*) – Saxon ealdorman of Northumbria and enemy of Mercia and Wessex.

**Turgesius** (*Tur-geese-e-us*) Deceased Viking warlord, alleged half-brother of Ragnar Lodbrok and founder of the city of Dublin.

**Tyr** – Warlike God of the Scandinavian pantheon.

**Ubba Ragnarsson** – Long-dead Viking warlord and leader of the Great Heathen Army, brother of Ivar the Boneless.

# CHAPTER 1

# THE RIGHT HAND OF THE HIGH KING FLANN SINNA (907)

A warm breeze blew around the Hill of Tara, ruffling the leaves of the few trees that surrounded the giant fort. Sihtric of the Ui Imair accompanied the ancient High King Flann Sinna as he strolled through the massive oaken gates that led to the northern Slige Midluachra road. Sihtric usually recognised the moods the King displayed and what they portended, but today the combination of downcast head and pensive aloofness concerned and confused the young Viking warrior. The King usually did not hold court on Fridays, preferring to observe the Christian fast day in peace and solitude. He would not usually see any guests or entertain petitioners in his hall; instead, he would pray in the humble cell at the rear of his living accommodations at the back of his abode. In the five years Sihtric had lived in the fort of the High King he had noticed that Flann Sinna, more and more, thoroughly observed his Christian faith. One day Sihtric had summoned the courage to question the King upon his increasing piousness, but Flann had just smiled and said that he was an old sinner who needed to make his peace with God before he met him personally.

Today was an auspicious day though and very politically important, Sihtric knew. There were five extremely important people here to see the King and it just wouldn't be optimal to rebuff them on religious grounds, as many lives were at stake. Sihtric watched the King move slowly down toward the trees to the left of the road, hands clasped behind his back. The advance of years could no longer be denied; the King looked old, weather-beaten, and white of hair. Even his iron-grey beard was evolving to snow white.

The events of the last number of years were taking a visible toll on the King. Before Sihtric had been captured and had arrived in Meath in 902, a rogue under-king in Connaught had captured Flann Sinna's son Mael Ruanaid, trapped him in a church and burned him to death. Queen Mael Muire had confided in Sihtric that it had been a terrible blow to the King. He had been Flann Sinna's heir apparent and the most favoured of his sons. Donnchadh Donn, his eldest son, did not see eye to eye with Flann for some ancient grievance that Sihtric had never heard, but the bad feeling had been compounded when the High King had named another son, Oengus, as his new heir designate, yet again ignoring his eldest. The prince's resentment had boiled over two years previously when he had attempted to rally the under-kings and chieftains of the Southern Ui Neill to his cause in an attempted coup, but Flann Sinna had discovered the plot and cornered Donnchadh Donn in Kells. Sihtric had been there carrying the King's standard into battle before him. The fighting had been swift and decisive, and Flann Sinna had executed most of the nobles and minor chieftains that had supported the prince before letting Donnchadh Donn go. Sihtric himself had been given the honour of putting two of the minor chieftains to death by beheading, the first men he had ever killed. He had also been handed the scourge with which to punish some of the minor nobles whom the High King felt required a harsh lesson rather than being put to death, or were too politically connected to execute outright, and from the use of that weapon, Sihtric had been known by the moniker "The Scourge" ever since.

In the same year, Flann Sinna's greatest companion, Aidan mac Fergus, had passed away after a short illness, another terrible blow for the King. Flann Sinna had relied upon Aidan's council for more than thirty years and now Flann's favourite shoulder to lean on, had passed from this life into the Christian heaven. Strangely in the last two years, it was an outsider in Sihtric, a young member of the Viking Ui Imair, that Flann Sinna adopted as his new companion. Flann's sons Oengus and Conchobar had forts of their own and did not reside in Tara exclusively. Although only a very young man, barely having reached manhood, Sihtric had proved himself in battle during the subjugation of parts of Osraige and the raids on Munster. His fighting skills, his stoicism and his unswerving loyalty had impressed the King and because of this, their relationship had blossomed.

Flann Sinna had admitted as much. It was true that initially Sihtric had been taken as a captive and made a ward of the High King, but those days had gone. The Ui Imair prince had very little memory of the events of the fall of Viking Dublin in truth, only fleeting images of his brother Godfrith hiding while Sihtric tried to defend his mother, and of Ragnall, his older brother, being banished by the High King. His memories were jumbled and confused but he bore no ill will toward Flann Sinna. It was just Irish politics, and he accepted his life for what it was. He now ate at the High King's table, practised with his weapons in the yard with the elite Ui Neill household guard and stood at the King's side when petitioners came to court. He protected him night and day and fought beside him in his battles. When he looked at the old king pondering the enormity of the upcoming day's events, he didn't see his captor, oppressor or jailor; he saw his mentor, King and friend.

The High King meandered further amongst the trees lost in his own world, stopping occasionally to examine a leaf or to listen intently to the warbling of birds. Sihtric hated to interrupt him or intrude upon him when the King took these walks in the countryside. He stayed back behind him, ever watchful. The old king bore such massive burdens that moments of peace and clarity, however rare, could only do him good, Sihtric felt. Flann Sinna's never-ending quest to unify the island of Ireland under one king was a constant struggle. Under-kings repeatedly revolted against his authority or fought amongst themselves for land or livestock. The Eoghanachta of Munster were in open rebellion, refusing to pay tribute to the Southern Ui Neill. while the Viking towns of Linn, Dublin, Wexford, Waterford, Cork and Limerick to all intents and purposes paid only lip service to Flann Sinna's overlordship. It seemed to Sihtric's understanding that every step forward taken by Flann Sinna through a political agreement or well-matched marriage, was nullified by some rebellion somewhere in the land. To control the shifting tide of politics in Ireland was to try and herd cats.

Every battle season the High King inevitably had to campaign across the country, not necessarily to fight, but to show the myriad other petty kings that he was still powerful, and he was to be feared if crossed. At length the King discovered a moss-covered tree that had been felled and he turned to Sihtric and beckoned for him to sit as well. The ancient king and the young Viking just sat in silence; the King closed his eyes and listened to the sound of his lands. On opening his eyes again, he addressed the young Ui Imair prince.

"I have something to tell you, Sihtric. I have received very bad news overnight, but I did not want to wake you from your sleep. I wanted to bring you to a quiet peaceful place to inform you of what has happened."

Sihtric's heart sank. *Something is hugely wrong here,* he thought.

"There was a battle in Mercia a week ago. Your brothers and cousins in alliance with the Kings of Yorvik attempted to take Chester from Queen Aethelfled. They were betrayed by some of their Irish allies."

Sihtric's heart was in his mouth. *Please Odin not Godfrith, please let him still be alive.*

"Ingamundr King of the Ui Imair was slain when he and his vanguard were trapped in the town and surrounded. They lost hundreds of men."

Sihtric let out a sigh of relief. He felt guilty about it but really Ingamundr was a distant memory for him. He had only occasionally seen him in his youth in Dublin and if truthful with himself could barely remember his face. He was always raiding or fighting the Saxons, his visits to the hall of his mother and father infrequent. The last time Flann Sinna had taken Sihtric to a quiet place to talk, he had informed him that his father and his brothers, Ivar the Young and Amlaib, had been killed in battle with Constantine of Scotland and his general Niall Glundub of the Ui Neill. Sihtric had shed tears of sadness and anger and the High King had understood and consoled him. This time he was better prepared, he was a man now after all.

"Your brother Ragnall I believe will be made king at the next *Thing*," Flann said.

A *Thing* was the word used for a meeting of import on serious matters in the Viking world. The High King placed his hand on Sihtric's knee and stared into his eyes.

"Sihtric, it is my intention in several years, when you are more mature, to make you the King of Dublin. You will only answer to me."

Sihtric's heart leapt in his chest at the king's pronouncement.

"When you are fully mature and have learned all that you can at my side, I will install you as leader of the city. The Norse-Gael people of the city are unruly and hate having to bend the knee to the Kings of Leinster or Brega, or even myself. I want you to be a bridge between our worlds, Sihtric. You are already for such a young man, one of the most incredible warriors I have ever seen, virtually unbeatable in a fight, but you must learn that there is a difference between being a great warrior and being a great leader."

The King paused to compose himself while Sihtric listened engrossed, hanging on every word.

"Look at your brother Ragnall, he is mighty but before he has finished one fight, he is off raiding or fighting somewhere else. He cannot give his people peace. But you can. Even Niall Glundub, the most famous Irish warrior of our age, he only solves problems by the edge of his sword. Eventually he will encounter someone who will defeat him, and it will be over for him. You need to have nuance, a blend of strength and flexibility. Ragnall, Glundub, Cormac mac Cuilennain the Eoghanachta king; they are all just wolves upon the land and sea, but you can be more than that."

Sihtric digested all of what the High King said, absorbing these teachings like a sponge. The High King looked downcast once more and then met Sihtrics eyes.

"I have one more truth to tell you. I had meant to tell you over the years but my memory, as you know, has depreciated badly. It was only when I received the report from the battle at Chester that I recalled it. You are old enough to know. The man who betrayed your brothers and cousins in Mercia and the man who I was informed was the one who slew your mother, were one and the same."

Sihtric's heart hammered in his chest as he waited for the High King to speak, the memories of a powerful young Irish warrior impaling his mother to the bench in their hall stabbed his memory.

"It was a prince of the Ui Dunlainge of Leinster, Augaire mac Aililla."

Sihtric's hands instinctively grasped his sword. His anger and need for revenge rose like a volcano inside him. But the old king grabbed his wrist to calm him.

"Steady yourself, young Sihtric, you must be able to endure loss. In the next couple of years, we will force this entire island into submission. You, me, my sons and my allies. Once we have won, I will install you as King of Dublin and I swear, as not just your High King but as your great-uncle too, you have my permission to seek your vengeance upon Augaire mac Aililla and the Ui Dunlainge, although I can never publicly condone it."

Sihtric ever so slowly nodded his head in agreement and understanding. As his rage abated, the picture became clearer now. *There is a reason why Flann Sinna has been King for thirty years,* he thought.

Several hours passed quickly for Sihtric as he dreamed of all the ways he would take his vengeance upon this Augaire mac Aililla, who also happened to be his brother-in-law by marriage. The old memory of his mother being filleted by her Irish murderer haunted him and enraged him in equal measure. The vision of her being impaled to the bench made him grind his teeth in fury, old memories harsh and only half buried. The creaking of the doors of the main hall in Tara snapped him from his reverie and a familiar face approached the dais where Flann Sinna held court, with Sihtric standing at his side. The old High King shifted imperceptibly in his seat, a sign Sihtric recognised that he wasn't best pleased with the first of the dignitaries to address him. The man in question was Flaithbertach mac Inmainen. He was chief advisor to the King of Munster and allegedly the voice of dissension in the court of Cormac mac Cuilennain in Cashel, a warmonger, and an agitator.

In the previous battle season, the Munstermen had campaigned as far north as Connaught and some of the chieftains of Meath had felt their presence also. They had even possessed the gall to demand tribute and hostages from those same minor chieftains, who all owed their allegiance to Flann Sinna and the Southern Ui Neill. *What happens here will decide the fate of Munster,* thought Sihtric. Flaithbertach was a small but broad man with a red face and even redder hair. He was renowned for having a fierce temper and little patience but Sihtric knew that any sort of outburst here by the Munsterman and he would possibly have to step down off the dais and shorten him by a head. The High King spoke first which quietened the court.

"Flaithbertach mac Inmainen, you have successfully petitioned my son Oengus to speak to me, but before you begin, know that you will be held accountable personally for your words, even if these words are spoken at the behest of your king."

Flann Sinna looked and nodded toward Sihtric before continuing.

"If you in any way threaten my person, my chieftains or even the lowliest of my people, my grandnephew Sihtric of the Ui Imair will cut you down here and now on front of my whole court."

A great hush fell on the crowd which were quiet to begin with, on the promise of violence. Even Sihtric himself was surprised as the king was usually far more tactful and diplomatic to both foe and ally alike. The brazen Munsterman went beetroot-red in the face, even ruddier than was normal, but he got the message. His response was careful and meek.

"High King Flann Sinna of the Ui Neill, I have been sent to Tara to discuss a redrawing of the border between north and south. King Cormac has commissioned me to respectfully request a movement between the Leath Cuinn and Leath Mogha, the two sides of the country. For our mutual benefit and security, King Cormac and I feel that the line should be redrawn further north to Uisneach in the South of Meath and also the rule of Dublin and all of its incomes should be fairly split between the Ui Neill and the Eoghanachta of Munster."

The crowd began to stir in outrage at this request. Uncaring, the Munsterman continued:

"We also believe that the lands of Osraige should also fall back under our control as they did in centuries past."

The hall erupted at this suggestion. The sound of a sword being unsheathed alerted Sihtric to possible danger and he leapt down from the dais, his eyes searching for the source of the drawn weapon. Ceallach mac Cerbaill, the King of Osraige and cousin of the High King, emerged from the crowd. Sihtric cursed himself for not realising this and the potential for trouble his presence could pose knowing that the warmonger Flaithbertach would be addressing Flann Sinna. The Osraige king flew at the unarmed Munsterman but Sihtric interposed himself, parrying his sword with his axe.

"SHEATH YOUR WEAPON, CEALLACH, BEFORE YOU DISGRACE YOURSELF," roared the old High King which stilled the violence instantly.

Abashed, the King of Osraige bowed and stood back into the crowd. Sihtric turned before returning to the dais to see that Flaithbertach was smirking, delighting in the fact that his words had caused such anguish in Flann Sinna's hall. Flann Sinna turned in the direction of King Ceallach.

"You will have your chance to address me once Flaithbertach is finished and has left my hall, until then hold your peace."

He turned to face the Munsterman. "Your demands are unreasonable. You have no cause or reason to claim these lands from my control. The rule of Dublin is mine and no other. Osraige is mine, Leinster is mine, Connaught is mine and the Northern Ui Neill will answer if I summon them in a time of absolute need. But you Munstermen do not seem to understand the bigger picture."

Flaithbertach's arrogant smile curdled, Sihtric saw. *By Odin's grace allow me an excuse to bury my axe in his face,* he thought. A glance at the High King revealed to Sihtric that Flann Sinna was thinking the exact same thing.

"You Munstermen seem to think you are deserving of some sort of independence from my rule, but I am the High King of Ireland and not just the

High King of the Leath Cuinn. You will pay me tribute like all the rest, or I will gather my armies and invade."

The Munsterman was angered at that pronouncement; he puffed out his chest before issuing a retort.

"This is unacceptable, King Flann. We in Munster are tired of bending the knee to Tara or any of the Ui Neill, a ruined line of bullies long bereft of nobility. You will grant us control of these lands and our independence from your rule, or we will seize it for ourselves!"

Flann Sinna rose up to his full height. Even in his old age he was still a tall man and on the dais, he towered over Flaithbertach.

"You will take these terms to your King. He will adhere to the existing borders. He will refrain from attacking the lands of my allies. Dublin, Osraige and Leinster are mine and will never fall under the rule of the Eoghanachta. He will resume paying me tribute at Easter and at Samhain and he will come himself to pay fealty to me at the winter solstice. If he does not agree to these terms, Munster will burn."

The Munsterman snarled furiously and was about to shout in response but one step from Sihtric toward him saw his retort wither on the vine. He simply spat in disgust and stormed from the hall. Sihtric looked across at Flann Sinna with an unspoken request to follow him and slay the man, but the High King shook his head. *War then,* thought Sihtric calmly.

The next petitioner was the aforementioned son-in-law of Flann Sinna, Ceallach mac Cerbaill. He began his petition by apologising profusely for his outburst minutes earlier, which Flann Sinna accepted graciously. To Sihtric's eyes, Ceallach was an oaf, but a likeable one. Flann Sinna often told Sihtric that Ceallach was nothing like his fearsome father Cerbaill mac Dunlainge, who had died after the Battle of Pilgrim long before he was born. His biggest quality in fact was that he was loyal. Whatever Flann Sinna required of Osraige, Ceallach leapt to obey. He wasn't much of a fighter or general but the two or three thousand fighting men that he ruled in Osraige were very useful when placed at the High King's disposal. The High King for minutes on end placated his son-in-law with assurances of their ongoing alliance and how Meath would always come to the aid of Osraige; be they under attack from the south against Munster, from the east from Leinster, or through the river systems against the occasional Viking foray. Sihtric felt slightly uncomfortable when his older brother Ragnall was discussed as a potential threat to Osraige's security. The boorish king went on at length to Flann Sinna about how best to respond should the Ui Imair attack. At length the King of Osraige was mollified and eventually dismissed and the High King called for the penultimate petitioners to enter the hall and approach.

Two of the strangest-looking men Sihtric had ever seen in his life advanced toward the dais. He had campaigned around much of the country already in his young life at the side of the High King but Sihtric had never laid eyes on men as exotic as these two. They were introduced as Amir Ibn Hafsun of the Umayyad Caliphate of Cordoba in Al Andalus and Dyabbi Cisse, prince and envoy of the Ghanaian Empire of the Aifric. Amir Ibn Hafsun wore fine silks and a turban around his head. He smelled, even from a few feet away, of spices and perfumes, both exotic and exhilarating to Sihtric. His beard was luxurious, and he wore black coal beneath his eyes, bequeathing him a feminine air. The second man was even more mysterious if that was possible. He also wore the finest silks, but he wore a luxuriant fur of some wild beast draped across his shoulder and he positively glittered with gold and diamonds. He was tall and spare and wore a turban also to protect against the cold. Although he sported no beard his skin was as dark as night and Sihtric could sense great cunning and intelligence emanating from his expressive eyes. To Sihtric's surprise both spoke excellent Gaelic as they introduced themselves and their lineages to Flann Sinna and both laid gifts at the High King's feet. The Umayyad vizier began the official business.

"Oh great High King Flann Sinna, even in the court of Cordoba your wisdom and leadership is spoken about in loving terms."

Sihtric could see the hint of a smile play across Flann Sinna's mouth at that outright lie.

"I come as a humble servant of the great Sultan, looking to do business with you, as has my colleague and friendly competitor, Prince Dyabbi Cisse."

The Ghanaian prince nodded in agreement.

"For many years, we did extraordinary business with the people of Dublin that benefitted all concerned. We understand, as is your right as High King, that you have expelled the ruffian element from the city and have taken over management. We would like to explore business opportunities once more with both you and your subjects. What say you, good king?"

The King rubbed his chin, leaned forward and asked a simple question.

"What is it that you wish to purchase that you two esteemed men feel you must appear at Tara to petition me for? The Norse-Gaels of Dublin are free to trade as they see fit as long as they pay tribute to me. I do not interfere."

The Ghanaian prince spoke next.

"High King Flann Sinna, the Bregans and Leinster men that you have placed in charge of the city, to rule in your stead, refuse to sell… certain stock… that we require. We have decided to approach you directly as the foremost authority in this land, to… eh… perhaps reconsider certain policies around the trade of certain… eh…goods?"

The High King shifted imperceptibly on his bench and Sihtric could sense immediately that something was wrong. He had grown so attuned to the mannerisms of the High King that he could tell when Flann was enraged. The thought hit him like a thunderbolt: *they are talking about slaves!* Flann Sinna stood from his chair and stared down at the two dignitaries. His fury was tangible and everyone in the hall could feel it.

"You call yourselves ambassadors and traders and dare come to my court looking to purchase Irish men, women and children from the slaver's block. The Irish people are mine to protect, not to sell to the Aifric and to the Caliphates of the Middle East. You dress up in silks and finery and use subtle words but in truth, you are no less barbarous than the Vikings. At least they don't dress up what they are. You claim civility and nobility, but it is just a lie."

The King stepped down off the dais and faced them up close.

"The day may come when it is my descendants and kings like me who are purchasing your people from the slaver's block and your descendants will understand slavery for what it is. It is an atrocity not a business. So leave my court at once and count yourself lucky that I do not summon Sihtric of the Ui Imair to collect your heads and send them back to your lords and masters in boxes. If I ever see you two again, I will have you crucified on the shore as a warning to your kin."

The two traders smiled unctuously and bowed low, but the Umayyad vizier fired a parting shot.

"Of course, good King Flann Sinna, we will relay your message to our betters. But know this; King Alan of Brittany, a king of the same… ah… vintage as yourself, had a similar… ah… policy position to you, but he has unfortunately passed away due to its unpopularity. His successor has been more… ah… amenable to our terms. We witnessed your audience with the Munstermen, perhaps the next king after you may… ah… understand our business interests better, with our help of course."

Sihtric stepped down from the dais, axes in hand; despite the implicit threat Flann Sinna shot a warning glance at him to stay his hand. The two viziers retreated from the hall rapidly before anything could spiral out of control.

The High King looked visibly drained at that point and his wife, Queen Mael Muire, insisted that he take his meat at the board and retire to his quarters for a rest. The final visitor to Tara was the most illustrious and one that Sihtric had longed to meet, if only to take his measure. Niall Glundub was here in Tara, the great warrior of the Northern Ui Neill, the great slayer of Vikings and the man who had killed Sihtric's father and brothers. The King had agreed that he had to be at his best when treating with Niall Glundub and that any mistake could be diplomatically costly. Sihtric had so many conflicting feelings about Niall Glundub mac Aed Findliath. He was the killer of his kin, yet he was a warrior of such renown that Sihtric couldn't help but respect and admire him. Growing up in Tara, Sihtric had heard so many stories about the legend of Niall Glundub that he almost feared that he would be disappointed when he met him. All the young boys dreamed of becoming like Niall Glundub. He was the modern-day Finn mac Cumhaill, Cuchulainn or Niall of the Nine Hostages. He was a warrior prince who had defeated armies of Vikings in two different countries. He was the hero of the Battle of Pilgrim, who had held the old footbridge single-handedly while the High King retreated to safety. He had defeated many foes in single combat, and it was said that no man from any land that bordered the Irish Sea could face him and live.

Sihtric though, his inner Viking stirring, almost salivated at the prospect of one day facing him. He knew that his brothers would be thinking the same, particularly Ragnall from memory, who would probably cut ten men down just to get into a fight with the great Glundub. He was rabidly excited to meet him, the great prince of the Northern Ui Neill and now heir and somewhat joint ruler of the northern throne. Excitement warred with vengeance within Sihtric and until he took the Northern Ui Neill prince's measure, he could not say for sure what would win out. Flann Sinna would demand silence and obedience when Glundub came to court and Sihtric would of course acquiesce, but in the dark part of his mind he couldn't help but imagine scenarios where the High King commanded him down from the dais to face the mighty Niall Glundub, sword to axe.

At dusk Sihtric accompanied the High King back to the great hall at Tara and made sure he was safely ensconced on his bench with a drink of mead close by. The hall was packed as the elite of Tara crowded in to witness a famous meeting of two of the most powerful Ui Neill nobles of all time. Only when the King was seated comfortably did Sihtric turn to stand at his side and face the giant in the centre of the room, his heart beating rapidly in his chest as adrenalin coursed through him. Niall Glundub was a veritable monster amongst Irishmen. He had relatively short brown hair and was clean-shaven which was unusual. His tunic was a bit too small for him, Sihtric thought, but it did expose his bulging muscles for all to see. He had lines in his face and a stray grey hair or two but he looked incredibly fit and strong for his age none the less. Absolute authority and confidence exuded from every pore of the Ui Neill prince and the attendees in the hall shrank many feet away from him, being simply overawed by his presence. Sihtric weighed him up with his practised eye. He was already by far the best fighter in Tara, more than a match for the princes Oengus and Conchobar, the half-brother of Niall Glundub. Conchobar was of the same build as Niall Glundub and Sihtric had put him flat on his back in the practice yard many times. That line of form served to infuse the young Viking with confidence. *I could take him,* he thrilled. The sobering thought that Sihtric had only ever fought in three battles, that were barely skirmishes in truth, compared to the dozens of battles Niall Glundub fought in, simultaneously gave him pause. The High King spoke first and Sihtric strained to listen:

"Niall Glundub, it is a great honour to receive you, the great prince of the Ui Neill and son-in-law of mine. I have summoned you here for a specific purpose; I wish you and your brother to join your strength to mine if I campaign next summer. I would have your allegiance and submission as your High King and overlord of the Ui Neill."

Glundub crossed his arms and a hint of a smile curled upward on the side of his mouth.

"King Flann, my brother came to terms with you many years ago and acknowledged you as High King. When my time comes, I intend to do the same and will honour that arrangement. I will be frank; my brother is not the same man he was. He is diminished. His time is nearly done. The death of his son and heir has broken him and to all intents and purposes I rule in his stead already."

The High King interrupted. "Yes, I have heard how you have dealt with your subjects. Did you not massacre the warriors of Dub Sinna son of Eilge, the King of Mag Itha? Your heavy hand is there for all to see, Niall Glundub, but I will not tolerate this sort of behaviour even in one so mighty as you, even if you are my wife's son!"

Glundub laughed at that. "I will rule my lands as I see fit, with all due respect, Flann of the Shannon." Sihtric railed at the lack of respectful honorific in his retort but made no move. "I nominally accept your overlordship of the Ui Neill and Ireland too, but I will not tolerate you interfering in our own politics, nor will I pay you tribute."

This shocked the court and the volume of conversation rose at the prince's declaration. Three thumps of Sihtric's axe on the wooden floor of the dais silenced the crowd.

"I will accept that it is the Northern Ui Neill's responsibility to keep your own affairs in order, but I beg you, Glundub, to consider the diplomatic solution in future or your own kings will come to me to aid them against your tyranny, and it would only lead to war."

Glundub bristled at that., "Careful now, High King, I have faced far more dangerous rulers than you and foes with larger armies. Don't make enemies out of allies."

Sihtric's hackles rose, and he stepped down from the dais. The Northern Ui Neill prince turned to face him.

"What's this now? You are no Irishman."

He turned to Flann Sinna, "This is one of the Ui Imair, or do my eyes deceive me?"

Sihtric slowly unsheathed his axe and spoke. "I am Sihtric son of Ivar, of the Ui Imair. If you threaten the High King once more in this hall, your head will roll free from your torso, lord of the Ui Neill or no."

The hall went deathly quiet. Glundub faced Sihtric.

"Careful now, boy, be careful who *you* threaten. I don't want to kill you but I will if I have to. You wouldn't be the first Ui Imair prince I have sent to Valhalla and you probably won't be the last."

The High King beckoned Sihtric to retreat beside him on the dais. Sihtric could see by the High King's body language that he was pleased with Sihtric's confrontation with the Glundub. As fearsome as Niall was it was good to let him know that there was power enough to threaten him if it came to violence. Sihtric could feel the stare from Glundub boring into his back and even when he turned to face him once more on the dais, Glundub still stared at him. Sihtric met his gaze undaunted; his point had been made.

"Prince Niall, will the Northern Ui Neill join me on campaign if I call upon them as is my right as High King?"

Glundub answered, "On one condition, King Flann, that after your passing you reinstate the old tradition of alternating the High Kingship between the Northern and Southern Ui Neill once more. Your son Oengus is the heir designate I know, but let him be the lord of the Southern Ui Neill alone. If you agree to this, my sword is yours in future."

Flann Sinna sadly shook his head. "I am afraid we are at an impasse then, Glundub, as I have sworn before the Bishop of Clonard on the succession. Your brother Domnall has burned that bridge with his outrageous attack on Meath. Before God I cannot renege on my promise."

Glundub gloomily nodded his head. "Until you reinstate the old way then, High King, you will have no help from us on your campaigns."

Hours later in his bed, Sihtric thought back to the day's events and pondered, *Has Flann Sinna started two wars in a single day?*

# CHAPTER 2

# THE BATTLE OF BEALACH MUGHNA (908)

The wind whipped the hair from the shoulders of the upstart Connaught under-king Cleirchen mac Murchadh and revealed to Sihtric Ui Imair, the face of someone who had accepted his fate. Sihtric was the only guard present, as both he and the High King Flann Sinna were supremely confident in the young Ui Imair warrior's ability to handle himself against anyone. Cleirchen mac Murchadh had risen in rebellion against the King of Connaught and attempted to usurp power from the ruling Ui Briuin Sil Muiredaig clan. Cathal mac Conchobar the King of Connaught and staunch ally of Flann Sinna had moved his forces from Rathcroghan his capital, to meet the forces of the ever more powerful Niall Glundub on his northern borders. Too late, he had realised that it was a feint purely designed to draw Cathal mac Conchobar away from his stronghold and allow Cleirchen mac Murchadh, the King of Maigh Seola, to take Connaught for his own. The token force left to defend Rathcroghan under the command of one of Cathal's nephews, had sent riders north to King Cathal and east to the High King Flann Sinna. It was Flann Sinna who had received word first and he had sent a relieving force under the command of his son Oengus and Sihtric Ivarsson, the Scourge of Ireland. Sihtric had advocated a night attack and Oengus had listened. They had encircled the forces of Cleirchen in the stygian darkness and at the break of dawn they had surrounded and massacred the Connaught rebels. The King himself had submitted to capture and had been marched to Tara for judgement. Prince Oengus was eager to put the usurper to the question. But this was just another symptom of the fact, that across the territory of the Southern Ui Neill, Flann Sinna's allies were under pressure.

In Connaught, the Ui Briuin Sil Muiredaig had battled twice with the Breffni men in the last year and had almost lost their capital to Cleirchen. For the first time in many years the Vikings of Limerick were active on the Shannon, raiding villages and taking captives and livestock from the minor Connaught chieftains. In Brega, on the plains of east Meath, Flann Sinna had to deploy his old ward Fogartach mac Tolarg, to put down a rebellion from one of the minor under-kings, Mael Ograi son of Congalach the Stern. In north Meath, the fort at Tlachtga was sacked and burned by Niall Glundub and his brother Domnall. Tlachtga was an ancient place steeped in history and strong in the ways of the old gods. Not all of Flann Sinna's people were Christians and many folk loyal to him still paid respects to Dagda and the old pantheon at certain times of the year. Glundub had sent word that this desecration of a place of the Gaelic gods was to show the people how Flann Sinna trucked with demons and heathens and that he, Niall Glundub, was a Christian ruler who would turn every pagan site in Ireland to ash. *He will do the same to the Viking holy places,* Sihtric knew. Flann Sinna was also a devout Christian, but his rule was secular. Whether his subjects worshipped Jesus, Dagda, Lugh, Allah, Brigid, Odin or Tyr was irrelevant; if you bent the knee and paid tribute, he did not care. In Munster, the armies of Cormac mac Cuilennain ravaged Osraige and Leinster and had raided across the Shannon into Connaught on occasion. From all sides, Flann Sinna's territories and those of his allies were under siege. Both Sihtric and Flann Sinna suspected, however, that what was really happening was all connected and they perceived the dark machinations behind the scenes. Niall Glundub was flexing his muscles militarily and politically, stirring up rebellion across the entire island. It was a play for power; he was coming.

The Connaught under-king Cleirchen was chained to a bench in a small enclosure adjoining the outside of the fort in Tara. It was usually used for housing the horses of noble guests but had been converted to a prison stockade on this occasion. Flann Sinna had been called to convene a council with his three surviving sons: Oengus his heir, Conchobar, and even his estranged eldest son Donnchadh Donn. Sihtric had been given the task of guarding the captive. The defeated Connaught King looked up from his bench and spoke.

"I suppose you know that you and your great uncle can never win. The Southern Ui Neill have held power for too long. King Flann's forces are spread too thin; he cannot be everywhere at once. If it's not Cormac mac Cuilennain who defeats him, it will be Niall Glundub or your brother Ragnall."

Sihtric laughed at this. "My brother Ragnall has not set foot in Dublin for six years, he is no threat. He raids upon the Irish Sea and the Saxon coast. Flann Sinna has been king for more than thirty years; he knows how to deal with rebellion."

Cleirchen spat on the ground in disgust. "Aye, yes, I have seen how he deals with anyone who dares question him. He sends Oengus or Conchobar or that fat lickspittle from Leinster Cerbaill mac Muirecain, to harass and intimidate good Irish people or worse; he sends you, his pet heathen savage, to slaughter the innocent. They call you Flann Sinna's scourge and they are right but not in how they mean it. You are a scourge upon all of the people of this island and when Flann Sinna dies, either by the sword or the slow decay of time, your time will come as well, Sihtric of the Ui Imair."

That touched a nerve with Sihtric and he smashed his fist into the Connaught King's mouth. Cleirchen spat a mouthful of blood and teeth onto the ground but smiled as if irking the young Viking warrior was some sort of victory. Unheeding of his own personal safety the captive continued taunting Sihtric.

"All of those under-kings and chieftains looking on obsequious and submissive to Flann Sinna and seeing a barbarian like you at his right hand. Tell me, Scourge, do you not feel their eyes upon you? All the people under Flann Sinna's control have suffered under Viking tyranny for a hundred years;

do you think that when Flann Sinna passes you will be left to your own devices? No, Sihtric, you will be put to the sword and probably by one of his own sons."

Sihtric was about to strike the prisoner again, but Flann Sinna appeared before he could bury the butt of his axe in his face. The High King looked down at the bloodied prisoner who smiled sickeningly up at him with a ghastly visage of blood and broken teeth.

Flann Sinna's face darkened. "This was ill done, Sihtric. He is a prisoner of mine, not some sparring partner to practise your fighting skills upon."

Sihtric shrugged his shoulders apathetically.

"He made some threats against your life, my King; I was forced to try and silence him."

Flann Sinna nodded impatiently "Well, it makes no difference now anyway."

He addressed the chained prisoner. "Cleirchen mac Murchadh, you are sentenced to die. How do you wish to meet your end? By drowning, hanging or the axe?"

The Connaught under-king shakily stood to his feet. "By the axe, Flann of the Shannon, but swung by yourself or another of the Ui Neill, not by this Viking son of a Dublin whore"

Flann Sinna's face darkened again. "I will allow you to end by the axe. But I shall decide who shall swing it."

Sihtric dragged the prisoner down the hill toward the secluded spot where Flann Sinna executed his captured foes; a perfectly shaped stone where a prisoner could kneel and rest his chest thus protruding their extended neck out over the edge. Children and other ordinary folk stared curiously at events as they unfolded and some attempted to follow before being shooed away by some of Flann Sinna's personal guard. A copse of trees covered the clearing were the executioner's stone lay, obscuring it from prying eyes. All that were present were Flann's three sons with Flann himself, the Bishop of Clonard and Sihtric with the prisoner. Cleirchen met his end like a warrior and Sihtric couldn't help but be impressed. The Connaught under-king stripped off to the waist and received Holy Communion from the bishop who also doused him in holy water.

The High King then spoke to him. "King Cleirchen mac Murchadh, you leave sons behind you and a wife. Your remains will be sent to Galway upon your death for burial. You are of the Connaught branch of the Ui Neill and will receive your due respect as a nobleman and Christian. My sons and my grandnephew bear witness to my judgement and your passing. For the crime of conspiring with Niall Glundub to usurp the crown of Connaught, I, Flann Sinna mac Mael Seachnaill, the King of Meath and of all Ireland, sentence you to die. Have you any last words?"

The captive King looked in the eyes of each of the witnesses present, including the Bishop and surprisingly it was to the Bishop that he spoke first.

"Bishop Padraig of Clonard, the High King trucks with Vikings and allows his subjects to worship the old gods and yet you stand here and condone it?"

The Bishop did redden under the collar a little bit, Sihtric noticed, but the clergyman was wise enough to say nothing.

"You three sons of Flann Sinna, your father allows the Vikings to survive in Dublin and surrounds himself with fiends and monsters like this Sihtric Ui Imair. Are you Irish princes or worms to ally yourself with such as him? If so, Niall Glundub is the better option for Ireland. Flann Sinna has had power for too long and he has not the best interests of Ireland or the Ui Neill at heart. He should be long retired and one of you three should rule if you won't bend the knee to the Glundub."

Sihtric saw that Conchobar and Donachadh Donn were angered at this; Oengus shook his head in disgust. The High King had had enough.

"Sihtric, end this farce and put this man to death!"

Sihtric didn't need to be asked twice. He kicked the back of Cleirchen's knees, and they buckled. He landed with a thump on the execution stone. Sihtric didn't even wait for Cleirchen to stretch his neck out. With an expert blow he severed his head from his shoulders and it rolled free onto the grass. Oengus and Sihtric accompanied Flann Sinna back up toward the fort but Donnchadh Donn and Conchobar quickly outpaced them, leaving them behind. *The traitor's words have struck a chord with them,* Sihtric thought worryingly.

*

Three weeks later in the main hall in Tara, Sihtric attended the High King as he hosted the largest meeting of his major allies seen in a dozen years. The issue of Niall Glundub had come to a head and Flann Sinna, as was his want, called for council from his most powerful warlords, chieftains, and under-kings. One way or the other Shitric knew war was coming, but with who first and when was undecided. On the night that Sihtric had taken the head of Cleirchen mac Murchadh, the High King had sent out riders throughout Meath, Leinster, Osraige and Connaught. Niall Glundub had certainly roused the country against Flann Sinna's power and it was going to be answered in some way.

The braziers were lit in the hall to ward off the night's chill and everybody of unimportance was expelled from the hall. From Meath alone, there were Donnchadh Donn, Oengus mac Flann, Conchobar mac Flann, Bishop Padraig of Clonard, Fogartach mac Tolarg of South Brega and Mael Mithig mac Flannacain, the High Kings son-in-law and ruler of North Brega. From Connaught, the King Cathal mac Conchobar and his eldest son Tadg sat on a bench by the fire, but the Ua Ruairc clan had no representative present as they held the border with the Northern Ui Neill and couldn't risk leaving their territory undefended. From Osraige, Flann Sinna's ever fateful ally Ceallach mac Cerbaill was there and from Leinster stood the under-king, Aililla of the Ui Dunlainge, as Cerbaill mac Muireacain held the eastern bank of the River Lerr in Leinster against the rampaging army of Cormac mac Cuilennain, the King of Munster. Above them all on the dais sat High King Flann Sinna with his elderly wife Queen Mael Muire, the mother of both Prince Conchobar and Niall Glundub himself. Sihtric stood in his accustomed position to the side of the King. Flann Sinna slowly rose to his feet to address the hall.

"My loyal kings and princes, I have called you here and told you to gather your men for I mean to make war upon our enemies. The question is, do we move north and break the growing power of my son-in-law Niall Glundub? Or do we march south and relieve the Kingdom of Leinster and destroy the Munstermen under Cormac mac Cuilennain?"

The King slowly sat back down into his chair looking as weak as Sihtric had ever seen him. *These events are taxing him heavily,* thought Sihtric. *Will he even survive another campaign?* The Bishop of Clonard addressed the King first.

"High King Flann Sinna, it has come to my attention that King Cormac of Munster has recently become a bishop of our holy Christian faith. It would surely be unconscionable to attack a man of the cloth like this. Perhaps a peaceful solution should be considered or if warfare must be waged, maybe north is the direction you should look, my King?"

This made Sihtric smile. Bishops had always fought in the armies of the Irish, he knew, and rival kings often sacked the churches and monasteries and religious centres of rival kingdoms. The thought of a warmonger like Cormac of Munster suddenly finding God as he sacked and plundered the lands of Kildare was ludicrous. And yet Sihtric was surprised how Flann responded.

"Perhaps, Lord Bishop, if I was to offer gold and livestock to the monasteries at Clonmacnoise and Clonard, and began building further churches in my land, Holy God would perhaps forgive me for what I have to do?"

The Bishop adjusted his Christian attire and mumbled a response.

"Ah yes… well… I do believe that our Lord Father and his son Jesus Christ would find that tribute ah… suitable… to nullify any possible… problems… with the holy faith that any warfare could cause."

Sihtric almost laughed out loud at the hypocrisy of it. As long as Flann Sinna kicked back a share of any spoils to his pet priests and bishops, all would be well with the Christian God and their servants on earth.

Mael Muire the Queen was next to speak. Her hair had gone to grey in the last few years, but in Sihtric's opinion she still possessed an intimidating air of nobility that commanded respect whenever she deigned to speak. In many matters of governance within Flann Sinna's realm, it was actually Queen Mael Muire who held court and made the day-to-day decisions. She turned to Flann Sinna, resting her arm on his own.

"Perhaps we should sue for peace? Niall Glundub is no barbarian; he doesn't pursue violence for violence's sake. It is a means to an end, not an end in itself. Let me speak with him and convince him to come to negotiate. If we placate Glundub, perhaps the Munstermen will retreat upon knowing that your forces will be free to march upon their lands without worrying about the threat from the north? Our people have suffered enough over the years. If war can be avoided, I say you should pursue that course, husband."

Flann Sinna nodded sagely at his Queen's thoughts in the matter and Sihtric could see the Bishop of Clonard nodding his head in agreement. But Donnchadh Donn, Flann Sinna's eldest son, disagreed with the Queen almost immediately.

"Father, Niall Glundub assaults our borders with impunity. It is my lands in North Meath that he regularly attacks. His minions from Argialla, Breffni and the lands of the Ulaid are sacking and burning our smaller settlements. If we do not join and march north, how long will it be until our smaller chieftains and under-kings turn away from us and give their allegiance to the Glundub? He must be faced!"

Cathal the King of Connaught agreed.

"King Flann, you have our eternal allegiance forever, but our lands are being raided constantly. You saw what happened last month. Glundub and his brother are stirring up unrest across our collective lands, telling aggrieved and greedy under-kings what they want to hear, subverting them with dreams of power and wealth. He is coming. We need to join forces. I say we march north into Argialla and devastate the land. The Black Fox is no more and his savage son Maol Craoibh needs to be put to the sword. If we wipe out the Argiallans, our lands and those of your son Donnchadh Donn will be saved from Niall Glundub and we will have a buffer zone between us and the Northern Ui Neill. The Ulaid and the Dal nAridi will fall into line and if we have to march west and wipe out the Breffni, so be it!"

There was a chorus of *Ayes* from Donnchadh Donn, Conchobar mac Flann and Oengus the heir designate. Sihtric found himself nodding in agreement too for the chance to clash with the allies of the Glundub. Conchobar, Flann's youngest son, was the next to speak.

"I agree with King Cathal on this but with one small deviation. I say that we attack the Breffni instead of the Argialla. In a direct attack, Flann mac Tighernain the King of Breffni will fold quickly and we will be at Glundub's doorstep. I will then negotiate with my half-brother from a position of strength. I am certain he will listen to sense and desist. At the end of the day, Father, we want the Northern Ui Neill and the people they rule to bend the knee, we do not wish to massacre them. The poor people of Ireland have suffered enough hardship and death. Let us keep war and death to a minimum and bring my brother to heel."

The chorus of *Ayes* was even louder this time. Both Donnchadh Donn and the King of Connaught were happy with this plan and Oengus clearly considered it sensible too. The Bishop of Clonard nodded his head ponderously and even Queen Mael Muire, although clearly dismayed at the inevitable violence, was satisfied by the course of action suggested by her youngest son. The two warlike Bregan kings were also pleased with the chance to march north and give Glundub and his allies a taste of his own medicine. At this point King Aililla of the Ui Dunlainge stepped forward to say his piece.

"My Kings, I must respectfully intercede. You all speak of Niall Glundub as the main problem, a looming threat to be answered through warfare. But my lands are under attack as we speak. We are subjects under your rule, High King Flann Sinna, and we pay you tribute. In return we ask for your protection. King Cormac mac Cuilennain of Munster ravages our lands, now, today! My liege lord the King of Leinster, Cerbaill mac Muireacain, and my son Augaire lead our forces, but they are in full retreat. The Munstermen are camped at Bealach Mughna and are devastating the lands around Kildare and on south and even as far as the coast. My son Augaire is a brilliant warrior, but he has been reduced to hitting their supply lines and retreating into the hills. He does not have the men to risk open battle against Cormac."

The name of Augaire raised the hairs on Sihtric's neck. This was the man who had slain his mother and captured him, according to Flann Sinna, and in Sihtric's private thoughts, he hoped Cormac caught and butchered him. King Aililla continued:

"The Munstermen are reinforced by Viking longships from Limerick and Cork who help resupply them from the river systems. One of my own chieftain's entire clan was wiped out, every man, woman and child, by one of these roving bands of marauders allied to King Cormac. I say to you, King Flann Sinna, that you all must respond to the enemy that openly wages battle against your people rather than the threat from the north that may or may not materialise at all."

Sihtric looked around the room at the reaction to the Leinster King's opinion.

All the Southern Ui Neill and Connaught kings and princes grumbled in disapproval. It was obvious that they cared little or less for what was befalling the Leinster men and were only concerned with their own interests. The sycophant Ceallach mac Cerbaill simply waited for Flann Sinna's decision. The old king sat in his throne staring into the middle distance. He had heard all the council available to him from his allies and Sihtric could perceive Flann Sinna's great mind churning through the potential scenarios and outcomes of every decision. At length he stood up from his chair and addressed the people in the hall.

"Here is my decision. We will split our forces into four parts. Donnchadh Donn, you will martial the Caille Follamain and deploy them at the point where the borders of Connaught, Meath and the territories of the Breffni and the Airgialla meet. You will engage Niall Glundub and his allies if they invade Meath."

Donnchadh Donn looked displeased but did not raise any argument.

"King Fogarthach and King Mael Mithig, you will join the armies of North and South Brega and camp at the point where the lands of the Ulaid and the Argiallans border with Meath."

Both men touched their foreheads with three fingers in deference and respect.

"Oengus my son and heir, you will hold Tara in my absence. Should Glundub or his allies slip past our garrisons, long may you hold Tara in my absence."

The Queen interrupted Flann Sinna to his annoyance.

"Husband, you cannot mean to march south yourself, you are past seventy years of age. You have three mighty sons by your side; send them in your stead. Even Sihtric the Scourge would suffice to defeat Cormac in open battle."

Flann Sinna sadly shook his head.

"My dream of a united country is so close yet so far away, my Queen. It must be me who leads our forces south to cleanse Leinster of the Munstermen. I will go south with a large part of the forces of Clan Colman of the Southern Ui Neill. My scourge, Sihtric Ui Imair, will bear my standard and be my champion in the field. The armies of Connaught will venture south with me to join forces with the Leinster men and the Kingdom of Osraige. My son Conchobar, I will not ask you to fight your own half-brother; you will command the vanguard of my army instead against King Cormac. Together – Connaught, Meath, Osraige and Leinster – we will smash the armies of King Cormac mac Cuilennain and his allies or die in the attempt."

\*

It had taken four weeks but on the morning of the thirteenth of September, 908, the forces of Flann Sinna had surrounded the camp during the night of the Munstermen and their Viking allies. The scouts had successfully assassinated any enemy scouts and avoided all the other sentries that were set by King Cormac. They were few in number which suggested that the Munstermen did not expect to face any significant foe in the field. *They were very wrong about that,* thought Sihtric.

Flann Sinna's scouts had numbered the foe at roughly five thousand warriors in total, almost matching Flann Sinna, but their camp was haphazard, and their long occupation of the area had reduced their camp to a mucky unorganised mess. Discipline was almost zero. On receiving the full report from his scouts Flann had set about deploying his forces. The camp of the Munstermen was on the east bank of the River Lerr a couple of miles from the monastery at Castledermot, at the burned-out village of Bealach Mughna. A high ridge surrounded the river in a crescent from the north to the south. Flann had sent riders to the embattled forces of the King of Leinster, Cerbaill mac Muireacain, with a command to move his warriors to the east of the high ridge. He had told the King of Osraige, Ceallach mac Cerbaill, to circle around undetected to the south to prevent any escape for Cormac. The forces of the Connaught men were to hold the west bank of the River Lerr, which was neither wide nor deep, but should suffice to keep the Munstermen from fleeing west easily. Flann's son Conchobar would lead the bulk of the forces of Clan Colman of the Southern Ui Neill from the north of the ridge and attack the camp at dawn. Flann Sinna himself would command the reserve of two hundred men with Sihtric Ui Imair and reinforce any part of the battle line that came under pressure, or, if there was some decisive blow that could be dealt by this reserve to Cormac's forces, they would also enter the fray. Everybody was in position; all was in readiness and all it would take would be a single horn blast from Sihtric and the battle of Bealach Mughna would begin.

The dawn light fast approached as the sun threatened to rise in the east above the ridge. Sihtric was almost sick with excitement. The Irishmen around him were shivering in fear and inhaling massive and rapid breaths as if within the thick of the battle already. Sihtric could almost hear the teeth of some of the men around him chattering in pure fear, but he was confident that when it came to it, these warriors would not let the High King down. A sound from above in the sky drew his gaze. A murder of crows circled lazily at high altitude in the very early morning light as if anticipating the slaughter to come.

All along the ridge, which was about three miles long, Sihtric could see the line of battle formed, ready to charge down the hill and into the camp of the Munstermen. He turned to Flann Sinna, his horn at his lips in readiness. Flann Sinna appeared to be listening to the wind, perhaps hoping to hear some words from his Christian god, but maybe just waiting for the ground running down to the river to illuminate further in the dawn light. The High King had never looked as regal as this in Sihtric's memory. He wore a long cloak, green as the colour of the Southern Ui Neill, and in this moment on the utmost cusp of battle the years fell away from him, and he looked like what Sihtric Ui Imair imagined the legendary Irish conquerors of old had done, like Finn mac Cumhaill and Cuchulainn. Flann turned to Sihtric and gave him the most imperceptible of nods. Sihtric placed his horn to his lips and blew like he was the avatar of Thor the Thunder God himself, and the sound echoed around the lands of the River Lerr. It was answered by horns from the different sections of the army. A great inhalation of breath was collectively drawn and then five thousand men screamed and charged as one upon the Munstermen. And so began the Battle of Bealach Mughna, the great battle of the time.

The Munstermen were caught unawares and hundreds of them were slaughtered as they rubbed sleep from their eyes, but in less than a minute, hardened Irish veterans and Viking berserkers had formed islands in the sea of Flann Sinna's onrushing forces. Even from several hundred feet away, Sihtric could see perfectly the visceral slaughter occurring as blood and shit and intestines combined with the muck of the camp into a primordial soup of gore. The screams of rage and dying entwined into a cacophonous chorus that surely the gods could hear. And the crows circled ever so slowly in the sky and in greater number, waiting to feast on the slain.

Sihtric passed the banner of the High King to a young lad and eased his axe and shield to the ready. His scourge was strapped to his back and he was festooned with other daggers across his person. He placed his heavily spiked helm upon his head. Prince Oengus had warned him that wearing such fearsome and ostentatious wargear would single him out for the enemy, but Sihtric felt that the fear his recognisable presence exuded amongst the enemy was worth the risk of standing out. The young but already giant Viking prince bearing the spiked helm subliminally told any enemy that Sihtric of the Ui Imair had come and your life was forfeit should you face him in the field. The messengers came thick and fast to Flann Sinna and were despatched back to the various kings and sergeants on the battlefield.

The Munstermen had attempted to retreat across the river immediately, but Cathal mac Conchobar had beaten them back for little loss, his archers having done terrible damage. However, another message had come with grave tidings as a bunch of Limerick berserkers had smashed their way through the ranks of the main force from Osraige and King Ceallach mac Cerbaill had been cut down and his body hacked to pieces. His men had rallied and driven the Vikings back into the ranks of the Munstermen. Better news had arrived minutes later when a runner revealed that Fogartach son of Suibne, the King of Kerry, had been slain in single combat by Flann's own son Conchobar and that Conchobar's vanguard was reaping a terrible toll amongst the Kerrymen. The worst news of all arrived next when a breathless messenger boy informed Flann Sinna that those same berserkers that had tried to break through to the south had tried the eastern ridge next and Aililla son of Eogan was killed in the fighting. Those elite berserkers had finally been surrounded and put to the sword, but to lose a commander of Aililla's experience was a savage loss to Flann Sinna. It was apparent after an hour's fighting that the men from Munster were about to make their last stand and finally Flann Sinna commanded Sihtric forward with his two hundred men with orders to go straight for the banner of Cormac mac Cuilennain to deliver justice. And so Sihtric Ui Imair, the Scourge of Ireland, entered the fray at the Battle of Bealach Mughna.

The ranks of Clan Colman parted as Sihtric went through and a roar of exultant savagery rose from the Ui Neill ranks and then he was amongst the slaughter. He buried his axe in the chests, heads and bellies of his opponents and severed limbs as if cutting through butter with a knife. The Munstermen began to break on his approach, some fled before him while others threw themselves down at his feet begging for mercy. He had none to offer and slew them all. Cormac mac Cuilennain, who was mounted, came forward to meet the Ui Imair prince and charged. Sihtric hacked the leg of the horse clean through while blocking the overhead blow from the Munster King. The stricken animal threw the King from the saddle and he toppled to the ground. Sihtric approached, savouring the chance to land the killing blow, but frustratingly he saw that the King had broken his neck in the fall and was dead already. In a furious rage, denied the finality of delivering the fatal blow, he hacked the head from the Munster King's shoulders and raised it up for all to see. On sighting the grisly demise of their king, the Munstermen almost as one, threw down their arms in surrender. And as quickly as that, the battle was over.

"FLANN SINNA ABU! FLANN SINNA ABU!"

The victory chant echoed around the ridge at Bealach Mughna. The men of Munster were defeated, and their fighters were either captured or slain. Notably they had successfully captured Flaithbertach mac Inmainen, the Munster prince who had initiated this conflict in Flann Sinna's hall a year ago.

Sihtric, covered in the blood and entrails of his foes, strode up the hill to Flann Sinna and threw the head of the Munster King at his feet. The High King's face changed from jubilation to one of sorrow.

"That was an evil deed, Sihtric, you should not have despoiled his corpse so. Cormac mac Cuilennain fought bravely. I witnessed his last stand against you, a mighty Ui Imair Prince. He knew that he could not defeat you, but he faced you none the less. I shall honour him and leave his soldiers in peace. There will be no more death this day. Give the command to take hostages and send the survivors of the Munster forces home with food for the journey."

Flann picked up the head and kissed the dead king's forehead.

"We shall bury him with full honours at the Monastery of Castledermot."

Sihtric took a cloth and cleaned his axe of the blood that drenched it. The crows were circling uncounted, thousands of them. *Perhaps one for each warrior slain today,* thought Sihtric. *Odin is here.*

In the halls of Ireland, a short time after the conclusion of the battle, a poem was repeated about the faithful day, of the Battle of Bealach Mughna and who fell there:

*Cormac of Feimhin, Fogartach, Colman,*
*Ceallach of the hard conflicts,*
*They perished with many thousands*
*In the great battle of Bealach Mughna*
*Flann of Tara, of the plain of Tailteann,*
*Cerbhall of Carman without fail,*
*On the thirteenth of the Calends of September,*
*Gained the battle of which hundreds were joyful.*
*The bishop, the soul's director,*
*The renowned, illustrious doctor,*
*King of Caiseal, King of Iarmumha;*
*Oh God! Alas for Cormac.*

# CHAPTER 3

# THE RESCUE FROM TARA
# (909)

Sihtric rode beside the King at the head of a column of retainers on the road from the monastery at Clonmacnoise, to the fort of Flann Sinna's people at Lough Ennell. These lands were the heart of the territory of Clan Colman and they were where the Southern Ui Neill predominantly drew its strength. The fort at Tara had only been rebuilt during the early days of Flann Sinna's reign and it was actually here on the banks of Lough Ennell, that Flann Sinna had grown up and where his father Mael Seachnaill had ruled Ireland from. Flann Sinna's son Conchobar ruled Lough Ennell now, with Oengus, his heir designate, ruling by his father's side at Tara. Donnchadh Donn ruled the eminent clan the Caille Follamain, who controlled the lands north of Lough Owel and further east. Lough Owel itself was the place where Flann Sinna's father had executed the first great Viking invader of the land, Turgesius, or Thorgest as he was known amongst the Norse and Danes. For his crimes he was tied up in chains with hempen bags full of rocks hung from his shoulders and tossed to the bottom to drown. In the three days since they had left Clonmacnoise, Flann Sinna had decided to tell that story to Sihtric five times already, but Sihtric preferred not to point this out and allowed the old king to relive his memories and the stories of his youth. They seemed to give him joy.

The land was full of tales for the King. Sihtric allowed himself to be immersed in the great stories and sagas known by Flann Sinna. One time he pointed out to Sihtric a small valley where Diarmuid and Grainne had evaded the great Finn mac Cumhaill when they had eloped. By a stream that trickled through a certain glen, Flann Sinna eagerly pointed out that this was the place where Niall Noigiallach received oaths of fealty from the Kings of the Leath Mogha, having defeated them in battle. The land was infused with history, magic and mystery and the High King knew all the stories. Flann Sinna had travelled to Clonmacnoise for a variety of reasons. Firstly, he wished to deliver on his promises to the clergy to provide them with gold, silver and livestock as a mark of respect on supporting his cause in his fight with the Eoghanachta and their allies. Had he not done this, it would have caused problems with the common men sworn to fight for him. If they believed that Jesus Christ was not on their side, many could have deserted. The second reason was a sad one. One of the under-kings of Connaught, Sochlachlann mac Diarmata, a second cousin and childhood friend of Flann Sinna, had passed away from sickness and the infirmities brought on by extreme old age. One by one, Flann Sinna's peers of his youth were falling by the wayside, dying in battle or suffering the afflictions of time and sickness. Only a month prior to that, word had reached Flann Sinna of the death of Cadell ap Rhodri, the Welsh King of Seisyllwg. They had never met but had corresponded with written letters of mutual respect and were of an age. Each death, Sihtric could see, diminished Flann Sinna further. *The day will come when he is all alone,* thought Sihtric.

The final reason for the trip to Clonmacnoise was a political one. The border disputes between Connaught and the Breffni, under-kings of the Northern Ui Neill, had exacerbated over the year and warfare was now rife. Flann had to council the King of Connaught on policy before anything ill-judged could occur. Niall Glundub had devastated the land belonging to the Ui Fiachrach, a clan based in North Connaught also. King Cathal mac Conchobar, who was also attending the funeral of Sochlachlann, was adamant that both he and Flann Sinna should march north and wipe the Breffni from the face of the earth, but

Flann had decided against it. Flann had insisted that the next year's crop of young men could do with another year's seasoning before they campaigned once more. Although the battle of Bealach Mughna the previous year had been a resounding victory for the High King and his allies, their armies had taken hundreds of casualties. To appease Cathal the Connaught King, Flann gave his leave for him to take revenge whenever the Breffni dared cross the border with retaliatory attacks into their lands.

All across the island of Ireland and the Irish Sea, the tides of war were ebbing and flowing and Flann often used Sihtric to bounce his ideas and opinions off on how he should position himself geopolitically. From the lands of the Saxons, news had come to Tara that Aethelfled, the War Queen of the Mercians, had joined forces with her brother Edward once more and devastated the lands of Northumbria. The attack had culminated in the plundering of the monastery where the bones of Saint Oswald lay. The saint's remains were taken as spoils back to Mercia and Aethelfled had commissioned the building of a great church to hold the relics. Flann Sinna had told Sihtric what he really thought was going on. Although ostensibly the reason why the Saxons had marched north and broken the truce with the brothers who ruled Northumbria from Yorvik, was to rescue Christian relics from heathen hands, the excuse was flimsy at best in Flann's opinion. Many of the settlers of Danish or Norse heritage had taken Christ as their God and abandoned Odin and even though the brothers Ingvarr, Eowils and Halfdan were as heathen as Sihtric himself, their people were mostly Christian. Flann perceived Aethelfled's actions as an attempt by the Saxons to provoke war with Northumbria because if they could destroy the forces of the brothers, the Saxons could focus all of their attention on taming the Danelaw and East Anglia for once and for all.

Inevitably, when King Flann ran over the same story again and again with Sihtric as he never remembered telling him in the first place, his thoughts would then turn to Ragnall. Speaking about his brother as a potential enemy with the King made Sihtric deeply uncomfortable. He had not seen his brother in almost eight years yet the King repeatedly quizzed Sihtric on what he thought his brother might do in the future. Flann always came back to the issue of would Ragnall lead the Ui Imair Vikings into battle beside the three brothers of Yorvik against the Saxons, or would he keep his warriors out of it? And if Ragnall entered the fray, would he begin recruiting young men from Dublin, Cork and Limerick to join him? Flann Sinna had often remarked that he suspected that every year many of the young Norse-Gael men would quietly slip out from Dublin in their longboats to seek their fortune at the side of the great sea king Ragnall Ivarsson. Flann had conceded that not once in almost eight years had his lands been attacked by any of the Ui Imair or raiders affiliated to them. They had kept their word. But the allure for young Norse-Gaels in Ireland to join Ragnall's forces was still concerning. Allegedly, the Northern Ui Neill had not been as fortunate as Flann's territories.

The Ulaid and the Dal nAridi on the eastern parts of Niall Glundub's kingdom had endured dozens of raids and on several occasions, Niall Glundub himself had to march forth from Aileach to deal with the Vikings. Ragnall in the past year had been rampaging up and down the Irish Sea. The Norse-Gaels of the Hebrides had been hit many times and even as far south as the coast of Francia had felt Ragnall's wrath. His fleet and his armies grew ever larger, and it was only a matter of time before Aethelfled, Constantine of Scotland or even Niall Glundub, would be forced to act and purge these wolves from the Irish Sea before they became too powerful. Everything revolved around what the Kings of Northumbria did in response to the Saxon raid and how involved the Ui Imair would be in the inevitable conflict that Flann Sinna foresaw.

At home as well, events were moving apace, and Sihtric knew that Flann Sinna was even better informed of events on Irish soil. Cerbaill mac Muirecan had died of a sickness at a young age in Leinster. His son had been deemed too young to assume the kingship of Leinster yet, especially as the province was sorely wounded from the ravages of the Munstermen and the southern-based Vikings. The kings and chieftains had elected Augaire mac Aililla as the King of Leinster. He was a proven battle commander having fought against the Ui Imair for years and he had led men in the sack of Dublin in 902. He had covered himself in glory leading the defence of Leinster against the forces of Cormac mac Cuilennain and he had also allied himself with the Saxons in the defeat of Ingamundr at Chester in 907. A cold fury rose when Sihtric ever heard the name of Augaire mentioned by the King, but Flann Sinna either didn't remember whom he was talking to or didn't care and ploughed on regardless, irrespective of Sihtric's feelings. Sihtric suspected that although the King's memories were depreciating rapidly with old age, it was in fact the latter and the King expected Sihtric as a prince of the Ui Imair to be able to look at things objectively, undiluted by personal grievance and thoughts of revenge.

In Munster, the former strength of the entire Leath Mogha, the southern half of the country, was much diminished. At least fifteen hundred fighting men had been killed at Bealach Mughna and now Flann Sinna and his allies had a responsibility to protect them while also stopping old grievances from emerging as various factions vied for power in the vacuum that was once Munster. Flann Sinna had of late repeatedly told Sihtric in confidence that he dreaded the idea of word escaping out into the Viking world of the fighting shape of the most southern province. The Ui Imair had stood by their oaths to him but there were many other rogue elements out there on the high seas. Bairid mac Oitir held court on the Isle of Mann. Harald Fairhair's sons, including the Bloodaxe, reaved and pillaged internationally. Many Independent war bands infested the river systems of Francia, only nominally allied to the barbarian known as Rollo the Walker. There were rich lands in Munster and thousands of unprotected women and children, and Flann Sinna knew that it was up to him to defend the province. To this end he went against the advice of his son Oengus and released the treacherous snake Flaithbertach mac Inmainen. He needed a leader under his control who could keep the peace in the south, as the people there would never listen to a King from Osraige, Connaught, Meath or Leinster. It had to be one of their own and although it was a bit of a gamble, he owed Flann Sinna his life after all as the King was perfectly within his rights to execute the Munster prince after the battle of Bealach Mughna.

In Meath an even more worrying development had occurred in North Brega. Amalgaid son of Congalach had been defeated in battle alongside his ally Inneirge mac Mael Teimin in a dispute over tribute. Conaille mac Muirteimne, a minor chieftain, had made common cause with the Northmen of Linn and defeated the Bregan nobles, decapitating both in a grizzly execution. In normal times, Flann Sinna would have raised a force of men from Brega and the rest of Meath and marched north to decimate his foes, but with the uneasy situation with his son-in-law Niall Glundub ongoing, he did not want to drive these Vikings from Linn into the arms of the Northern Ui Neill, however unlikely that was. War made for strange bedfellows. They were unaligned with anybody and to rock the boat now would have consequences that Flann Sinna believed he could not endure currently. Niall Glundub continued his relentless crusade in the northern lands, punishing any dissent against his rule. His latest opponent was Becc, grandson of Lethlobar of the Dal nAridi, whom Glundub's young son Muirchertach mac Niall captured and executed on the shores of Lough Neagh. Glundub's son had already garnered a serious reputation as a warrior and as hisgrandfather, the King took a perverse pride in his achievements, despite him being effectively his enemy. Many times, he would tell Sihtric with delight that the men of the Northern Ui Neill had taken to calling his grandson *Hector* after the hero from the ancient Trojan legends; Muirchertach mac Niall, the Hector of Ireland. Whenever he heard his name, Sihtric always felt a spasm of desire to cut this Hector down personally if or when the time came.

The days rolled on, and the convoy of retainers that Sihtric and the King spearheaded meandered through the countryside of Meath. Forests of oak, rowan, ash and black alder densely covered the more sparsely populated regions, but close to the forts of chieftains this scenery gave way to ploughed fields and cultivated lands for grass and barley. Every chieftain and leader whose lands they passed invited them to feast, and the King obliged, but he never overstayed his welcome as a retinue as large as his could impoverish a lowly chieftain very quickly. Sihtric always stayed in the background, not just searching for threats to the King but observing how he behaved, taking in how a King should treat his subjects. Flann Sinna was clearly a master at it, as these very same chieftains gladly sent forth their young men every battle season to fight and potentially die for Flann Sinna's causes. They worshipped him. Sihtric noticed that before Flann's convoy left, he would always lavish some great gift upon the hosting chieftain, gold, silver or livestock. Every word Flann said, every move he made, Sihtric catalogued it into the back of his mind for future reference.

Seven days after leaving Clonmacnoise, the train of retainers arrived at Clonard and Flann Sinna took Holy Confession and Communion with the Bishop there. Bishop Paudi, as King Flann affectionately called him, had been a regular visitor to Tara over the last year or two and had become a favourite of the King. Sihtric had suspected that the Bishop was trying to sway the King to be buried in the grounds at Clonard when he passed rather than beside his father at Kells where the rulers of Clan Colman had been buried for over fifty years. That would allow Clonard to perhaps eclipse Clonmacnoise in terms of religious importance, which would result in higher incomes there for the clergy. Sihtric had brought his concerns to Mael Muire but she had dryly responded asking how it had taken him so long for it to dawn upon him and Sihtric had abashedly retreated. *Nothing occurred within the court of Flann Sinna that Mael Muire did not see or have a hand in.* On the fourteenth day, the large caravan of the High King finally arrived at Tara Hill, its magnificent, whitewashed palisades gleaming in the early autumn evening, a beacon of the rule of Flann Sinna towering over the plains of Meath.

When the convoy had been settled and quartered and the men had been sent back to their families, the King invited Sihtric to join him by the fire in his main hall. It was late at night and the fire was roaring but Sihtric could see that the King was in one of his retrospective moods.

"Sit down beside me, Sihtric, and I will tell you a tale and hopefully through it you can see why it is I do what I do, and how I do it."

Sihtric poured them both a cup of mead and sat down on the bench before the flames. The King stared into the fire as if searching for inspiration.

"Many years ago, Sihtric, when I was still a boy I found myself in the house of a seer alongside my father. My memory is bad, but I will never forget the name of this seer; his name was Finegas."

Sihtric paused for a moment; the seer's name was the same as the one from the epic tale of the Salmon of Knowledge, where Finn mac Cumhaill had gained access to all knowledge known to man through the taste of that very salmon.

The King had witnessed the look of recognition that had crossed Sihtric's face and smiled at him, guessing his mind.

"I know what you are thinking; was this the same Finegas that advised Finn mac Cumhaill? The truth is, who knows such things? Maybe it was, maybe it wasn't. Maybe it was just some charlatan who had convinced my father he had truths to tell. Either way, I know what he said and I believed him, both then and now."

He drained his cup and placed it down before continuing, nodding at a servant to refill their cups from the secluded corner the servant had secreted himself in.

"He told my father, that an Irish king must emerge to unite the entire country and not just the Irish but the Norse and Danes as well, and that it must happen soon within a few generations or calamity would befall this country as has never been suffered. A foreign power will come and for centuries we will be forced to kneel to it and pay tribute unless we are united. My father assumed it was him who must unite the country under his rule. If not him who else?"

Sihtric recalled all the stories he had heard about the mighty High King, Mael Seachnaill mac Mael Ruanaid. He had defeated and captured the Viking warlord Torgesis and forced Ceitl Flatnose the King of Limerick to bend the knee. He had even given Aed Findliath no choice but to acknowledge him as the High King of Ireland for a time. But it had not lasted.

"My father in his hubris stretched himself too thin and eventually his power was spent trying to subdue all of the unruly kings of Ireland. I had to bide my time, waiting for Aed Findliath to return power to the Southern Ui Neill and I have taken up my father's mantle. I am so close to achieving this dream, but I must move fast before old age and frailty rob me of the vigour and mental capacity required to rule. I cannot tolerate Niall Glundub defying me any longer. I will march north next year and subdue him. If he won't yield, I will be forced to make my daughter a widow and install my grandson Hector mac Niall as the Lord of the Northern Ui Neill."

He turned to Sihtric. "But not before I announce you as King of Dublin, answerable only to me. And when I pass, you shall answer to Oengus. Will you lead the Norse-Gael of Dublin, Sihtric, and save this country from the fears of an old man?"

Sihtric sat back and absorbed all of what Flann had said. So many thoughts and emotions rolled through his head that he was almost dizzy. Was he ready at such a young age? Would the Norse-Gael accept him as their ruler? He was Ui Imair but Ragnall and even Garangr, his cousin, were more senior. Haltingly, he nodded his acceptance.

"Yes, High King Flann of the Shannon, I will rule Dublin in your name and become the King of Dublin."

The King sighed and seemed to shrink, possessing that faraway look he sometimes bore. At times Sihtric felt that Flann Sinna was perhaps half a seer himself. He always seemed to be a step ahead of his rivals, anticipating their moves and uncannily predicting the effects faraway events would have on his lands.

"Sihtric, I have told you of the events occurring for years now, the whys and hows and the what ifs, but let me now foretell to you my version of the doom the seer prophesied. He predicted the foreign invasion of Ireland and subjugation of our people, but I don't believe this potential enemy will be the Danes or the Norse. It is the Saxons that we must fear. The Vikings, as they have proven, will mingle in with the natives of whatever land they invade, marrying the local women and so forth. You yourself are the proof of that. The Saxons are different. They will consume and conquer and force their neighbours to adopt their customs and accept them as overlords or they will massacre them. I have corresponded with my Queen's nephew, King Constantine of Scotland. He and I are of one mind in this. It is a pity that your grandfather, my brother-in-law Ivar the Boneless, did not commit to battle one more time to finish off the Saxons for good, God forgive me. He allowed Halfdan, Ubba and that barbarian Guthrum to fight Alfred the Great and retreated to Dublin. Had Ivar led the Viking armies I have no doubt that the world would have been a different place. A more dangerous place to be sure, with Viking power unchecked across the Irish Sea, but a landscape that I could have more easily united my country within."

Sihtric could see the look of regret that passed over the King's face. He and Sihtric's grandfather were close, as close as neighbouring rulers could be. There was a question that continued to plague Sihtric's thoughts, and he decided that now was the time to ask it.

"King Flann, your vision is one that, it seems to me, could be multigenerational. It could be one of your sons or grandsons or even rivals who could complete this task. How come you keep overlooking Donnchadh Donn for your heir designate, as perhaps he could be the man to succeed?"

A flash of anger briefly registered on the King's face but it changed to sadness.

"Initially I swore to the King of the Northern Ui Neill that it would be a son of mine that shared blood with both him and myself that would succeed me as King of the Southern Ui Neill. At the time I agreed as the arrangement between the two houses of Niall of the Nine Hostages still stood at the time. I thought Donnchadh Donn would never get the chance to inherit the title. But when Domnall mac Aed unveiled his capacity for treachery to me, I reneged on that ancient agreement on the grounds that the Northern Ui Neill were bereft of honour and no longer deserved the trust of the people of this island. When Mael Ruanaid my son was murdered by that rogue faction of the Connaught men, I was not beholden to old promises and could have chosen Donnchadh Donn to replace him. But I didn't and I will tell you why."

Sihtric could see the heartbreak and sadness on the features of the High King as he sagged in his chair.

"Donnchadh Donn is a powerful warrior and has ruled the Caille Follamain well. But he will not rule after me for the same reason I will oppose Niall Glundub. They are both wolves who solve problems with the sword. Men like that cannot unite the country and will only sow despair in the long run. As a commander of men, Donnchadh Donn is almost peerless, but as a High King to rule this country, there are men better suited to the task. My son Conchobar reflects both of his warlike brothers also; only Oengus possesses the temperament to rule."

A noise broke their conversation and muffled shouting could be heard outside the hall. Prince Oengus burst into the room.

"Father, we are under attack! The Vikings have come and are attacking Slane. Longships have been sighted on the Boyne. The Vikings have come for the first time in years. We must defend the people."

The King rose steadily to his feet.

"Go, my son, raise the household guards of Tara and go to Slane. Send out runners to Brega and to Donnchadh Donn and Conchobar. Sihtric, if this is your cousins or your brothers, I will ask you to stay with me, I will not ask you to fight your own kin. Defend me and my family in Oengus' stead. Fly now, Oengus, defend our people."

*

Many hours later in the depths of night, Sihtric paced up and down the hall, his mind wandering and wondering what was happening in Slane. His first thought was if it was Ragnall or one of his captains who had struck Slane; would all these years beside Flann Sinna and protecting him mean anything? Would his life now be forfeit? The other prominent thought in his head was would Oengus and a couple of hundred men be enough to drive the raiders off? Sihtric knew his name carried weight, even abroad. It was possible that the sight of the spiked helm he wore and the scourge at his back or hip would be enough to discourage the Vikings from holding their ground and maybe it was a mistake for him not to have gone.

The settlement at Slane had grown over the last number of years and had dwellings on both sides of the River Boyne, but even if the relieving force outnumbered the Vikings, it would be very difficult to engage them in a way where numbers would count. Upon the water the Vikings had no equal.

As the night progressed Sihtric could find no ease. It would take hours for the force to reach Slane and night-time battles were generally frowned upon due to the obvious difficulty in visibility. The High King was just as anxious as Sihtric for news of events and had elected to await the outcome in the hall with Sihtric, but the late hours had proved too much and his head had nodded to his chest in slumber upon his chair. The accommodation of the extended royal family was located in an adjoining hall from the main hall, and all there were sound asleep with one exception: Sihtric knew that Queen Mael Muire would be awake and feeling the same apprehension that both he and her husband felt. The children of both Oengus and Flann Sinna's dead son Mael Ruanaid were also present in Tara too this night, to greet their grandfather on his return from Clonmacnoise.

A sound caught Sihtric's attention. At first he thought it was the wind, but when it arose again, he knew it for what it was; a muffled scream. Sihtric slowly drew his axe and slung his shield onto his forearm, his scourge loose and ready upon his back. The third similar sound erased any doubt – a guard outside the hall was clearly being strangled to death and even the King awoke from his slumber. One look from Sihtric was all it took for Flann Sinna to rise to his feet and draw his weapon. The victims outside were being expertly murdered in such a way as not to raise an alarm, and the best men had been drawn away with Oengus. A cold fury rose in Sihtric; whoever stepped through that door would, he swore, die brutally. *Niall Glundub has come to slay the King,* he thought. Flann Sinna, forty years past his prime, stood beside him, the firelight revealing the grim look of determination on his face. Mael Muire opened the door at that moment and stood in the doorway. She was fully armoured and armed and looked terribly fearful. The whimpers behind her revealed why; it was not for herself she was scared but for her adopted family and stepgrandchildren. She was a Queen of Meath and a Princess of Scotland, and she was willing to sell her life dearly in defence of her family.

The door quietly swung open and two men entered, cloaked in the shadows cast by the fire. The second man paused to close the door behind him. Sihtric retreated ever so slowly backward, interposing himself between them and the King. As the two men approached into the light, Sihtric could see their faces. The first was shockingly Ragnall of the Ui Imair, his white stripe of hair dissecting the long-plaited lengths of black hair on his head. He bore the dual axes he was famous for in a menacing fashion, twirling them over and back in a hypnotic display. The second Viking was the mirror image of Sihtric, identical in fact; the same size, shape and even armed similarly. Sihtric stood up straight y lowered his arms.

r," he said gently in Norse, the word for brother and the two attackers froze. For the first time in almost eight years, the three surviving sons of Ivar son of Ivar, son of Ragnar Lodbrok, stood together in the same room.

Ragnall was the first to speak.

"We have come for you, Sihtric. Our men have drawn the forces of Tara away and we have killed all the guards outside, my men stand outside the door. We control a route back over the walls and we will be gone from here. No longer will this cretin," he pointed at Flann Sinna, "have the Ui Imair over a barrel. Let us kill him and his family and have done with it. The Ui Neill have slighted us for the last time."

Flann Sinna took a step forward ready to swing a blow at Ragnall but Sihtric shouted "NO!" which halted all potential violence. Flann Sinna stepped back, unsure.

"We will shed no blood in this hall. Flann Sinna has treated me with kindness and respect and taught me how to be a warrior at his side. I will not allow his or his family's deaths to occur while I have been sworn to protect him."

Godfrith stepped forward and embraced Sihtric. The twin brothers had not seen each other in many years and yet it was like they had never been apart. Sihtric could almost read his mind, the questions, and the excitement at seeing him, but also the confusion at Sihtric's inability to act when the entire royal family of the Southern Ui Neill were at their mercy. Ragnall went left toward the Queen instead and raised his axe to strike her but Sihtric hauled him back, shouting, "I SAID NO, RAGNALL!"

The Ui Imair sea king hissed his annoyance and spat a response.

"We have come to free you and slay your gaolers, why do you deny us our revenge? For years we have had to endure this stain upon our honour as the Ui Imair, but no longer."

Sihtric shook his head. "I cannot allow you to just slay a man like Flann Sinna. At the minimum, when his sons learned that you had killed him like this, they will march on Dublin, and slay every man, woman and child. Do you want innocents to die because you acted spitefully? We would know no peace and you would unite the entire Irish Sea against you, on both sides of the water."

Ragnall snarled his impatience. "We have given Viking lives to rescue you, Sihtric, and now you must choose, are you one of us, or are you one of them?"

Sihtric looked to Flann Sinna who returned his stare. The King lowered his weapon and spoke.

"Allow me to speak, sons of Ivar," he asked of Ragnall and Godfrith.

Ragnall was about to raise his weapons again, but Godfrith raised his hand to his older brother and nodded curtly at the King.

"Sihtric, you know I had great plans for you, to unite this nation; but now your brothers have undone my vision at least temporarily. I ask you, Sihtric, and you, Ragnall, and you who must be Shitric's twin Godfrith; please honour your pledge of peace to me at least while I am alive. I beg you, do not attack the lands under the control of the Southern Ui Neill. Go with them, Sihtric, my scourge, for my sons will blame you for this as much as your two savage brothers, but know that I am proud of the man you have become under my tutelage."

Sihtric sadly bowed his head to Flann Sinna who then embraced him. Queen Mael Muire, who had stowed her weapon once it was clear that Sihtric would not allow his brothers to slay them all, acknowledged him gratefully, with the three fingered forehead salute of the Irish. Ragnall, with a snarl, was the first to exit the hall and began to bark commands at the raiding party that guarded the hall. He contemptuously kicked the corpses of the dead guards as he passed them on being denied the chance to collect the head of Flann Sinna by Sihtric. The two twin brothers exited the hall arm in arm, tears shed in happiness at being together at last, leaving Flann Sinna alone in his hall with his wife, bereft of his scourge... but still alive.

# CHAPTER 4

# THE AFTERMATH OF ODINSFIELD (910)

The sea crashed against the prow of the Drakkar boat of Sihtric's brother Ragnall, splashing the crew with spray in the wind. The boat was of a new design that had spread rapidly around the Viking world and with Ragnall's newfound infamy and wealth, he now possessed one with another two under construction. The Karvi, Snekkja and Skeid designs were all still employed by the fleet of the Ui Imair and the Kings of Yorvik, but one look at the formidable Drakkar type longboat revealed, even to a layman, that this design was the future. Sihtric had never even set foot upon the deck of a longboat in more than eight years before being sprung from Tara and all his seamanship skills had atrophied. He humbly had to take instruction from the lowliest Vikings on what to do and where to be on the ship at any given time. His twin brother Godfrith was particularly merciless with his jibes, berating Sihtric tongue-in-cheek on everything from his rowing technique to his sailing skills and even his less than graceful balance on deck.

"Are you Viking or are you an Irishman, Sihtric?" he had more than once publicly shouted at his twin brother to howls of playful derision from the crew.

As the months went by, he had improved his seamanship bit by bit until he was at least passably competent compared to the other Viking warriors of the ever-growing Ui Imair war bands. He did not yet feel confident enough to take command of a longboat himself and was content to sail alongside his brothers, his cousin Garangr or, on occasion, the ageing warrior Brunbolg Headtaker. After his flight from Tara six months earlier, Sihtric had not wasted any time acclimatising to the Viking way of life and immediately began earning his reputation on raids. It was all well and good being a member of the Ui Imair dynasty, but you had to prove that you were what you said you were; the Vikings after all admired strength above all.

Ragnall had led two raids over the winter and early spring with part of his forces. The first raid had been on a town on the coast of Brittany, a province loosely affiliated with Francia, and the second had been a surprise attack on Gwynedd, on the fleet's return to their headquarters upon the western coast of Northumbria. Both times Sihtric had insisted on being the first man from the longboat and each time he had slaughtered several warriors in combat. His spiked helm and the unusual scourge weapon he occasionally employed when fighting, immediately caught the eye of the warriors of the war band and his foes alike and his infamy grew. Word had reached the Viking world for years of an estranged Ui Imair prince that had grown up a fierce fighter amongst the Irish and Ragnall had encouraged Sihtric to prove that the tales were true and that his prowess was not exaggerated. Ragnall always led from the front from his Drakkar dragon boat, which he named Jotunn, after the giants who were enemies of the gods. Sihtric had witnessed first-hand the sheer terror the boat sowed as it approached the shoreline of their foes, as to sight his brother's sails was to see your death approach. But Sihtric wanted more. He wanted to be part of the legend. *When people see Jotunn attack they will know that Sihtric Ui Imair is aboard and has come for your soul.*

In the previous year, the armies of Aethelfled the bitch queen of Mercia and her merciless brother Edward, had invaded Northumbria and had devastated the land owned by Norse, Dane and Saxon Christian alike. The lands controlled by the Ui Imair on the western coast and inland from there had remained

d, but when the three joint rulers of Yorvik – Eowils, Halfdan and
came to Ragnall's hall looking for an alliance to wreak revenge, there
was never going to be any answer given but yes. Sihtric had only heard of the
battle of Chester anecdotally from the High King Flann Sinna and his sons,
but for Ragnall and Godfrith it was fresh in the mind and the treachery and
loss they had suffered that day had fuelled their desire for vengeance. Ragnall
had previously confided in Sihtric that even if the Saxons had not attacked
the lands controlled by Yorvik, he had been considering an invasion by the
Ui Imair alone into Mercia anyway. They could now command almost three
thousand warriors and given time, Ragnall was confident that they could
call upon another three thousand from disparate war bands from across the
Danelaw, Ireland, Francia and even Scandinavia.

Godfrith was now married to the daughter of Ingvarr, one of the three kings
too, which made the Ui Imair in a way beholden to Yorvik, in a similar manner
to their father Ivar formerly being beholden to Harald Fairhair on account of
being married to the Norse King's eldest daughter. The time had come and
on *Midsumarblot*, the Viking summer harvest festival, the combined fleet was
assembled on the mouth of the Mersey River. The three brothers intended to
sail around Wales and up the River Severn and do as much damage as they
could to Northern Wessex and Western Mercia. The fleet was comprised of
predominantly Northumbrian Norse and Danes and the Ui Imair, with some
aligned war bands. A handful of Saxon ealdormen who owed their allegiance to
Yorvik sailed as well, eager to take their revenge upon their southern brethren.
The Ui Imair agreed to send two thirds of their entire strength south with the
Kings of Yorvik, almost eighteen hundred warriors on fifty longboats. The
entire fleet numbered almost two hundred ships in total and as they entered
the estuary of the River Severn, Sihtric was informed by his brothers that they
had not lost a single one on the journey south. One way or the other, the Saxons
would surely suffer.

The Viking fleet took the Mercians completely by surprise and several
villages were overwhelmed and sacked in the first few days. The forces of
Ragnall and the Yorvik brothers did not bother to venture far along the western

tributaries of the Severn, which saved the Welsh kingdoms of Gwent and Glywysing from destruction. Splinter fleets rowed up the Tern, the Teme, the Warwick Avon and the Worcester Stour. Hundreds of Saxons were put to the sword and only the comeliest women and hardiest children were spared, the former to entertain the warriors and the latter to run errands and help set up various camps on land. After two weeks of rampaging around the countryside, the easy targets had shrivelled away. Every village, town and monastery that lay within three miles of the river system had been sacked and plundered, and any settlements slightly further away were abandoned and their populations fled with all their wealth, grain, and livestock. Only in a handful of the larger walled towns did the Northumbrian and Ui Imair force encounter any resistance at all, and of the major chieftains only Benesing the Bulky lost his life when he was skewered by a spearman. Great caches of spoils were laid down under guard, for loading when the fleet made its retreat out the way they came. The force was not foolhardy though and left the major power centres of the region alone. Tamworth, the great capital of Mercia, was left alone as were Lichfield and Worcester. The plan was to devastate the land and its people rather than look for prolonged conflict.

After three weeks of raiding, the people of the countryside began to burn their own lands ahead of the Northumbrian forces, denying them food or shelter. In the fourth week, Ragnall sent their cousin Garangr back north with three ships filled with the spoils of Mercia, but Sihtric could feel his frustration mounting. His brother was itching for battle and although the Ui Imair were rampaging successfully on the eastern bank of the Severn, crops could be regrown, and villages could be rebuilt. Aethelfled was nowhere to be found or seen. On multiple occasions the various commanders of the force had witnessed scouts on horseback, observing the army as it rolled over the countryside, but they always fled on the first sign of pursuit.

On the fifth week of the campaign, the countryside was well and truly pillaged and very little booty was left to be claimed. It was at this point that the leaders of the invasion force were called to the burned-out village of Kidderminster to decide what to do. Ragnall voiced his displeasure at the

and advocated going home as it was clear that Aethelfed and her
⁀w the land far better than they and that every day they waited gave
her time to gather her warriors to her, perhaps her brother's warriors as well.
Godfrith made the point that with the land being burned before them and
stores of food being moved, foraging for a force as large as theirs had become
difficult. They had perhaps two weeks of food left before they would have to
retreat anyway. The brothers and their Saxon allies had been adamant that they
must stay as long as they could to inflict as much damage as possible upon the
Saxons so as to reinforce the notion that to attack Northumbria was to invite
invasion and retaliation.

At length, it was agreed that they would only stay one more week, with a sole
target in mind. When Northumbria had been invaded, in a last spiteful act, the
Saxons had seized the relics of Saint Oswald. Aethelfled had begun building
a church near Tamworth to house them but while the building was being
constructed, the relics were being held at an abbey. It was called the Abbey of
Saint Mary at Wolverhampton. It lay several miles from one of the tributaries
of the Severn, the River Stour, and many captured prisoners had confirmed
this intelligence to be true. The River Stour was far too small to accommodate
more than two longboats abreast after less than three miles north of where
it was swallowed by the mighty Severn. Brunbolg, Sihtric and Godfrith were
left in command of most of the fleet there with a thousand Ui Imair warriors,
while most of the army marched northeast overland to sack the abbey. Ragnall
led seven hundred of the Ui Imair, with two thousand Northumbrian Vikings
and Saxons led by the three brothers. The remaining three or four hundred
warriors were sent south back along the Severn to await the army there rather
than clog up the waterways. And on the morning of the fifth of August, 910,
Sihtric found himself sharing a fire with Brunbolg and his brother Godfrith,
awaiting the return of his brother Ragnall and the forces of the three brothers
of Yorvik.

The fire crackled brightly, and the three warlords used it to roast a brace of
partridges to break their fast. Brunbolg and Godfrith sat legs crossed, unarmed
and unarmoured occasionally turning the poultry and debating over how

much seasoning to apply to it. Sihtric was staring upward. A vast murder of crows flowed like a river overhead in the direction of Wolverhampton. *Odin is here,* he thought, a shiver of anticipation descending his spine.

"Look at those crows overhead, Godfrith, thousands of them," he said.

His twin brother glanced up into the morning sky as did the giant Brunbolg, a steaming thigh of partridge hanging from his mouth, dripping grease onto his massive beard.

"Ah, 'tis nothing, young Sihtric," answered Brunbolg. "Where dead men fall, crows will follow."

Godfrith met the eyes of his brother and wordlessly the two rose to their feet.

"In the name of Thor," exclaimed Brunbolg, "can we not enjoy a bit of meat before we settle into another day of monotony in this damned country?"

The two brothers ignored him and began strapping on their mail and armour. While Sihtric reached for his spiked helm and scourge, his brother began bellowing commands at the warriors. As nervousness crept through the camp, even Brunbolg was not immune to the spreading disquiet and within minutes the entire camp, all thousand men, were packing away their tents and equipment onto the longboats closest the shore and simultaneously arming themselves. Sihtric deployed the archers on the first row of boats grounded on the water and sent a unit each to flank either side of the pathway taken by the force the day before. The remainder of the men gathered on the grass, their weapons at the ready and close to each other in case the shield wall must be formed rapidly. Godfrith sent out a trio of scouts with their few horses northeast to ascertain the wellbeing of the Northumbrian army.

"Perhaps it is still nothing, young Sihtric," mused Brunbolg, "maybe they are migrating north or something."

Sihtric shook his head. 'No, Brunbolg, I witnessed this phenomenon at the battle of Bealach Mughna in Ireland. Crows are carrion birds; a great slaughtering is happening or has happened."

Godfrith answered, "Perhaps you are right, brother, maybe Ragnall and the have killed everybody in the monastery and any warriors there?"

considered that line of reasoning for a moment before discounting it.

"Aethelfled has known we are in her lands for at least four weeks, brother, and yet we have prisoners and slaves telling us that the remnants of that Christian saint have not been moved and have remained at that abbey for all of this time. Why not just move them like they have their people and their livestock?"

Slowly comprehension dawned upon Godfrith and his face drained of colour. Brunbolg who was not known for being a particularly intelligent Viking reasoned it out, out loud, with a puzzled look on his face.

"She left the dead saint there, despite his value to the Christians, while we were ravaging the land... while stripping Mercia bare before us... which means she knew... or hoped... that we would come?"

A grim finality etched itself across the enormous warlord's face as it dawned on him. "Which means they are dead then, and they will come for us next."

Godfrith scoffed at the warlord's proclamation. "Do you think Ragnall Ivarsson, the greatest Viking in the world, is going to simply be slain in some ambush? No, Brunbolg, if Aethelfled has sprung a trap, I have faith that Ragnall will escape it."

Five hours later one of the scouts returned, galloping over the ridge, his horse lathered in sweat. He jumped down off the animal and rushed straight to Sihtric and Godfrith.

"Lords, there has been a great slaughter of the Northumbrian forces."

Many of the surrounding warriors edged in to hear the scout's report.

"On the march to the abbey, Queen Aethelfled's army emerged from the countryside and engaged our armies. Ragnall was sent to hold the rear, as the three brothers and the Northumbrian Saxons wished to seek vengeance upon her. Our armies outnumbered hers and the three brothers obviously thought they could win. Her brother Edward's Wessex army then hit our men from the south and Prince Aethelstan hit from the north with further reinforcements and enveloped them. Ragnall consolidated the rearguard on a nearby hill. The

Northumbrian army has been massacred, my lords."

A rumble of shocked surprise rippled out from the warriors surrounding the scout, but they quieted to hear the rest of his report.

"All three Kings of Yorvik are dead; Eowils, Halfdan and your father-in-law Ingvarr, Lord Godfrith. But they died well and are already in Valhalla."

Godfrith showed no emotion but somberly nodded his head in affirmation.

"Other notable eorls to fall were Ohter and Scurf. All the Northumbrian Saxon ealdormen have been slain also; Agmund, Othulf, Thunferth, Osferth and Guthferth. The only nobleman left is Anlaf the Swarthy and he succeeded in breaking out of the trap and joining with Ragnall. Prince Aethelstan took his third of the Saxon army and attacked Ragnall's position, but Ragnall defeated this assault and has taken the young prince captive."

A huge cheer rose from the Ui Imair on news that Ragnall had driven the Saxons back and defied the entire might of their army with a fraction of the men.

"King Ragnall sent me back as quickly as possible, you are to ready the ships and have your archers deployed. Ragnall and his surviving men are marching in good order, being pursued at a wary distance by the Mercians and Wessexians, for fear of Ragnall killing the Prince Aethelstan. They will be here within the hour."

Sihtric and his brother began issuing commands on what to do while Brunbolg bellowed at the archers to be in position to protect the retreat of Ragnall. Hooks and ropes were used to temporarily lash the longboats together to allow warriors to move from one to the other upon the water and not create a backlog of warriors looking to board. Despite having almost half of their warriors allegedly slain, the longboats themselves were far too valuable to be captured or even scuttled in the river. It would only take a handful of men to crew each one, leaving none for the Saxons. Once all was ready, Brunbolg, Sihtric and Godfrith waited fifty feet from the shoreline ahead of their massed ranks of archers.

At midday, the noise of hundreds of warriors moving could be discerned from the surrounding countryside. Brunbolg possessed superb sight if little

:r and pointed out hundreds of Saxon soldiers that had surrounded

'arriors while the remainder of the enemy wearily pursued them a

mile off. And then Ragnall himself appeared over the ridge, his men disciplined, marching behind him. Sihtric was dismayed to see many wounded Vikings amongst the ranks and even recognised the carcass of Anlaf the Swarthy being carried on a makeshift stretcher. *Perhaps his escape from the trap wasn't as successful as the scout had said,* he thought.

Ragnall had a length of rope in his hand, the other end of which was tied to a tall thin young man of noble bearing; *Aethelstan,* Sihtric guessed. As the men arrived, Ragnall wearily acknowledged his two brothers and Brunbolg, and told the men to board the ships while he turned and kicked Aethelstan down to his knees. In several minutes, the bulk of the Saxon army arrived upon the ridge. Two of their leaders approached on horseback and halted before the three brothers, Brunbolg and the prisoner. It was Aethelfled and Edward, sister and brother. The Queen spoke first.

"This is twice that you have evaded me, Ragnall of the Ui Imair," she began in Irish. "I curse myself nightly in my prayers for not having you hung for a reaver and a pirate in Tamworth years ago. Because of my inaction, you have been allowed to rampage up and down the sea at will."

She paused momentarily, gazing first at Brunbolg and then Sihtric and Godfrith. She addressed Brunbolg first.

"You there, giant, are you Brunbolg who is known in Francia as the Headtaker?"

Brunbolg just nodded and spat at her horse's hooves.

"I should have done the Francs a favour and destroyed you at Chester."

The massive Viking smiled at that affably, taking perverse pride in defying the Mercian Queen.

"And you two," she nodded at the twin brothers, "two more pups from the same rotten brood as this heathen savage?" she asked, pointing at Ragnall.

"We are," answered Godfrith arms folded defiantly.

"Well let's get down to business, shall we? If you give us back Prince Aethelstan, the King's oldest son and my ward and nephew, I shall permit you to leave these lands unhindered. If not, I will signal for our entire army to descend upon the river and destroy you before you can escape. I will then march north, capture all your women and children that live north of the Mersey, and crucify them all across the border of Mercia and Northumbria as a warning to you pagans never to return. I will then ally with the Welsh and whatever backward Irish kings I can find and burn Dublin to the ground. This I do swear to God as Queen Aethelfled of Mercia. Release the prisoner, or death? Choose, Ragnall."

The wind picked up and the Sihtric could sense the army of the Saxons and the remnants of the invading force hold their collective breath. To Sihtric's surprise, Ragnall was smiling. He stared directly at the Queen and she held his gaze, two of the most powerful nobles in Britain or Ireland. He dragged Prince Aethelstan to his feet.

"I agree," he answered.

He cut the restraints of the prisoner and held him by the back of the neck, a knife at his throat and waited. All the ships were told to cast off with Godfrith and Brunbolg among them to hedge against treachery, until just one remained to take Sihtric and Ragnall down the Severn with a crew of forty men. Once satisfied that the Ui Imair escape was unavoidable, Ragnall whispered into Aethlstan's ear, but Sihtric was close enough to hear.

"Remember me, boy," he hissed, "your aunt and father won't always be here to save you."

Quick as a snake he slashed the prince's cheek with his dagger and threw him forward to the hooves of his aunt's horse. The prince yelped in pain and the Queen jumped down to help him, concern etched across her face. But Ragnall and Sihtric had already turned and leapt to board the waiting longboat and in moments they had cast off, leaving the vast Saxon army behind.

In hours, the ships had reached the mouth of the Severn and it shocked Sihtric to see how few warriors remained. By his count they had lost almost fifteen hundred warriors in the campaign. The few surviving Saxons in the army were mutedly calling the great defeat the Battle of Tettenhall, the closest townland to where the confrontation took place, but the Ui Imair had a different name for it; the Battle of Odinsfield, as evidence of Odin's presence there could be seen by the thousands of crows that attended the fighting. A crisis meeting was called upon Ragnall's longboat. The last surviving noblemen of the Northumbrian army decided there and then who should become King of Yorvik on the brothers' deaths. They elected a Saxon Christian called Eadwulf to lead them as he had a Danish wife who worshipped the old gods, and it was agreed upon that he would be a unifying force in the difficult times ahead. Sihtric had told Ragnall what he felt Aethelfled and Edward would do next. They would not march north; they would go east and subjugate the Danelaw and East Anglia and force the Danes there to bend the knee. Only then when they had subdued the entire south, would the Saxons look north. Ragnall had shrugged his shoulders and smiled at Sihtric's prediction, uncaring. It puzzled Sihtric and so he put his brother to the question.

"Ragnall, you do not seem dismayed at this catastrophe. The Saxons have won a massive victory this day. It will be years before the Northumbrians can regather the manpower needed to launch another assault upon the Saxons. Are you not concerned what is in store for the Ui Imair as a result?"

Ragnall placed his arm around his brother.

"Look around you, Sihtric. The three brothers placed the Ui Imair at the rear in their own haste to get at the enemy. You and Godfrith were in the rearguard guarding the boats with the rest of our warriors and Garangr has gone home with the treasure. We have lost perhaps eighty men on this campaign, that is all, and Yorvik has no way to enforce tribute or warriors from us any longer. Before long we shall rule them in all but name. Through Godfrith marrying Ingvarr's daughter, we have claim to the throne of Yorvik now however tenuous. Sihtric, we are the last notable independent Viking power in Britain or Ireland. We are too strong to be challenged. Every young warrior from Limerick to London, with even a piece of Viking blood in him, will want to join us and nobody else."

He placed his other arm on Sihtric's other shoulder and looked into his eyes.

"I can now look to Ireland, with you and Godfrith at my side, and take back what is ours. The time of the Ui Neill is over; the time of the Ui Imair is here."

Sihtric was captured by the vision painted by his brother, a vision of revenge, plunder, adventure and legend. He was already sold, *but not while Flann is alive.*

# EPILOGUE

# THE PROPHESY OF EITHIGEN
# (910)

A sharp stinging slap from Brother Padraig brought the young monk
Aonghus of the Ui Maine to his senses. His mind still reeled from the
fact that the venerable Bishop of Treoit, Eithigen mac Fingen, was on his death
bed and would soon meet God face to face. The blow stunned him into focus,
and he dipped his head in obeisance to his superior. "Aonghus! Fetch the slaves
Bran and Sceolain and bring cloth and pails of water immediately." Brother
Padraig then slowly turned to the stricken and ancient Bishop on his cot and
sadly caressed his weather-beaten face. Without turning around to young
Aonghus again he simply whispered the word, "Go."

Aonghus quickly fled the cloister and emerged out into the storm-lashed
night. He raced to the slave quarters and peered through the door of their
humble barn which served to shelter them. A gaggle of men were warming
themselves by a fire but when he appeared, each tapped their three fingers
to their foreheads in respect despite several of them being four times his age.
Aonghus tried to sound aloof and attempted to deepen his voice to give force
to his command, but when he ordered Bran and Sceolain to come with him to
fetch pails of water and cloth, he sounded like a girl in his own ears and cursed

himself for his weakness. He was a man of sixteen after all.

The three of them ran in a crouch toward the stream at the back of the grounds snatching the required pails on the way, each trying to protect their heads from the rain by drawing up the hoods on their respective cloaks. But it was all in vain and in moments they were collectively drenched. As the two slaves carefully picked their way down the banks of the lively stream, Aonghus thought back on all his time with Eithigen. He was the fourth son of the King of the Ui Maine of Connaught and had been sent to the monastery to become a monk. Even then as a small boy, he knew that he was a political pawn in the machinations of his father who had tried to ingratiate himself with the High King Flann Sinna through sending his son to Treoit and not Armagh or Kildare. Aonghus had been terrified at first being sent away from his family but after a while he had grown to love the monastic way of life. Eithigen had always been a kindly master and teacher, wise and caring and constantly protective of Aonghus as he grew up amidst older aspirants. Eithigen was hugely respected in Meath and Leinster and had counselled the kings of Brega and Tara for almost fifty years. He had even fought at the side of the High King in his wars with the Northern Ui Neill and the Eoghanachta of Munster, and Aonghus had always hoped that he would be called to fight alongside the bishop in one of the High King's legendary battles. But as age and infirmity had overtaken Eithigen, that likelihood had evaporated away. And now his time was at an end.

The three men, once the pails were filled, sprinted through the lashing rain back toward the cloister where the bishop lay dying, with a brief stop at the back of the main church proper to secure some wool and silk. In moments they reached the cloister and re-entered. Brother Padraig sent the two slaves away and began dipping the silk into the first pail and attempted to wipe the sweat from the feeble bishop's brow. Eithigen was a shell of the man Aonghus once knew and even in the last week he had depreciated precipitously. He reached a frail hand toward Brother Padraig and Aonghus and beckoned them closer. In a rasping voice he whispered, "I have had a vision. Padraig, take that quill and parchment at my desk and heed my words." A dull rumble of thunder from outside seemed to send a spasm of pain and fear across the features of Eithigen.

Each intake of breath the old bishop inhaled was a battle now and Aonghus privately worried that he would pass away mid-sentence. But the old man gathered himself once more, a fervent look of determination etched across his ragged features. "Two suns passed by each other today and it is a sign. Brothers will come to these shores, and it will be brothers who will be the ones to face them." Padraig grimly scratched the words on the parchment. "This celestial alignment was proceeded by the storm that assails us now; the rain is the sea, and the lightning is the violence that it brings." The ailing bishop's voice was barely a whisper now and both Brother Padraig and Aonghus had to strain to hear. "The Wolves of the Irish Sea approach and Flann Sinna must be ready. The Ui Imair will return with blood and fire and the savage demons they worship will dance in the skies above them, the wolf, the dragon and the storm. They are coming."

As if to punctuate his statement a titanic peel of thunder pulverised the evening with its cacophony and Aonghus knew there and then that his Lord Bishop Superior had received a true vision of the future, handed down by the Lord himself. Brother Padraig handed the quill to the bishop and in a weak scrawl, Eithigen signed his name to the parchment. Once done he lay back into his cot and Brother Padraig and Aonghus sat the final watch for the master of Treoit. Before midnight, he passed away. Within the hour, Aonghus was sent on horseback to Tara, which lay only two miles away. In his ears rang the instructions given him by Brother Padraig, to not only inform the King and his advisors that the great Bishop Superior of Treoit, Eithigen son of Fingen son of Conchobar had passed away, but that he had received a true prophecy from God and that it must be relayed.

"The Wolves of the Irish Sea approach... and Flann Sinna must be ready."

*To Be Continued...*

# ACKNOWLEDGMENTS:

Writing a book, I have learned is a bit like an iceberg. What you see above the water (writing it) is all well and dandy, but 90% of the danger lies under the water. There are so many other elements to getting a tome like this over the finishing line. There are many people I wish to thank and acknowledge as a result. My partner Gillian has project-managed *Wolves of the Irish Sea* and basically become my de-facto boss throughout this project. During the project she was my sounding board as I read through endless sequences of five thousand words at her to see what she thought. Her relentless pursuit of victory and her indomitable organisational skills have won us the day here. To my editor Robin Seavill and my artist Mark Thomas, you lads have effectively converted the ideas of a mindless barbarian (myself) into a book that would not look out of place in my view, on any bookshelf. Robin, your depth of knowledge on the period I have written about surpasses my own and you have expunged every dumb anachronism from the work. Mark, the piece of art for the cover is phenomenal and did exactly what we both wanted; it captivates the imagination immediately.

When Gillian and I started shopping my work around, we received a few offers, but it quickly became apparent that we would have to go it alone. There are myriad costs in producing a book for sale and we elected to rely on our friends, family, and connections to back us through Kickstarter. Their generosity has been integral to the finishing of the book as it covered many of our costs. Catriona Black, Natasha Anderson, Michaela Craddock, Paul O'Farrell, Kathy Jankovic, Benny Alary and Stephen Martin; I want to thank you personally, here, for your support. Without your collective effort, *Wolves of the Irish Sea* has come to fruition much earlier than otherwise possible. To Jarrett Budworth, Adrian Granaghan and Susan Loughran what can I say except I owe you. I had business support also from both Henry Loughran's bar in Navan and the Pictish king of the Delta (you know who you are), I will never forget. And finally thank you, the reader, for taking a chance on a novice author and adding this book to your collections.

# NOTES

The idea for *Wolves of the Irish Sea* occurred to me whilst watching both "Vikings" and "The Last Kingdom" wildly popular television shows. I was extremely aware through my reading and tales from older folk I knew in Meath of Ireland in the 9$^{th}$ and 10$^{th}$ century, and I felt that what was occurring simultaneously in Ireland and Scotland, in the plots in those wonderful shows, had been abandoned. What occurred in the early Middle Ages effectively forged Britain and Ireland into what they are now and the connotations of that period echo into today. The Saxon and Danish perspective has been done to death in a historical fiction context, but Ireland and Scotland had been abandoned. *Wolves of the Irish Sea*, I hope, will rectify this somewhat. I have used the same sources to create my picture and through the eyes of my five main characters I hope the reader can catch a glimpse of the economics and politics of the era. I was as chronologically accurate as I could be. In the same way we all know the iceberg defeated the Titanic, one can't take any liberties with historical events. However, as a work of historical-fiction, I could use my discretion to add characters and alternate between Irish, Norse and Anglicised place names to make them as computable as possible. With some names I just picked what I thought was the coolest one. I am exploring history, but I am not here to be your teacher either.

I am not here to teach a history lesson per say and I am sure that some of the PHD guys will argue for different versions of events, but this is my best interpretation of how, why, and when the main geopolitical events of the Irish Sea in the 9$^{th}$ and 10$^{th}$ century occurred. I want for the reader, especially of Scottish, Irish, and Norse-Gael descent, to feel a sense of pride and a connection to their ancestors of the past. I hope that *Wolves of the Irish Sea* is perceived as a tale of hope; that when times are darkest in the Celtic world, great leaders emerge. But I also want to convey the message that when we are divided as a people, we are vulnerable to the mercies of ferocious enemies. In the 9th century it was Vikings, in the 21st century Ireland and Scotland, it is hedge funds, corrupt politics and the utter hegemony of the elite. Although a thousand years apart, each of those foes of Ireland and Scotland, have invaded, demand tribute and have no qualms about inflicting suffering for gain upon the peoples of the Irish Sea.

# ABOUT THE AUTHOR

Conor Brennan grew up on the slopes of Tara hill, in that landscape so heavily draped in history, but now lives in Perth in Western Australia with his partner Gillian and daughter. He has studied economics, geography and has a master's in public policy, as well as having an avid interest in sports, history and politics. He works in the financial sector. Having (possibly) reached the end of his sporting career, Conor has since been writing prolifically; already having self-published a book on gambling and two quiz books, as well as currently documenting the first six months of parenting his new daughter with a view to publishing a light-hearted reassurance to other fathers of a similarly barbarian ilk. He is now determined to pursue this endeavour; to publish books and have them read. He says he'll keep going now until the day he dies and already is cooking three more ideas (at least!) and getting ready to set them in motion next.

To discover more about Conor and *The Wolves of the Irish Sea*, please visit:

**conorbrennanauthor.com**

# REFERENCES

Bachrach, D. (2012). *Warfare in Tenth-Century Germany*.
London: The Boydell Press.
Retrieved from: https://en.wikipedia.org/wiki/Henry_the_Fowler

BBC. (2004, December 20). *Brunanburgh: Birthplace of Englishness*.
https://military.wikia.org/wiki/Battle_of_Brunanburh. London.

Bill, J. (2008). *Viking Ships and the Sea*. Oxford Illustrated.

Broun, D. (2020, August 20th). *The Chronicles of the Kings of Alba*.
Edinburgh, Scotland.

Byrne, F. (1973). *Irish Kings and High-Kings*. London: Batsford.

Connolly, S. (1998). 10th Century Ireland.
In S. Connolly, *The Oxford Companion to Irish History* (p. 329).
London: Oxford University Press. doi:ISBN 0-19-211695-9.

Downham, C. (2004). *Eric Bloodaxe - Axed? The Mystery of the Last Viking King of York*. Mediaeval Scandinavia, 51-77.

Downham, C. (2007). *Viking Kings of Britain and Ireland: The Dynasty of Ivarr to A.D 1014*. Edinburgh: Dunedin Academic Press.

Duffy, S. (1998). *Irishmen and Islesmen in the Kingdom of Dublin and Man. Eriu, 1052-1171*. Retrieved from: JSTOR 30007421.

Foot, A. (n.d.). *Aethelstan: The First King of England*. Retrieved October 1st, 2020, from https://en.wikipedia.org/wiki/%C3%86thelstan%27s_invasion_of_Scotland

Hader, S. (1997). *Tennyson's Translation of The Battle of Brunanburh*. New York, United States. Retrieved from: https://victorianweb.org/authors/tennyson/brunanburh/brun.html

Ingram, J. (n.d.). *The Anglo Saxon Chronicles*. London. doi:https://www.gutenberg.org/ebooks/657

Killings, D. (2008). *Anglo Saxon Chronicles Translation*. London: Project Gutenberg. Retrieved from: http://www.gutenberg.org/cache/epub/657/pg657.html

Lancaster, P. (2018, May 27). *The Unknown Region*. Retrieved from: https://theunknownregion.wordpress.com/2018/05/27/a-lament-for-aethelflaed

Mac Niocaill, G. (1975). *The Medieval Irish Annals. Irish Historical Studies*, 20(77), 3-20. Retrieved August 1st, 2020

Mark, J. (2018). Flann Sinna. *World History Encyclopedia*, 1-2. Retrieved from: https://www.ancient.eu/Flann_Sinna

McCarthy, D. (2002). *The Chronological Apparatus of the Annals of Ulster.* *Peritia*, 256-283. Retrieved August 10th, 2020

NFB. (2012, January 30). *Ireland's Wars: The Second Viking Age.* Retrieved from: https://neverfeltbetter.wordpress.com/2012/01/30/irelands-wars-the-second-viking-age/.

O' Corrain, D. (2006). *Celtic Culture: A historical Encyclopedia.* Denver: Oxford. Retrieved August 20th, 2020

Reuter, T. (2002). *History of the Archibishops of Hamburg-Bremen.* Columbia University Press.

Smyth, A. (1987). *Scandanavian York and Dublin.* Irish Academic Press, 2-62.

UCC. (2000, June 1). *Chronicum Scotorum.* Cork, Munster, Ireland. Retrieved June 1, 2020

UCC. (2000, December 1). *The Annals of the Four Masters.* (CELT, Ed.) Cork, Munster, Ireland. Retrieved June 1, 2020

UCC. (2000, December 1). *The Annals of Ulster.* (C. -c. Texts, Ed.) Cork, Munster, Ireland. doi:https://celt.ucc.ie//published/T100001A/

Ulster-Series. (1999). *Kingdom of Argialla. Belfast, Northern Ireland, United Kingdom.* Retrieved August 19th, 2020, from http://sites.rootsweb.com/~irlkik/ihm/colla.htm

Wiki. (2020, September 1st). *Amlaib Cuaran*. Retrieved from:
https://en.wikipedia.org/wiki/Amla%C3%ADb_Cuar%C3%A1n.

Wiki. (2020, October 5th). *Constantine mac Aed*. Retrieved from:
https://en.wikipedia.org/wiki/Constantine_II_of_Scotland.

Wiki. (2020, May 2nd). *Flann Sinna*.
Retrieved from: https://en.wikipedia.org/wiki/Flann_Sinna.

Wiki. (2020, August 2nd). *Niall Glundub*. Retrieved from:
https://en.wikipedia.org/wiki/Niall_Gl%C3%BAndub.

Wiki. (2020, September 1st). *Ragnall Ui Imair*. Retrieved from:
https://en.wikipedia.org/wiki/Ragnall_ua_%C3%8Dmair.

Wiki. (2020, October 1st). *Sihtric the Scourge*. Retrieved from:
https://en.wikipedia.org/wiki/Sitric_C%C3%A1ech.

Wiki. (2020, November 1st). *The Year 918*. Retrieved from:
https://en.wikipedia.org/wiki/918.

Printed in Great Britain
by Amazon

13780432R00195